Tales of the Obeni

Other Books published by Writersandpoets.com

* *Schemin'* by Andrea Blackstone
* *Zero Debt* by Lynnette Khalfani
* *Investing Success* by Lynnette Khalfani
  With a foreword by investing legend, Charles Schwab
* *Ready Set Grow!* by Veronica Holcomb
* *Smoking Cigarettes* by Reginald L. Hall
* *Memoir: Delaware County Prison* by Reginald L. Hall
* *Threesome: Where Seduction Power and Basketball Collide*
  by Brenda L. Thomas
* *Daddy Big Bucks* by Robert Waite
* *Just Between Us* by Wyndy Adkins
* *Drama Factor* by Wanda Toby
* *Diamond Dynasty* by Brandon McCalla
* *Diamond Drought* by Brandon McCalla
* *She'll Learn* by Sybil Barkley Staples
* *Intimate Soul - Embracing the Passion* by Surreal

Tales of the Obeni

Leon Allen Bryan

Writersandpoets.com

Writersandpoets.com

Book Design:'Damola Ifaturoti/ AMV Publishing Services
Cover Design: Dapo Ojo-Ade
Back Cover Photography: Demetrice Burgess

Printed in the United States of America

Library of Congress Catalog Control Number: 2007934488

ISBN 10: 0-9762710-3-6
ISBN 13: 978-09762710-3-1

Writers and Poets.com
P.O. Box 1307
Mountainside, NJ 07092
http://www.writersandpoets.com

First Printing

Dedication

This book is dedicated in loving memory to
my fiancée
Sandra D. Burgess.
Because of her I believe and know for sure love exists.
I am grateful for the time we had together.

Acknowledgements

I would like to thank the creator of all things for staying with me through the difficult times. I would also thank Sandra D. Burgess for all her technical support. I very much need to thank Mr. Steve Harvey for his morning words of inspiration.

I would like to thank my editor Pam Brown. I would like to thank Earl Cox, founder of Writersandpoets.com for his guidance. I would like to thank all my co-workers and extended family at the Brooklyn General Mail Facility who surrounded me with love, hugs, and support when I needed it the most

Thanks to Dr. Charles Finch of Morehouse College who helped me see with proof the wondrous seldom discussed achievements of black and African people. Thanks to the late Dr John Henry Clark for helping me understand the history of my ancestors did not start in the United States. I would even give thanks to the ones who came just to cause confusion for me because they have made me stronger. Some of my favorite artists who sing and play songs of love I give many thanks:

Dianne Reeves for *We Belong Together.*
Prince for *Pink Cashmere.*
Bobby Watson for *Love Remains.*
George Duke for *Just for You.*
And last but not least, Angela Bofill for *Tonight I Give In.*

If you have never heard these songs I urge you to listen to them.

About the Author

Leon Allen Bryan was born in New York City and grew up in the Sugar Hill area. He attended Manhattan Community College, and York College in Queens. Leon is blessed with three children. This is his first novel.

Chapter 1

My father Benjamin Reeves Sr. would often tell me encouraging stories from his life and mine in hopes of inspiring me. He was born in the early 1900s the fourth of ten siblings. He'd escaped the horrors of slavery by two generations, endured severe hunger and many sleepless nights during medical school to become the family's first doctor. He received care packages from his family while working odd jobs to make ends meet. Many times he told me how he divided a box of oatmeal into thirty equal portions to make sure it would last a month.

My mother Laval Daniels was born in 1927 in Augusta, Georgia. She was the youngest of four children. Mom became an orphan near age five after witnessing the agonizing death of her mother in the family kitchen. A jealous neighbor poisoned both of Mom's parents for reasons that remain unclear to me. After spending some years in an orphanage she came to New York at the age of eighteen and found work as a cashier.

Mom pretty much became independent during her teens and preferred making decisions for herself. In addition to her many strong qualities, she was beautiful. Mom's skin was velvety smooth, dark brown, and evenly toned. Strangers on the street would compliment her and she accepted them gracefully. When I was with her I felt like she was a movie star or even better a Queen, and I was her ten year old bodyguard. It was my duty and privilege to protect her. And by age eleven I felt if it were ever necessary to fight and die for her protection, I'd give my life willingly. When any man approached her, they could look into my eleven year old eyes and know I wasn't afraid to execute them at the slightest provocation.

My mother and father were never married nor did they live together. They both worked and had very different lifestyles. My father was the reader and researcher while my mother was the negotiator and speaker. Together each was very dominant and stubborn. Two people born under the sign of Leo would find it very hard to live together, but in their own way I knew they loved each other.

So it was natural after the death of my parents to ask myself what would they do or what would they say to me in times of trouble. This strategy helped me during some of my most trying times. By examining their views, I found comfort and strength when I was alone. I would later find out after their deaths that being alone and being by yourself have two radically different meanings.

This morning I awoke feeling very upset and thought of a story my father told me. That Sunday evening my father, mother and I went to Brooklyn to have dinner with my father's sisters Maude and Marion. They lived in a four-story brownstone my father had purchased for them. It was a corner house on Gates Avenue with a three foot high black wrought iron fence. The fence started in front of the house and continued around the side past the backyard and ended at the two car garage.

The dining room was on the first floor in the front of the house and the next room had a large eat-in kitchen with two refrigerators. When I was young I loved being there. My aunts also did the cooking and washing for my dad because he rarely had time to cook. So each week his meals were prepared and picked up as a Sunday ritual. He was given four days of home cooked meals and desserts and the other two days he fended for himself. Food was prepared with love and never from cans. I swear there wasn't anything Maude couldn't make taste good.

Maude was light skinned and the same complexion as my father, but Marion was dark like me. Marion's job was to wash the clothes, do the housecleaning and be the joke teller of the family. And as long as I can remember she was most comfortable when standing near the breakfront watching T.V.

The story my father told me happened on a Sunday. My mother joined us at Gates Avenue for dinner, and the television was tuned to "Wild Kingdom", a nature show where two experts capture wild animals for study. That night's menu was rump roast with white rice and mixed vegetables. My aunts would fix the plates in the kitchen and bring them into the dining room. That night my mom got up to cut my slice of roast when I politely tapped her on the wrist and said,

"I'll do dat."

The family roared with laughter and pride at the bold statement from one a little more than a year old. And to this day I still want the chance to do it for myself. I thought of his story and felt no comfort this time. Every idea I had came to the same conclusion, I needed help.

I decided to hire a private detective to find my younger sister Linda. Trying on my own for months with no success, I was desperate. The last time I saw her was almost a year ago, April 27, 1987.

Larry, my next-door neighbor, witnessed Linda leaving the house that morning in April shortly before 7:00 a.m. He said she seemed very distressed as she threw a black duffel bag into a waiting taxi. When Larry said good morning to her she was startled and angry with herself for being observed. He said she wiped a tear from her face, said good morning and jumped in the cab. When I returned home that same evening I was opening the car door when Larry called from across the street. He did not wait for me to get out of the car. He started crossing the street and loudly asked,

"What's wrong with your sister? I saw her early this morning flying out the house."

He told me everything she'd done and asked why would she be in such a hurry to leave that morning? I looked calmly into his face and told him I had no idea. He looked at me in disbelief and said,

"I've seen people run from burning buildings that couldn't catch her."

I told him I would find out and left him standing next to my car. Then I went to the front door and instantly realized I was to blame.

After repeated attempts to find Linda, with no success, a private detective was the next logical step. I couldn't take many more sleepless nights without her. If the whole world had to be searched city by city, I had to find her.

I'd been on the phone before the sun rose making the usual calls to see if the stores were open, and there were no problems. Several years ago my oldest childhood friend Ronald Jefferson and I started a business together. Against the odds, it grew from one laundromat to a chain of twelve spread through out the five boroughs of New York City.

We also learned silk-screening and hired neighborhood youths in the summer to sell T-shirts when summer jobs were scarce. As long as their messages were uplifting they could put it on a shirt. I will never understand how our people can walk around with their children with T-shirts that say, "Fuck the world," and, "don't ask me for shit." Ronald and I were determined to run those products out of Harlem.

Then there was the pride of our company's venture, R and B Investors. This was established in late 1987 and was the fastest growing leg of our business. Harlem was a real estate gold mine for us, so we bought properties and renovated them. Some were sold only to people who were living in or had grown up in Harlem. Other brownstones were sometimes rented with an option to buy at the lowest possible interest rates. You see we got tired of hearing the same sad story on the news about banks that wouldn't give mortgages to black people with the same income and good credit as anyone else. So we made an effort to change that policy by becoming lenders.

Following a long-standing African tradition of honoring the elders, we had another jewel in our crown. This was a six floor eighteen unit apartment building reserved for our retired relatives. Ronald had half of the apartments and I had the rest. Our families stayed in the building rent free with only gas and electric to pay. As we gained economic security, they would eventually pay nothing at all. We wanted to repay them for all the love and support they'd given us. Next year, we planned to put a thirty-foot pool in the backyard and a satellite dish on the roof. Ronald and I were doing good things for the neighborhood we grew up in. We were financially secure, yet I was miserable.

I called my Aunt Dot in Detroit around 3:30 a.m. last night. Whenever I couldn't sleep, it was always good to hear her voice. We talked about Linda and how much I missed her. I told Aunt Dot I was hiring a private detective to help in my search. Last night she told me I shouldn't blame myself for Linda's disappearance. She knew how much I loved Linda and assured me one day she would return. I asked Aunt Dot what Uncle Paul was doing and she said he fell asleep with the TV on. Auntie asked again if I knew what made Linda run away and I gave the same response I gave Larry, I said I didn't know. I wasn't sure if she believed me, but she told me she loved me and after a few more minutes we said goodnight.

This morning it was very hard for me to concentrate. I hastily called all the stores, and no problems were reported. By 6:50 a.m., I was pouring a glass of pineapple, orange and mango juice. I took the phone and the glass into the bathroom to brush my hair. When I looked in the mirror I could see how the sleepless nights were adding up.

I put on a brown suede jacket and checked my .38 revolver making sure it was loaded. I had a business carry permit for the gun for the last two years and was happy I never needed to use it; I switched on my answering machine and grabbed my house keys. It was my habit to drive almost everywhere I went, but it was such a warm day for the middle of March I decided to walk my dog Mister to the park for my meeting with Mr. Queen.

Mr. Queen and I never met but I did know of him. Ronald mentioned one day in passing how good a detective Mr. Queen was for the New York City police department. During the pursuit of a serial killer he fell from a three story window into a backyard. After months of rehabilitation Mr. Queen took an early retirement, and started his security firm. We spoke on the phone yesterday and agreed to meet inside the park on St. Nicholas and 140th Street at 8:00 a.m. I figured if anyone could find Linda Mr. Queen could.

While walking through the 600 block of St. Nicholas I tried to retrace my steps. What was it I was overlooking? I'd searched for Linda for months after she left but she was always one step ahead of me. I went everywhere she'd been or ever talked about. And the day I went to the bank I learned she'd closed both of her bank accounts, which totaled $218,000 dollars. A huge sigh left my throat as I fixed my eyes on the concrete while I walked. The last night I saw her was such a huge mistake. If she'd just come back I'd promise never to touch her again.

I entered the park using the ramp and turned left, picking a bench facing towards the playground near the chess tables. Looking around I remembered sitting all over this park at one time or another during my life. As kids, we played basketball here and had neighborhood fights with other kids. The swings and the seesaws are still here, but the monkey bars are gone. I wondered if the lines for the handball court were still on the other side of the wall and went to investigate. When Mister and I walked around it was still there.

Straight ahead was the 141st Street hill Ronald and I used to ride our bikes down. To this day I still don't know the name of that church on the corner. I bet Ronald would know; he remembers stuff like that. Those small details weren't important to me, but Linda was. I began to feel guilt about the love we'd made and shame in the way I'd desired her and kissed her tender lips. Was I one of the few people who've felt love like this? If I could find her and convince her to come back I would never touch her again!

A brown-skinned man with a short hair cut came up the ramp as if he were looking for someone. When he saw me he walked in my direction wondering if he should approach with Mister growling. Mister was a 120 lb. Rottweiler I raised from a puppy and he was the best guard dog anyone could have. I told Mister to sit and the man came over. He was carrying a black briefcase, and wearing a gray suit with a white shirt and pin striped tie.

"Mr. Reeves," he said.

I stood up from the bench and extended my hand and Mister continued to growl.

"Let him smell your hand and it will be ok," I told him.

"Are you sure?"

"Yes its fine just let him smell your hand and he will calm down."

Mr. Queen held his hand out carefully then Mister smelled it and sat down.

"I am Mr. Queen," he said with apprehension.

We shook hands again and continued until we sat down. Mr. Queen was a tall slender man and looked too young to be retired from the police force.

"That's a beautiful dog," he said.

"Thank you, Mr. Queen. Would you mind showing me some identification?" I asked.

"No, of course not."

He reached inside his jacket and took out his wallet and handed over his investigators license and his driver's license. I caught a glimpse of a strap that could only be a shoulder holster. I gave him his license back and went for my wallet.

"No need Mr. Reeves I know who you are."

Looking at him, I remained silent.

"I've seen you at a few community board meetings, and I approve of all the work you're doing in Harlem. I'm just sorry we had to meet like this."

Well I definitely wasn't going to tell him the truth now.

"Thank you very much Mr. Queen. I have grown up in Harlem and been here all my life."

"So have I, I went to Rice High School and we lived on 143rd street, not too far from here."

He picked up his briefcase and rested it on his knees pushing two buttons then the latches popped open. Before he opened it he asked,

"Do you object to me taping your information, or would you prefer I write it?"

"I don't know. Maybe you should write it," I said.

He opened the case and retrieved a pocket-sized note pad flipping the cover open to the first page and began to read.

"Your sister Linda Reeves and your niece Tiffany Reeves have been missing since April 27th 1987, is that correct?"

"Yes."

"Do you suspect kidnapping?"

"No!"

He gave a peculiar look and continued.

"Who was the last person to see them?"

"I saw her last and it was a Sunday night on the 26th at home about 8 p.m. Tiffany was sleeping. My neighbor Larry saw her leave the next morning."

I was trying to relax because this was just the beginning and more personal questions were coming.

"How did you discover her missing?"

"Monday evening when I came home, Larry said he'd seen her leave in a cab that morning."

"I'll need it speak to him," he said writing Larry's name down.

"And that evening they never came home and..."

Damn it! I almost mentioned the note Linda left me. In the note she said her feelings were growing for me in ways that were totally unacceptable. She wasn't sure who was to blame but it had to stop. She also expressed her fear of me being around Tiffany. When I read that sentence it made me sit down. How could she think I'd go after a small child?

"Mr. Reeves, did you hear me?"

"Yes I'm sorry. It's just very painful to think about," I said deciding to make all of my statements short.

"When I went through the house a few of her things were gone."

"What did she take?" Mr. Queen asked.

"Some clothes for her and the baby, her bank books and later I noticed a picture of my mother and father missing from the mantle. The next day I went to the bank and she'd closed both of her accounts."

"The police didn't help you?"

"I never called the police."

I was beginning to regret calling Mr. Queen with every new question.

"Your sister and niece have been missing almost a year and you haven't been to the police?" he asked loudly.

"Mr. Queen keep your voice down."

"Mr. Reeves, your sister may have been abducted," he said calmly. I knew my story was full of holes and then he said it.

"Is there something you're not telling me?"

"No!"

"Mr. Reeves, do you understand I need to know everything. Even the smallest clues can help!"

I looked into the street at the cars creeping to the red light, and assured myself he didn't need to know the truth, and the emotional pain I felt made me regret at times I'd ever gone to Egypt.

"Mr. Queen, this is between you and me," I said sternly, "It is a personal family matter."

He flipped the pad closed and inched down the bench closer to me and poised to listen.

"My sister had a nervous breakdown some time ago. She had some personal problems and was working them out."

"What kind of problems?"

"Slight emotional problems, Mr. Queen, nothing to worry about."

"Very strange," he said as he shook his head.

"Did she have any arguments with anyone in the last week or so before she left?"

I paused for a minute and said, "No!"

"So why does she wake up one morning and decide to leave?" He looks at me for an answer and I just shake my head.

"That's what you'll tell me when you find her."

I reached inside my jacket and gave him an envelope. It had pictures of Linda and Tiffany and other useful documents, like a copy of her passport, social security number, and the numbers of her bank accounts.

"Does she have a driver's license?"

"No, she doesn't."

"What about a credit card?"

"No."

I gave him another envelope with $5000 in cash and told him if he needed more I would set up an expense account for him. He looked puzzled while he wrote my receipt. I could see the wheels turning inside his head.

"And when you find her, don't approach her. Just inform me. That's all I want you to do," I said hastily.

"So, you don't think she's in any danger?"

"No," I replied, "Linda's not helpless. I taught her a few moves to protect herself."

I did explain however that Linda was a gentle person. She never picked fights but if she was ever assaulted and the police asked what the assailants looked like Linda could say roll them over and see for yourself.

His eyes were focused on me when he continued his notes. Now and then he would look up then continue writing. This went on for several minutes, and I sat quiet and watched. He lifted his head and took a deep breath,

"Does your sister have a boyfriend?"

"No."

"Are you sure?"

"I'm sure."

"Is your sister gay?"

I just stared at him and said nothing.

"I need to ask," he said.

"What's wrong with a woman being able to defend herself?"

"Mr. Reeves I meant no offense. You said she didn't have a boy-friend."

"No, she's not gay," I said looking into the street.

"What about her friends?"

"She doesn't have any."

"None at all?"

"She knows people but doesn't socialize much," I told him.

"Mr. Reeves everyone has a best friend. Someone they can talk to."

I was her best friend, her only friend, and this was true. In the whole world I was the one she trusted the most, and I broke that trust. Dear God I hope he finds her. If I never saw her again I don't know what I would do, or how I could live. I had plenty of time to sink into my own sorrow but now wasn't the time; it was however time to change the subject.

"She likes the water," I blurted out, "you could look in coastal cities or on cruise ships."

"Good, that's a start."

"And she also likes to paint, so you can check art supply stores."

There was some degree of truth about Linda having emotional problems. I decided to share with him without telling the whole story, so I went carefully.

"When Linda stands in front of a mirror she becomes confused momentarily. Her doctor, Dr. Donnell Jase, said Linda becomes some-how detached from herself. With more time, he was sure she might make progress."

"I'll need the Doctor's phone number."

Reluctantly I gave Mr. Queen Dr. Jase`s telephone number.

After a moment, Mr. Queen stopped writing. He folded his pad and told me he would call every two days; sooner if there was anything new to report. I had his telephone and beeper numbers with his busi-ness card in my pocket. To my left a young man came into the park with two children; a girl of about four or five years old wearing a pink wool jacket, blue jeans with white sneakers and the other child he carried in his right arm. When he walked by us, we smiled at the children and nodded hello to him. The girl caught sight of the swings and took off running. Mr. Queen told me, it was good to see a man taking care of his children. I was about to agree when I thought of more clues for him to follow. This one I thought was the most important of all.

"I almost forgot the most important place she likes to go."

"Where's that?"

"Linda loves the library. She had an insatiable appetite for books and reads at least one or two books a week."

"What types of books does she like?"

"Everything, there's no telling what subject peaks her interest."

Mr. Queen stood up from the bench, shook my hand and told me not to worry he would find her. He told me he'd been able to locate people who were missing much longer and with a lot less information. We shook hands and then he walked away. His confidence and positive attitude gave me some relief. But I needed a plan B. If he couldn't find her, what would I do next?

I watched Mr. Queen walk down the ramp, out of the park, and then across the street to a dark blue Toyota Camry. He pulled from the parking space and sped uptown. He had to be suspicious. If it were me, I wouldn't believe that line of bullshit I just gave him. And if I thought telling him the whole truth would help him find her I would.

There was an incident a few months before Linda left. I discovered her in a trance-like state standing in front of the mirror in the hallway. My brownstone had a first floor entrance and another one the second floor. When you enter the house from the second floor past the alcove to your right is a huge mirror mounted on the wall. It is four feet across and four feet high starting two feet from the floor.

That day when I came through the door she was standing there and when I spoke to her she said nothing. I went closer and she still didn't seem to see me. I called her again and she wouldn't answer. I stood next to her shoulder and she was a statue. I asked her what was wrong. She gave no movement or acknowledgment. Her expression was one of frozen disbelief. I touched her and she didn't move. I whispered her name softly, while nudging her shoulder. This had happened before and each time I always felt helpless. There was a time I tested her to see how long she would stand there and it was more than two hours. This time I reached up and put my hand in front of her face. Her eyes focused on my hand and across my arm to my face. Sometimes she came out of her trance and didn't know who I was. And there were times she went outside and had the same experience. She would be late occasionally with no explanation or recollection. I could imagine her on Fifth Avenue lost in her reflection.

One time she smiled when she saw me and jokingly told me to get my hand out of her face. Each time was a little different. Now I stepped in front of her. Her eyes focused on mine, and a pleasing smile came to her face. Her arms rose to embrace me with a hug. Her head sank into the crest of my neck as my arms wrapped around her waist. She felt so good a hunger started to rise and I hugged her tighter. I thought today she would finally be mine again, mine forever. She pulled her head back and this time, I saw a twinge of distrust. She quickly let go and ran upstairs and that was the last time I saw her.

At 3:00, children began filling the streets. Where had the time gone? I walked to 125th Street and St. Nicholas with Mister then down to Seventh Avenue towards home. Several months ago Linda expressed a desire to paint. So we went downtown to an art supply on the west side. We bought some paints and brushes and two books on painting for beginners. The book for beginners was a guide with helpful hints from other artists. When we got home Linda started to work immediately. Like most artists, she never let me see her unfinished work. After two days, her first painting was done. It was a river flanked by green grass. The next one hung in the living room and was a great conversation piece. Linda painted the pyramids of Egypt in great detail surrounded by grass and trees.

For those who are interested, I'd show them books from my personal library about Africa. So many times I would hear people say they didn't know Egypt was in Africa. I thought it was in the Middle East they'd say. I'd shake my head and refer them to the map of Africa.

Egypt was not the original name of the country. The indigenous people of the country were known as the Kemites and they called their land Kemit. As a teenager, I was always curious about the history of Kemit. Over the years I built a fine library in a room upstairs on the third floor. It contains books I've purchased and includes audio and videotapes on African history. Friends will come over and read the titles of my books and ask to borrow them. Only because I felt knowledge should be shared, I reluctantly agreed. After awhile I began to notice the books or the videotapes I'd loaned remained in their possession unread or unwatched. Some of my books were just lost through carelessness. From then on I politely refused to lend from the knowledge center. It was my ambition to leave this important asset to my children when I had some.

It seems as if as quickly as my excitement for history grew, it fizzled out. My fascination with Egyptian history got me into the mess I was in now, and took me to the extreme. Maybe it was possible in Kemit for a brother and sister to marry, but it wasn't acceptable today. If I hadn't gone to Kemit years ago my heart wouldn't be breaking right now. I wouldn't feel the kind of love I have for Linda, or the longing to make love to her again. If I hadn't gone to Africa two years ago, I think I would have married Terri. If I had given myself the chance I could have fallen in love with her. Most likely we'd have children by now. Back then she loved me totally, now she has a new man and hates my guts. It's understandable, I guess. I could have treated her better.

As long as I can remember, the land of my ancestors called to me. Like a mother's call to a child or a gentle tugging. Call it crazy but if I was walking east my life was easier and free of obstacles. Kemit was for me a faint spiritual sound few could hear. But once heard, it was always calling you. The voice carried across the winds whispering,

"Don't forget me; don't stop loving me, because I long for your touch. You are my child and I've never seen you. Never felt your unique footsteps. From your feet I can feel your heart beating and I know it's you. Come to me and receive this love. The love I have been saving for you since that time you were taken away."

Just like an ignorant child I rebelled against her. Yes, Mother Africa I trusted you and you showed me mysteries. You gave me love and then you took it away. Was it fair to blame you? You showed me secrets Mama that changed my life for the worst. You introduced me to events that altered my values and twisted my perceptions of reality forever. Every time I start to feel like my first meeting with you was a dream, my love for Linda was the proof I was fully awake.

Finally reaching home I took my keys from my pocket, and stared at the door. Home was not where I wanted to be. It was different without Linda and Tiffany. I promised myself if Linda came back, I would never touch her again. I would forever put out of my mind the feelings I had for her.

I went into the living room and sat on the couch across from the painting of the pyramids, a scene all too familiar to me. It was unreasonable for me to blame my trip to Kemit for my predicament now, but there were times I wished I'd never gone.

Chapter 2

About two years earlier shortly after my birthday in the beginning of 1986 I considered the path my life was taking. No, it wasn't greed, it was an attitude. One could compare it to building a successful house of cards. When others would quit I would stack just one more card and persist.

In other words I wanted the most out of life. I was still young almost six feet tall not overly muscular but I kept in shape. Dark like my mother I was teased when I was a kid. In my adult life I learned to counter the jokes by saying my dark skin was pure and I was proud it wasn't diluted.

I wanted children with a woman I loved, and who loved me. When the kids came my goal was to teach them to be self- reliant, and to search for the secrets of life and happiness. I was lucky enough to have parents who knew they weren't perfect, but through me they set into motion a system of advancement. The plan was simple; be a better parent then your parents. Learn from their mistakes and don't repeat them. At times this meant my parents would share their most intimate disappointments and blunders with me. While others kept their family skeletons in the closet, my mother and father accepted their blunders and talked about them with me. They didn't tell me every mistake they made, but I believe they were horribly honest about most of them.

I was also taught that success doesn't fall into your lap, and everyone can't hit the lottery. The successes in your life must be chased, hunted and captured. Rarely will you find happiness without some trial, effort and error. Yes I wanted children with a woman I loved and I never wanted her to ever worry about finances. I wanted to live in a world without fear with a woman who was discrete, intelligent and courageous. Add too that a thin slice of freakiness reserved for me and her picture would be complete. She would know how to turn up my flame. She would be one who could say, show me yours and I'll show you mine. Kiss me there and I'll kiss you back. Hold me and I will never let you go. Love me, and I'll love you forever. This was the dream I pursued and until she was found I was unfilled.

It was March of 1986 and I had just turned twenty seven last January. I had no children of my own and no love in my life. Yet, there were a few good things to be thankful for; good friends, my health and a growing business.

With some money Ronald and I saved we started our first coin-operated laundry four years ago. Now we have four stores in the Harlem area. The Nicholas Avenue Kleenit laundromat was the first to open with fifteen washers and the same amount of dryers. By November of 1983, we paid off our loan and had enough capital to open the Amsterdam Avenue Kleenit that was twice as big. When 1984 rolled around, we had even better ideas. The Eighth Avenue Kleenit was the size of a small supermarket. It had enough space to hold fifty dryers and seventy washing machines, with dry cleaning done on the premises. During one of our monthly meetings, we decided there was enough room for an indoor play area for the children of customers. Within five months, Ronald and I had made enough money to open a fourth store on Seventh Avenue exactly like the one on Eighth.

Ronald worked out a schedule for us to take turns managing the stores on a weekly basis and it worked out well. When it was his week off I made sure all the stores were open for business and the money was deposited in the bank. I took care of employee payroll, and placed orders for merchandise. We loved this idea because except for the morning calls we made to check-in with each other, it amounted to working six months out of every year.

Today Ronald was waiting in the back office of the Eighth Avenue store to hear a new proposal to earn more capital. My idea was to become a lending institution after buying real estate in the Harlem area. It was my dream to have everyone living well and working, zero unemployment in the Harlem community. It was probably more fantasy than a dream, but we had to start someplace.

This was the third day in a row that it had rained and the sky was still dark gray. What had begun as little puddles on Tuesday were now lakes that took forever to walk around on Thursday. I parked my car in front of the beauty salon halfway down the block from the Eighth Avenue Kleenit. It didn't seem like it was raining that hard a minute ago but it always seems to happen that every time I'm ready to get out of the car or walk to a building it starts to rain harder. The rain falling against the roof of the car sounded like hundreds of little drummers, and the water cascaded across the windshield to make visibility non-existent. I opened the door and looked down the street to make sure no cars were coming. In those few seconds my face and jacket were soaked, so I closed the door. I thought maybe if I sit a few minutes the rain would lighten up. That thought immediately changed to,

"Hell, I'm already wet; I might as well go for it."

I opened the door, took a look at the traffic and when it was clear, I got out and started running. Before reaching the curb, I was drenched. I ran down the block to the entrance of the Kleenit and went inside. People were standing inside behind the door with their laundry baskets looking outside waiting for the rain to let up. Greeting them with a hello I sprinted past and saw Chris reading a book behind the counter.

Chris was one of twelve employees who helped open the stores during the week. He'd been with us from the beginning when we opened the first store on St. Nicholas Avenue. Employees who showed up on time and worked hard got regular raises and as much responsibility as they could handle. Chris was five feet eight inches tall or maybe five-nine and the product of a black father and a Spanish mother. Chris is light complexioned, while his Brother Raymond's skin is dark like mine. Chris looked up from the counter when I walked by and said hello. He let me know Ronald was in the back office, and he was expecting me. Speaking to him in Spanish, I asked how his family was? He answered that they were fine.

Shaking the water from my jacket, I knocked on the door. Light shone from the peephole. The door opened and Ronald walked toward the desk and sat in the chair behind it. I removed my jacket and draped it across the back of the chair on the other side of the desk. It was a comfortable office with three chairs, a desk, two filing cabinets, and a black leather couch. There was a wall unit with a 20-inch TV and VCR, and two closed-circuit television monitors hooked up to four ceiling cameras in each corner of the laundry. The two monitors had split screens and recorded 24 hours a day. One camera focused on the front door and the change machine. The other pointed to the rear exit and the two remaining ones swiveled to watch the customers.

Today I would tell Ronald about my idea to start an investment company. R. And B Investments had a nice ring to it or even R and J investments. We could make low interest loans or start a Harlem merchant's bank.

"So homey, what's up?" I said.

"Give me one second, Ben," he said as he continued to write.

"I need to make a memo about Chris. He asked to work the weekend and take Wednesday and Thursday off. He has a test to study for at the end of this month. So his brother Ray is working in his place."

"Take your time."

Ronald closed his daily reminder and took a momentary recess. He looked at me for a moment then sat up in his chair to lean over and shake my hand.

"So what's up, man?" He said.

"Awh you know same old thing."

I could never tell what Ronald was feeling by trying to read his facial expressions. He had a deadpan look even when he was angry.

Ronald and I grew up together in Harlem and have been friends ever since. I recall meeting him for the first time like it was yesterday. It was the summer and we were six or seven years old. I was walking past a building up the street from my house and I heard commotion from a nearby hallway. I peered in and saw a little dark-skinned boy with blue jeans and a white T-shirt hitting another boy on the steps inside the hallway. I'd seen this kid on the block before and I asked him why was he hitting that boy. Ronald told me in a calm voice,

"Mark was at my house and he stole these Hot Wheels cars."
He came out of his pants pocket with two racecars in his hand. Before I could stop myself, we were both beating Mark up on the steps of the hallway. We left him sobbing and went down the street. We all made up a few days later and Ronald and I have been best friends ever since. So his statement came totally out of the blue.

"How long have we known each other?" he asked.

"Awhh shit, what is it now?"

Whenever we needed to discuss a serious problem, one of us would always say,

"How long had we known each other?"

We were both smiling. I shook my head from side to side and said, "What is it?"

"How long we known each other?" he asked again.

"Since we were six or seven," I replied.

"So what's up with you?"

This is our time for confession. The only words spoken between us now had to be the truth.

"I don't know, I've been a little edgy lately."

"Are you and Terri OK?"

"Yeah, you can see for yourself., She's meeting me here."

"When?"

"Soon," I said.

"It's not just me who noticed. Terri called the house looking for you two days ago. Your sister called because you had her waiting at her house all day and never showed."

"Everything's cool man, it's just well..." Then I took a deep breath, "I was thinking about asking Terri to marry me."

"Yeah!"

"Yup."

"What about Paula?" he asked.

"I stopped seeing her last week."

His mouth dropped open, "Get outta here! Paula? Not Paula?!"

He seemed more disappointed then I was.

"All that stuff you told me about her!"

"Yeah, I am gonna miss her."

"How did she take it?"

"I tried not to hurt her feelings, but she didn't take it very well. But hey, you know she's not the one. I care about her and that's it. She's just not the one."

He just kept saying,

"Paula, no more Paula."

I know he wanted to fuck Paula but I didn't care.

"Love's supposed to make you forget everybody else. Terri's a good woman you know that. She's intelligent, independent, has her own money, she looks good, and she's good to me. Plus I know she loves me," I said.

"So what' the problem?" he asked

"When I get married I want to know I can look her straight in her face and mean it when I say I love you. She suspects I see other women but she's never asked me."

"Why?"

"Because she knows I would tell the truth, and I'm tired of pretending it doesn't hurt her."

He sat there and waited for me to continue.

"Truthfully, I don't want to cause her anymore pain."

"Well yo, between you and me, Lorraine told me Terri doesn't think she can put up with you much longer. She told Lorraine she loves you but she's getting tired of waiting."

"Yeah Ron I can feel it. We argue more about little stuff."

"I hear you man,"

"And last week I really messed up."

"What happened?"

"I told her if she found someone who loved her she should leave me."

"Damn! What's wrong with you?" he said jokingly.

"Yeah I did, and that was a mistake. She got out of bed crying and I felt like shit. Why did I think saying that could make her feel better? I was trying to be straight with her you know? I just want her to be happy."

We stopped for minute to look at the monitor. Two men walked into the laundromat. One man wore a trench coat and the other a solid green army jacket. We were always careful a few hours before closing time. Our eyes studied the screen but they were only trying to sell jumper cables. Chris confronted them politely and asked them to leave.

"Does he think he can get rid of those cables in here?" Ronald said.

"Hey nothing surprises me any more."

"So what are you gonna do?"

"I think I need a vacation," I said as if it were a blessing.

"That's a good idea, where to?"

"I'm not sure, maybe I'll go to Africa."

"Africa! Are the Bahamas out of style already?"

"No, I have always wanted to go to Africa ever since I was a kid."

"What part of Africa?"

"Egypt, the pyramids, the Sphinx, and whatever else there is to see."

"When are you going?"

"I'll call the travel agent first thing in the morning and if I can leave next week I will. That is if you and Lorraine don't have any plans."

"We'll work something out. Who knows Lorraine and I might join you two."

"Terri's not going," I said.

"You and Paula?"

"What did I just tell you? There is no more Paula."

Now he was smiling at me like I was fooling around. So I refreshed his memory about Paula. As far as I was concerned Paula was just for sex and nothing more. We rarely had a conversation about anything meaningful.

"Ron, you've seen Paula, and you know how she is. I told her I wanted her and her roommate Karen and what did she do? One night when I went to pick her up the three of us went to a club in the village danced for a while, had a few drinks, then spent the weekend together." There were times I didn't tell Ronald everything right away because he would tell Lorraine my business, but he was my best friend.

"Now could I seriously marry Paula? "

"Yeah you're right," then his eyes went to the monitor when I spoke.

"Every time I see Paula she's been," I was interrupted.

"Terri's here," he said hastily.

Her figure floated across the screen to the direction of the office door. I got up and walked to the door and opened it before she could knock. I could only wonder after seeing her smiling face what kind of fool I'd been. Any man would be proud to have her.

Terri was a petite 5'8" with caramel colored skin. Her hair was shoulder length and when she wore it up I knew she had been in court. She was dressed in a brown double-breasted suit with a white blouse. Her face was still wet from the rain when she kissed me. I told her I missed her and with a smirk of disbelief, she said she missed me too. Her fragrance excited me and when she walked past and into the office I was even more aroused.

I met Terri one evening when she and my sister were walking home from the train station. They had become friends after seeing each other almost every day on the No. 5 train. And after months of talking and laughing they started hanging out. One day I surprised my sister at the train station and she introduced me to Terri. At that time Terri was involved with a man who was an alcoholic. After a few months they broke up. From that day I started making any excuse to meet my sister when she got off of the train. Sometimes I'd say I was just in the area shopping or visiting a friend nearby, anything just to talk with Terri. Our first date was a brunch at the Blue Note and we've been seeing each other ever since.

Terri sat on the couch and looked around the office. There were times she would enter this room like a detective searching for clues. She removed her right shoe and fumbled with the strap. I told her I was waiting for her so we could leave. She said she'd be ready as soon as she fixed her shoe. Terri was just like me in some ways because she knows just what she wants, where she is headed, and what price she had to pay to get there. As I watched her put her shoe back on I knew there was just so much she'd be willing to put up with from me. Terri stood up and said goodbye to Ronald and asked him to remind Lorraine to call her. I held the door open and she walked out and I told Ronald we'd talk later

We reached the front door and I told Chris to have a nice night. The wind was blowing hard and the rain was the same as when I came in so I offered to get the car and bring it to the front. Sarcastically, Terri told me she wouldn't melt. Instead she unfolded a plastic rain scarf and tied around her head. Then she frowned at me and said let's go. I started running and when I looked back she was just walking slowly. I stopped to wait for her and the rain started running down my neck.

"Come on baby," I said.

"Did you forget my shoe was broken?"

"I didn't know it was broken."

"I told you it was broken in the office!" she said with her voice was rising.

I knew she didn't tell me it was broken and I didn't argue. I would have a hard enough time explaining why she couldn't go on this vacation with me. My keys fumbled in the lock. I opened the door and waited for her to get in. I was drenched now so there was no need to run to the other side. Now I just took my time opening the door and got in. I started the car, looked over at her and could tell there was something on her mind. I told her again how much I missed her and she smiled, leaned over and kissed me.

"Is there anything you want while we're outside?" I asked.

"Do you have any shrimps in the freezer?"

I had to think for a minute, "no."

"Do you have any lettuce or tomatoes for a salad?"

"I'm not sure, I think so."

"It doesn't matter, let's just go," she said abruptly.

Terri had a major attitude and I knew I was in for it tonight. When she was upset she got quiet, but when Terri got pissed off she treated you like you were in the courtroom. You were asked a series of questions as if a judge or jury could hear them. You had no choice but to tell the truth because the girl had a great memory for details. In her personal courtroom she made the law and enforced it.. It was one of the many qualities I respected about her and which eventually drew me to her. All in all she was fair and in time my conscience forced me to be fair and equal with her. The last time we argued she asked me so many questions at once I couldn't keep up. And then she answered them for me before I could speak. And she always used the same closing statement, Isn't that right, Bennie?

I made a right turn into my block and looked for a space. The car behind me stayed too close for me to park right away, so I pulled to the side to let that idiot pass by.

"What time do you have to get up tomorrow?" I asked.

Terri never looked at me when she answered. She stared out the car window and watched a single drop of water roll jaggedly down the glass.

"I'm free tomorrow," she replied.

So I looked for space on the left side of the street. Cars on the right side had to be moved on Friday before 9:00 am. Further down the block I saw a space not too far from the house. The wind and rain tapered off and the sidewalks were empty. Terri was still silently looking out the window. I took hold of her hand and squeezed it gently and told her I missed her. She turned and looked into my eyes in disbelief. Squeezing a little tighter I repeated myself, and painfully she told me she missed me too. Leaning over I kissed her on the lips for just a second and she smiled. Then I suggested we go running in the morning. Most of the time when Terri didn't rush off to work we would run three or four miles before breakfast. I took her nod as a yes then opened the door and got out.

My mind and my attitude about life had been steadily changing. I was twenty-seven years old and I wasn't entirely happy. My love for one woman and trust of one friend were missing. I was sure my feelings for Terri were growing stronger. And each time I thought about asking her to marry me my fears decreased. I wondered if she would always love me. There were times when I thought she just wanted to be married because I was good in bed, or because she thought I was attractive and would make a good provider. I've seen it happen to couples before and I didn't want it to happen to me.

Would she change once I put a ring on her finger? Not only do the women change, but so do men. For some men you're just a cute piece of ass to come home to. To some women you're just a brainless chump who pays the bills. Yes, my fears were diminishing but until I was sure I loved her I had to wait.

Once inside the house, Terri took off her shoes. I walked around her and into the kitchen to look in the refrigerator. There was enough lettuce and tomatoes for a salad and some leftover turkey thighs from the night before. From the corner of my eye I saw her walk from the hallway and up the spiral staircase to the bedroom. With my jacket still on, I washed my hands in the sink and prepared her salad. She walked to the doorway of the kitchen but didn't come in. Her blouse was unbuttoned exposing a white bra.

"Your salad will be ready in a minute," I said.

"OK, I think I'll take a shower first."

When she turned to walk away I called her. "Baby," I said softly. She stopped and took a step back. My arms opened wide beckoning to embrace her. Hesitantly she walked towards me. My arms closed around her. Her face lay flat on my chest as I held her. She felt so good in my arms. At that moment I wondered when would be a good time to tell her I was going to Egypt and she couldn't come, before or after we made love.

Terri pushed away,

"Where's the new nightgown I left here?"

"Did you look in your drawer?" I said.

Her smile was bright now and I wasn't about to chase it away. Before the night was over I would have to tell her about Egypt.

Almost an hour passed since we got in. After my shower I wore the dark blue pajamas Terri brought me for Christmas and added a touch of cologne to my neck, and went back downstairs to the living room. Terri was on the couch in front of the cocktail table. The room was quiet with no television and no music playing. She sat there on the couch with her legs folded under her in a yoga position. When the phone rang she leaned over and answered it. I knew it was Ronald calling to say all of the stores were locked up for the night.

Whoever was managing that week would check-in between 9 and 9:30 pm. We carried no money at closing time but the threat of robbery was very real. We made these nightly calls to each other without fail. Terri spoke to Ronald briefly and handed over the phone. I asked if she would mind fixing a drink for us.

Ronald told me there were no problems closing up for the night. Then he asked if I told Terri about my trip. Before I could answer she returned from the kitchen with two glasses. She handed one to me, and stood there waiting for me to taste it. I took a sip and told him I was working on it, then said goodbye.

I took a long slow gaze at her new nightie. It was gold and silky looking. I could see the impression of her nipples protruding through the fabric.

"You look good baby, I like it!"

My hand reached out to touch the material starting down her back until I reached the hem. She walked away from me around the coffee table and sat in the corner of the couch. My drink was good not too strong, just the right blend of rum and Coke.

"Why'd you sit all the way over there?" I asked.

"So you could be sure this was what you wanted."

Then she smiled at me and took a sip from her glass.

35

"You know it is," I said.

Terri looked at me in a stern manor and said,

"I wasn't coming back after the other day. I was going to drop you, and put your keys through the mail slot."

"Why?"

"Why! After what you said to me?" and she put her glass down.

"Bennie you think my feelings are a joke!"

I saw the tears roll down her face. I put my glass down and moved closer.

"Baby I don't think your feelings are a joke. I care for you more than anyone."

"Then why don't you want to see me anymore?"

"Huh?"

I had to think for a minute, "I never said that!"

Terri was calming down and the lawyer was coming out.

"You never said that?" She repeated.

"No I didn't," I said quickly.

"Do you remember telling me I could see anybody I wanted to?"

Before I could answer she said,

"Do you remember me opening my heart and telling you I loved you?"

She just stared at me. When my mouth opened to answer she interrupted.

"What kind of man tells a woman who is in love with him she can see other people!"

"That's not how I meant it"

"Is that what you said to me?"

"Yeah but."

"Yeah but what?"

"That's not what I meant. Baby, whose stuff is here? Yours! And who has keys to my house? You."

"Did you or did you not tell me I should sleep with other men? My last man treated me like I was stupid and he's real sorry! I'm not stupid Bennie! Do you think I'm stupid, huh? Answer me!"

She'd never been this mad before, and I damn sure wasn't going to mention Egypt now. I moved across the couch to sit next to her.

"Terri, as long as we've been together, have I ever lied to you?"

Her eyebrow rose when she looked at me but she didn't answer.

"I may tell you things you don't want to hear, but do you feel when you ask me something important I lie to you?"

Still she said nothing.

"Do you think I've ever tried to make you feel bad on purpose? Do I wake up in the morning and try to make you feel like shit?"

I took hold of her hand cautiously and wouldn't let go.

"I want you to let me talk for a minute, just hear me out."

She refused to look at me, and sat there pretending to be bored. Softly I said,

"Any man would be lucky to have you. You've been wonderful to me. Every moment I've spent with you I've wanted to be with you and I've never pretended when I'm with you. You've been so very good to me. Whenever I need your help and your support and comfort you're always there. I'm not trying to get rid of you!"

I shook her hand to make her look at me.

"I am not trying to get rid of you! I was trying to be unselfish when I told you about seeing other people. The truth is I couldn't stand to see another man touch you!"

"So why'd you say that? You have no idea how much that hurt!"

"I didn't mean it like that. I just want you to be happy."

"I am happy you idiot!"

I let go of her hand and put my arm around her shoulder. I could take all her pain and sadness away by looking deep into her eyes and saying I loved her, but I didn't. I knew why I was too scared to trust. She could never break my heart if I didn't give it to her.

"Terri, I care more for you than anyone in a longtime."

She let me kiss the corner of her mouth where there was the salty taste of tears on my lips.

"If I tell you something now will you believe me?" I asked.

"What?"

"Will you believe me?"

"Maybe."

"I've been thinking about you all week and you need to know you're the only one in my life."

She frowned and put her hand on her chin.

"Do you believe me?" then I kissed her lips again, "I mean it baby, just you."

Through the silence we looked at each other. The anticipation of her response created a lump in my throat. Her hand formed a rake as her fingers spread apart and dug into my hair.

"You need a hair cut baby," she whispered.

"I've been busy."

Terri stood up in front of me still raking my hair.

"Let me close the blinds," she said.

When she got up to close the blinds I followed and caught her between the loveseat and the window and kissed her. We held each other tight and kissed passionately. I squatted down placing my arms under her hips and picked her up until her belly button was near my chest. Rocking slowly her feet dangled in the air as I kissed her breasts through her nightie. She pulled the shoulder straps down to reveal herself. Willingly I took each breast into my mouth as her fingers rubbed the back of my head and then down my neck. Effortlessly, I held her in the middle of the living room. My arms folded under her and her legs slightly straddled me. One hand rubbed the inside of her thigh until I turned my wrist upward to touch her. The nightie was down around her waist while my lips found their way between her breasts. She moaned softly as my finger searched for her opening. She asked me to put her down and I ignored her. Instead I kept probing her secrets until her passion dripped down my fingers. We made love slowly to the sounds of the night and our own voices. I was such a fool. Beneath me lay a woman who gave every inch of her body freely and all her trust exclusively to me. Why wasn't it enough?

I was awakened by a soft kiss on my cheek and then another. The first thing I saw was Terri smiling at me. It was a strong clue that I hadn't mentioned Egypt last night. I pulled her close and hugged her. This would be the last time I see her for sure.

"There is something I've got to tell you baby," I said while I stretched. Then she pulled away from me. I didn't notice she had a firm grip on my wrist. With a strong yank she pulled me almost out of the bed. I was laughing and telling her to stop but she kept on pulling. Terri pulled me out of the bed and across the floor. She was dressed in purple bicycle tights with a gray hooded track sweater. Her running shoes gave her good traction to pull me across the carpet.

"Yeah I know," she said, "you want to tell me you're too tired to go."

She let go of my wrist then stood with her feet on each side of my head so I was looking up at her.

"Look at you. I give you a little bit and now you can talk."

"No baby, I need to tell you,"

And before I could finish my sentence she came crashing down on my chest like a professional wrestler.. Then she quickly rolled to her feet and resumed her position. I began to laugh while holding that spot on my chest.

"Yo woman, are you out of your mind?"

"You need to go running with me. The last time you couldn't keep up," she bragged,

"And what about my flowers? You owe me three dozen roses, or did you forget? You said whenever we raced if you lost you'd buy me a dozen roses."

"Damn baby, you ran track in college. How do you expect me to keep up with those long legs of yours."

"What's wrong with my legs?" She asked jokingly.

"Nothing, nothing," I said.

"If you don't get up off the floor you're going to feel my knee."

"All right I'll get up." I looked at the clock and said, "Terri its six-thirty in the morning."

I saw her walking down the staircase,

"Where are you going?"

"I'm going downstairs to do my stretches."

"Not in those tights you're not."

I could only see her bust when she stopped on the stairs. She rolled her eyes at me and said, "well hurry up."

The air smells so sweet after a heavy rain. It was a damp brisk morning with a temperature of around 48 degrees. Terri was talking with Larry, my neighbor from across the street. He was probably try-ing to get free legal advice like everyone else. Terri was accustomed to people asking her for legal advice once they found out she was a law-yer. She didn't mind giving the advice and I didn't mind her talking to Larry. Larry was a good friend and neighbor to everyone in the block. I heard the tail end of their conversation. Terri was saying how it was a shame and Larry was saying those sons of bitches have to pay.

"Who has to pay?" I asked.

"Someone keyed my car again!" Larry said angrily.

Then he turned crossed the street and went home. I asked Terri did Larry have any idea when it happened and she said no.

"So how far are we running today baby?"

"I don' know, make it light on yourself," I responded.

"How about from here to Yankee Stadium and back. First one to come back and touch this rail wins."

"And what does the winner get?" I questioned.

"Whatever the winner wants."

"I know what I want," I said looking eagerly at her.

"Well you have to work for it."

I knew if we ran three or four miles she'd win so I suggested we run further than the Stadium.

"I'll take your bet," I said, "but the stadium is too close."

"Where to?" she asked.

"Let me see, how about from here to 110th Street and Seventh Avenue, as a warm up. Then from there we'll circle Central Park and come back home. The first one that touches this rail wins." The smile melted off her face.

"Well talk to me, what's up? What's wrong? No juice?" I boasted.

"How long is that gonna take?"

"It'll take you longer than me baby," I laughed.

She agreed and after we warmed up we were off. Terri was an excellent runner. She had at least a dozen first-place trophies in track and field from college, and more for second place. She kept a quick pace that wasn't easy to keep up with. When we ran together Terri would keep me on a fast pace to burn me out quickly. Most of the time her strategy worked. But I noticed when we ran more than five miles I was able to hold my own. It still wasn't easy to beat her but this way I stood a chance.

"How are you feeling?" She asked.

"This feels good, when was the last time you went running?"

"Three days ago."

"Really, how far?"

"I don't know, six or seven miles," she said.

I wasn't gonna look worried I just said, "That's good baby."

"Bennie I keep forgetting to tell you I got a promotion."

"Congratulations," I shouted, "partner?"

"Not hardly," she replied.

A man was walking a large Rottweiler without a leash in the next block, so we crossed the street.

"What does the promotion mean?"

"It means I'll be in charge of the new lawyers hired by the firm who recently passed the bar exam."

"When did you find out?"

"Last week."

"Why didn't you tell me before?"

"I wanted to come over and tell you in person but I couldn't catch up with you," she said cynically.

"What day was this?"

"Last Tuesday."

Tuesday was the night I met with Paula and told her it was over.

"Where were you?" She asked.

"Tuesday I think I was hanging out with some guys from the neighborhood."

"Well anyway, they hired four new lawyers and I'll be training them for the next eight weeks starting Monday."

I stopped running; I couldn't believe this was happening.

"What's wrong," she asked.

Before I put my foot in my mouth I asked her if she was sure she was taking the job and she said yes.

"What's the problem?" She repeated.

"I was planning a short vacation," then I waited for her to speak.

"Bennie I can't leave, I just took the job."

There we were Seventh Avenue and 113th Street close to the park.

"I can't go, why didn't you tell me before? When did you decide to go?"

"You know how much I needed a vacation. I talked with Ronald yesterday and he's going to cover for me."

I quickly changed the subject, "Why didn't you tell me about the promotion? You could have called."

"I just never got around to it."

I stopped and hugged her, "well, congratulations baby."

"Where were we going?" She asked.

"Egypt," I said.

Everyone on 7th Avenue heard her yell "Egypt!?"

"Yeah, Egypt," I said pleasantly.

"When did you do this? How did you do it so fast?"

The lie I was about to tell made me feel uneasy, especially after reminding her last night about my honesty.

"While I was at work yesterday I made plans with the travel agent."

"And when are we supposed to leave?"

"I don't know the exact date, but it's soon."

"You put the money down already?"

"Yes, I put $2000 down."

"Honey I like surprises but damn! You should have talked to me."

"I know, I know."

We couldn't discuss our business in the street like this so we walked to Central Park. Terri was quiet while we walked until we reached the park. She took my hand and with hope and the willingness to believe me on her face, she asked if there was more I needed to tell her? It's been said that love hurts but sometimes not loving someone can hurt more. If I were truly in love with Terri I would have been comfortable telling her about what was happening to me. The tugging in my spirit, the feeling I was missing someone or someone was missing me. Almost as if there was a place I was needed and someone was waiting for me. And if I believed in myself and followed my heart all my questions would be answered. If I loved Terri I could trust her with the deepest part of me, my soul. It was times like this when I'd ask myself how long it would take for me to trust her.

She turned to me and said, "I tell you what we can do. I will speed up the training so I can be finished in six weeks. Call the travel agent and tell him we'll go later."

"Honey I can't wait that long. I've been under a little stress. Maybe it's the money or all the things I'm not doing to help people in the community."

She interrupted me, "You're just one man. You can't save the world. I know you'd like to try, but you can't! Bennie sometimes I think you won't be happy until every nigga in Harlem has his own business! You do a lot for people, a lot more than most. Aren't you setting your sister up with her own bakery?

"Yes."

"So, you do so much. You have nothing to be ashamed of."

She took a deep breath and looked into my eyes,

"Bennie I'll be very honest with you. Sometimes when I tell you I love you and you don't say it back I just want to slap the shit out of you. But after last night you said things to me to make me believe you do love me. You said I would be the only woman in your life, and I want to believe you. In time I will believe you, but I can't help thinking if I don't go with you now you'll take someone else."

"There's no one else in my life, only you. And if I tell you I'm going alone I am. Terri I don't want to lose you, and I'm not trying to chase you away. Believe me I do know how lucky I am to have you."

Terri looked into the clouds scanning the heavens for an answer.

"When I get back it'll be different you'll see, it will be better," I said. Truth be told I've had women who after a few weeks refused to deal with my bullshit. They said goodbye and I never lost any sleep over it, but Terri and I had become more. She was the only woman I'd ever given keys to the house, and the only one I'd ever taken on a vacation.

She was the only one I'd made an effort to keep.

Finally she turned to me as if it were my last chance and asked,

"If you need me to do anything for you let me know."

"It would be great if you can stay at my house a few nights a week," I said.

"How long do you think you'll be gone?" she asked.

"No more than two weeks."

Once again I changed the subject, "will you stay with me tonight Ms. Anderson?"

"Yes, Mr. Reeves."

The day crawled by and when we reached home only blocks separated us, but I did win the race. I won because I ran away from the look on her face and the lie I'd told in Central Park. Once home we changed clothes and planned to spend the whole day out.

In the evening we went to the village for dinner. Before we went home I stopped at a corner store on 6th Avenue and bought a dozen white roses with streaks of pink in the petals and gave them to Terri. That night it was my intention to please her as never before. To do anything she wished for as long as she wanted. This was not unusual but tonight had to be different. If she wanted to have multiples on top of her multiples, she would get them tonight. I would make love to her as if my life depended on it, as if it were our last time.

Sometime during the night I got up to use the bathroom. When I returned Terri was awake and sitting up in bed. I got under the covers put my arms around her and she was asleep again. But I never went back to sleep that night. The light trickled slowly into the bedroom. I even contemplated asking her to marry me while she slept, and then the sun came up.

Many thoughts went through my mind that night. A part of me believed if I went to Egypt upon my return I'd never be the same. A chill had replaced the warm gentle tugging feeling associated with my trip. It was like when they say a person steps on your grave. It ran icy cold down my neck and into my stomach and I got the same feeling every time I thought about what lay ahead.

Chapter 3

Rows of silver scales moving in effortless rhythm up one side of the glass tank and down to the gravel at the bottom relaxed me. There was no time to test the automatic feeder I purchased yesterday. All I could do now was follow the directions and hope it deposited the food each day for two weeks until I returned. I would have left a note for Terri asking her to feed the fish but I changed my mind. Ignoring the facts and believing my lie was all I could ask her to do. The answering machine was on and all the bills were up to date. Since I'd booked my trip with such short notice my airfare was a fortune and I didn't care. After all of my longing, I'd finally be in Egypt on March 11th.

As a child I was always interested in history but not the lessons from those boring books in elementary school. Unlike some, my mind expanded with my body. So by the time I got to high school I pretty much figured out the history books we read as children were lies.

Oddly a joke on a Flip Wilson album triggered my quest for the truth about history. In school we were caught early that Christopher Columbus discovered America. Flip Wilson said when Christopher landed here he stepped off the boat and once on land proclaimed he had discovered America. Just then and Indian walked up to Chris and said, "You better discover your ass away from here!"

The dictionary defines discovery as finding the unknown or previously unseen. And that's what sparked my interest in history, the lies. How many more lies would I find? I was going to the land of the Pharaohs and as an added bonus I would see Halley's Comet. The newspaper said the comet has traveled around the sun and is headed out of the solar system, and there were only three maybe four weeks of good visibility left. I'd read about the comet for years and my fascination would soon be satisfied. Two people who'd seen the comet once before had been interviewed on the evening news and both were extremely old. The gleam in their faces describing the first time looking at Halley's Comet was one I hoped to soon possess. With all the secrets of the universe and the mysteries of the unknown I would be happy to see it just once. The stars held an attraction for me and I often speculated when man would ever get to the nearest star or find planets like ours. I could look into the night sky for hours wishing I had a chance to see what was out there.

My bags were packed and my flight leaves Kennedy airport in three hours. I said goodbye to my sister and Aunt Dot early this morning and gave them my itinerary. Aunt Dot expects a postcard with a beautiful scene from Egypt as soon as I arrive.

This morning my phone call to Ronald was unusual and I wished I'd never made it. I dialed the Eighth Avenue Kleenit to say goodbye to Ronald last night. He hinted that he and Lorraine might join me in Egypt in a week or so. So I was really calling this morning to see if he was kidding. The three of us have never been on a vacation together before so why would he and Lorraine think of coming now? The phone was answered by a female voice, a voice I knew all too well.

"Hi Lorraine," I said.

"Hi Bennie," she responded.

"How are you?" I asked.

"Fine, I am waiting for Ronald, he's in front refilling the coin dispensers. So Bennie you're going away today?"

"Yeah."

"Why aren't you taking Terri?"

"She can't go. She can't get away from work."

"Uh huh, did you ask her?"

"Believe me she can't go."

"So who are you taking?"

This was a very strange question for her to ask, because I never mention my escapades to her.

"What?"

"Who's going with you?" She said as if I were deaf.

"I'm going by myself."

"Why?"

There was no way I was telling her the truth either. Even though we'd been friends since we were teenagers. No one knew my inner feelings and I wasn't starting now.

"Bennie you know if you ever take my husband and help him cheat on me like you do with Terri, you know I'll hurt your ass. You know that right?"

"What are you talking about Lorraine?"

"You still didn't tell me why you're going to Egypt? Why can't you go to the Bahamas or Mexico like everyone else?"

She was getting on my nerves and I wanted to hang up on her.

"Look I got to go," I said quickly.

"So now you don't want to speak to Ronald?"

"No I gotta go. I'll call when I check into the hotel."

"Whatever," she said, and hung up the phone.

One brown leather shoulder bag had all my carry-on items. My passport, traveler's checks, and credit cards always stayed with me. The new issue of the Amsterdam News was in the side pouch of my bag, and the plane tickets were in my inside jacket pocket. The other piece of luggage was not very full because I intended to buy most of my clothes when I arrived.

The ride to Kennedy Airport was slow due to a three car accident in Astoria, which backed up traffic for miles. An hour after I left home I still hadn't crossed the Triborough bridge. Everyone sat in their cars until the police and emergency vehicles moved the injured and cleared the highway. By the time I arrived at the international terminal, it was fifty minutes before departure time. When I finished checking my luggage I heard the boarding call and went to the gate. I meant to use the extra time at the terminal to call Terri but there wasn't enough time.

It was the first occasion I'd flown first class and once I boarded a stewardess at the door directed me to the front of the aircraft. Then my own personal stewardess showed me to a large comfortable seat by the window. Not long after I took my seat I watched the men through the window working to push the plane out of the gate next to us. A young shapely woman with brown hair stood next to my seat. She said her name was Dari and she would be my stewardess. Dari informed me we would depart shortly and she should put my bag into the overhead compartment. Then she went to each passenger and introduced herself. One of the crewmembers went up the spiral staircase holding a flashlight and went into the cockpit.

The last time I was on an airplane, Terri and I went to Bermuda. And the day before we talked about all the plane crashes we could think of as our sick way of blessing the trip. Like a friend telling an actor to break a leg on opening night.

The week we spent in Bermuda was a lot of fun. We went to a few shows and skinny-dipped in the hotel pool at night, then made love in a reclining chair on the beach. So what would have been the harm in taking her with me now?

There was a backward lurch and we were moving. Dari did the usual speech before take off, and I found myself looking and thinking of her sexually for a brief moment. Once the plane was in the air and we'd had out first snack I closed my eyes and fell into a light sleep until it was time to eat. The first-class meal was a tender piece of brisket served with diced peas and carrots and garlic potatoes. After dinner I put the seat back and took off my shoes and Dari placed a glass of dry white wine on the tray next to me. Some magazines were in a pouch behind the seat in front of me so I searched for something else to read and found a magazine on the wonders of Egypt. The cover had the Giza pyramid in the background with an Arabic-looking man wearing a turban in front. Then the whisper of a stray thought in my mind,

"Touch the pyramid with your right hand."
What would happen if I touched it? The thought left almost as quickly as it had come. Another stray thought flowed through my mind, which made no sense at all. It says here the pyramids are between five and six thousand years old. The largest and most famous one was forty stories tall and I couldn't wait to see it. Imagine a building forty stories tall and four hundred feet high. How did they do it? This wasn't the first time I'd read books about Egypt but the phrase Middle East always bothered me. Why do they say Egypt is in the Middle East? I see it in the continent of Africa. And if it's in Africa, Africans must have had a hand in building it. To my knowledge these were the oldest structures in the world.

Dari came over to ask if I cared for anything else. I told her no, but she didn't leave right away.

"Is this your first visit to Egypt?"

"Yes."

"How long are you staying?"

"Just two weeks."

"You must see the pyramids, and the temple of Karnic," she said standing with her hand on the seat next to me.

I smiled at her longer than I should have and then she asked,

"Why didn't your wife come with you?"

"I'm not married."

"Your girlfriend?" she asked with a raised eyebrow.

"She couldn't get away from work, new job and all."

Where was this leading I wondered. Then she sat down next to me.

"So what are you going to do all by yourself?"

The conversation wasn't going in the direction I wanted and I blamed myself. I shouldn't have looked at her the way I did. And then I couldn't believe I said,

"Do you have any ideas?"

"I might," she said with a warm smile.

A buzzer rang and Dari went to the cockpit door and knocked. The crew was finished with their meals and she went back to work. Dari was attractive but I had no intentions of cheating on Terri. If the flirtation goes any further I'll have to find a way to get out of it. Now might be a good time for me to go to sleep. If I were sleeping she probably wouldn't wake me. I finished the wine and felt a little better. We were more than half way there, not much longer to go. I turned off the overhead light and pulled the window shade down. Then I pressed the button so the seat would recline some more.

A gentle hand lay on my right shoulder without shaking me. Dari held me firmly squeezing all the bones and muscles in my shoulder. I had fallen asleep for four and a half hours and the plane was on final approach.

"Mr. Reeves, we've begun our descent. You need to put your seat in the upright position and fasten your seat belt."

In that first minute of waking I recalled the dream I just had. I sat up slowly and tried to remember. For me waking from a dream happened in two ways. Sometimes the dream would dissipate slowly and I'd be pulled out by the sounds of reality. The backgrounds and colors would fade and the characters looked at me with sadness. This was usually unpleasant especially when the dream was a blissful one.

The nightmares were different, and never let go of me quickly. In those dreams it was a fight to wake up. I was always running and defending myself from zombies, vampires, witches and robbers. If I had a baseball bat or a machete and I was chopping them up it wasn't so bad. But sometimes the dream wouldn't allow me to have or find a weapon to defend myself and the only choice left was to run.

This dream however was new and gratifying. I was a Pharaoh in Egypt, a leader of many people. I was standing on a hill overlooking a valley and it started to rain. I wanted to stay and was pulled away and then I woke up. Strange as it seemed it was the best dream I'd ever had.

When we reached the gate everyone clamored to exit the plane except me. Since your luggage was never there when you hurried I couldn't see the point of rushing. When I did reach the baggage area I found my luggage easily and went in the direction of taxis.

Once outside I felt like I walked into a wall of dry dusty heat. It was 10:00 am and I was well rested. I slept most of the flight and was eager to look around. Excited to be in Egypt, after all my years of waiting I would finally see and hopefully touch the pyramid of Giza. And that wasn't all; I would witness Halley's Comet for the first and last time. To glimpse it again I would need to live another seventy six years and though not impossible it was unlikely.

It last came to earth in 1910 and most people who saw it were scared to death. It was one-quarter of the size of the moon with a long streaking tail behind it. People thought they would die from poisonous gas particles left by the comet. It never surprised me how people seemed to grow less smart and more fearful of the unknown as the future progressed.

Before I left the plane, Dari slipped me the telephone number to her hotel. Then she gave me some tips on getting around. First she told me to get a conversion chart so I wouldn't get cheated then exchange my American money for the local currency. She said I should find out what places give the best rate of exchange for your money. The hotel staff would be very helpful when explaining how much a taxi should charge or how much you'll pay for souvenirs. Her advice would come in handy later but I decided to change a little of my money in the airport.

I went back inside the terminal to the counter with the exchange sign on top and waited in line. When it was my turn I exchanged $200 for the equivalent in Egyptian pounds and was told what it would cost to get to the El Gezirah Sheraton hotel.

The bills were not what I expected. I thought there would be a face in the center like American money. The ten-pound note had a picture of a building with four columns and a huge chandelier suspended in front. The right of the bill had three lines in Arabic. The one-pound notes had thick black borders with a different building in the center resembling the Taj Mahal. I counted fourteen of these ten-pound notes and the teller suggested I only ride with drivers who spoke English to avoid any language problems. In addition I should tell the driver I know how much the ride will cost and how long it will take.

After twenty minutes of driving, my taxi made a right turn down a narrow street that led to a slight upgrade. Then a turn left into a loop in front of the hotel. The driver put my luggage on a cart brought out by the doorman. I paid the driver the agreed upon fare and a nice tip. In return he gave me a card with his cab number.

The air-conditioning in the lobby felt good. A large floral arrangement filled with orange and purple flowers was displayed on a white marble table. I walked to the front desk on my left to check in. The clerk asked for my passport and gave me the hotel register to sign in. The bellboy wheeled my luggage to a waiting elevator and pressed the ninth floor. When he opened the door to my suite I thought I was in the wrong room. It was huge and spacious. The walls were off white with red carpet. There was a living room next to the bedroom with a white couch and matching loveseat. The bellboy told me how to use the phone while he turned on the air conditioner. Next he showed me the safe hidden in the closet. The directions were written in different languages including English. I could change the code to the safe at any time if I chose to. When he finished the tour he handed me the key and I tipped him. He said thank you and closed the door behind him.

I had made no plans or travel arrangements yet but I could speak to someone later. I wanted to see the pyramid of Giza and the comet. Anything else I did here would be on the spur of the moment. I unpacked a little then took a quick shower. My green Harlem T-shirt should go nice with these baggy sand colored shorts. I slipped on my sandals then changed the code on the safe inside the closet. I put $1500 and the money I got from the exchange in my pocket and placed the rest of my cash and travelers checks into safe. I placed the rest of the contents from my pockets on the dresser. I grabbed my watch and my hotel key and Dari`s phone number fell from the dresser onto the carpet. I procrastinated and put it back on the dresser. When I got back to the room I would throw it away. When it was time to leave like always I took a last look around then closed the door.

At the lobby I talked with the hotel tour guide and purchased a ticket for an all day trip to the pyramid of Giza. The bus would pick me up from the hotel in the morning on 15th. The trip included breakfast and dinner. When I finished with him I left the lobby and stood out-side. My plan was to walk around the city when I got a better idea. I wanted to see where the ordinary people lived, the people I could relate to. The doorman hailed the first taxi on line. He looked pleasant enough so I asked him did he speak English and he said yes. The taxi had no A/C and the afternoon sun baked the back seat until it felt like an oven. It was a good thing the seats were made of cloth.

The driver asked, "Where are you going?"

"I don't know yet, just drive for a little while."

He looked a bit confused then drove out of the loop. Once the air flowed through the windows it wasn't so bad. But still it was a dry dusty heat.

It felt good to be in Africa and I did feel that spiritual connection I'd heard about.

"What's in that direction?" I asked.

"Little markets and buildings, where working people live."

His English was broken but I understood him.

"Take me down there. I'd like to see."

Small two story houses made of brick lined both sides of the street. There was barely enough room for two cars to pass each other. After we'd gone several miles away from the city a store came up on the right that looked like a gift shop. Whenever I went away I looked for the shops away from the city. Most times you got better prices there than in the tourist traps.

"Hold on, I want to stop here and look inside."

I got out of the car and walked to the front window. There was a sign in Arabic atop the building. I had no clue to what it read. The door was in the center of the building with two huge picture windows on each side. I told the driver I was going inside to look around and he turned the engine off. I walked past the wicker chairs and wooden tables on the sidewalk and opened the door. A bell attached to the top corner of the door tinkled announcing my entrance. It was hot inside even though two ceiling fans slowly stirred the air.

An old woman walked slowly from the back with her head crooked to the side. She came down a narrow path through the center of the store. Her shoes clicked softly on the wooden floor and her dress had a faded flower pattern. Her skin was dark like mine. Her hair was white like snow but not straight like the driver's; it was curly like mine. When she stopped walking she looked up at me. Her eyes focused sternly and then her face became distorted. She spoke to me but it wasn't in English. I couldn't understand her; and she repeated herself and got more excited.

"I just came inside to see what you're selling," I said.
She only gaped at me with astonishment, like she'd seen me before. The old woman closed her mouth and took a deep breath.

"What name?" She asked.

"My name is Reeves. I came here from the United States."

"America?"

"Yes, I was riding by in a taxi when I saw your store and thought I'd look around."

The old lady's constant staring made me very agitated,

"Did I do something wrong?"

"No," she said, "no, you look like...."

"Like who?"

Totally ignoring my question she kept staring. Abruptly she turned to walk away and said, "look, you see, call me."

Normally I would have left but she didn't seem afraid of me so I took a look around. The store was not large but it was fully stocked. There were lamps and wooden statues with Egyptian faces I did not know. Actually I didn't know any except for King Tut, Cleopatra and Ramses. I knew Ramses from the movie the Ten Commandments. There was a large wooden desk facing me with three drawers on one side and one big drawer on the other. It had a chair to match and a small lamp on top. There were masks of horned animals and racks of jewelry made of beads and semi-precious stones mixed with small shells.

The borderline rudeness I felt from the old woman made the shop unimpressive. I turned to walk out and I saw a strange looking object in the corner. I walked over for a closer look. It was appeared to be a standing full-length mirror made with a dark wooden frame. But it wasn't a mirror. Instead of reflecting glass it was clear and hollowed out yet filled inside with sand and reddish colored specks. It looked like a big flat hourglass but the sand was filled all the way to the top. It rested on four wooden legs carved into the shape of paws. The top was arched with two holes carved in the center. Symbols were also carved into the surrounding wooden frame above and in the wooden borders. I had to know what this was so I called out for someone I could ask, "Hello, hello?"

A hand reached between the stained brown curtains at the end of the aisle. A young woman in her thirties came out and walked up to me.

She had a receipt in her hand and a smirk on her face as if I was keeping her from business elsewhere.

"My grandmother said you'd want to buy the Obeni."

"The what?"

"The Obeni, O...ben...eye," she said slowly pointed to the strange hourglass.

"An Obeni," I said curiously, "what is it?"

"It's Egyptian, its old, and it has something to do with the sands of time. Do you want to buy it?"

"No, I just asked because I've never seen anything like it before."

I instinctively said no but I really did want it. "Then call me when you want to buy something," she said rudely and turned to walk away.

"How much is it?"

"$1000 American dollars," she said.

Looking at her I reached out and touched the wood.

"What do these markings say?"

"I don't know," she replied roughly.

"Does your grandmother know?"

"She doesn't know either."

I could lie to her but I couldn't lie to myself, I wanted it as soon as I saw it.

"Ok I'll take it."

"You will," she seemed surprised, "you want this? you really want this?"

"Yes."

I didn't want to seem too anxious and I was eager to examine it but I wanted to get it out of the store before they changed their minds. She went to the counter in front of the curtain and made a phone call. When she finished she returned and handed me the receipt. Then she took a roll of spongy material from behind the counter and began to wrap the sides. When she finished she got a footstool and did the top. After it was completely padded she took a spool of cloth resembling an eight-inch wide ace bandage. Standing on the stool she started from the top and began to wrap it again. Eager to leave, I stood on one side passing her the spool from behind the Obeni. When it was finished she said,

"Where are you staying?"

"At the Sheraton," I said.

The bell tinkled above the door and a man walked in. She spoke to him in her language pointing to the Obeni. He said something to her and she simply replied, Sheraton.

"This man is called Abdel. He will take the Obeni in his truck and follow you to your hotel. The delivery fee is $100 American dollars." I gave the woman $1000 and put the rest back in my pocket. I wasn't going to pay Abdel until we reached the hotel. I looked at the receipt and asked for the name of this store. She told me it was called Aswan.

The taxi driver and Abdel wheeled the Obeni out of the store with a hand truck and laid it down on a thick bed of blankets in the back of the pickup truck. Before I could close the door to the shop I heard the old woman's voice from behind the curtain. I'd had the feeling she'd been standing behind it watching me all the time. Her granddaughter went through the curtain and I continued to walk out. When I reached the taxi door I heard her call me.

"Mr. Reeves wait! My grandmother said this goes with the Obeni." She gave me a small leather pouch with a drawstring. Then she abruptly turned around and went back inside.

The entire ride I kept my eyes on the pickup truck until it turned into the loop of the hotel behind us. My driver helped Abdel remove the Obeni and position it on the hand truck and then I paid him.

Curiosity filled the faces in the lobby of the hotel when we wheeled it in but no one asked any questions. I smiled and led Abdel past the front desk and to the elevators. Abdel said nothing the entire time. I assumed it was because he probably couldn't speak English.

It was warm when I entered my suite because I'd forgotten to leave the air-conditioner on when I left. I invited Abdel into the room with hand gestures. He brought the Obeni inside and slid the hand truck out from under it. Together we carefully lifted it and placed it between the wall and the foot of the bed. I gave Abdel $100; he smiled and nodded his head then left the room.

I was like a kid on Christmas not knowing what to do next. I washed my hands and went to the safe to get another $500. This time I'd go back out look around some more and have something to eat. And this time I left the air conditioner on when I closed the door. The lady at the front desk recommended a nice restaurant within walking distance, and inquired about the piece I brought in. I told her it was a big hourglass and asked her suggestions on how I should ship it home. She told me to go have dinner and she would leave the information in my box by the time I returned.

Normally I would have tried a local dish but for dinner I ordered a steak with a baked potato and a salad. The steak was cooked medium rare and very tender. And then it hit me. I never called Terri to let her know I had arrived safely. As soon as I get back to my room I must call her and tell her I miss her, and find out how the new job is going. But before I leave I think I'll have one more glass of the house wine.

The sun was making its descent yet, it was still hot. Once back at the hotel the woman at the front desk told me I had a message from the states. She handed me a card folded in half. The outside of the card had my name and room number on it. It was from Terri. The note said to call no matter what time it was. I just need to hear your voice. It brought a smile to my face so I went upstairs to call her.

The maid had been in the room because there were fresh towels on the rack and the bathroom had been cleaned. I could tell she turned the air conditioner off because the room was hot once again and it smelled like the Aswan shop. I wanted to see the Obeni again and decided to unwrap it starting from the top. I began looking for the beginning of the cloth. Once I found it I peeled it around in a circular motion until it was uncovered. Maybe I should have left it wrapped. It would be a pain in the ass fixing it back when it came time to ship it home.

When I finished I stood in front and looked it over slowly now with a closer look at the legs that resembled lion's paws with the claws exposed. It was six feet high and less than four feet wide. The wood was dark colored and had small cracks throughout. The wooden frame that held the glass in place was four inches wide on each side. The symbols were carved along the side in between the frame and stopped at the arch on the top. The arch had two circular doughnut size holes carved side by side separated by a four inch gap. The carved symbols stopped at the first hole and started again after the second and ran back down to the bottom.

I got some towels from the bathroom to wipe the dust from the wood. Rubbing gently I worked my way from the bottom left side to the top. Then, I had to stop. The dust was making me sneeze. My eyes fell on the leather pouch the girl gave me and I wondered what was in it? I walked to the bed picked it up and opened it. Inside were two round metal disks reddish and color. They were a quarter of an inch thick with long flat bases.

I began to wonder why did they sell this mirror to me. It looks very old and possibly valuable. I know why, because it's not real. A person in the souvenir business could make one of these for fifty bucks. Yeah that was it; you never get something for nothing. There's a sucker born every minute and right now that sucker was I.

By now the room was nice and cool and I held one disk in each hand. They weighed and looked the same except one of the bases was shorter than the other. I looked at the Obeni and wondered two holes and two disks; they must go in the holes. Yeah she said they go with the Obeni so I took a chair and stood on it to look at the holes more closely. They had slots cut in the top of the arch where the disks should go. I placed one disk in and it fit perfectly. When I went to place the second disk in a thought washed over me. Maybe I shouldn't put the second disk in. I found myself laughing aloud, what did I think what happen? Was the room gonna blow up? My fear was silly and my lack of courage felt pathetic. It made me furious and I immediately put the second disk in place. Then I got down from the chair and stepped back to look. I touched the glass and the sides then pulled the chair back a few feet to sit down. I kept looking and nothing happened. Nevertheless, it was a beautiful piece I thought to myself. Just don't tell anyone how much you paid for it. Then I decided to take a shower and call Terri, then go out for the night.

I looked at the Obeni many times while putting my clothes away and doing little things around the room. On my list of things to do tomorrow was to get some postcards and send them to my aunt, sister and some of the store employees.

It was 7:02 pm and I still hadn't returned Terri's call. There was a sound in the bedroom. I stuck my head out from the bathroom and saw nothing. Maybe it was the air-conditioner. I put my sand colored cotton dress pants on with a matching cotton short-sleeved shirt, then walked out of the bathroom and went to the closet safe to put back some of the money I was carrying. When I went to the dresser in front of my bed and there it was again; that sound! It was like someone was in the room with me. I stood still and listened, it was the sound of breathing. I spun around to face the bed, and then out of the corner of my eye I saw her. To my left at the Obeni there was a woman looking right at me.

"Damn lady! You scared the shit out of me!! How'd you get in here?"

She said nothing, she didn't move. She just looked directly at me. I looked closer and her eyes widened with fear. She wasn't in the room she was in the Obeni. There was no sand inside just this black woman looking at me like a reflection. My heart was beating so fast. I closed my eyes tight and opened them. She was still standing there in a white dress that covered her ankles. I could see her standing on the ground with gold sandals on her feet. Her dress was a wraparound or loose fitting robe with a colorful red and green pattern bordering the neckline. Her braided hair was short in the front and the sides came down to her chest like a Rick James wig.

Get a grip Bennie; it's a reflection from somewhere. I walked over to the Obeni and waved my hand back and forth. I saw no shadow and her image didn't distort. Then I walked around the room to see where this projection was coming from. I looked in the back of the Obeni and saw nothing was plugged in. There was no light source or heat, and no mechanical sounds. There must be a projector hidden in the room. Then I understood someone was playing a joke on me like that old Candid Camera show. Yeah that's it they've been taping me I thought looking around the room. That means they could have been watching me while I showered and got dressed.

"OK guys," I said. "It's not funny anymore. You're invading my privacy now. The joke's not funny."

The image interrupted me before I could speak in the tinny delayed voice of and badly dubbed Chinese movie.

"I am no joke spirit!"

I ignored her remarks and kept looking for the source of the projection. Standing on the bed I looked at the entire ceiling and the light fixture then jumped off in front of Obeni. This scared her and she took a step backwards.

"I fear you not spirit!" She yelled.

Still ignoring her I kneeled down to look under the bed and nothing was there. Then I sat on the edge of the bed thinking it might be compulsory to play along for a minute and get this over with. As I looked directly at her, she spoke again.

"Who are you and, where dwells you spirit?"

I still didn't answer as I heard her words seconds after her mouth stopped moving.

"Be you God or demon?"

Sucking my teeth I said, "Oh please."

I pinched my nose with my fingers and shook my head. I am going to sue somebody cause they think black people won't sue their asses.

She repeated, "Are you a demon?"

"Can't you say something else?" I said.

I can't believe I just answered her. Maybe it's Terri playing a joke on me. She found out some of her actress friends were staying here and called them up.

"Be you God or demon?"

"Neither," I said.

"Neither," she repeated, "what is neither?"

I wanted to laugh but I didn't. Where did they get this girl?

I reiterated, "I am not a God or a demon."

"You are a spirit," she replied like a person teaching class.

"Why are you watching at me, Spirit?"

"Would you stop calling me that?"

This sister was getting tired and I was about to get up when she said, "Thou has been sent to do my bidding spirit! I command you, tell all secrets to me."

I got up from the bed walked closer and reached out my hand to touch her. When I did the glass felt soft and there was a numbing cold in my fingertips so I withdrew my hand quickly.

"You will not depart, Spirit."

If she called me a spirit one more time I would take this chair and smash the glass into a thousand little pieces. But who was I kidding I paid a lot of money for this damn thing.

So finally I said,

"What's your name?" as if this lunatic was going to tell me.

"I am Princess Sakatet Whende," she said proudly.

"Well You just hang on sister. I'll be right back."

I was pissed now and the prank had never been funny. My playing along had gone nowhere. I snatched my keys off the dresser and went to the door. I was almost running when I got to the front desk in the lobby. They saw me talking to myself and yelling but I didn't care. I walk up to the front desk and asked,

"What the hell is going on in my room?"

"May I help you sir?"

She acted like she didn't hear me so I said it again,

"What the hell is going on in my room?"

"What's the problem sir?"

"My room is bugged, that's the problem."

"You say there are bugs in your room?"

"Not bugs, my room is bugged, people are in my room watching me."

Three people were behind the counter now two men and the young lady who helped me earlier.

"You say there are people watching you in your room?" the gentleman said.

Simultaneously they looked at each other in disbelief.

"Hey, you think this is funny?"

The short dark haired man came from behind the counter.

"No sir I'll call hotel security immediately and we will go upstairs."

We rode the elevator to my floor and got off and there was know one in the hallway. I asked the clerk from the lobby where was hotel security? He told me to relax; security would meet us in the room. We got to my door and I gave him my key.

"Are you sure you locked your door when the left?"

"Yes."

"OK," he said.

Then he turned the key and pushed the door open. When we got in I looked at the Obeni and it was filled with sand. He walked in and looked around past the Obeni into the bathroom.

"I don't see anybody," he said.

"Are you in on this gag too?"

"I don't know what you mean, Sir."

"There was a woman in my room like a movie. Like someone was showing a movie on the wall."

"On the wall Sir?"

"There was a woman in my room talking to me."

"Have you been drinking, Sir?" He asked politely.

"No, well I had some wine at dinner but it was just two glasses."

"Oh two glasses!"

"Yeah two glasses so what! Do you think that's a lot?"

"I don't know Sir," he looked around then asked.

"I'm telling you there was a woman in here," I said pointing to the Obeni.

"Would you like to change your room sir?"

I sighed in disappointment, "no that won't be necessary."

"If you have any problems please call downstairs."

Then he closed the door on his way out. I sat on the edge of the bed in the same spot I had been earlier.

My first day in Egypt and people were fucking with me already. No problem, it wouldn't be the first time I thought. I began trying to calm myself but only succeeded in making things worse. I came all the way here to go through a home invasion? Someone was always trying to get over on me and nobody had ever done it more than twice! I knew what to do. That eccentric old lady from the store was expecting me for some reason and I was gonna find out why. So the first thing tomorrow I'd be knocking at her door.

Chapter 4

Tuesday morning at 7:10 am I opened my eyes and the light was bright inside my suite. The sun gleamed off the glass coffee table near the terrace window and the beam shined directly in my face. I rolled over lying on my stomach facing the head of the bed and stretched grateful for a good night's sleep. I stopped in the middle of my stretch recalling the night before, and how it took me forever to fall asleep. The sense of being watched was hard to shake, but it was coming back to me now.

Turning around violently to face the foot of my bed, a sheet still covered the Obeni. I stayed in that position frozen and thinking. I never went out last night. I remember getting angry and considering smashing the Obeni to pieces. Instead I covered it with a sheet after I removed the two disks and put them in the safe. Then what did I do? Oh yes, I planned my revenge. Someone had to pay and she said her name was Whende something and already I couldn't stand her. She was playing head games, talking that thus and thou bullshit trying to screw with my mind. They call me Princess Whende. Yeah right, I got your princess swinging right here sister.

I got out of bed and went to the Obeni reaching for the sheet from the top and pulled it off. Grains of sand inside the glass were all I saw. Somebody could have drugged me. They say LSD gives you hallucinations. Maybe I was drugged and thought I saw her? I'd rather go with that then believe what happened last night.

She was standing in the Obeni and the sun was in the sky behind her and it looked so real. Last night I had no plan of action, but this morning it was clear. I would start at the Aswan antique shop. That old lady had some explaining to do. It was that old bag and her granddaughter who were responsible and before I knew it I was dressed and in a cab. I didn't even brush my teeth, just threw on the same clothes I wore yesterday, grabbed the receipt and was on my way.

Because of my hastiness I didn't get a driver who spoke English. I came down in the elevator, walked straight through the lobby and pass the front desk and never waited for the doorman to hail my cab. I walked to the first one and got in showing him the receipt with the name and address. He started the car and pulled off and when we reached the end of the loop the driver turned right on to a different street from the one we took yesterday. So I asked him why? It was then I determined we had a language problem. I showed him the receipt again and he nodded his head quickly.

The streets were filled with people. Most were walking and some were riding bicycles. Two men were arguing at a passing corner and a third man stepped between them. The men arguing made me think of Terri. I had done it again, neglecting to call my baby. I was distracted last night and I rushed out this morning. I must call her when I get back and explain the whole thing. I know she'll understand.

We arrived at the street with the two story brick houses and I never noticed we were on a dirt road yesterday. For a minute I thought we were on the wrong street and then I saw the shop on my left this time. We made a U-turn and stopped in front but it didn't look the same. The awning wasn't there and the sidewalk was empty. No chairs outside and no furniture or baskets in front. I walked to the door and when I knocked I heard the cab leave. He was paid and I never told him to wait. So here I was alone on the block except for a woman in the distance sweeping the sidewalk. She stopped for a moment to look at me and kept sweeping. I looked inside through the glass all the way to the back and behind the curtain was a little sliver of light. There was no bell outside so I started knocking. Now the woman with the broom was still looking in my direction. The shadow of a face broke the beam of light shining through the curtain but nobody came. Waiting a few more minutes I made up my mind they were going to let me in. I started knocking and yelling this time. The woman with the broom spoke loudly to me from up the block but I couldn't understand her. From the ground floor a window opened from across the street and a teenage girl poked her head out. I turned back to look in the store and said,

"Hello, hello is anyone home? Hello!"

The curtain opened from one side and a shadow came closer. Finally the granddaughter who gave me my receipt moved closer. She wore a burgundy robe tied at the waist with a coffee cup in her hand. When she got to the door she said,

"We're not open, come back at 10: ooam."

She turned to walk away so I started knocking again.

"Excuse me; do you remember me from yesterday?"

She answered without looking at me,

"Yes I know you, Mr. Reeves but you still have to come back at 10: ooam."

She turned her back on me and began walking away. This time I knocked so hard on the door the glass rattled and the sides shook with each pound from my fist.

"If you don't' talk to me now, I'll call the police!" I yelled.

I looked past her and saw the curtain in the back move. Someone else was watching. The granddaughter spoke to someone behind the curtain then walked to the door and unlocked it. I went in and she locked the door behind me. With the curtain drawn and no lights on the few shadows that were cast made the entire shop eerie. The granddaughter brushed past me almost knocking me down in the process. Then she turned and stood in front of me.

"Call the police for what? What have we done?" She asked angrily.

"Let's start with bugging my room and invading my privacy."

"Bugging your room, who bugged your room?"

"Miss, don't play with me! It's not funny and where is Whende?"

"Who?"

"Whende, I saw her yesterday is she here?"

The old woman came from behind the curtain walked up to me and took my left hand.

"Young man, did you see someone yesterday?" she questioned.

"Yes," I said as if she didn't know.

"What did you see?"

"I saw a woman in my room."

She squeezed my hand a little tighter and asked,

"Where? Where did you see her?"

"I saw her inside the Obeni."

"You get out of here now!" her granddaughter said.

"You think I'm playing around?" I said yelling back at her.

"You get the hell out of here right now!! You hear me? Now!" she said again.

But the old woman held my hand never looking away from me and said,

"Calm down Farisha, set another place at the table for Mr. Reeves." She then led me behind the curtain.

The room behind the curtain was thoroughly opposite than the front of the store. It was so unbelievably bright my eyes took time to adjust. There were four windows, two on each side that allowed the sun to flood this room. Plants hung from hooks in each corner of every open window allowing a steady breeze of fresh air. The walls were white trimmed in yellow. And in the center of this small but spacious kitchen was a wooden table painted jet black with a quarter inch thick sheet of glass covering it. Ahead of me a white stove stood next to an old fashioned double-sided sink with a white refrigerator in the corner. The old woman never let go of my hand and it made me feel uncomfortable. I was taught to respect my elders and I always did. But I was also taught to speak up for myself. No matter what happened I knew I wouldn't lay it on thick like I planned. When we got near the table I pulled out a chair for the old woman and she sat down. I took the seat next to her with my back to the curtain. From here I could see through the window into the yard outside. They had a small garden with rows of tomatoes and other green plants. This kitchen made me think of my aunt's kitchen in North Carolina.

The grandmother got up from the table abruptly.

"Farisha fix Mr. Reeves some coffee, I'll be right back."

She went into the hallway in front of me and up the stairs. Farisha walked to the table with a pot of coffee and a cup in her hand. She put the cup down in front of me but didn't pour.
Warning me hastily Farisha said,

"My grandmother is more than eighty years old. Don't ever upset her like that again!"

She poured some coffee into my cup and put the pot back on the stove. Her grandmother returned holding a bottle of liquor and a small faded brown metal box. She set the box on the counter next to the stove then went to the cabinet for two glasses. Farisha stared at me as if her grandmother bringing in the liquor bottle was my fault. She poured the tea colored liquid in two glasses and sat down. One glass she put next to my cup of coffee. Her face had such concentration. Suddenly with a heavy sigh, she lifted her glass and drank from it.

"Mr. Reeves this isn't going to be easy to believe and I'm sure when I finished telling you what happened to my family, you'll think I'm crazy. It's been many years since I thought about it but the pain is still there. Some of this I remember but the rest was told to me by my mother before she died."

"It all started with my father in the Valley of the Kings. My father's name was Remi Ali and when he was a child he would go with his father on excavations of tombs. My grandfather Omar Ali worked on most of the important finds in the Valley of the Kings. He was always distressed by the attitudes of the British, French and American scientists who worked the digs. He complained to the family and a few close friends about the way they lacked respect for the workers and showed an even greater lack of respect for Egyptian history. Several times, a find was kept secret from the workers until important or extraordinary articles were removed, altered or destroyed. Omar would speak about books and scrolls, which held information about Egyptian achievements being copied and later burned. Sometimes artifacts were taken never to be seen again. When statues of Egyptians in wood and stone were found the noses and lips were knocked off.

Back then powerful men and racial hatred of African people wouldn't let archaeologists divulge the truth about what they discovered. It was revealed to the world in small columns in the back pages of newspapers the newfound knowledge that African people were the creators of civilization. Many scientists and scholars took great offense when they uncovered tomb centuries old and saw the unmistakable features of African men and women. During my grandfather's time, slavery still existed in America, and it created a feeling of jealousy to know the first ancient civilizations were made up of African people. Napoleon who wandered upon the Sphinx in the desert was confronted with a huge African face on that statue and ordered his men to disfigure it with cannon fire. Since then countless acts of vandalism have been performed on Egyptian artifacts."

"I wondered about that," I said, "How a statue that's been buried underground away from the wind and rain have all the noses knocked off. I need to ask you a question," I interrupted,

"Your English has gotten better since yesterday, why was that?"

Farisha looked at me as if I were discourteous.

"Mr. Reeves I speak Latin, Greek, Spanish, French, four or five African dialects, and English. I don't speak English much so I was a little bad."

"So what happened to Omar?" Farisha asked.

"Omar decided to do something. He formed a secret group with a few trusted friends and family. They would copy the scrolls and make molds of the faces before they turned them over. Other times they would find artifacts and just hide them. Plus they put money together to fund digs of their own."

I took a sip of coffee then added more sugar. So far it was unlikely I'd cuss these two out today, and then she continued.

"Remi loved his father and looked up to him and when he was ten years old he started exploring the desert on his own against his father's wishes. Omar warned him that excavating was dangerous and should be done in teams but my father was very headstrong. One day in the desert Remi`s foot got stuck in a crevasse under the sand. Often this was how tombs were discovered, purely by accident. The harder he tried to pull his foot out the deeper he got sucked into the sand. Alone and stuck he had no choice but to dig his way out. He took off his shirt and filled it with sand and threw it as far over his shoulder as he could. After an hour in the hot sun he'd removed most of the sand to find his foot stuck in the crack of a stone block."

"How'd he get out Grandma? Farisha asked.

"He had to lubricate his foot." she demonstrated by sticking her finger down a throat.

"He stuck a finger down his throat forcing himself to vomit then he pulled his foot out. Remi covered the spot up leaving his shirt as a marker and went for his father. Omar called their group to a meeting and it was decided to protect this site and keep it to themselves. To do this they built a small house on top of it and each night they would move sand and dirt.

About the time of Remi's eleventh birthday all this sand had been removed and the entrance found. With chisels and hammers they cut a seven ton block of stone to get inside. Because Remi found the site Omar thought it only fair that his son be the first to see inside. They lowered a lantern through the horizontal opening until it rested on the floor below. A second rope was then tied to my father and he was lowered down. They found no treasure, no jewelry, no mummies, no carvings and no statutes. This was not a tomb at all but a study chamber with a wooden chair and a rotten cushion. Adjacent to the chair was a table with an oil lamp and scroll. The thrill of discovery had claimed my father right then. He was addicted to it like a drug and this rush was what took him away from me," She said clearing her throat.

"He never heard the men on top calling him asking him what he saw. Moving the lantern closer to the table to look at the scroll he carefully unrolled it. The first thing he saw was a drawing of the Obeni. Then there was a tap on his shoulder and he tried not to tremble. He refused to turn around, refused to breathe feeling the fingers tighten. Omar was lowered down on another rope because Remi never answered their calls. Near the table he found Remi frozen in place. They both looked at the drawing of the Obeni and the surrounding symbols but Omar couldn't read them. He could read Egyptian hieroglyphics but couldn't understand these."

We all sat silently at the kitchen table, Farisha looking at her grandmother and her grandmother looking out the window.

"Grandma are you all right?"

She looked away from the window and smiled at Farisha.

"Yes child I'm fine," and then she continued.

"The Obeni was a mystery that would never be solved by my grandfather. After fifteen years the only thing Omar could figure out about the room was the scroll in it belonged to an Egyptian man who called himself the keeper of the known and guardian of the Obeni. A few months passed by and in 1889 Omar died. With the death of my grandfather, Remi was given the responsibility to maintain the secret society and solve the mystery of the Obeni. Remi was consumed with guilt because after sixteen years of study he was unable to give his father any new information about the Obeni before Omar died. The mystery addicted him and he would explore the most remote places for clues. Just two years after his father's death while looking in the Valley of the Kings, Remi lost his balance fell down a steep embankment, and into a huge hole in the ground. He wasn't hurt from the fall but he was trapped. There was no sticking his finger down his throat this time. Luckily he'd learned to carry a small tool belt with a hammer, chisel, and small pick which came off during the fall."

"So how he get himself out of this one?" Farisha asked.

"He didn't," her grandmother said, "He stayed there trapped for close to two days. Because he was so stubborn it wasn't unusual for him to go out exploring alone. His friends didn't start looking for him until the second day when he didn't return home. But what really saved him was the shape of the whole he fell in. It amplified the sound of his voice and carried his cries for help further. Remi called out now and again and near the close of the second day they found him. Against the advice of the local doctor and his friends, he did not rest and was out searching the next day. He believed the odds were in his favor that he would stumble on a clue to the mystery of the chamber in the desert.

More years passed and he decided that the answers must be right under his nose. All of the members including his father must have overlooked something inside the tomb."

She looked away from me and turned to Farisha and said.

"Make a sign and put it in the window to say the store will open at 12:00 today."

When Farisha went to the front her grandmother poured some fresh coffee for me.

"What is your name?" I asked.

"My name is Candice," she answered.

Then I added two teaspoons of sugar to my fresh cup and stirred it slowly. Farisha sat back down in her chair waiting for her grandmother to continue.

"Now where was I?"

She thought for a moment, "oh yes, my father started spending his time in the underground room. Another two years went by and he'd learned nothing more. Each day he spent there was more depressing than the last. One night he put his foot on the ladder to climb out and a coin fell out of his pocket and he listened to it roll along the bottom of the stone floor. He took the lantern and started to look for it. When he couldn't find it he became indignant and left. During the night he couldn't sleep. He figured if he couldn't find a coin he just dropped how he could solve an ancient mystery. Remi had a lot of regrets about his life during the night. He was approaching thirty years old and he'd never married. There were no children and very little money. More than half of the members in their secret society had left to find more profitable work. All night he considered giving up the search and then losing the coin and not being able to find it was the worst. Sometime during the night when his mind was almost clear a feeling of loneliness that had been with him since the death of my grandfather suddenly went away. He reviewed scenes of the two of them reading the scroll. Then he heard or thought he heard one simple sentence. If you find the coin you'll find the secret. Now whether it was his mind playing tricks or the ancestors talking to him I can't say but he swears he heard it?"

"It must have been the stress," Farisha said sadly.

"Call it what you want," Candice said.

"So Remi got dressed and went back to the underground room. It struck him as strange his pants pockets had no holes. How could he have lost anything? He was convinced what he heard in his room was just himself thinking out aloud and not realizing he'd been moving his mouth. In the middle of the night he went out alone again. He reached the house soon after and went back down the ladder and into the room. If you find the coin, you'll find the secret. He knew it had to be here so he went back upstairs and brought down two more lanterns. After he lit those he decided to get two more and after he lit those two he figured two more would make it as bright as day down there.

He started near the ladder and went in a straight line to the end of the room. If he searched in sections it would be easier. When he walked back to the ladder he turned to go in another direction when he saw faint lines in the stonewall behind the ladder, lines he'd never noticed before. He moved the ladder over and took a small wire brush from his tool kit. He lightly brushed the wall following the path of the lines. Before he could finish he recognized the shape immediately. Carved in the wall was the shape of the Obeni as it appeared in the scroll. All these years they never saw it behind the ladder.

Remi examined the section of wall from top to bottom. He took a thin piece of metal and began to remove the hard dry sand from the joints. As he scraped with frenzy he lost his grip on the piece of metal and it fell through the space between the walls. It was obvious there was something on the other side. He got more tools and many hours later he removed all the dried sand to reveal a stone panel five feet across and six feet high. No way was he going to sleep until he found out what lay beyond this panel. When he got on his knees he could see a quarter inch gap between the floor and the panel where his coin had to be. An iron shaft one inch round stuck through the floor and up inside the panel and into the stone above like a primitive hinge. Remi pushed on the right side of the stone slab. When it didn't move he tried the other side and it moved slightly when he pushed. He was able to open it enough to slide a wedge inside and force it open to get in. What he found in that small hidden space was the Obeni."

Farisha and I looked at Candice with skepticism. Here was an item in her family that was an authentic Egyptian artifact and she sold it to me.

"Yes it's real!" Candice said.

"But let me finish, there was nothing inside this hidden space but the Obeni. Remi removed it and brought it here to his home in 1898. He never went into the desert or the Valley of the Kings to search for anything ever again. He was determined to find out what the Obeni was and unlock the meaning of the symbols. Five years later he met my mother Laneie, married her and she gave birth to me on August 23rd 1905."

Candice got quiet and a sad look came on her face. Her eyes filled with tears. Farisha held her hand and said, "what's wrong, Grandma?"

"I've lived with this secret for so long," she said.

Candice took the glass of liquor in her hand. This time she turned the glass upward tilted her head back and drank all of it.

"My mother told me my father acted very bizarre the first few days before he disappeared. He wouldn't eat or drink anything when he worked."

Candice was visibly upset and Farisha went to her side and placed her arm around her.

"Grandma you've had enough for one day. Mr. Reeves I think you should leave now," and this time her voice was compassionate. I pivoted in my seat but Candice said,

"No! I have to finish."

"Then I think you should have some more coffee," Farisha said removing the bottle from the table. Candice with her hands shaking wiped her watering eyes and continued.

"I can recall that day like it was yesterday. Shortly after sunrise I woke up and got out of bed. I was maybe four or five years old but I remember. I heard my father talking downstairs and went to him. He was sitting in a chair facing the Obeni. There was so much light coming from it I crept closer. From the bottom of the stairs I saw a man inside, a black man inside the Obeni. He wore a white cloth around his waist and nothing on his chest. When I walked closer the man saw me and smiled, causing my father to turn around. I remember him saying everything is all right when he scooped me in his arms and took me upstairs. I wasn't frightened so he hugged me tight for a long time kissed my forehead, and then put me in bed with my mother. I watched him leave the room and listened to his footsteps going back downstairs."

She took a deep breath and said, "we never saw my father again after that day."

"What happened to him Grandma?"

"I don't know Farisha. I think the man I saw had something to do with it."

They both looked at me to see what I would do, but I didn't know what to say. My first reaction was to not believe any of this shit. This was a long way to go to get me to forget about suing them. But then again, why would she lie? She saw a man inside the Obeni when she was a child. No, I didn't believe her. Hell, she was over eighty years old and probably senile or in the early stages. I drank my coffee without saying a word. Then Candice told Farisha to fill my cup again.

"Miss Candice, I have a question. The Obeni`s been in your family for so long it must be valuable. Why did you sell it to me?"

"It was your face," she said.

She put the metal box on the table close to me and opened it. Then she pulled out a small wooden figure about seven inches high. It had a faded white cloth dress similar to the one that actress was wearing. It had four carved fingers and a thumb on each hand. The little statue had jewelry on the wrists and earrings and it stood on a base with symbols carved around it. The feet were in a walking position with the right foot ahead of the left. Candice told me this meant the person was alive when the statue was made. If the feet were together in a standing position it meant the person was dead when it was carved.

"Is this the woman you saw?" Candice asked.

Glancing at the face it could've been the woman I saw in the room but I wasn't sure.

So I humored her saying,

"It's kind of small but it could be."

"This was Queen Kymeka. She lived in Egypt in the fourth or fifth dynasty and before you say anything." She stopped talking reached in the box again and placed an object on the table.

"And this is the face of someone who is not known."

She turned it toward me and I was speechless. My mouth just hung open and Farisha almost dropped the pot of coffee.

"Grandma it's him! It looks just like him!"

The face was round and protruded like a mask. The eyes were painted to look normal but the overall color was gold. The more I tried to think it didn't look like me the more ridiculous I felt. It would've been like seeing a picture up yourself and telling people it wasn't you. Now I took the glass of liquor from the table and drank. I wanted to say it just resembled me and how two of every three or four million people could look alike and never be related. The shocker was it looked exactly like me. The face had my goatee and my hairline. There was a chain etched around the neck like the one I had on and the left ear had a hooped earring just like mine.

"What are you people trying to do to me?" I yelled. "I don't believe any of this shit!" And stood up from the table, "You made this yesterday after I left!"

Without getting up Candice reached for my hand. I could see her shaking and didn't want to be the cause of scaring an old lady to death.

"Son, the pieces have been in my family since I was a little girl. I didn't make them yesterday or any other day."

Disbelief was the only look I could give her.

"No one is trying to deceive you," she said.

"Oh yeah, then how did you know I wanted the Obeni?"

Her granddaughter seemed curious to know the answer too.

"Because they are all connected," she said.

I might have been in shock and couldn't tell. I was pacing around the kitchen like a caged animal. I only knew I wanted to leave now. I didn't want to hear any more, I didn't want to see anything else. I just wanted to leave before she showed me a picture of my mother and father.

In a whisper I announced my departure and split the curtain with my hand. I was upset because when it came down to it, I believed her. What reason would she have to bug up my room. I stumbled upon her shop she didn't call me there. But still it was impossible and I refused to believe it. There must be some other reason I am not thinking of.

"Will you let yourself out Mr. Reeves?" Farisha said.

"Sure."

I unlocked the front door and Farisha came behind me placing her hand on my arm. For the first time in two days she reflected kindness.

"Be careful Mr. Reeves, please be careful."

An hour or so later a waiter brought me a glass of water I ordered two scrambled eggs with corned beef hash, and white toast. He suggested other Cairo specialties but I wasn't in the mood for any more surprises. I needed food I could recognize. The eggs should be yellow, the toast light brown. That's all I wanted to see. Hopefully, once I ate my headache would go away.

Was this what it's like when you're in shock? I remember leaving the Aswan shop and walking not knowing how long or how I got to this restaurant. It must have been the aroma of food, which brought me out of my trance. In my haste this morning, I left my watch at the hotel and had no idea of the time. When the waiter comes back I'll ask him.

These weren't hunger pangs I felt. My head was hurting from confusion. I couldn't explain why but I believed Candice's story. I believed she was telling me the truth. And if she was telling me the truth than the spirit I saw was real. And if the spirit I saw was real, well that was the source of my headache. How could it be real?

What would my father do in this situation? He told me once when he was a child he'd seen his dead sister in the hallway of their house and he said he wasn't afraid. She smiled at him and then he didn't see her anymore. And the wooden spinning top he was playing with moments before was gone. He told me he looked in every inch of the hallway and in every room, but never found the spinning top. Sure there were times when he teased me but that story wasn't one of them. The honesty in his face that day said he believed what he had seen, but he was just a child. It might have been a dream and he was too young to know the difference. Of course there are things in the world that can't be explained and the hardest thing to do is except them. So what would he do if he were in my shoes now?

My mother would never go back to the hotel that's for sure. She'd send someone for all her belongings and leave immediately. Each of my parents had different strengths and exploration of the unknown wasn't one of hers.

Then I remembered my father telling me how he overcame his fear of the dead. When dad was eight years old he was afraid of the dark. His father, Henry, told him if he could walk through the town cemetery at night past all those graves and come out on the other side he'd have no reason to be afraid of the dark anymore. I pictured my father walking alone at night in North Carolina through the cemetery. When he was a boy in the South, there were no streetlights. He stumbled through the graveyard with just the light of the full moon and came out the other side. Henry was waiting and after that dad wasn't afraid of the dark again. I sat there and called on his guidance and it came. If he had that much courage when he was a child, how could I be scared now as a man?

The waiter came back and for the second time since I'd gotten off the plane I smelled something familiar. My eggs were yellow and my hash was slightly crispy, and toast was light brown with a wad of butter melting in center. Then I found out I'd been walking more than two hours it was ten minutes after four.

My food was good and making me homesick with every bite. Why had I walked so long? Was it because I didn't want to go back to the hotel? What was I so scared of? If that woman was dead she couldn't hurt me I reasoned. After all, she was just a spirit. And that's why she called me a spirit; she's in a place where spirits stay. There was nothing to be afraid of she was just a reflection on or inside a glass. How could she hurt me? The woman is dead, just a ghost. There's nothing she can do to me.

The fear was making me angry when I thought of the possibilities. I might learn from her if she was willing to cooperate. I could find out things no one knew. Secrets she could answer about death or life. My appetite was destroyed with my next thought. If the Obeni is an object through which spirits could communicate with the living maybe my mother and father were in there. I could talk to them again and, I stopped myself right there. This was the craziest idea I ever had. Candice had really gotten to me and I was believing all kinds of shit! My folks are gone and nothing was bringing them back.

Either way it was time to stop being scared and find out. I took the equivalent of $20 American dollars and put it under my glass of water and got up from the table. Then I went outside and caught a taxi and headed for my hotel. The temperature was 97 degrees with no breeze just a dry, dusty heat. The skin under my knees stuck to the seat of the taxi and made me sweat more. The only air came through the window and that was hot.

The doorman opened the taxi and greeted me with a smile. The cool air and the lobby felt so good and I stopped at the front desk to check for messages. I had one from Ronald and one from Terri. They both read basically the same way, "Haven't heard from you. Call as soon as possible."

The ninth floor hallway was quiet. No maids were in sight and no people were walking around. I opened the door to my room but didn't go in right away. I looked inside, my bed was made, and the floor was vacuumed and fresh glasses wrapped in plastic on the dresser. Everything looked fine. The clothes I wore yesterday when I got off the plane were draped over the chair next to the bed just as I left them.

I refused to look at it at first. I walked in slowly and looked in the bathroom and the spare room. I turned on the air conditioner then glanced at the Obeni as I went to close the door. When I did look at it I couldn't take my eyes off of it. African hands had exquisitely made it and I felt proud to own it. I walked around behind it to see if it had been disturbed but the maids had not touched it. Maybe I should keep it covered so there wouldn't be too many questions the next time I leave the room.

My energy was high with expectation and if she appeared what should I do? Maybe a pen and paper to write down what she says. Or write down what I'm trying to do in case something happens to me. Maybe it might not be her and I could see someone else.

I found a pen in my carry on bag and some pads in the drawer. Wait a minute; I have a voice-activated tape recorder in my suitcase. I ran across the room unzipped my bag and took out the recorder inserting a new blank tape. This way someone would have to believe me. Too bad I didn't bring my camcorder. I checked the batteries even though they were new and tested the player anyway. The tape was working fine and now I would have proof.

I sat on the bed and waited staring at the stand behind the glass still feeling unwilling to believe what I saw. Then again if all this was true it could only happen to me. My life has been one close call after another. Like the day Ronald and I were riding our bikes in the rain and almost took a tumble off the 59th Street Bridge on the Fourth of July, 1976, the 200 year anniversary of our country's independence. Ronald and I decided to ride our bikes to what I referred to as the bicycle highway. We crossed the Triborough Bridge into Queens and rode to Flushing Meadow Park from Harlem. It was a warm summer day and we peddled from one side of Flushing Meadow Park to the other until it got late and we started to ride home. When we got back to the Triborough Bridge a police officer told us the pedestrian path to the bridge was closed. There were boats from many countries in the East River, which came to join in the celebration. The police feared people would throw objects from the bridges so they closed the walkways. With no money for the train we rode to the next bridge south to 59th Street. It was beginning to rain when we caught sight of it. We saw a policeman in the distance guarding the bridge's entry. Thinking he would also stop us from crossing we pedaled up a single lane outer roadway and passed the barricades as quickly as we could. Behind us we could hear the officer yelling for us to come back but we ignored his call.

The rain poured heavy so we kept our heads down as we shifted into a lower gear and pulled up the steep grade. Halfway across the bridge I felt a need to stop. Ronald stopped next to me and asked what was wrong. I wiped the water from my brow and said I didn't know. It turned out six or seven feet in front of us was a missing section of the bridge. The outer roadway was under construction and all that was left in our path was a gaping hole fifty feet across. We looked at each other and said nothing. We finished the ride across the bridge in the center roadway with the cars at our backs.

The sun was shining when we got to Second Avenue and exited the bridge. We never said a word until we got back to our block and I never told Ronald what really made me stop that day. But if I hadn't, we would have ridden off the bridge plunging to our deaths. So strange things have happened to me most of my life but so far I've always landed on my feet.

I didn't know when I fell asleep. I lay with my head at the foot of the bed looking into the sand disappointed. I know I saw a woman before. When I saw the holes, the slots were empty. I went to the safe inside the closet and opened it. Then took the disks out of the leather pouch and closed the closet door. I took the chair and moved it back in front of the Obeni. Then stood on the chair and put the disks inside the slots and stepped down. Pulling the chair a few feet away I sat down and waited. Another half hour had gone by and nothing happened. I sat back in the chair to get more comfortable. I looked around the room and was startled by the phone and went over to the nightstand and picked up on the fourth ring. It was the front desk with a long distance call from America.

"Mr. Reeves your party is on the line go ahead."

"Hello who is this?" I asked.

"Hi baby, how ya doing?" The voice said.

"Who is this?"

"It's me, who do you think it is?"

"Oh, hi Terri."

"What are you doing over there? It's been almost two days since you've talked to me."

"I know Terri."

"What's the problem?" She said.

I didn't want to tell her what's been going on yet.

"I'm sorry baby I was having so much fun I forgot."

Damn why'd I say that?

"You're having so much fun without me? I was worried about you."
I looked up and saw an image. It was very cloudy but it was there, a
tree with the top branches blowing in the wind.

"Are you listening to me?" Terri said.

The image was becoming clearer. There was a building in the background and curtains in the windows where the glass panes would be.

"Hey! What are you doing over there? Who's there with you?"

"No one is here."

"I've been telling you how much I miss you and you don't say
anything. If you don't want to talk to me just say so!"

It was so strange. I could see small birds flying in the distance.

"You son of a bitch! You have a woman there don't you?"
I couldn't hide the happiness in my voice.

"Honey there's nobody here!"

"Then what's your fucking problem?" She yelled.

"Let me call you right back," I said.

There was a pause followed by a loud click. I wasn't surprised she
hung up on me, but it just didn't seem important now. I wanted to have
a closer look at the Obeni and then I'd call her back.

I put the phone down and went closer. There wasn't much I could
see clearly. It was like trying to read letters on the bottom of a pool
while the water was being splashed on the surface. In the right corner
the ripples dissipated enough for me to see a single story house with
four columns outside. Before long all the distortion in the Obeni went
away and I could see the house clearly. It was white polished stone
with a doorway in the center between the second and third column,
and a window on each side of the door. I could see the sky in the
background over the horizon. The sky was deep blue with white clouds
scattered about. I couldn't be sure of the distance but I could see a
mountain range in the background. I found myself trembling and
ashamed. Candice told me the truth and I tried hard not to believe
her. Across the yard was a tree in the middle left corner with a thin
sturdy trunk and big green leaves like elephant ears swaying in the
breeze and the ground had a dirt path worn into the grass leading to
the door of the house.

I took a seat at the foot of the bed and watched. The path from the doorway forked in two directions. The left fork came in my direction and the right fork went near the tree and disappeared over the hill. I didn't notice it at first but there was a chair under the tree. It was white with small green designs. The back was in a slightly reclined position. What the hell was this thing? Could it be a way to see into another dimension or planet? Or maybe it was something simple like heaven. If it was heaven why were there footpaths worn in the grass? Didn't people just fly instead of walk? And why was there a chair under a tree? If I were in heaven I'd sit down in mid-air. And I also saw birds in the distant sky. Do all the dead birds go to heaven too? If it were heaven the woman I saw wouldn't have been afraid of me, unless when you die you go there and don't actually know you're dead. But that's the whole point of going to heaven, knowing you're dead. And she called me a spirit so she thought I was the one who was dead.

More then an hour passed and I hadn't seen her or anyone else. I walked around the room glancing at the Obeni every other second. If anyone did come back I needed some proof because I would never be believed. Oh man, I just remembered I brought a camera. I could take a picture and that would be enough proof. Now where did I put my camera?

Whenever I traveled by myself, I never fully unpacked. I lived out of my suitcases because I never knew what had been in the dresser drawers. I kept my dirty laundry in a plastic bag inside the dresser and my clean stuff in my suitcase. It wasn't until Terri and I started traveling together that I took all of my clothes out from my suitcase and packed them away. I went to the closet and zipped my carry on bag. I have a Polaroid camera that takes instant pictures. When I looked on the back in the little window, and saw five pictures were left. I opened the camera and watched for the light to appear. When it turned green I stood about six feet away and pushed the button. Right away the Obeni image became wavy and distorted like in the beginning. The picture cranked out slowly from its slot and I placed it on the dresser. I wasn't going to risk taking any more right now so I closed the camera and put it on the dresser next to the developing photo.

When the photo started to develop, I could see there was a prob-lem. The wooden frame of the Obeni was there but inside the frame was bright light as if I had taken a picture of the sun. Getting proof with the camera wasn't going to work. So the tape recorder was all I had left. If I couldn't get a picture a conversation would have to do. The proof would be in my questions and her possible answers.

Two hours had gone by and I hadn't seen her or anyone else. I paced around the room wondering if I should call Terri back now? I went to the phone but did not reach for it. If I saw someone in the Obeni while I was talking to her and she heard a woman's voice in the room that would make it worse than it already was. Terri had an apology coming from me but not yet. I didn't want to take my eyes away from the Obeni for a second.

The sunset here was unforgettable. The sky was changing colors ever so slowly. The sun was a ruby red color and close to the horizon. It seemed as I went back and forth from the terrace I noticed the sun in the Obeni making similar color changes. Behind the chair under the tree the sky had the same beautiful sunset. When the last sliver of the sun sank into the horizon I came from the terrace and looked at Obeni. It was dark and filled with sand. Why hadn't I seen her? Maybe she'd been there watching me and I couldn't see her. One thing had become apparent, I wasn't angry with the Princess anymore.

I placed an overseas call to my house hoping Terri would pick up. My answering machine came on and I called out her name and waited but she didn't pick up. The next call was to her apartment. Terri should be at work now but she'd hear the message when she came home. The phone rang four times and the answering machine came on. Her machine was like mine; it gave you more than a few minutes to talk.

"Hello I know you're at work now but I want you to know there was no one in my room last night. Something strange happened here and it upset me but I am okay. If I told you what it was you would never believe me. It's an Obeni and I bought it from an antique shop."
I wasn't prepared to give Terri any more details so I said,

"And I was looking at it when you called. I know it's no excuse but if you never believe anything I ever say again believe me now, there was no one in my room."
Now was the time to tell Terri I loved her but I couldn't.

"Well that's what I wanted to say and I miss you. I'll be in the room all night. Call me when you get this message, bye."
Then I called the front desk and asked for a wake up call at 4:00am.

I would not miss Halley's Comet tonight. I should have taken the time to return Ronald's call; instead I took a shower and went to bed. I couldn't fall asleep right away and I wondered why I couldn't see the house in the Obeni at nighttime? Did it work with light or rays from the sun? And why was the sun setting at the same time here as it was there? That might be a clue someone was playing a high tech game with me. I stretched long and hard and took a deep breath. For the first time since I became a man I slept with the light on.

The phone rang; it was the desk waking me at 4am. I got out of bed opened the terrace door and looked outside. There at the right lower corner of the horizon was the comet. My dream had come true at last. It was very small but I could see its white streaks pointing upward. I watched until the sky grew lighter and the comet couldn't be seen anymore. Now I was one of the few people who could say they actually saw Halley's Comet.

When I got back into bed the Obeni was still dark and I wondered if I'd ever see Whende again. I longed to talk to her and oddly enough I missed her. I'd seen her only once but felt like her face was familiar, and I had to see her again.

Chapter 5

Back in New York it was an ordinary Wednesday afternoon. On lower Broadway the race began with no time to waste in the pursuit of a lunchtime fix. The day's pace seems faster because there is only so much you can do in an hour. If you purchase your lunch in the first twenty minutes, you can use twenty five minutes to eat your food in a civilized manner and avoid indigestion. That leaves you fifteen minutes to return to work. So anyone who didn't have a legitimate reason to be in the city when the office buildings let out for lunch stayed away.

Lorraine was out shopping early this morning and by afternoon she was entering the office building along Broadway a few blocks past Chambers Street. She took the elevator to the seventh floor, walked down the hallway, and pressed the doorbell outside the two huge oak doors. Once inside, she gave her name and took a seat in the waiting area.

Terri came in some moments later, greeted her and quietly escorted her to her office. What should have been a friendly lunch date was a deception, not unlike a CIA covert maneuver. Information and secrets would be shared and propaganda would be spread. Once inside the office Terri closed the door and took a seat behind her desk. Lorraine put two shopping bags near a couch in the corner and took a seat and then the operation began.

"Terri, you have too many books in here and girl your desk is a mess. I'll bring you some plants the next time I come."

"Honey don't bother, I'm too busy to water them. They'll be dead in a few weeks."

"Well, how about a cactus? It's pretty hard to kill a cactus."

Terri thought for a moment but did not respond.

"It would look nice right there on that table," Lorraine said.

"Thank you," Terri said graciously.

"So how are you doing, girl?" Lorraine said solemnly as if she were in the hospital visiting a sick friend.

"I am fine, I got a little raise and everything's been great."

Lorraine smiled for a second then asked, "So how's Bennie?"

"He is fine I guess."

"You guess, when did you hear from him last?"

"Sunday night before he left for the airport," Terri said sadly.

"Sunday!? That was three days ago! Ronald called his hotel yesterday but he wasn't in his room, and he never us called back."

"I forgot. I did speak with him yesterday," Terri said.

"So what did he say?"

"Nothing much, he was doing something in his room and I got mad and hung up on him."

"What was he doing?"

"I don't know."

"Well what do you think he was doing?"

"I don't know!" Terri said trying not to lash out at her.

"He said he purchased an item and was looking at it when I called." Lorraine opened her purse and took out a pack of cigarettes. She struck a match then gave herself a light. After she exhaled, she shook her head.

"Let me tell you something girl, I've known Bennie since he was eighteen and he's always been a dog. I'm telling you you're not the first.

"I think he's changed, I mean, I know he's changed. We had a nice talk before he left. And when he comes back, I know things will be different."

"Has he asked you to marry him?"

"Not yet but he told me things would be different when he got back."

"What's that supposed to mean?" Lorraine said, as she reached for the ashtray Terri was handing her.

"Why do you put up with this?" She continued.

"I know he loves me, I can feel it. I see it in the way he looks at me.

85

He's the first man to ever give me keys to his apartment. And he told me I was the only woman in his life."

"Did he say that?"

"Yes!"

Lorraine was back in the hospital speaking to Terri like she was on the critical list.

"Honey, I didn't want to tell you this because I was hoping he'd get his act together."

"Tell me what?" Terri said quickly.

"Has anyone ever called the house named Paula?"

"No, and he lets me answer the phone whenever I want. It's either you or Ronald, his sister or his Aunt Dot, or friends from work."

"You've never heard the name Paula?" She said again.

"Who is Paula?" Terri asked.

Lorraine sat quiet in the chair taking the last drag and putting the cigarette out.

"He's been seeing some freak stripper bitch named Paula the same time he's been with you. I didn't want to tell you girl, but I can't let him treat you like this."

Terri closed her eyes and sat silently in her chair. Lorraine had to be wrong. She put all her trust in Bennie, so there had to be a mistake.

"How do you know?" Terri asked.

"I know a lot of secrets," bragged Lorraine.

Terri felt like she was being held underwater, deep water that puts pressure around your body making it hard for you to breathe. She fought to hold herself together. She was at work and wasn't about to lose her job for any man.

"I'll find out for sure when he gets back from Egypt."

"And when you talk to him ask him where he was last Tuesday."

"Tuesday he was hanging out with some friends from the neighborhood," Terri said.

"He was with her last Tuesday," Lorraine said.

"How do you know? Did you see them?"

"You think I would lie to you about something like this. I've been watching him for a long time and he's always been full of shit."

Lorraine stood up from the chair and brushed off the flakes of ash from her pants. Then she walked to the couch for her shopping bags.

"I just had a thought," she said, "Don't say anything to Bennie until he gets back. I think Ronald and I are going to Egypt next week. He should still be there, so don't say anything OK."

"No, I won't say a word."

"Good, I'll call you tonight."

"You're not staying for lunch?" Terri asked.

"No I am not hungry."

Terri got up to escort Lorraine to the elevator. She held it together until she returned to her office. She fought back the urge to leave work and take the first flight to Egypt, or cut up all of his clothes, pour Clorox in his fish tank, and totally trash his house. But the lawyer in her would give him a chance. He was innocent until proven guilty but right now as far as she was concerned he was on death row.

Many hours later the Egyptian sun rose to begin the start of my next day. When I opened my eyes it was morning. I rolled away from the light and saw the terrace door with the curtains drawn. Where was that sunlight coming from? I sat up and there she was with her hand on the bottom of her chin like that statue of the thinker. Her eyes were so serious and intimidating, and then she stood up.

"Why do you sleep, Spirit?"

I didn't mind her calling me a spirit this time. I wanted to talk to her but her face was so intimidating I just looked at her.

She was wearing a short sheer silky white dress tapered at the waist, which stopped above her knees. It rippled in the breeze and when the sun shined behind her I could see the outline of her body. Her hips had nice curves and her legs were long and slender. The sandals she wore laced in a crisscross fashion up to her ankles.

With these mounting details came the irrefutable evidence I had never been dreaming and therefore was forced to believe. And with the belief came the deserved respect.

"Princess, I want to talk to you."

She looked around as if talking to me should be done surreptitiously. And this time she was less apprehensive.

"What do you want of me?"

"I would like to know who you are, and where you come from."

"I will answer a question and you answer me," she said.

"I," she gestured pointing to herself, "am in back of my dega."

"What is a dega?"

"Dega is where I dwell and do my studying. Now you, where are you from and what garments are those?"

"I am from a city called Harlem in a place called New York and these are called shorts." I turned around pulling my pockets inside out and stuffing them back inside. Now what should I ask her?

"Princess is there anyone else inside with you?"

"Inside? Yes there are people all around the city and in the temples but this is my own dega."

"What are they doing?" I asked.

"Anything they want. They are working, raising families, studying, and exploring. They do what they want."

I'm wondering to myself why people in heaven need to explore. Why do dead people work or raise families? This makes no sense. "I don't understand Princess, what kind of work are the people doing?"

"My brother is building a tomb for our father, the Pharaoh, near the other two tombs. Many workmen in the city and adjoining lands will be there. The tomb will be ready before Pharaoh's death. When finished it will be a site to behold. Three tombs near the Gomon."

"What is the Gomon?"

"The Gomon is a testament to man's elevation of self and control over his animal mind."

I had to keep asking,

"What does the Gomon look like?"

"It is the head of Gomon on the body of a lion."

I think the Princess mistakes the Gomon for the Sphinx. And she says there are two tombs near the Sphinx instead of three. I must not be hearing her right.

"So you say you are the daughter of a pharaoh and your brother is building a tomb near the Sphinx, I mean the Gomon."

"Not just his daughter, his favorite daughter," she said proudly.

My mouth dropped open and I immediately sat in the chair.

"What troubles you, Spirit?"

I didn't answer; I just patted the air in front of me with an open hand while shaking my head.

"I was wrong to think I could learn anything from you, Spirit."

"You don't understand I think you are alive, and you are thousands of years in the past!" I said.

She was staring at me now in disbelief and I replayed what I said to her in my head. Maybe in my haste I said it wrong, so I tried again.

"In my time right now there are three tombs near the Gomon and they are thousands of years old." This time she took a seat on the ground.

"I'm telling you the truth!" I yelled.

She took a deep sigh. I could tell she didn't believe me. It was the same look I'd given to Candice in the kitchen.

"How is that possible? You are attempting to deceive me, Spirit. You have the tombs wrong. What do they look like? She asked.

I made a triangle shape with my two hands. "But they're big and they have four sides made of stone blocks." She nodded in agreement.

"I don't understand how you can be in the future?"

"Maybe it's what the Obeni does," I said.

"What did you say?" as if astounded.

"It must be the Obeni," I repeated.

Now her mouth opened wide and no words came out. Then softly she said,

"You have the Obeni?"

"Yes I do!"

I waited for her to say something but she jumped to her feet. Her eyes were moving like she was thinking of something to do.

"Do you know what it is?" I asked.

"I can't tell now. I must go. Wait for me, I will return."

All my ideas about the Obeni being a hoax disappeared when Princess Whende walked away from me and down the footpath into the doorway of the house I saw in the background. It was not a computer projection. It was not a high tech hologram and this was not Candid Camera. I sat in the chair next to the bed in front of the Obeni for several hours and Whende didn't return. I knew she would come back but when? This was not heaven I was looking into Whende was alive. She did not fly away from me or fade away. She walked. I sat in the chair next to my bed and watched her world until the sun went down and the images faded away.

It had been days since I'd seen Whende and when I woke Saturday I couldn't spend another day trapped in my suite. I had no doubt she would come back but where was she? Why did she rush off and how could she speak English? Were the Egyptian people speaking English then? It didn't seem possible, English was a new language compared to Greek and Latin. That would be my first question when we spoke again.

In the morning I went to the Museum of Cairo searching for answers. My mind was made up not to tell anyone in the museum what I purchased at the Aswan shop. I was here to get answers if possible. When I reached the second floor I found a surprise in the room to my left. Behind the glass display case was the top half of an Obeni. I immediately recognized it. Even though it was just the wooden frame, it had the same arch with two holes carved in the top. The sign next to it said it was an Egyptian hourglass from 4600 B.C. obviously they had no idea what it was either. Further down on the opposite side of the display case were two discs like the ones in my safe at the hotel. The sign next to them said Egyptian jewelry. It was now apparent to me the museum would be of no help.

North Kemit was several miles from Cairo. I'd been to the Kemit University at noon and spoken to Dr. Morrison who was here from Hunter College. I did not tell him about the Obeni but I asked him if he'd ever heard of an object that could look into the past. Of course he never took me seriously but the hours spent with him were very enlightening. He gave me a brief lesson on Egyptian history and recommended several books I could read. One such book was called "Black man of the Nile and His Family". It was written by Dr. Yosef A A ben-Jochannan. Surprisingly I'd seen this book many times before he shared it with me, but I'd never purchased it.

Cheikh Anta Diop was the author of another book he recommended. The title was "African origins of civilization: myth or reality". Dr. Morrison told me these books among others would give me a true representation of African history. Written by men who had no desire to mislead or trivialize the great accomplishments of African people.

After leaving the University I went shopping for my friends and family back home. I brought Terri some gold wristbands with matching anklets. I took ten T-shirts in different colors with Egypt written on the front. I also purchased a few carved wooden figures of animals. My

Aunt Dot liked lions and elephants and these were mahogany works of art. I saw a crystal pyramid six inches high and purchased it also.

My shopping bags were not heavy so I asked for directions to the hotel by bus. The longer I stayed in Cairo the more I felt at ease. Walking to the bus stop I thought about the talk I had with Dr. Morrison at the University. I went there because I wanted to see if anyone could tell me about Princess Sakatet Whende and if she ever existed.

It was my fortune to find Dr. Morrison at that time. He was here with a group of students from the teaching on Egypt and the civilizations of the Nile. He told me the recorded information on Princess Sakatet was fragmented. Her father Pharaoh Afermose had many wives and Princess Sakatet was the daughter of his most treasured wife Queen Kymeka. Afermose died in 3287 B.C. and was by all accounts a wise man. He built many temples in her honor expressing his love for the Queen.

The bus pulled to the curb bringing a trail of dust behind it. It was small; only half the size of the city bus with twenty seats. I paid the driver and took a seat in the back. I settled down and thought more about my conversation with Dr. Morrison. He told me the Princess asked permission to study in the temples with the priests. This was unheard of because only men were allowed to study the sciences. The Queen and the Princess pleaded with Afermose to change the rules regarding women and he did. In the year shortly before her birthday Princess Sakatet had knowledge of geometry, medicine and astronomy. Princess Sakatet married Kfaru and had some children. Her husband died young possibly of a disease or in battle. It is believed she became a great queen but that was all speculation. No more records of her life have been found.

The bus stopped at the curb near the entrance at the bottom of the loop to my hotel. I stood up with my bags and went to the door. I thanked the driver and stepped off making sure I had not left anything. Once again I was glad to enter the lobby of the hotel. The walk from the bus stop was not long but it was all up hill. The woman at the front desk called to give me a message from Ronald. The message said he might come down with his wife Lorraine in a week. I know I could show him my discovery and he would believe me, besides he was the only person who was not a family member that I trusted.

The suite was cleaned while I was away. The maid must think I'm strange because I stayed in my room most of my visit except for today. She was a nice lady who followed my instructions faithfully. I asked her only to clean my bathroom, vacuum, and make up my bed. Under no circumstances should she move anything in my room. Before I put my bags down I went to the Obeni and looked at the legs to see if there were new impressions in the carpet. Glad to see the Obeni had not been moved I went in front of the dresser and put the bags down.

Next I went to the safe and removed the discs and inserted them into slots and waited. After a few minutes I decided to take a quick shower. When I was about to shave when I heard someone call out,

"Where are you?"

She was back, I ran to the Obeni to find her sitting in a chair. The same chair I'd seen under the tree. On her lap with two objects resembling rolling pins with paper wrapped around them. They appeared to be scrolls used to store information long before books was invented. She looked at me and for the first time she smiled,

"I've been here most of the morning, where have you been?"

"I was waiting princess."

"It took some time and don't call me Princess. My name is Whende."

There was a change in her attitude and I liked it.

"What do you call yourself?"

"Oh, I am not a spirit anymore?" I said with some levity. I didn't wait for her answer; I was just pleased she wanted to know.

"My name is Benjamin Reeves, and you can call me Bennie."

"Bennie, that's a strange name," she said with a hint of a smile, "I thought you were a spirit because you live in my pool under the water."

"But I am not underwater," I said.

"I know you don't live underwater but that is where you appear."

"Whende, tell me what you know about the Obeni?"

Whende was very excited now and said,

"The Obeni was a story told to me by my mother when I wouldn't sleep. She said the Obeni would swallow me if I stayed awake. Everyone here tells the story to the children for as long as anyone can remember."

"Whende, how can you speak English?" I asked.

"What is English?" She said.

"It's the language we are speaking now," I said.

"I was to ask you how you speak Kemetic so well." She replied.

We looked at each other in silence neither having an answer to that obscurity... Then she opened one of the scrolls and finally answered,

"I do not know."

"Whende,"

"Yes,"

"What is the Obeni?"

She picked up the first scroll leaned back in the chair and unraveled it.

"I will begin," she said calmly.

"I know not what age you are in so I start from my age. The scroll I wrote this from could not be taken from its resting place. I wrote everything from it here," (this is awkward and confusing and you have switched to modern English. I have no idea what she is trying to tell him here.) gesturing to the scrolls on her lap. "It was written in the age of the Popic 1096 mala before the age of the beetle."

She spoke slowly as if she was a teacher and I was a student and I interrupted, "what is a mala and a Popic?" I asked.

"One mala is Samae`s circle around Ra and,"

I interrupted again, "What is Samae and what is Ra?"

"Samae is the land," she stomped her feet on the ground and with her hands together they slowly parted until her arms were outstretched. "Ra is the light in the sky."

The words were different but I understood her and started once again to believe this was a hoax. Samae was the earth and Ra was the sun and a mala must be one year. How could they know back then the Earth resolved around the sun?

"How do you know the Earth I mean Samae moves around Ra?"

Whende looked puzzled,

"Every child knows Samae dances around Ra!"

If what she said was true everything I was taught or saw on television about Egyptian people was wrong.

"Please go ahead," I would try not to interrupt her unless absolutely necessary.

"In the age of the Popic 1096 mala before the age of the beetle or 3728 mala ago a sika was seen close to Samae. The Sika Yemot flies the sky tonight and will not come back for 76 Mala. A priest named Jonen saw the Sika glowing red in the night sky. Sika Jonen it is said could be seen even in the morning. Not long after another sika appeared in the night sky glowing white. It was the Sika Yemot sent by the creator to bring peace."

Whende looked up from the scroll and seeing she had my full attention continued, but once again I interrupted.

"How much time are you talking about?"

It was hard to phrase the question I was trying to ask.

"How much history do you have? I mean how far can you go back in time?"

By the perplexed look she gave made me rephrase the question.

"How far do the scrolls go back? How many Mala ago do the scrolls go back?"

Finally I think she understood my question and paused for a moment,

"The oldest scroll tells of the time in 11,300 Mala ago," she answered.

That was a long time and I think she was estimating it from her present, which made the thought of how far Egyptian history went back so overwhelming all my questions were put on hold.

"Please finish, Whende."

"Jonen said the two Sika would meet and battle in the sky. When the battle was over Jonen named the small Sika Yemot after his son. Then told the people the Sika Jonen would not return for 14,820 mala. The Sika Yemot would keep watch over Samae once every 76 mala."

She rolled the scroll up and placed it on the right side of her chair near her feet.

I was astounded by their knowledge of celestial movement and speculated how they could know all of this. And then I remembered Candice telling me about the jealousy that ran through the hearts and minds of the people who first opened the ancient tombs. Who knows what artifacts were kept, hidden or destroyed giving testament to this great civilization of astronomers? With that in mind it wasn't hard to except Sir Edmund Halley as the second person to discover the comet.

Something else was happening I hadn't expected. The anger associated with the feeling of being spied upon was gone, replaced by a longing to spend more time with her. Yes it was becoming an addiction. That was the only explanation for it because I hadn't called Terri anymore or anyone else. I loved the intelligence and grace of Whende. Why couldn't I find a woman like this in my time? Then I thought about Candice's warning and the pain in her face. Candice said the Obeni was responsible for her father's disappearance. I had to be careful, dealing with something I knew absolutely nothing about. If this is an addiction that would lead to my death, I must have the common sense to break free.

"Do you wish me to continue?" Whende asked.

"Yes," I smiled generously, "I want to know more."

"Men here don't listen to me when I try to teach them something they don't know."

"I am not like them," I said flirtatiously.

She sat back in the chair and opened the second scroll. This time I took a seat at the foot of the bed and clasped my hands together in eagerness.

"In the battle of Sika Jonen and Sika Yemot fireballs fell from the sky. Jonen walked for many mala looking for fireballs that fell to Samae. When they found them Yemot kept them safe and so did a son Mentu. Tafnekhet son of Mentu moved the fireballs from their resting place. And Ept son of Tafnekhet was born he had the gift of knowing. He was called a pomice before he could walk and,"

I understood the fireballs were fragments of the two meteors but I had to stop and ask,

"Whende what is a pomice?"

"A pomice is one who is quickly able to know. Great thinkers they are born as man or woman, servant, or queen and only after many, many mala."

It took only a few moments to understand a pomice was a genius, their equivalent to Albert Einstein. An article I read somewhere said a genius was born every couple of hundred years and that it knew no gender or racial barriers.

Whende found her place on the scroll and continued,

"Before Ept could walk it was known he was a pomice. Tafnekhet told Ept in 6 mala Sika Yemot would return and together they would move the fireballs to another place. Before the 6 mala passed Ept studied the movement of the sky and the circles of Samae around Ra and Samae herself. He went to the temple of the knowing and read every scroll."

"When Sika Yemot came back to Samae Ept and his father went to move the fireballs. They took food and tools on three horses. The journey to the hiding place of the fireballs would take six risings of Ra. The place was found and they began to dig in Samae when the first fireball was seen. When Tafnekhet touched the fireball he had a vision. He saw his wife giving birth to Ept and then he saw his father Mentu as a young man. Each time he touched the fireball he had a vision. He saw Ra rise and fall in the sky. He saw the rain come and go. Tafnekhet held the fireball long enough to see the battle of Sika Yemot and Jonen and then let go."

Whende looked away from the scroll and towards the sky.

"Soon Ra will be leaving," she said.

I went to the entrance of the balcony and pulled back the curtain. Time for me had gone by so fast but she was right, the sun was setting.

"Will you come back Whende?"

"Yes, but I must tell you now!" She closed the scroll then told the rest from memory.

"With all manner of study and many mala later Ept made three Obeni from the grains of the fireballs."

Then with a deliberate and slow voice Whende said,

"The Obeni is a doorway to the past."

Her eyes were piercing me looking for a reaction, but she did not let me speak. She took the same commanding tone like the first day we met.

"I can tell you how many mala we are apart when you find what age is there? Or when was the last time the Still star moved?"

"Which star is the Still Star?" I asked.

She looked up to the sky again and said,

"All stars circle the Still Star but each 26,000 mala the Still Star leaves and another one takes its place."

The connection between us was being broken and Whende`s voice was a bit louder,

"Samae rocks," she made a pitching motion with her hand, "every 26,000 mala Still Star Bennie."

I sat motionless and dejected staring into the sand. My stomach was upset and I was finding it hard to breathe. This was overwhelming and I began to doubt. No one would believe I spent most of my day talking to a woman who by all rights should be dead. There has to be a logical explanation. There is no history of mental illness in my family so I must be the first one. My head felt like it was between a vice and with each thought the pain grew. Something was very wrong. Maybe someone was pumping an odorless gas into my room to make me have hallucinations. I stood up to go to the balcony then changed my mind. For some reason I thought I might accidentally fall off. I ran to the door and opened it so fast the do not disturb sign fell on the floor. I couldn't even remember putting it there. It was time to get out of this room so reluctantly; I went to the dresser picked up the keys and went out.

Walking in a fit of confusion I went to the elevator glad to be in the hallway alone. When the elevator reached the lobby I didn't want to get off but other guests in the hotel were waiting and I dreaded riding back up with them. While walking through the lobby though no one knew me I was hoping they didn't see me. I even gave the front desk a wide berth and I was still seen. A young man called out to me and I pretended not hear.

He called a little louder and different heads from various positions sitting and standing looked up all focusing on me.

"Mr. Reeves please," he motions for me to come to the desk.

"I'm sorry we tried to contact you this morning. The tour bus arrived and we could not locate you."

With all the excitement I'd forgotten about the tour to the pyramids.

"Well what should I do?" I said uncaringly.

"We cannot refund your money but I can book that tour for you another day."

"I'll let you know," and I turned to leave.

"And one more thing Sir, you requested we hold your messages."

He gave me four pieces of paper then asked if I was all right. I said yes and asked him to point me in the direction of the hotel bar. I had no intention of going to the bar but I needed a reason to walk away.

I was slowly getting a grip on myself fueled by not giving anyone the satisfaction of seeing this young man from Harlem out of control. There was a small table in the back away from everyone so I took a seat. The waiter came to the table to take my order. When he left I moved closer to an overhead light to read my messages. My aunt Dot called, the next paper had my sister's name, and the last two were from Ronald. All the messages said basically the same thing we haven't heard from you and call us soon. I had to return these phone calls so nobody would worry but it was the last thing on my mind. I could still hear Whende's last words about the mala and the still star.

The waiter put a napkin on the table and then the Rum and Coke. He asked if I wanted to charge it to my room and I said yes. I took a sip knowing alcohol was not the answer. What should I do? Where could I draw strength? My indistinctive response to the confusion and fear was to face it. The grip from the vice was loosening from my head. Then I took one more sip and left the bar. I had found a remarkable once in a lifetime discovery. And I was determined to explore all the possibilities. But I had to be cautious. Suppose Whende wasn't all she seemed? What if it was something evil that snatched souls and because she was there trapped she needed me to help her escape. Then I thought about those movies with monsters and haunted houses I'd seen over the years. If the people would have stayed away they would be alive. Instead they go into that scary house, or crawl into a dark cave that's littered with bones and rotting flesh and meet their demise. Every time I watched those movies I was so happy when the monster got them. I laughed when they brought King Kong to New York City and he smashed up everything. During the movie I would say to myself, leave Kong where he is he's not bothering anybody. And now I was doing the same thing, taking a risk that wasn't necessary.

Chapter 6

On the other side of the world Terri woke up in a cold sweat Saturday morning. It was another addition to the string of consecutive nights of tossing and turning since he left. She wasn't sure if the days were worse than the nights. At the same time brief thoughts of getting a guard dog so she could sleep better at night were contemplated. In the year or so she and Bennie had been together with each passing month more nights were spent with him. A dog's paws could never replace the arms that wrapped her in a blanket of sanctuary, or challenge her intellectually through stimulating conversation.

She walked to the mirror in front of her bed and looked at herself starting from her head down to her toes. Bennie always made her believe she was enough woman for him. So what was missing, what wasn't she doing right? Men came on to her everyday when she walked down the street, or rode the subway. They'd hit on her in the morning from the time she left her apartment building in the Bronx, until she reached lower Broadway. There wasn't one time since establishing a relationship with Bennie that she even flirted with anyone. She couldn't understand why he said things would be different when he got back.

Terri went to the bathroom to brush her teeth. When she turned on the water she thought about the fish. Today was Saturday and she had not been to his apartment since Tuesday night. And something else didn't make sense. Bennie hasn't called his aunt, his sister or Ronald. If it was one thing she knew about men she knew they covered their tracks. If he took that bitch Paula on a vacation he would have called someone.

Terri thought about all the people who might have lied to her. Could she believe his sister when she said she knew nothing about a

woman named Paula? And what about Bennie? He looked so convincing the last time they were together. You are the only woman in
my life he said. Who has keys to my house? Whose clothes are here?
His message on her answering machine did sound sincere. And even if
it were a stupid thing to say, she did understand why he told her if she
would be happier with someone else to leave him. Or should she believe Lorraine? She was her friend so why would she lie?

Terri decided to play it straight. She would be the good little
woman and go to his house to feed the fish and water his plants. Maybe
she would spend the weekend in his bed for a good night's sleep. Again
she would temporarily pardon him for his stupidity and wait for his
return. She walked briskly from the bathroom to look at herself in the
mirror again. And if he were lying she'd scratch his fucking eyes out.

Ronald sat in the office of the Eighth Avenue Kleenit by the telephone. Some minor problems were discovered with three washers at
the Amsterdam store yesterday. Two machines were stuck on the
wash cycle and the third machine's coin slot was jammed with paper or
something. It was our intention to replace them with newer models at
the beginning of the next quarter. He watched the monitor in the
office to see when Chris wasn't busy then called him into the office.
Ronald told Chris of his plans for a vacation next week. Though not
sure of the day he and Lorraine would leave, Chris would receive a
temporary pay increase for managerial duties effective immediately.
This would not be the first time Chris was left in charge during both
our absences. While it was rare for Ronald and me to be away at the
same time it was a relief to know we could trust Chris.

When Chris left the office, Ronald stopped writing and thought to
himself for a minute. Bennie had never gone away and left so many
people wondering if he was all right and it began to force his concern.
Deep down he knew Bennie was all right but his latest stunt was
altering his life in two ways.

First Ronald had no desire to go to Egypt and second he didn't
want to take vacation in March. They always took their vacation in
June and he wanted to go to Paris. It was a wish he shared with Lorraine
for a long time. Just to stand under the Eiffel Tower and take pictures,
then ride the elevator inside and take in the view. Because of the
actions of his best friend the dream would be postponed.

The office phone started to ring; it was the mechanic calling to verify the address for the machines that were out of order. Before he could completely give the address the other line rang, "I have another call could you hold for one second please," then he pressed the button for the other line and said,

"Kleenit, Ronald speaking."

"Hi honey it's me," said Lorraine.

"Is everything all right," he said hastily.

"Yes, what do you want for dinner tonight?"

"I can't talk right now. I have someone on the line."

"Is it Bennie?"

"No, I'll call you right back"

"Okay, you can have steak or chicken. Potatoes with the steak or rice with the chicken, and any kind of vegetable you want."

"Give me ten minutes,"

"Okay bye," she said.

Ronald pressed the button on the telephone to return to the previous call but there was no answer. He reached for the Rolodex to find the mechanic's telephone number when the phone rang again.

"Kleenit Ronald speaking."

"Mr. Jefferson you hung up on me."

"I'm sorry," Ronald said, "I tried to put you on hold and must have pressed the wrong button."

"I've done that once or twice myself," the mechanic said pleasantly, "I was about to tell you I didn't really need the address. Just tell me if it is the store on St. Nicholas or Amsterdam."

"It's the store on Amsterdam," Ronald said.

"Now what was the problem and how many machines are down?"

"It's three washers and let me find the paper so I can tell you which ones."

Ronald sorted through the papers and the bills looking for the memo when the phone rang again.

"Jesse can you hold on one more time please?"

"Sure go ahead."

"Kleenit Ronald speaking."

"Hi honey."

Ronald uttered a low moan of frustration than softly said,

"Yes."

"What's wrong?" Lorraine said.

"Nothing I'm still on the phone."

"Well I was ready to go to the market and I wasn't sure what you wanted?"

"Whatever you decide is fine. Look honey I got to go," he said.

"I really called to ask if you made the arrangements with the travel agent and what day we were leaving." She said.

"I made the call yesterday and they didn't get back to me."

"Ok baby I know your busy," Lorraine said.

"Call me later bye."

"And don't forget make sure we stay at the same hotel Bennie's booked in."

"Yes I know," Ronald, pressed the button again.

"Hello Jesse, are you still there?"

"Yes I'm here; you did it right this time."

"I'm sorry for the interruptions," Ronald said, "I won't take any more calls until we finished."

"Sure," said Jesse.

"Now where were we?"

"The numbers of the machines and what the problems were."

"Oh yes, now let's see." He found the memo and began to read.

"Washing machine No. 2 and machine No. 17 are stuck in one cycle, the wash cycle. And machine No. 6 has the coin slot jammed with something."

"So it's just three machines on Amsterdam," Jessie said.

"That it."

"I got it Mr. Jefferson. I'll be there in less than two hours and call you when I finished."

The phone rang again but this time Ronald ignored it then looked at his watch.

"If you call and I'm not here you can leave a message or you can beep me and I'll call you back. Do you still have the beeper number?" Ronald asked.

"Yes I do,"

"Well thanks a lot and I'll wait to hear from you."

"Fine," said Jesse.

"All right bye."

Ronald continued to sit in the chair behind desk. With a small amount of energy he used one foot to make the chair swivel from side to side. He thought to himself, if Bennie would call before his travel agent does he could cancel the trip and go to Paris in June. Last night he thought about calling the police but decided against it. Only because every time he left a message the hotel staff assured him Bennie was all right and had just left. Why was Lorraine so hell bent on tracking him down on his vacation? Every time those two got together they disagreed on something. It wasn't because of Terri's feelings she felt the need to confront Bennie, Ronald knew for a fact Lorraine didn't care much for Terri. And that was a mystery too. Terri was an attractive, independent hard-working woman who got along with every body. Why didn't Lorraine like her?

Back at the hotel in Egypt I received my usual and 4:30 A. M. wake up call went to the bathroom and got myself together. I didn't want to open my eyes with her looking at me. It was Saturday morning March 16th. Changing into my clothes I thought back to yesterday. Whende faded as gracefully as the sun went down. She told me then that the Obeni draws its power from the sun and uses the gravity of the moon. She spoke as fast as she faded away I'd forgotten her saying only the present can return to the past.

After returning from the lobby last night I called Dr. Morrison with a few questions. He was just about to leave the University but made time to answer them. I believe he was intrigued by my inquiries into the subject of Egyptian history and offered to make me part of his tour group. Any other time I would have jumped at the chance, but I could learn more from Whende about history then he could ever teach me.

Dr. Morrison explained the earth's precession like this. The earth spins or rotates while it orbits around the sun, and spins on a 23 degree axis like the spinning tops kids play with. Every 26,000 years the Earth wobbles like a top and it's called a precession. At the equator the heavens are broken into twelve parts called a zodiac. At the poles the heavens are broken into seven parts called ages. The polar constellations and the equatorial constellations work together like the long and short hands of the clock. Each 2100 years or so brings a new age. There is an age of the beetle, and age of the fish, and age of the ram and so on. Dr. Morrison regretted he could not remember each age but suggested some books I could read on the subject. Around 2,100 B. C. was the age of the ram. Then we entered the age of the fish with the birth of Christ. The next age to come is Kefeius the black king. Somewhere between 2003 and 2015 A. D. the North Star or the pole star will move out of position and another star will take its place and this will represent the age of Kefeius.

The Egyptian people believed, as do some who study astrology, that the stars are maps to future events if you know how to interpret them and changing these events are impossible. It would be like stopping the sun from rising. Just as the stars are marked in the heavens the future of mankind is also destined. The star that will take place of the North Star will remain until the next new age. The North Star in ancient times served two purposes. Also referred to as the Still Star it remained constant in the sky for thousands of years, used as a navigational guide on land and sea. Some believed the movement of the star served as a bookmark for each new age.

This was more information than I could absorb in one phone conversation. Although I found it interesting I felt bad because I never bothered to read about this subject. But the fact that Whende and her people knew these things so long ago was unbelievable.

At 4:45 in this morning I was high as if I'd smoked a joint. Was this what it was like to be intoxicated from newfound knowledge? If it was it felt good, and I needed to have more. I couldn't wait to talk to her again. As for Terri, she was nice but I knew I didn't love her. At the moment I didn't care about Ronald, Terri, my family, or my business.

I went to the terrace and looked outside. The streets were quiet at this hour. My eyes focused on Yemot`s comet and not Halley's for the first time. Who would ever believe the comet had been discovered and named so long ago? Before I could tell anyone I needed some proof. Yes the Obeni was proof enough but if the Egyptian authorities discovered its power I'm sure they would take it away. And then I remembered my tape recorder. It had been on since Tuesday. If I had Whende's voice on tape, that would be some proof for the time being. I rushed to pick up the tape player and pushed rewind and waited for it to end.

I heard my voice say, hello who's this? It was my phone call with Terri. I fast forwarded it and stopped again. It was my voice again, Princess I want to talk to you. I would like to know who you are and where you come from. Then my voice again, I am from a place called Harlem. I know she was talking to me, why couldn't I hear her on the tape? I fast forwarded again and again but my voice was the only one I could hear.

The sun rose slowly over the horizon, as did my excitement. About 7:20am the sun started shining from the Obeni and the cloudy image of the house in the background was becoming clearer with each second. Whende was sitting in the chair reading and there were two more scrolls near her feet. I couldn't open my mouth. I sat on the corner of the bed and just looked. Her hair was parted down the center forming two braids on each side of her temples that drifted behind the base of her neck until they formed one thick braid that snaked around over her left shoulder. She wore an off white top and matching skirt that stopped three inches above her knee, seemingly made of soft cotton. Her fingernails and toes were painted red like the color of minuet roses. What would it be like to have a woman like her as mine? Yes she was pleasing to look at but there was more to her than most women. Maybe it was her mind, or the way she held her head so high. Was she the mother from Africa who was waiting to embrace me? Thoughts of Whende were filling my head more each day. The respect she commanded was always at hand. I could say safely, I'd never met anyone like her and probably never would again.

Her eyes focused on me and she smiled.

"I was thinking of you last night. Are you a king, and how many wives do you have?"

"I'm no king Whende. I am just a man with no one special in my life." I couldn't count the number of women I'd said that particular line to.

She smiled again and said,

"Did I tell you not to disturb the Obeni?"

"I think so."

"You must not move the Obeni," she said abruptly. "Mark the spot so you can know where it belongs."

"Why?" I asked.

"It is like holding a shiny piece of metal up to Ra. When you move the metal a piece of Ra moves."

I understood her perfectly; if I moved the Obeni it would open a door in the same time but in a different place.

"Yes, I'll mark the spot somehow. So what else have you learned?"

From then on Whende began to teach me more about the Obeni. She said it always goes back the same number of years. We hadn't figured how many years separated us yet, but she told me it was at least 5000 years. And the distance between our times never changes. I could never go back to the first day before a met her. Each day that is lost is gone forever but the amount of years between us will always stay the same. If Candice knew what the Obeni really was I don't think she'd be so afraid. It didn't do anything evil to her father. He probably got information about hidden treasure from the man he was talking to and had some fatal accident in the desert.

Whende stood up and took a step forward. I could see now her outfit was a short blouse showing some of her navel and a matching silky emerald green skirt. Her locks were pulled back into a pony tail and held in place with a matching green scarf. The skirt stopped above her knees and the sun shined through it. Yes I could see the outline of her body and felt no shame in looking. She picked up the next scroll and looked at me with the sun behind her and said,

"I see men's desires have not changed."

I didn't know whether to be embarrassed or to keep looking. Was it something she saw in my face? A momentary expression of lustfulness I forgot to hide. Could she see in my eyes that I'd give anything just to touch her?

Once again she took a seat and opened the scroll. While reading silently to herself she said,

"I was coming to your time but this scroll warns against it."

"So it is a doorway to the past!"

"Yes," she said.

"How is that possible? People can not go back in time."

This was the part I absolutely refused to believe. You would need a spaceship or a machine with fancy gadgets, and lights flickering on an off. And you'd need a power source, or a generator like in the movies.

So I found myself humoring her.

"You can't come to me, but I can come to you?"

With a very alluring smile she said,

"Yes you can."

"So how do I do it? How would I get there?"

I wanted her to describe something so impossible I would have to say no. But she never asked me to come in the verbal sense. It was only a hint with the eye and a pouty mouth. This time I wasn't sure of her intentions. If she were a woman in my time I would suspect I was about to be played for a sucker, and act accordingly. If Egyptian people knew about the stars and the rotation of the earth did they know how to use psychology?

Whende did not ask me to come but she stood in front of me knowing I could see through her skirt. Could she be reading my mind and not tell me? Was this why Candice told me to be careful?

Then Whende eased my racing heart by saying,

"I do not know how. The Obeni needs the power of Sika Yemot and will only work when it is here. When the sika leaves the doorway is closed and will not open for another 76 mala."

Never believing for a second I could travel back in time I said with a smile and little emotion,

"Tell me what to do and I will come."

I pretended to be unmoved by the notion of time travel but I was very troubled. What scared me more than the unknown was myself? I never knew when to stop reaching for the impossible and this time I felt compelled without explanation. The tugging in my heart and the sense of connection when I stepped on African soil was a feeling of being watched over and protected.

How is it possible for Candice to have the image of my face? It had to be a coincidence because she'd never seen me before. It was like fighting a losing battle. I wanted to go back in time. My bones wanted to go, my heart wanted to go, and so did my black skin. For days I'd been denying my destiny but no longer. If it was possible for me to return to my origins without killing myself I would.

My doubts were like ice cubes melting in the hot sun. My room was never bugged and the Obeni was not a movie projector. Whende was as real as the birds that flew past her in the background. No one drugged me, and this wasn't candid camera.

"Bennie are writings, on the Obeni?"

"Yes, in the borders."

"Tell me!" She said anxiously.

"They're symbols; I don't know what they mean."

"What are they like?" She asked.

"Where do I start?"

"Begin at the bottom."

I've been watching her read the scrolls for some time. It seems she read them from right to left. I kneeled down close to the right leg of the Obeni and looked.

"There are wavy lines like triangles and,"

"What are triangles?" She interrupted.

I made the shape for her with my hands and she acknowledged and said, "How many."

"Six, six triangles connected with a circle over each. There is a comet I mean sika on top."

I looked into the Obeni to see Whende writing feverishly. In her right hand was a slim brown cylindrical object six inches long but I couldn't see the tip?

"There is a line on top of the sika with a bird sitting on top of an eye. Then a feather inside of a half circle."

"Which bird?"

"I don't know," I said.

"How does it sit?"

I described the bird as best I could until she was satisfied.

"There's one more bird and another sika. Oh, and the first bird is bigger than the next."

The description of the symbols took hours. The variations were intricate and not easy to explain. Whende asked questions like how many waves within each line and how many feathers did the birds have? All the circles and symbols were confusing to me but I continued with my descriptions until there were no more questions.

"Is that all?" She said.

"Yes that's all."

She stood up from the chair and said,

"The writing is very old. I must go to the elders to know it all. I will be back."

Whende started to walk away when I called out to her,

"Wait I found out what age I'm in."

She walked back so close until her body blocked the view of everything behind her. Damn that's nice I thought to myself.

"We are coming into the age of Kefeius in 17 or 30 mala," I said.

The skirt stuck to her skin from the sweat and when she was this close I could see her perfectly, from every hair that grew from her head, to the shape of her ear lobes. The small beads she wore around her neck, and the shape of her breasts. Beneath her skirt the underwear resembled a thong. I think she enjoyed the way I looked at her. Once again she smiled and walked away, and I watched her every step.

I'd completely lost track of the time. It was almost noon and I hadn't had breakfast yet. While I was giving the descriptions to Whende I recalled hearing the maids in the hallway cleaning the rooms. The night before I hung the do not disturb sign on the door. It was the only thing that kept them from coming into my room. It seemed all the employees noticed me whenever I went out. The word must have spread concerning my hysterics that first day. If I did decide to make this trip it wouldn't matter, they'd never see me again.

Preparations would have to be made and what should be my priorities? I shouldn't disappear without some explanation. My family and my friends would worry and they would look for me. I needed to figure out a way to make them understand what I was about to do. But first I needed some breakfast. I went to the phone by the night table and called room service. I ordered two bottles of spring water, and some fresh fruit. Then I placed calls to the states. I found out through Ronald and Lorraine's son Jimmy, they would be arriving here on the 23.

Next I tried to call Terri at home and got her answering machine. I said hello softly only once hoping she wouldn't pick up. Guilt was an emotion I rarely experienced but one you never forget. She was my one regret through all of this. And if she picked up the phone I had no idea what I would say to her. The truth was I was leaving her without so much as a goodbye, or a dear Jane letter.

I had just about finished my lunch when I saw Whende coming in the distance. She stopped within a few feet from the doorway of her house and surveyed the land as if she were looking for someone. Then looked over her shoulder and briskly walked up to her chair.

When she saw me she said,

"Did you eat?"

"Yes I did."

With a sigh she said,

"Then I am too late."

"Why what's wrong?"

"The teachings say to make the flight or fall into the Obeni you must not eat nor drink for three risings of Ra!"

I stopped chewing the apple and swallowed,

"Are you sure?"

"Yes."

"All I have to do is not eat or drink for three days?"

Whende looked puzzled when I said the word days but she did say yes. It was too late now so I finished my apple.

"You can do it, Bennie?" she asked.

"Sure," I replied, "no problem, it's a piece of cake."

Chapter 7

The 4:30 a.m. wake up call startled me in the darkness but served as a reminder to cancel the calls in the future. If I was successful in my journey I didn't want the desk calling my room each day and getting no answer. When I didn't show up to check out they would find out soon enough.

I shot my hand out from under the blanket into the cold morning air to accept the phone call. I hadn't used a blanket as a protective cocoon in that way since I was at least four or five. One night my parents took me to the movies to see "Hush, Hush Sweet Charlotte". Some adults in the theater covered their eyes when the scary parts came but I couldn't. Even at that age I felt it necessary to confront my fear. I watched the headless man walk slowly down the stairs calling Charlotte's name, and when it came time to go to sleep that night I covered myself under the blanket in a fetal position. As long as I didn't stick my head out Charlotte's man couldn't get me. Years passed and I could still see the headless man in my darkened room. Each time it turned out to be my suit for church on Sunday or a sweater on a hanger. Many times I wondered if my folks knew how much the movie scared me? Now here I was a grown ass man in a fetal position with a blanket over my head.

Yesterday shortly after my conversation with Whende I removed the disks. It was hard to concentrate with her watching me. I began to have the feeling she had control over me and that she couldn't be trusted. She said there were people around but I'd never seen them. She said the scrolls warned against her coming here to this time but how could I know this was the truth? Her calculations put the years between us at 14,820 give or take 100 years and that could be a lie too.

In my life I could not remember reading or hearing anyone say Egyptian history was that old. I thought about this last night under the blanket in the darkness. Was it possible that Whende was my "headless man" coming to steal my head?

Yesterday while I was alone I planned to cover my disappearance in two stages. The first and easiest one was done yesterday. It was my plan to be seen by everyone so there would be no suspicion. I left my suite when I heard the maids in the hallway. Approaching mine pleasantly I spoke to her saying, good morning and asked how she was doing? The word spread in the hotel that I was eccentric and needed to be watched because of my outbursts that first day. For most of the week anyone who worked at the hotel watched me momentarily. So the morning chambermaid was the first person I felt needed the most convincing. I apologized to her for my strange behavior and hinted that I was a bachelor and had female company in my room. Then I gave her a generous sum of money as a tip and asked her to clean my room. This was absolutely necessary because no one had seen my room in days. I was not worried she'd move the Obeni because I had marked the legs and masked the Obeni with a sheet. It was also essential to leave her alone in the room so she could take her time without being watched, to see everything was normal.

Next I went down to the lobby and stopped at the front desk. Again I was apologetic about my behavior the first day. My excuse was I had been under a lot of stress from work and needed this vacation. I didn't tell them the maid was cleaning my room because if my theory were correct they would know soon enough. I asked if there were any messages and once I received them I went to the desk where the tours were arranged and spoke with the agent. I purposely stayed in the lobby to be seen and for almost an hour I looked at brochures of the tourist attractions without being able to decide which one to take. Hinting again of an upcoming sexual encounter and not knowing what day I would be free, I said I'd come back and book a tour tomorrow.

Everything was going according to plan until an elderly couple came through the lobby doors with a bottle of water. I couldn't take my eyes off if it and I watched them walk to the front desk. The tour guide asked if I knew them and I said no. Upon seeing the water I closed my mouth and ran my tongue in a circular motion up to the roof and down to the sides of my teeth. There was no doubt I was thirsty. Each word seemed to make my mouth drier and the conversation about tours was over. Trying not to seem strange and destroy the excellent work I'd begun in public relations I said firmly I'd see him tomorrow.

I stood up from the chair not knowing where to go next. I started towards the lobby doors but the steady climb in temperature made me change my mind. Going outside would be a bad move so I turned away from the doors and calmly strolled in the opposite direction. This would be the perfect time to take a walking tour of the hotel.

Down the corridor past the bar was the dining room. It was a large room with a sunken floor. There was a dance floor in the center and a stage in the corner for the band. Past the hotel restaurant was the entrance to the swimming pool downstairs. I was tempted to see how large the pool was but visualizing all that water turned me around. I'd done enough socializing for the day and headed back to my room.

The first part of my plan yesterday was successful, but how was I going to get through today? I lay in bed doubting I had enough willpower to finish. Not because of yesterday or even today for that matter, but because I had two more days to go and I wanted to eat so badly.

Still I accepted the challenge on behalf of my father who always reminded me I'd never gone hungry a day in my life, and had no idea of what it was like. But he never said anything about not having water. If my grandmother and grandfather didn't have food for them to eat they damn sure had some water. Maybe I could stay right here in bed and sleep until Tuesday. If I were asleep I couldn't be hungry or thirsty. I only needed to leave the room one more time and make an appearance Monday morning or Monday night.

So I stayed in bed this morning and tried to go back to sleep but it was futile. There were things going on around me that couldn't be ignored. I began to think about my journey and the excitement crept in. Then there was that god-awful tang in my mouth. My tongue and teeth had a sticky film that tasted nauseating. If I gargled with water would I have the strength to spit out? The last time I'd eaten or sipped any liquid was Saturday afternoon almost twenty four hours ago. Could I take a chance on brushing my teeth?

Yes I thought, yes I can because I was the ruler of my fate, and the commander of myself. I needed a pep talk from the only person here I could truly trust. No one rules me except me I thought, and no one has power over me except God. My two feet stopped the slide down this path of cowardliness. Nothing in this world could ever hurt me with the Lord guiding me. I threw the blanket off and stood up on my feet with my chest out like a warrior ready for battle. I breathed deep and slow afraid of nothing. I will do this I thought, I would make it until Tuesday.

The bathroom tile was cold under my feet. I looked at the sink and knew I would not drink any water. I removed the plastic wrapper from the glass and squeezed some toothpaste on my toothbrush. Then brushed my teeth and my tongue furiously and spit the toothpaste out. Next I filled the glass halfway and gargled the water for a few seconds and spit it into the sink. Then I turned on the shower and while the water heated up I went back inside the room and turned off the air conditioner. I showered quickly making sure not to drink any of the water that ran into my mouth. When I got out I got dressed and stood near the edge of the bed in front of the Obeni.

In my heightened state of aggressiveness I stared at the Obeni as if it were my opponent. From the lion shaped paws that made up the four legs to the top of its arch. Like two fighters in the ring before the first round I looked at every symbol and every blemish of the wood. I touched the glass that held the grains of odd colored sand and sat down. There was no need to go through with this I thought. I could let the disks stay in my safe and go home wondering what would have happened. What other reason could there be for me to risk my life?

Then I realized returning in time with my knowledge of the future had to have some advantage. Beyond going for my own selfish reasons what contributions could I make? Would I be able to change history with my knowledge of the future?

Once again I regretted not paying attention to history while I was in Manhattan community college, or even visiting the library on my own to read. My facts about Egypt and who were the first invaders were sketchy and I had no dates. With my limited knowledge of history I would tell Whende and her people not to trust the Greeks or the Romans. They would come as friends to learn architecture, and the sciences only to claim them as their own inventions. Then somewhere after the Roman invasion came the Arabs. Yes I was sorry now I didn't pay more attention to history. I should know these things because this was the continent which brought the birth of my ancestors.

Many times a brief struggle erupted in me. Not as serious as a tug of war between good and evil, more like dedication and shiftlessness. The battle never bothered me because the creaking of the slave ships and sounds my ancestor in clanking chains always won and held me to a steady path.

The first time I heard stories about the abduction of African people sold into slavery and descriptions of the middle passage touched me more than most. Attaching feelings of empathy and potency to my spirit like an extra molecule. Sometimes I didn't know what saddened me more the creaking of the ship, or the thought that no one in my circle of friends could hear it too. Any time the subject of slavery came up it was never explored at the same length as the basketball game or who was on TV last night. The blood of these tortured souls ran through my veins and at times I hated to be around people who didn't care. It was an empty gut wrenching feeling of helplessness that further distanced me from my family and friends.

I could close my eyes at night and see the rapes of thousands of African women, or feel the whip across my back. It would be worth risking my life if I could somehow stop the slave trade by warning the ancestors what was coming. Even without anyone knowing my sacrifice, I could be another Malcolm or a Dr. King and add my name to the list of individuals who stood up for the freedom and rights of African people.

This intriguing thought brought more happiness now than anything I'd ever dreamed, but I only had one chance. I would never live another 76 years to find out if the Obeni works. Sure longevity ran in my family but no one had lived over a hundred years. Most of my relatives met death obstinately in their eighties and nineties. Who was I kidding? It was my nature to take the hard road and in my character to be different. I wasn't going to wait 76 years or risk 76 more hours by drinking some water, and never finding out if I could make changes.

Retrieving the disks from the safe I placed them in their slots. Slowly just like before the sunlight filtered into my room from the Obeni and the distorted picture became clear. Everything was there just like before, the stone structure in the background and the chair under the tree in the distance.

Whende sat in her chair in a reclining position like a sunbather at the beach. She looked into the sky like a birdwatcher squinting only when her eyes looked toward the sun. And then I called to her,

"Whende, I'm here."

Her face lit up like a child receiving a birthday present and she sat up. She seemed honestly happy to see me then asked, "Did you eat?"

"No I have not."

"Will you come to me?"

"Yes, I will."

"Will you talk with me?"

"Yes."

Now was my opportunity to find out more about her. If she was deceiving me or controlling me I would need to find out now.

"Tell me about life in your world." She asked before I could speak. I thought about where I should begin. Then I started with cars and told her on how we travel. I described airplanes and ocean liners, bicycles, motorcycles and she was not impressed. Then I explained television, radio and how we listened to music on records and cassettes and got the same reaction. I thought surely my description of airplanes and how people flew across great distances would impress her but it didn't. Then she asked me one simple question. How close have we gotten to the Creators? It was my understanding she meant God so I told her that we worship and love Him! Whende asked if I had ever seen the Creators and if we are still in their favor? Her phrasing of the question was a revelation. We never had a problem with singular and plural so why did she keep saying creators? It was my understanding Egyptian people worshiped many Gods so I didn't want to get deep into religion with her yet.

"Do you have any children?" I asked.

Sadly she said,

"No, and you?"

"No I don't."

Something was wrong with her and the conversation wasn't what

I expected. She looked over her shoulder toward the house a few times as though perplexed then came back to her original question, "tell me of the Creators?"

Religion and politics were not conversations I avoided with anyone except in a bar or in the presence of the person's home. I have always taken the stance that individuals have the right to believe and worship whomever they choose. It didn't matter to me if they called him Abraham or Allah. We live in the world of many languages where people have different names for the same thing. It was my choice to believe what my mother and father believed so I called him God.

So how would I interpret her meaning of being closer to the Creators? Were we following the teachings of God? I didn't think so. From the sermons I've listened to in church and the Scriptures I've personally read, no. Even with television sermons and newspaper articles of current events I could say no. My world was full of murderers and crooked politicians and ministers who stole from their congregations. Most people thought about themselves, and the ones in power were the greediest of all.

Then I looked at myself and had to say no. I personally hadn't done anything to move closer to God. Yes, I was a nice guy who never bothered anyone who didn't bother me first, but I was short on forgiveness. Had we moved closer to the creators? I answered Whende's question by saying,

"We try."

I felt she deserved a better answer so while I thought of what more I could say, she asked about music.

"What music is there?"

That was simple enough and I responded, "We listen to a lot of music. Men and women sing together or by themselves. There can be as many as thirty men and women playing instruments and..."
She cut my answer short by asking about instruments. I started by demonstrating a drum with my hands and then a guitar,

"We make music with instruments."

"We do too," she said.

"What about a horn?" I put my fingers in front of my face and blew as if I had a horn.

Again she said,

"We do too."

"What about a piano?" I started my description by telling her a piano was as large as my bed and supported by three legs. Then I kneeled down in front of the bed and began to play at the edge with my fingers.

"I wish I could hear it," she said.

My throat felt a little scratchy now but I continued,

"Men and women play many instruments and sing songs about life, love, sadness and revolution. Because there are so many different people singing we call them groups."

"What group do you favor?" Asked Whende.

"Wow, there are so many, I like a lot of them."

"Sing for me."

"I'm not much of a singer," I said shyly, "but let's see."

There were so many good songs I'd heard in my lifetime. Songs I heard as a child my mother played like Nat King Cole and the Drifters, to songs I listened to as a teenager. There was Al Green, and the Stylistics or James Brown and Minnie Ripperton. I wouldn't dare try to sing a Minnie Ripperton song. Of all the music I heard in my lifetime I couldn't think of anybody. Maybe I could do the Commodore's Brick house, no that's a bad idea. I'd have to explain the words and although it was a good song now was not the time. What was that song they played every night before 8:00pm on WBLS? I couldn't remember so I decided to pick something fast,

"Okay I have one, just give me a second."

Whende was excited and I wasn't sure I knew all the words but she'd never know.

"Daa dump dump daaaa, daa dump dump daaaa da daa daaa, da dump da daaaa, dadump dump da daa daaa, Hearts of fire, creates loves desire. Take you higher and higher, to the world you belong."
I sang this song as best I could sporadically substituting the word world, for Samae so she could better understand. When I finished I told her that group was called Earth, Wind and Fire.

"It is very pleasing," she said, "I wish to hear all of the groups."

"You will, I will tell you everything I know."

There was nothing sinister about Whende that I could see and I looked forward to singing more songs to her.

Only when my interests were sincere would I ask a lady personal or intimate questions about her life. So I asked Whende to tell me a fond memory of her childhood. She seemed surprised at my question but looked up into the sky and then smiled. She explained it as the day shortly before she became a woman.

Whende's father Afermose took her fishing on his boat. Whende's mother Kymeka came into her bedchamber shortly before sunrise to wake her. It was a night Whende spent in restless anticipation. Since her father's decisions affected so many people, there were times she would go for days without seeing him. Last night while they were having dinner Afermose told Whende he would take her fishing the next morning if the weather was good. In her face I saw how fulfilling this memory was and I could detect no subterfuge. During the night she woke up a few times listening for sounds of rain. The next morning her mother was there by her bedside telling her it was time to get dressed.

She jumped out of bed and put on her clothes quickly like any other excited child. When she finished dressing she ran straight out the front door to see her father standing by the family carriage. The first sliver of a deep red sun peaked over the horizon and the dirt road ahead was barely visible. The birds were singing songs to the dawn from the nearby trees as she ran into the open arms of her father. At this age she stood slightly taller than his stomach and to her it was like standing at the base of a mighty tree. He lifted her magically by the waist until her feet touched the floor of the carriage. Kymeka briskly walked down the path to the carriage with a bag containing a round loaf of fresh baked bread and a gourd filled with berry juice. The driver gave his signal and the horses headed in the direction of the rising sun. Whende watched her mother fade quickly into the darkness until all she could see were the two oil lamps that burned over the doorway.

The day was warm and the water was calm. She said it was that day she fell in love with the water. Two men on each side rhythmically lifted their oars in and out of the water. While another man steered from the stern. Whende and her father sat in a bench seat near the bow. By now the Sun was bright in the sky and other boats of different sizes were leaving the shore. When he saw the area he wanted to fish he stood up and told his crew to go there.

The four men took their oars from the water placing them on the sides of the boat behind their seats. Carefully they lifted a chiseled stone with four points tied to a long rope and threw it into the water. Their boat rocked gently anchored not far from shore. On her left side in the center of the river were many boats of all sizes. Some were heading upstream against the current while others went in the opposite direction.

Many times before, Afermose turned a simple experience into a time for teaching. Often when she was enthusiastic about a project he used this time to slip in related facts. If she picked up a stone while they were walking he became her geology teacher. When she looked up in the sky at night she got a brief lesson on astronomy. So before she ever put her line in the water she got a brief tutorial on the different types of fish and what bait to use. He also instructed her on how to get back in the boat if she went overboard. That day she learned about the tides and the effect the moon had on them. Anything Afermose could think of to stimulate her curiosity he told her. But the little girl was scared of this new experience until she caught her first fish.

I looked at her in the Obeni holding her hands apart demonstrating the length of her first catch. Her smile was like the homegirl next door. A smile I could relate to because I had the same experience with my father at Sheepshead bay. We were simultaneously in a moment of cheerfulness and I felt myself trying to be the gentleman. Ignoring the need to look at her breasts, or the shape of her thighs. The growing subtle craving I have for her was excused because of similar happy childhood moments. And I reconciled, I liked her much more than I realized.

For the next hour we touched briefly on what I would leave behind. A flourishing business I helped build and the life I could never return to. I tried to recite my lineage and the places I'd traveled. None of this compared to what I would hear from Whende next.

Whende's grandfather Amadonen sailed to the North American Continent and back before Afermose was born landing somewhere on the southern tip of the Florida coast. At that time a few of the southern coastal regions were inhabited by families from Egypt. No doubt they explored more than just the coast. And it is conceivable some families chose to stay and make a new life for themselves on this continent, and multiplied through the generations.

As I listened and speculated on what happened to all of the people who came before Columbus my stomach tightened with hunger and the scratchiness in my throat grew. I tried not to think of how many hours I had left. I had to limit my talking and find a way to make the hours pass more quickly. There was a special mission I was taking and I would need to look and act normal as I walked around the hotel for the last time. I told Whende I would sleep now and would not speak to her again until midday tomorrow.

I stood up and walked towards the Obeni and did not speak. Using only a hand gesture to wave goodbye, I then removed the discs and returned them to the safe. A strange sadness fell across her face. She did not seem as excited about my journey as she was previously. I lay across the bed wishing I could take an aspirin to rid myself on this headache. I closed my eyes and thought about the past, which would become my future. Relaxing a little more the thirst subsided replaced by the vision of Whende fishing with her father and the sunlight overhead. She must take me to the exact same spot where they fished, and after that, I will sail to America and see what the landscape looks like before my neighborhood is built.

Someone else in my place might think of more historic places with greater importance. I just want to walk down to Riverside Park on the Hudson, and stand at the same spot Ronald and the rest of us hung out when we were teenagers. There we would smoke reefer and drink beer while looking at the Jersey shore. This is gonna be great I thought as I melted into the darkness. Will Terri ever forgive me? Will all of them ever forgive me?

Meanwhile back in New York Terri walked with a quick pace down the street this Sunday afternoon towards Bennie's house. From the time she'd turned the corner her eyes fell on each car in the block searching for his chocolate brown Honda. She swore to herself she would stay calm until hearing his outrageous explanation, but it wasn't easy. He said he would leave his car at the airport and she wasn't sure if he did. The anticipation of seeing his car made her feel like a stalker. Each building she walked past had her wondering how many women he'd had in this block? Terri always sensed from the start he was a fucking whore, but she believed he would one day love her enough to change.

Larry was under the hood of his car tinkering as usual and   she hoped to make it inside the house before he looked up. Reaching in her purse for the house keys she got to the first step and heard some-one call her name. The happiness she once felt when she came in the block was replaced by her feeling that everyone knew she was getting dogged.

Larry began to cross the street wiping his hands with a dirty rag.

"Hey sweetheart, how are you?"

Terri greeted him with a forced smile.

"How's my girl?" He said loudly.

"I'm fine Larry, how are you?" She had no desire for conversation but would give him a minute or two.

"Is Bennie still on vacation?"

"Yes he is," she said reluctantly.

"And that bum didn't take you? What's wrong with him? He can't leave a fine looking woman here by herself."

"It's all right Larry he would have taken me, but I got a promotion and couldn't leave; besides the tickets were already paid for."

"Yeah but damn, why hasn't he called you?" And he waited for an answer.

In that split second she was back in the courtroom. How could he know that? Did Ronald or Lorraine tell him, and how long has he known? How many more mother fuckers knew about her business or her pain? Like the professional she was Terri quickly regrouped,

"I forgot," she said jokingly, "he has called and left me messages."

Larry stared at her for a moment with a look she knew all too well. It was the same stare of stone a jury gives when they've heard false testimony.

"Okay, as long as you're all right," he said with the strangest look.

"Yes I'm fine, I mean we are fine and everything is good."

Then she turned to walk up the stairs to the front door and said, "I'll see you later."

"All right then," he waited for her to reach the top before he said loudly,

"If that boy ever messes up you can come with me. And I'll tell him myself."

Then he laughed and went back to his car.

Terri closed the second door to the alcove then stood in front of the huge mirror in the hallway. She went inside the living room and sat down on the sofa without taking her coat off. What the hell was she doing here? Truthfully she was too upset to trash his house and too embarrassed to cry. So she sat looking down at the keys in her hand, the hand that should have an engagement ring on it by now. Instead she rubbed the gold chain around her wrist Bennie had given her on Valentine's Day. Was this one of those gifts that men give when they want to buy your silence or cooperation? She'd always thought it was from his heart. Quietly she sat gathering her thoughts attempting to sort the facts from the circumstantial evidence.

Fact one, he said before he left I would be the only one in his life. Now do I believe him? She went back to that rainy day they drove home from the laundry. Though he acted a bit strange that day there was nothing about his attitude or his mannerisms that set off any alarms. When I come in with him he never runs around the apartment trying to hide things like my ex. She tried to think of his facial expressions that night he told her she was the only one in his life, and his eyes were filled with sincerity.

Fact two, the keys in her hand must mean something. Even Lorraine and Ronald have confirmed she's the only one who ever had keys to his house. My other boyfriends might throw the keys out of the window to let me in or insist I call before I pop over, but they never gave me a set of keys.

Fact three, Lorraine for some reason does not like him. And until I talked to him face to face I will not believe he had dinner a few weeks ago with some bitch. Her knowing about a dinner date is circumstantial until it's confirmed. She never said she saw them with her own eyes.

Fact four, he could have canceled that trip if he wanted to. It's possible he doesn't understand how much it hurts that he left me here.

Terri stood up to remove her coat then walked to the other side of the living room and sat in his favorite chair still holding the keys in her hand. Trying hard not to think about fact five because fact five was his love making which made her quiver with guiltless shame. She took a quiet breath and crossed her legs tightly sending a signal of passion throughout her body. This intimate pulse released her from the court-room and postponed Bennie's trial once again. At this moment, the facts were unimportant and the circumstantial evidence irrelevant. Terri wanted this man deeply and that was all that mattered.

Putting all of her questions aside Terri hung her coat on the wooden coat rack in the hallway and returned to the living room placing her keys on the coffee table. She walked through the living room to the kitchen and looked out the window into the backyard. A stray cat walked cautiously a top the chain link fence that separated the next-door neighbor's yard. She watched the cat walk to a small tree where it leaped off the fence and scurried down the trunk. It was obvious he knew his way around. He continued walking to the end of the back-yard and crawled through a small gap in the next fence and disap-peared.

Terri turned away from the window enjoying the silence search-ing for a sign of hope for a drowning relationship. Everywhere she looked in the kitchen she'd left her mark. On the wall near the refrig-erator was the cute little potholder rack she'd put up herself. And the assorted magnets she'd stuck on the refrigerator were her idea. As a matter of fact she convinced him to remodel the whole kitchen. A new ceramic tile floor with white kitchen counters. It was only fair she buy the kitchen table and the chairs. When she thought of what this kitchen looked like before he met her, she finally decided. If Bennie was com-ing home each night to her it was all that mattered. She had invested more in this relationship than any of her others. She'd done her re-search and knew what he liked to wear, the places he liked to go, the music he liked to listen to, and all his favorite foods. Damn it, she even knew his favorite position. Like in a courtroom this would be her de-fense for his case and she wasn't giving up now.

The sudden sound of the chimes startled Terri. It ripped through the silence like the sound of thunder. There was no reason for Bennie to ring the doorbell unless he'd lost his keys. Walking calmly to the door she pulled back the curtain and looked through the glass. It was Lorraine standing outside looking across the street. Terri opened the door and walked an extra yard to open the outside door.

"Hey girl what you doing here?" Lorraine asked running up the stoop.

"I told you the other day I was coming to check on the house."

"I know but I wasn't sure you would come."

Lorraine walked into the living room briefly scanning it.

"Are you all right?" She asked while placing her coat on the couch.

"Yeah I am fine."

Immediately Lorraine began walking around the living room without saying much. She leaned over the coffee table and thumbed through the magazines and then Bennie's mail.

"How long have you been here, Terri?"

"I don't know maybe an hour."

Lorraine was on her way to the kitchen when she spoke a little louder,

"Talked to Bennie?"

By now Lorraine was out of sight and Terri had a choice of yelling a response or walking to the kitchen to answer her. She reached the kitchen in time to see Lorraine close the refrigerator. What was she looking for? She was acting like she'd never been in his house before and was seeing everything for the first time.

"Well have you talked to him?"

"No," Terri said cheerfully as if nothing bothered her.

"Girl I don't know how you do it. If that was Ronald, I'd been on the first plane down there days ago."

"Well I've been doing some thinking," Terri said.

Lorraine closed the kitchen cabinet over the sink and waited for Terri to continue.

"I'm going to trust him and wait until he comes back."

"I hear you girl," Lorraine said walking from the kitchen towards the spiral staircase, "I'll be right back."

Lorraine went up the stairs and into the bedroom. Terri became annoyed following her around and stayed downstairs. She reached for the remote and turned on the television. She could hear Lorraine's footsteps in the bedroom from the ceiling above. She knew where the bathroom was so why is she walking around. Terri wanted to yell upstairs and ask what she was doing up there but she didn't. Lorraine's visit made her feel like she was the trespasser. She wouldn't be upstairs if she felt she didn't have the right.

Lorraine returned to the living room holding a small brown paper bag. Terri watched as she walked slowly to her chair and gave her the bag. Before she could reach inside Lorraine asked,

"Have you seen these before?"

From the bag came a stack of Polaroid pictures that were upside down. With her hands shaking she turned them around while Lorraine stood over her shoulder. The first picture was a dark skinned woman smiling wearing only a green garner belt with black stocking and it was taken with her left breast exposed and her back to the camera. The next picture was the same woman sucking him, and there was no denying it was he. The look in her eyes and the silver ring on his right hand was unmistakable.

"Where did you get these?" Terri asked.

"They were upstairs,"

"Upstairs where?"

"Look, just look at the next photo," Lorraine said without answering.

Terri took the first picture and put it on the bottom of the stack. This one was a white woman with dark hair taken in the kitchen. There was evidence in the background to prove it was his old kitchen. So far she'd looked through the stack and it was mostly the same thing. Women posing naked exposing everything they had.

"You see that one? I think that's Paula," Lorraine said.

This woman was the color of caramel and slender standing in front of his bed topless with red panties, and that same damned smile.

"Are you sure this is her?"

"I think so."

"Where did you find these?"

"I told you upstairs."

"Upstairs where?"

"Terri you've been alone in the house many times and you've never looked around?"

"Yes I look at stuff that I need, but I don't go through his stuff!"

"Look girl I am just trying to help."

"He trusts me and I never felt I had to go through his things!" She erupted.

"Well that's why you have to keep an eye on men. You can't let them do everything they want. And you sure as hell can't give Bennie all the freedom you've been giving him."

It just didn't seem right to put a stranglehold on a man. If I can't trust him I don't need him she thought. As much as the photographs stoked feelings of disdain Terri filed them under circumstantial evidence. But she was determined to know where they were and how Lorraine found them.

"Where were they?" She said calmly at first.

"I told you upstairs."

"Where Upstairs Terri said a little louder!

Lorraine walked away and Terri said,

"I am gonna rip this shit to shreds!"

"No, no don't do that!"

"Why?"

"He will know we found them."

"Do you think I'd give a shit now?"

Terri snatched the paper bag from the floor and stuffed it between the cushions. Then she quickly grabbed the first two pictures off the stack and made a tearing motion.

"Please girl calm down. You can't tear them up." Lorraine said as she thrusts her hands forward in a stopping motion.

"Oh I'm calm as a mother fucker!"

"They were in the back of his closet in one of his jacket pockets," Lorraine said quickly.

Terri released her grip on the pictures momentarily and continued the cross examination,

"How did you know they were there?"

"If I tell you, you have to promise you won't say anything to anybody."

"Sure."

"No I'm serious, you can't tell anyone."

Lorraine sat down across the living room on the couch to catch her breath. Terri folded her arms across her chest and waited.

"Ronald told me."

"Ronald?"

"Yes Ronald told me Bennie showed him the pictures more than a year ago. He said Bennie went in the closet and dug in one of the pockets and came out with a brown paper bag full of pictures. And you can't tell because Bennie will know that Ronald told me."

Terri sat silently staring at Lorraine.

"It's a girl thing you know? That's why I went upstairs and found them for you. I was trying to help you because I've seen through him a long time ago. As a matter of fact you should fly over there with us. We're leaving Friday and you should come."

"I don't think so. I'm not flying halfway around the world to chase a man."

"Well I didn't mean to upset you. I just thought you should know."

"I'm not upset; I'm not upset at all. If he took those pictures before he met me what can I say?"

"Well look honey I have to go. Can I take the pictures and put them back?"

"Yes and this time I'll go with you."

Two minutes hadn't gone by before Lorraine was out the door leaving Terri alone. It had become more of an uphill battle to stay true to her convictions. No one knew the horrible secrets Terri kept in her past, or about her violent alter ego. She'd thought twice before about killing Bennie, but was never able to confirm his infidelity. And the roses he bought her were dying in front of her eyes symbolizing their relationship. She said she wouldn't give up on him and she meant it. She had too much invested in this relationship. It wasn't even in terms of money anymore because her heart was priceless. Her heart was worth more than this house and everything in it. He couldn't acquire enough laundromats or make enough money in a lifetime to purchase something he already owned.

An hour or so before dawn back in Egypt I woke to the silence of my dark room. A slim beam of light escaped from the bathroom making it possible to only see the outline of the Obeni. There it stood in the darkness like the headless man from my childhood. Managing to sleep ten hours of the hunger and thirst away, I was thinking clearly but dared not speak. I stretched and yawned with my mouth closed. Nothing could have prepared me for the way I felt right now. There were no separate parts in my mouth. My tongue was stuck to the bottom and top of my mouth while the sides and front were cemented to my teeth. The air I breathed through my nostrils felt like small tumbleweeds rolling down a dirt path. Just half of glass of water could end this silly suffering. Why was I doing this? How could one man change the history of the world? This was an insane idea. Why would traveling back in time have any connection with dehydrating and starving one-self? And then I remembered falling asleep and imagining myself walking down to look at the Jersey Shore. I'd gone two-thirds of the way with only twenty six or twenty seven more hours to go. There was no way I could sleep through until Tuesday morning. Please father, tell me what should I do?

The reflection in the bathroom mirror held a hideous bombshell. My lips were so cracked and crusty I feared opening them would rip the flaky skin apart. Even my dark brown skin was turning ashy gray. I forced myself to move my tongue back and forth but my lips would not open. I turned on the tap and with just my pinky I touched my lips with three of four drops of water. My lips were so tight one drop of water wouldn't enter my mouth. With the same pinky I worked the moisture in until they were free.

Breathing through my mouth was even worse. My once pink tongue was now white like sandpaper. I can only imagine how my breath smelled, but I would have to make myself presentable today because I wanted no interference.

By the time I heard doors opening and closing in the hallway I'd finished writing my goodbyes and began to forge ahead with the last of my plans. The morning maid was at the other end of the hallway near the elevators. I removed the do not disturb sign from the door-knob placing it inside the room and locked the door. Casually I walked down the hallway forcing a smile on my face.

"Good morning," I said.

"Good morning Sir," she said happy to see me.

My previous mission had been a success. There were no more strange looks from her, but I had not anticipated her next reaction.

"Are you feeling all right Sir?"

Her question caught me off guard,

"Why yes, I feel fine."

"You look like you're catching a cold. If you don't mind me saying so, it's not good to leave the air-conditioner on all day. The room can get very cold. Saturday when I went inside to vacuum the air-conditioner was still running," she said caringly.

"You know, you're right I keep forgetting to turn it off when I am sleep, but listen I want to tell you something. I'm having a young lady over tomorrow and I don't want to be disturbed. We will be ordering breakfast and dinner from our room for a few days, and I will pick up the clean linen and make the bed myself."
Then I handed her a large tip and another envelope to give to the evening maid with the same instructions.

"Thank you!" she said happily, "I won't bother you at all."

"You're very welcome," I said then pressed the button for the elevator.

Next I went to the front desk and gave the clerk a sealed manila envelope with instructions for Ronald and Lorraine when they arrived on Friday. Its contents held the only explanation for my disappearance and my last wishes. I wrote down as much as I could about the history of the Obeni and how it worked. Ronald was further instructed to ship the Obeni to my home where it would remain in my family's control. I also made it very clear my sister was to inherit my half of the business, all of my property and the money in my bank accounts, and $75,000 was to be given to Terri. I'm quite sure Terri did not need the money but maybe it would help her to forgive me. Not knowing if this document would be legal or what kind of problems the family might face gaining a death certificate without a body I submitted in another solution. They could keep this secret between themselves and not bother obtaining a death certificate. My sister had a set of keys to the house, and she knew all of my codes and passwords. If they spoke to a lawyer and my so-called death was too hard to prove they had an alternative. Finally I told them all to be happy for me because something had been calling me all my life and I finally found my purpose.

Once that was done I sat in one of the cushioned chairs next to the couch across from the front desk. Again I had to make sure everyone who saw me could testify to my rationale. If possible I needed to sit here and flip through all of these magazines looking calm, healthy and confident.

If I just keep focused I'll forget about Sherman's barbecue on Seventh Avenue. I'm looking at the front desk, but I see that light skinned old man with the short gray hair wearing a white apron pulling the spaghetti out of the hot water, and dropping it on the white Styrofoam plate. Then the chopping sound the cleaver made on the wooden block separating the ribs from the slab. Then she took her hand, no tongs and no metal spatula, just her hand like we was home, and put it on the plate.

"Do you want sauce with that brother?"

"Hell yeah, I want sauce on every thing!"

She'd pick up the plate and take the big silver ladle and dip it in that huge pan of sauce. I must stop her before she pours the sauce. If she pours the sauce I am gonna eat it. The ribs and spaghetti was nothing without the sauce and my hallucination stopped.

My hunger pangs were becoming too severe and it was showing in my expressions. I had to forget about food. One deeper thought like that and I'd be in the dining room for real. It didn't matter if I'd been in the lobby for as long as I wanted it was time to leave. Ignoring the hunger and the thirst I stood up and walked to the elevator determined to see the Jersey shore in its infancy or die trying.

The maid did an excellent job cleaning my room except for the new glasses and the pitcher full of ice she left on the tray. I took the ice and dumped it in the bathroom sink and left the tray and glasses on the top shelf inside the closet. Next I went to the Obeni searching for signs of it being moved. The sheet I draped across the top was still securely fastened in the back. It was surprising that while she asked about my health, she never brought up the subject of the Obeni.

I turned the air conditioner on low then laid across the bed on my back staring at the ceiling. These past few days I pushed my fear aside. But fear has its place in the evolution of mankind. Why should I feel I could trust her more than my close friends or family? It had crossed my mind before she could be manipulating me in some unknown way. This journey was insane, and I wasn't sure of myself. I went to the phone to call Ronald one last time and tell him what I was planning and changed my mind. What was Whende doing to make me not trust my best friend? It was strange not to call him when he'd always been there for me.

Like when I got my first apartment and lost my job and was too stubborn to ask my parents for money to eat. They attributed my weight loss to drug abuse, but Ronald knew what was going on. He showed up at my apartment on Southern Boulevard with a large pizza pie with sausage and extra cheese. Before that time I had not eaten in four days and spent most of my time sleeping and drinking water. I'll never forget how happy I was to see him and that he was able to sift through my lies. My pride wouldn't let me tell my best friend I was hungry. How could I leave a person I loved and who had been a brother to me behind?

I lay staring at the blankness of the ceiling with only the hum of the air-conditioner and the sporadic clicking of the curtain cord tapping the wall. Nineteen hours more until sunrise was all that stood between my future. As I relaxed my hunger dissipated into the blankness of the ceiling. I would sleep a few hours then talk to Whende for the last time.

I drifted deep into a place where the thirst and hunger could not follow, never really awake but not entirely asleep. The sun was still up but it was cold. I looked at the clock hoping I had slept until Tuesday morning but only ninety minutes had passed. What was Whende doing now? Was she sitting in her chair by the pool waiting for me? I went to the safe again to retrieve the disks and place them on the edge of the bed. Then I walked behind the Obeni and unfastened the sheet and placed the disks in the slots. I stood closer this time than I've ever stood before staring at each grain of red sand. Slowly each grain rippled like water and became transparent like small crystals of class. Once all the grains were of the same consistency the image started to come into focus like turning the small wheel on your camera to make the picture clearer.

Whende was staring at me with no emotion. From her side I believe she was as close to the water as physically possible. Her body flooded the borders of the Obeni until nothing could be seen behind her. She was so close I could see the moisture between the rows of her braids and the jade colored beads in her hair. For a moment I thought she would reach through and grab me but she backed up slowly, sat down and look over her shoulder towards the doorway to her house. Only then did she become concerned,

"Are you in good health, Bennie?"

"Yes, I am fine. I'm very hungry, but I will make it."

"Bennie should not come. I wish you to stop now."

"Why?" I asked immediately.

She looked away from me in the direction of the tree but did not answer.

"I thought you wanted me to do it," I said.

Then she looked toward the house again as if someone was watching her.

"Whende what's going on?"

Shaking her head with a sigh she said,

"My woman servant knows I talk to you."

"I don't understand."

"She can make it bad!"

"Is that the only reason you don't want me to come?"

"Yes, I have desires for you," she said sadly.

This was something I hadn't thought of. It was obvious to me given the chance I would sleep with her but it was so far down on the list of things I planned to accomplish and places I wanted to visit I hadn't really thought about it.

"You are precious to me," she said.

I looked at her directly and forcefully,

"There's something you're not telling me, what is it?"

"Bennie I..." her head sank down to her chest and she continued, "all do not make it through."

We both sat silent for a moment.

"I should have told you before."

"It wouldn't have stopped me," I declared.

Her head rose with a smile of admiration for me.

"When you come I will treat you better than any king. You shall have your heart's desire!"

And now I'm thinking, did she say I might not get through?

"Rest Bennie, I will speak."

"Just one question Princess, how long did it take the slaves to build the pyramids?"

"What means slaves?"

"You know people you own like a house or a cow. You buy them and they're yours for life. They do your work and when they have children they are yours too."

"One cannot belong in that way!" sounding very upset by my question.

"Do you have slaves?" She asked.

"No, but this is what we are taught about your time."

"No slaves, Bennie."

We had to stop so I could discuss slavery with her. She told me people worked like we do to make a living and support their families. Then I told her how in the future men would come to the continent and steal people and force them to work. I wanted to go on but my throat was drying up.

"Whende tell me of your time, it's hard to speak now."

I lay across the bed on my stomach with my arms folded in under my chin facing the Obeni and watched her. In a very abstract way that was hard to understand she spoke about the earth as a seed spit forth from a distance star. She told me that every star in the universe was connected and belonged to each other like a family, like fathers and mothers giving birth to sons and daughters. In time, the sons and daughters become mothers and fathers spitting fourth a new seed, a new planet.

Whende said every planet had a spirit. Ra the father was the sun and Samae the earth was the mother and the last of their dynasty. Her words were like abstract poetry but I understood her. She said we should adore and honor Samae because her spirit has seen more than any of us could ever imagine. Her spirit is loving and patient but if provoked she could scratch her back and create an earthquake, or blow her breath and send a violent rain. Whende's warning said the people of my time would make Samae angrier then she's ever been.

Then she spoke about animals and plants. Whende said a long time ago before the time of man a Sika hit Samae and destroyed all life. In my time she said man would lose respect for life and the animals would lose respect for man. All of the animals are smarter than we believe and one day will secretly hate man because man will stop caring for Samae.

She said for every sickness there was a plant or tree that could cure it. There is nothing on Samae that can live longer than a tree.

There were times when it felt better to breathe through my nose. Then after a while the dryness of the air would irritate the back of my throat, and then I would breathe through my mouth. I turned my head away some moments ago so Whende couldn't see the difficult time I was having. There was silence in the room so I looked at the Obeni to see if she was still there. Her head was turning in all directions as if looking for a lost child in a crowd then she turned towards me again startled. My mind was asking her what was wrong but no words came through the cotton in my mouth.

"I thought you asleep," she said.

I only shook my head to say no then forced the words out of my mouth,

"What are you looking for?"

"Nothing, I will stay until you sleep."

Before I could ask another question, she began speaking again.

Whende said the conquerors in my time where their children who were looked down upon because they had lighter skin. As they grew and multiplied they began to dislike us and departed from this land. Ones who study the heavens said we have done an evil against our children and one day they would be the conquerors. The children turned away from everything spiritual and focused on what could be seen and measured. Prayers of forgiveness were offered from us to the creators and were answered. They sent one who was immersed in the spirit to right our wrongs. Like many people in this time and yours who stand for truth he will be ridiculed and killed.

Whende said she wished it were possible for her to come to my time and witness the rebirth of African people. She said she understands my people have become slovenly, and the new conqueror has put us into a deep sleep. A sleep so deep we cannot see our children's future taken away. Then she smiles at me and speaks of the day that will awaken us all. On that day we will bear witness to an act of unbelievable cruelty against us. The cries for satisfaction and justice will be heard around Samae and not be ignored. Many lives will be lost for the sake of true freedom, but the creators will be on our side. The sleeping warriors will awaken and the conquerors that resist will be destroyed. No power can stop it when the age of the dark King comes and Samae will be on your side. Like the sunrise or the movement of the planets no man will be able to stop the coming of the new age.

I listened to Whende until the hunger and thirst went away, and everything around me was quiet. For many hours she had given me a true history lesson. It had been filled with many words and phrases I didn't understand but I lacked the strength to ask her for clarity. I would be with her soon and understand it all.

The next morning I woke up on my own. The wake up calls had been canceled because I didn't want anyone coming into the room before Ronald and Lorraine arrived. I just lay in the bed unable to move accessing my condition. I did not feel well and my first thought was of water. My mouth felt like I had swallowed a cup of sand and I was scared. And then I heard her voice,

"You have done well."

My energy was rising and I was able to lift my head slowly. Whende was wearing a light blue one-piece dress with a half-inch gold colored belt around her waist.

"I had this made for you."

I didn't want to appear weak so I nodded my head in approval and forced myself up.

The room was cold and my vision somewhat blurry. My mind started playing tricks on me. I decided I should have something to drink because now I'm sure I'm strong enough to make it the next time. I'll have some water now and something to eat and go next week.

"Bennie are you well?"

"Yes Princess I'm fine."

My voice was scratchy and I was very confused. I needed to show her some confidence so I stood up and smiled. Her next words brought everything into focus,

"It's time, it's time Bennie."

Whende said it again,

"It's time, and you must come now!"

I had really made it to Tuesday without eating or drinking anything but I had one last call to make before I left. I walked over to the phone and dialed the front desk.

"You must come now!" Whende said insistently.

For a fraction of a second she was starting to sound like she did the first day I saw her.

"Hello front desk," The man answered.

"Hello this is Mr. Reeves in Suite 917. Please hold all my messages for the next few days."

"Why is that sir?"

"Because I don't want to be disturbed!"

"Yes sir, will that be all?"

"That's it thank you."

I hung up the phone and turned to the Obeni. Strangely I felt like a man taking his last walk on death row.

"What do I do now Whende?"

"Stick your hand in and see what happens."

I touched the Obeni with my left-handed and the reflection bent like one of those fun house mirrors at a carnival and the glass felt like soft plastic. I pushed harder and my hand went through.

"I see it, I see it, and it's under the water. Now come to me!"

I took a deep breath told myself there was nothing to be afraid of and pushed my way inside. My left foot never touched anything solid, I just fell in. it was like falling off a cliff into the darkness, and I was never prepared so I yelled,

"OH MY GODDDDDD!!!"

I was falling into a dark abyss. I could hear the wind rushing past my ears and the speed was increasing. What if I hit something in the darkness? My heart felt like it was about to burst and my stomach was in my throat. I'd been in about fifteen seconds when I stopped panicking and got used to the fall. I tried to take a breath but there was no air. I could hear it rushing past my ears and feel it hitting my face but I could not breathe. I tried again to suck some air into my lungs but it was no use. I was gasping for air but there was none and I was going to die.

In the distance I saw a small pinhole of light. Maybe that was the end; the light people see when they die. She had tricked me and I fell for it literally. Whende was really dead and she had lured me in with her. I'd been falling close to a minute but I tried to stay conscious. The circle of light was about the size of a quarter below me and I wasn't going to make it.

My mind was racing with thoughts of my life flashing before me. The woman at the Aswan shop saying be careful.

Now I see my plane on final approach. Suffocation was a horrible way to die, and still I fell. I saw Terri's face on Valentine's Day. She'd given me the best head I'd had from anyone in a long time. I was remembering so many events in my life. My first motorcycle and how much I missed my mother and the time we almost fell off the Queens Borough Bridge into the water below. The first girl I ever tongue kissed and my first flight on a plane. I saw my father's face and never realized how happy it made him to teach me to ride a bicycle, and I still couldn't breathe. I trusted you Whende! How could I have been so stupid? I'm three blocks from my house now walking home alone. There is that white kid who ran up to me and called me a nigger then spit in my face. I was so young and unaware someone could dislike me because my skin was different. My fist connected with his nose and the blood ran into his mouth. There is my first grade teacher Mrs. Dowling. I was getting closer to the light and the pain in my chest was easing. I knew this was the end. My mom was picking me up and washing me in the kitchen sink and I wasn't able to speak yet to tell her how much I loved and trusted her. But finally there she was holding me safely in her bosom.

Chapter 8

There was a cooing sound soft and faint in the darkness. It wasn't until I opened my eyes I realized I was not dead. My arms were attached and my ring was still on my finger. I was covered from my stomach with a soft black cloth with red and green wavy print along the borders. I pulled the cover off to make sure my body was whole. Someone had taken off my clothes and replaced them with a silky solid brown material resembling a hospital gown. I gazed at my feet then continued looking at my skin until it disappeared under the gown. With a flat hand I rubbed my chest and felt a sore spot in the center. Then I placed my hand around my groin let out a sigh of relief, and fell swiftly again into silent darkness.

The cooing sound was heard again and I opened my eyes. I was lying in a slightly upright position on something soft like cotton with slender arms cradling me. Around the room small flames flickered from white candles burning atop four foot high metal bases. I turned my head to see who was holding me and it was Whende. She took her other hand and caressed the side of my face. Her skin was warm and her hand stroked my ear gently.

From her right side she raised a white ceramic cup to my lips and I drank slowly. The liquid tasted like fruit juice, a mixture of pineapple and apple juice with another unknown flavor. She said something but I wasn't listening. I laid my head against her chest smelling her sweet fragrance, listening to her heartbeat, and feeling sorry I had doubted her.

The source of the cooing sound came from a big green parrot on a perch in the center of the room. On my left was a black wooden cabinet about three feet high with two swinging doors in the center. The floor was polished wood and next to the cabinet was a black bookcase with five shelves filled with scrolls. The sunlight cast a beam of light through a shutter in the window. It fell on one of four stone columns that supported the high ceiling. The air smelled sweet like air in the country and I took a deeper breath.

I'd seen my life flash before my eyes and really thought I was going to die. If I could get some food, I'd feel much stronger. I cleared my throat to speak then reached for her hand.

"I need some food, Whende."

This startled her. I could feel her body tense when I spoke. She looked at me with perplexed eyes. Then her mouth opened and I couldn't understand her.

"Salou me tume, Bennie?"

"What did you say?" I asked.

She said it again,

"Bennie, salou me tume?"

It sounded like a mixture of African and Latin. She spoke again and still it made no sense, and why should it? She removed her arm from my shoulder and made a motion with her hands pointing to her mouth, and we understood each other.

Whende returned from the hallway on my right carrying a large wooden tray. When she placed it before me my mouth began to water from its appetizing aroma. I sat up more and took a closer look then smiled at her. Everything on the tray was something I recognized. There were several brown ceramic teacup sized bowls on the outer edge of the tray. The first bowl contained brown rice in a light sauce and next to that was a piece of bread cut from a loaf. Another bowl contained string beans and near it some purple grapes. In the center of the tray was a large flat plate and Although, I thought I recognized the food on the plate. It looked like chicken though I might be mistaken. It was some kind of bird though because a drumstick was attached to the thigh. The pieces seemed too large to be from a chicken or a duck, but it was definitely some kind of fine smelling fowl. Whende gave me a wooden utensil with a cylindrical handle and a slender scoop on the other end and took a seat near my knees. I felt like grabbing that bird with my hands and eating like a man who'd been without food for days. Instead I reached for a drumstick and slowly took one small bite. It was seasoned so well I started to chew faster but

I caught myself and slowed down. Next I tried a small portion of rice on the end of my spoon. Can you imagine the restraint it takes to eat so slowly when you're as hungry as I was? If I was at home by myself I would be scoffing this meal down so fast it would be half finished. But I felt the need to show her I was all right and the experience had not bothered me. It worked. Her astonished smile proved she was impressed.

I wanted to believe everything that had happened to me so far but I was still not 100 percent convinced. Technology and mind altering drugs could make the impossible seem real. With all I had been through I felt the urge to reject my scenario. Without causing any alarm I stopped eating and slowly stood up with some dizziness. My chest ached and I began to cough. Whende stood next to me with the concern on her face. I felt like I had the flu because I was weak and my chest was hurting, but I had to see outside. Whende was standing close to me with her arms open in case I stumbled. I'd been three days without food or water and fell through thousands of years of time and made it. I was determined not to land on my face now.

I walked slowly but steadily to the red curtain rippling from a slight breeze and parted it. The door was actually a large full length shutter with a wooden latch in the center. I was forced to squint from the brightness of the sun so I put my hand over my brow and walked carefully down the dirt path away from the house and Whende followed. My eyes adjusted slowly to the brightness as we walked. Shivers of excitement and fear bubbled to the surface as I reached the end of the dirt path. There I found her chair at the edge of a reflecting pool. I heard the wind rustling the leaves from a solitary tree in the distance and looked back into the pool. I felt my knees become rubbery and I started to hyperventilate. Whende stood next to me and put her arm around my shoulder. I wanted to look at her but I can't. Inside the pool just under the water was the window into my time. I could see my unmade bed and the chair at the foot of it. Behind my bed was the door to the closet still ajar where I had kept the discs. There was no way to describe how I felt. It's almost like coming face to face with the creator and asking for corroboration of his existence. The unmade bed was my proof, and the chair my verification, and so was Whende. Aware of the shock to my system I tried to alter my thoughts. The reality now was I had a lot to be thankful for. I would start a new life here in a world with no complications. No threat of nuclear war or the growing sins of modern men.

When I looked to the north, I saw mountains in the horizon and her house was much further away than it looked. I turned to take a step and my legs came out from under me and I fell down in the dirt, but I did not hurt myself. Whende spoke to me and though I didn't understand her language I could only imagine her asking me if I was all right?

"I'm fine," I said dusting the dirt from my elbows.

She slipped her arm under mine and helped me to my feet as I held her around the waist. It felt good to touch her and as we walked down the path she didn't seem like the woman I'd first met in my hotel room. She wasn't the one I couldn't wait to curse out, or the one who annoyed me so by calling me "Spirit". This wasn't the royal stuck up woman I first met.

She was pulling me to come inside but I couldn't move. I was wondering how long it would take me to learn her language. We walked again and once inside I laid down on the bed and Whende went into the next room. I would have my whole life to see things no one else had seen and bring gifts of knowledge from the future.

My eyes focused on the smooth white ceiling above. It's funny I never associated the past with colors. Maybe it was because TVs were in black and white and so were the first programs I watched when I was a child. Somehow I thought the past would have an absence of color like those old movies.

A few moments passed and I felt much better. The bird stood on its perch looking at me with one eye and then the other. The excitement made it impossible to sleep so I sat up and ate a few grapes from the bowl.

The sun climbed higher in the sky and the gentle breeze that blew through the curtains in the morning felt warmer. I leaned over the tray placing the empty stem that was once full of grapes in the bowl when I caught a whiff of my underarms. I didn't smell bad but I would need to wash soon.

Whende's voice came from the corridor and it sounded like she was talking to another woman. I relinquished my curiosity and stayed in bed. When she came into the room, her face grew a bright smile and her pearly white teeth looked so perfect against her soft brown skin. She looked at the tray and spoke to me then pointed to her mouth, and I understood her gesture. The words she spoke sounded so beautiful and served only to remind me our people were once stripped of a language, a religion, and a culture. Except now it wouldn't happen because I knew the Holocaust that was coming, and I would stop it.

I shook my head and pointed to the food. Whende understood I was no longer hungry and removed the tray. It was then I noticed she wasn't wearing the same clothes she had been wearing when I left my hotel room. How long had I been asleep? Instead of blue she was now wearing an orange silk skirt that stopped above her knees with a matching low-cut top with orange and red squares around the neck. Her hair was in braids that stopped below her shoulders and as she reached for the tray some of the strands fell in her face.

"Whende! I want to go out, I want to see!"

I said energetically.

She looked bewildered by my tone of voice. I raised my hand and with two fingers touched my eyes and then made a sweeping motion with my arm. She smiled as she shook her head in acknowledgment when she turned to leave with the tray.

Each few minutes that passed brought an increased degree of heat. I pushed my hands far above my head and stretched hard into the air. The bird never took its eyes off me. I walked closer but not close enough to scare it. We looked at each other and I said,

"Hello birdie, hello."

He just kept twisting his head at me and when I turned away from the perch the bird said,

"Neia abeir, neia abeir."

For some reason, time seemed to be running away from me and the minutes seemed like seconds. I was fearful I would wake up from this dream without having accomplished anything. I wanted to look outside again now that I needed no assistance. The temperature was a little hotter then this morning, and the sun shone through intermittent clouds and bathed my skin. I walked over to the edge of the pool beside the chair and looked into the water and everything was the same. My bed was still unmade and the room was quiet. Whende came outside carrying more clothes and reached for my hand and squeezed it. Then she led me inside past her bed and into the hallway on the left side of her room.

It was a few degrees cooler in this part of the house. The 12'x 16' room had only one window and a few small candles in the corner for light. The wall across from the window had two black wooden dressers pushed together to make one long flat surface three feet above the floor. On the top of the dresser near the right side, was a large white ceramic bowl filled with water decorated with blue hand painted boats on the outer edge. I was never a person who paid much attention to small details, but I noticed them now. I could be in your home several times and not know what color carpet you had, or how many plants are in your window. However I felt different now because I was in awe. Everything caught my eye twice and I paid attention to it all.

Six or seven feet in front of the two cabinets was a rectangular white marble sunken tub filled with water. Kneeling down I tickled the warm water with my fingers. On the wall opposite the cabinets was a highly polished piece of metal oval in shape, which acted like a mirror. Behind the tub she laid out the clothes on a small black wooden bench. Then Whende pointed in the corner to a white and green striped curtain suspended from several hooks in the ceiling. Behind the curtain was a black wooden cabinet slightly smaller than a night table. She stood in front of the Cabinet and lifted the lid held by two hinges in the back. An unmistakably faint but tolerable odor rose from the small dark opening in the center. Moeda was the name Whende gave to this strange looking toilet. I repeated the name "Moeda" and she nodded with a smile. Then reaching for a cord connected to a small handle on a fish tank sized black ceramic container connected to the moeda and mounted on the wall four feet above the floor. She pulled the cord gently and released it. The water cascaded like a small thin waterfall inside the moeda just below the opening and disappeared into the darkness. I moved the curtain aside and walked back to the center of the room and stood near the tub. Whende took a blue ceramic bowl the size of the soap dish filled with a thick liquid and gave it to me. Then she made a rubbing motion with her hands over her skin. I put my fingers into the slippery liquid and smiled in compliance then she left the room.

There I stood silently with the cool marble under my bare feet watching the breeze rippling the curtains in the window. Again I considered the idea that I might be going crazy because it was impossible for me to be here. This all seemed too easy.

Recalling events in my mind I checked for discrepancies, after all I didn't want to wake up in a mental institution, wearing a straitjacket, only to have some doctor tell me I've been wandering around the hotel for the past week and a half like a lunatic and not having any memory of what I'd done. But I remembered the hunger and the thirst I went through all those days. And I remembered pushing through the glass into the darkness. And I remembered that fall into the abyss. That fall was no fucking joke-- that shit happened!

My heart raced and pounded inside my chest and my head felt like it was being squeezed in a vice once more. I walked to the cabinet against the wall and leaned on it. I wanted to scream or maybe break something. I spoke softly in earnest to one of the few people I had ever trusted in my life,

"Daddy, please help me. I don't know what I've done."

I waited for an answer that did not come and pushed off from the cabinet and walked slowly to the open window. In the distance I saw the mountain range with sparse green trees and foliage. I had to escape the confines of this small arena, and that was the key to my peace of mind. If this was some form of trickery or a well orchestrated illusion, it had to have a boundary. The world is a huge place and cannot be duplicated on a sound stage or a huge vacant lot. Seeing something other than these familiar surroundings would quench my suspicions.

The warm air smelled crisp and sweet and I regained control. I was my father's son and if anything were going to happen to me I would be on my feet standing, not all my knees. So long as he looked down on me I would never disgrace him or our family by selling my soul.

I undressed and got in the tub rubbing the water on my skin. Relaxing a bit I thought about the moeda. I didn't recall seeing anything that looked like toilet paper. But there would be plenty of time to find out. Scooping my fingers into the lotion I began to wash. The substance was more oily then soapy and soon my skin started to tingle pleasantly. Once I was finished I stood up and the breeze coming through the window made the room feel very cool. In the center of the tub was a small round cap with a nipple on top. I pulled the cap off and the water slowly went down the drain.

Now the bundle of clothes Whende left for me was another story. They were laid out nicely on a small bench behind the tub. One piece I knew was the top. It was a white silk T-shirt with short sleeves and a round open neck almost like what she wore except the pattern around the top was dark blue with white squares. The next garment was also familiar to me. It resembled a jock strap made of blue silk with a draw-string at the waist. The last piece was like an apron except it was long enough to cover my lower half. There with two long belts on each side and at first I put it on backwards but when I fixed it correctly the belts dangled in front and stopped just above the hemline. The sandals were made from the hide of some animal because they felt like leather. I sat on the bench and studied them carefully. There was a right and a left sandal and a slender piece of material separated my big toe from the other four. I tried one on and then the other tying the laces around my ankles. The clothes felt naturally comfortable and when I walked in front of the mirror I was proud to wear them. I looked like I was in a Charlton Heston movie or on my way to a costume party.

Returning to the bedroom I was startled by another woman. She was dark-skinned with salt and pepper hair parted in the center with one braid running alongside each temple. She appeared to be in her late fifties or early sixties and she was wearing a light brown dress. She bowed her head to me with a suspicious smile and continued sweep-ing. Whende entered the room immediately after with a white piece of cloth in her hand. She looked at me when the woman wasn't watch-ing putting her finger to her mouth as a gesture for me not to speak. After a few short words the woman bowed her head and left the room.

Whende seemed pleased by my appearance and she examined me from head to toe. She touched the skin on my forearm and looked deep into my eyes. For a second I thought I saw a worried look on her face and then it was gone. She noticed my hair and frowned slightly walking away in the direction of the bathroom. Rubbing both her hands together she stood in front of me and ran her fingers roughly through my hair. When she finished she went back to the bathroom and returned with what looked like an ordinary Afro pick made of wood and raked my hair.

The cloth Whende was holding turned out to be a scarf with a firm U-shaped piece sown under the material. I watched her carefully as

146

she applied it to her head and copied her motions. She held a scarf by the firm headpiece letting the material dangle under it. Raising her arms above her head she let the scarf fall against the back of her neck like a woman putting a wig. Then she adjusted the U-shaped piece in center on her forehead. Now the decorative band adorned her brow and only her face and none of her hair could be seen. I copied her movements to complete my wardrobe and could see she was pleased. Now I was ready to venture out and see the world.

I wanted first to see the great Pyramids and if one was still under construction. I pointed to my eyes and made the shape of a triangle with two hands. Whende spoke the word Beline then smiled and motioned with her hand for me to follow.

We exited through the corridor on the right side of her room and continued until it opened into an area the size of a ballroom with thirty foot high sand colored columns supporting a pearly white ceiling. Octagonal shaped wooden chandeliers lit by oil lamps hung from the ceiling supported by black chains. I could hear the echo our sandals made shuffling against the smooth white marble floor. The small room I'd been in most of the morning gave no hint to this mansion-sized structure. I behaved like a tourist taking a few steps and looking up and around while I walked. Four small steps led up to a hallway filled with sunlight and we emerged outside to steady gusts of warm wind. What I saw next took my breath away so that I blurted out,

"This is wonderful!"

The sun was on its downward slope and Whende put her arm around me to get my attention. She raised her finger to her closed mouth. I took a deep breath and relaxed a little but it was not easy. We were on a huge stone porch or sun deck. Her house was built into the mountainside eighty feet above overlooking the city. From the end of the porch on my right the view was truly spectacular. I could see dark gray clouds moving swiftly across the sky. Below one and two story buildings, clustered together in a grid like pattern and I fought hard to maintain my silence. One dirt road much wider than the others stretched north until it disappeared into the horizon. And as the road stretched away from the city, the buildings became sparse.

Nothing in my life could have ever prepared me for this moment and nothing would ever surpass what I saw next. I looked at Whende with erupting enthusiasm but said nothing. I was less than one hundred feet from the valley floor but I could see all these people, hundreds of them moving around. This part of town looked like any other busy street and like a kid who sees his favorite attraction at the amusement park I had to get down there. We walked to the center of the porch and down one flight of stone stairs to a dirt path. The path curved to the right with a slight downgrade another thirty yards until we stopped at a single dirt road. In front of us just a few yards away, two dark- skinned men wearing garments similar to mine but without the headdress, stood making the final adjustments to a carriage drawn by two large shiny black horses.

The carriage reminded me of the ones in Central Park. It was smooth polished dark wood with a padded bench seat in the rear. Most of it was open except for a white canvas type material suspended over the bench seat. In front slightly elevated was a smaller area for the coachman. When they were finished the first man, who was short in stature, led the horses to the road turning them in the direction of the city. Once the carriage stopped I could tell from his face he was a young teenager. He bowed his head to Whende saying,

"Osique Sakatet," and then to me.

The other man came from behind the carriage like one of the homeboys with an attitude. He walked past me with no acknowledgment and bowed to Whende saying nothing. This dude was no teenager. He made me wonder if they had fitness centers or did he just lift weights? His no nonsense look and cold stare reminded me of Jim Brown in "Three the Hard Way". Well fuck it; I thought to myself, I don't like you either. Then he started to climb into the coachman's seat and Whende stopped him. He still had one foot on the carriage step when he turned around. They began to converse until their voices grew louder. I stood silently but was unable to figure out what she was saying. Homeboy wasn't invited and he was getting pissed off. After some hesitation he removed his foot from the step giving me a cold look and walked in the direction of the stable. Whende spoke to me knowing I would not understand her, but motioned me to step up into the front seat. I got in the front seat hoping she would join me. The last time I'd been on a horse was when I was seven, and my parents took me to a petting zoo. Then the horse was tied to a pole anchored in the ground. There was nothing I needed to do but sit in the saddle and watch the horse walk a continuous circle around the pole.

In the direction of the stable I saw homeboy saddling another horse. If he couldn't go with us he was determined to follow. I watched him for a moment until he stopped to give me a hard stare. I stared back. Our gaze only broke when I felt the carriage shake and Whende sat next to me. Once she was situated the young man handed her the reins, bowed his head once more and stepped back. Whende tugged on the reins and we started to move.

Like a sightseer I watched everything. The scattered trees that went by and how the road which was almost twice as wide as the carriage continuously sloped slightly downward and to the right. I turned around before we got too far to see the pitched stone roof of Whende's house sink into the greenery. And there was homeboy in the distance standing in the center of the road with a horse. What was his problem or relationship to her? Were we breaking some type of protocol?

I could not remember the last time I felt this way. There was a smile on my face so wide my jaws began to ache and every tooth in my mouth could be seen. Whende noticed it too and smiled back, then gave the reins another tug and we went a little faster. I listened to the rhythmic sound of the hooves against the dirt. And watched the horse's heads bop up and down like a carousel.

A cool gust of wind blew across the side of my face making me take notice of the gray clouds moving across the sky. A mile or so down the road I started to hear the sound of inhabitants. Not voices but the resonance of activity like opening a window without looking out and knowing people were outside.

Then the dirt road became wider and blended into the street. I was feeling lightheaded standing on the precipice between absolute joy and total shock. Whende slowed the horses to a stop and held my hand squeezing it tightly but I did not look at her. I never thought there would be so many people walking around. The noise I heard was a mixture of everything that goes on in a city. The quiet sound of sandals walking on the dirt mixed in with the murmur of conversation and laughter, with one and two horse carriages moving up and down the street. I heard the sound cloth makes when it ripples in the wind coupled with the distant rhythmic sound of hammering. In front of us a young woman walked by reaching for her child's hand and speeding up as she crossed in front of the horses. The horses fascinated the little boy with coarse black hair and he looked them over slowly as he was hustled along, but found time to give a brief wave to Whende.

We turned left onto the street slowly at first. Upon reaching the center of the road, the horses began a brisk trot. The next thing I noticed was all the colors. Men, women and children were dressed in so many different colors it seemed to form a moving collage as far as the eye could see. Then we passed a storefront with live chickens waiting to be sold. That same spot had meat wrapped in cloth hanging up like the stores where my family and I bought the Virginia hams from down south. Then there were six or seven children standing in a circle kicking a ball seemingly made of leather to each other while one child stayed on the side and watched.

Next we came to a corner where the streets intersected. Two houses from the corner on the right side were people gathered in front of another market. I caught only a glimpse of what appeared to be vegetables and fruit as we rode by. An old woman sat in a chair in front of a window on a wooden porch with a tan blanket draped across her knees. Near her feet lay a brown medium sized dog with a short coat sleeping on its side.

There was so much to take in at one time. I searched for any word I could remember in Whende's language to verbally communicate with her. How did the Obeni make it possible for us to understand each other before? I wanted to ask her questions about the things I was witnessing and start learning her language now. But more than once she reminded me not to speak and it was clear I would have drawn undue attention to myself. Otherwise for all intents and purposes I blended in well. Everyone looked like me, and I looked like them. Most of the men and women I saw whose heads were not covered wore their hair in locks and a few men had beards.

One time out of curiosity I ordered a book about Egypt from Time Life magazine and was so disgusted I sent it back, because all the pictures of Egyptian people had skin like ivory. I wish they could see this now. Not one ivory colored person anywhere. Why would Time Life and other forms of media portray the oldest of African people with lightened skin? If anything it reminds me more of Harlem when I was a growing up.

Somewhere the soft lively sound of music played only to be drowned out by street noise. We passed another shop with clay pots of different sizes and colors displayed in front. A young girl stood outside resting a large clay pot on her hip while she talked to the woman standing next to her. Further down people sat at tables outside eating, drinking and laughing. At one of the tables, which were all made of wood, a woman sat talking to a man while nursing her baby. Beyond them there was a group of children that ran back and forth as if playing tag.

I don't know how long we had been traveling, maybe fifteen minutes. The shops and the buildings seemed to spread out with more space in between. In the distance a large canvas covered wagon caught my attention. Compared to the others, it was the largest one on the street. As we got closer, a team of six horses pulled the wagon until it stopped. The wheels were as tall as a man and the spokes were all made of metal as thick as my arm. The wagon was three car lengths long and eight feet wide. It had vertical poles for people to hold on to who were standing as they rode. In the center of the wagon others sat down. Three women and a man got off and began walking around the corner while one elderly gentleman with a cane stepped on. The driver pulled the reins and the big wagon was moving again.

Block by block, street by street, the traffic and the crowds diminished and the faint putrid unmistakable odor of garbage caught my nose. Ahead two men rode in a wagon designed like a pickup truck hauling garbage. After we went by, the smell dissipated and the road narrowed a little. Then Whende sent the horses into a thunderous gallop.

I looked at this woman who from the most unusual state of affairs had total direction over of my life. I watched her control these magnificent animals with the same concentration I'd have if I were driving on the highway. A small cloud of dust trailed behind us, and the city was now a small speck in the distance marked by thin rising columns of black smoke.

Our speed decreased when we came to a wooden bridge just slightly wider than the carriage. Whende slowed the horses to a trot as we began to cross and I found this experience disconcerting. They could have put some guard rails or made the bridge a little wider because when I looked over the side from my seat water flowed underneath. It seemed to be a man made canal because the sides that guided the water were smooth and hard like concrete and the water was crystal clear, but I wasn't impressed. I just wanted to get to the other side. Whende had a smirk on her face as if she wanted to laugh but held it back. Once the horses reached the other side I breathed a sigh of relief and we were thundering along once again.

In the distance ahead, the road resembled a snake stretched across a lumpy green carpet. Trees and foliage marked the road on both sides except for an occasional house surrounded by farmland. Uniform rows of plowed acreage surrounded each house we passed with only the green tops of unknown vegetables showing.

After many miles we slowed down again. The horses pulled us effortlessly uphill around a hairpin curve to the top of a clearing where we stopped. From here you could see twenty or more miles in any direction. A few miles ahead the road branched out in four or five different directions. One road headed straight to a small Mountain range spotted with green. Off to the right was a huge circular body of water two miles in circumference. Behind me lay only the faint memory of the town we left behind.

Whende watched me with enchantment. Although I could not express it verbally, she took reward from my pleasure. I looked deep into her beautiful brown eyes contemplating the sweetness of her lips against mine. Then I took her hand slowly raising it to my lips and kissed it softly on the knuckles. I thought about all the people I'd left behind and prayed they would understand how happy I was. The nagging and tugging at my soul was gone. The great mother hadn't lied to me. She urged me to come home so my destiny could be fulfilled. Every tree, rock and blade of grass felt like the hug of a loving family. I was home now and I was never leaving.

Once more a strong gust of wind blew until it lifted the manes of the horses. Our attention was directed upward to the ceiling of billowing gray clouds rolling ever closer. The smell of moisture that precedes rain was in the air. Whende pointed to a ridge straight ahead then put both her hands together to form a triangle.

"The pyramid, I mean the tombs are over there?"

Once more she made the sign of the triangle and said, "Beline."

One forceful pull and we were moving again until the horses were in full sprint. I looked at the sky now watching the darker clouds in the distance move closer. The temperature felt like a mild 80 degrees so if we got caught in the rain it wouldn't be so bad.

We arrived at a ridge went over and stopped. Whende seemed dissatisfied now. She pointed to a clearing many miles away covered by clouds and spoke the word Beline. I looked in the direction of her finger but couldn't see anything. On a clear day I might have seen it but not now. Still she insisted I look harder by jabbing her arm and pulling me closer. In the nondescript expanse of the clouds I saw a pearly white halo twinkle thru the haze many miles away and that was all.

We sat for a moment tolerating strong intermittent blasts of warm air waiting for a clearing in the clouds that never came. Around us the wind swayed the tops of trees while birds scrambled for shelter. And in the remoteness of the sky I heard the faint rumble of thunder. Our sites were drawn to the direction of a very dark cloud formation behind the mountains heading our way. We looked at each other and must have been thinking the same thing. It was time to leave.

Whende made a carefully executed U-turn urging the horses to go forward until we were facing the opposite direction. So I didn't see the pyramids the first time. It didn't matter they would always be there.

This time there was no slow steady acceleration. Those horses started running as if their lives depended on it. It seemed as though the moment we turned around the wind blew steady and hard. We raced down the hill toward the hairpin turn slowing down gradually until we came out and it was full speed ahead. We reached the tree-lined road, which offered a little shelter from the wind, but it was much darker than when we first passed. Overhead the dark clouds were catching up and the distant thunder grew louder. We were getting close to the huge pond and I thought about that rickety ass bridge ahead. I knew she wasn't going to take it at this speed.

Whende was in full concentration while she watched the road. The carriage roared on as leaves blew across our path and small grains of dirt hit the side of my face. When was she going to slow down? I could see the bridge a couple of hundred feet ahead. Now would be a good time to slow down I thought. Did this girl have a thrill seeking side to her? She had to know she was causing me some excitement. Fuck that, she was about to scare the shit out of me! I held on to the side of the carriage with my left hand and put my arm around the back of the bench seat. I looked at Whende then the bridge, then the distance from the bridge and then back at Whende. I wish I knew her language so I can say, yo, slow the fuck down. If the horses didn't run exactly in the center or one wheel came off the bridge we would fall. Less than fifty feet to go she finally slowed down but not enough for me. We flew across the bridge much faster than before and I did not look down.

I felt one drop of rain as we approached the first structure at the beginning of town. We rode down the middle at a slow gallop. Some places were now familiar to me. The people who were eating were gone. The shopkeeper was moving the pottery and jars inside. The few people who were out now were walking briskly. I forgot to look around the corner at the vegetable stand but the place where the meat was hanging was closed.

A bright flash of light appeared like a photographer's bulb followed by a crack of thunder so loud it vibrated through the ground. It startled the horses making them very nervous. They seemed to be looking around for a place to run. I could hear thousands of tiny drops coming closer. I turned around to see a thick drape of rain advance toward us until we were engulfed. In a matter of a few seconds we were both soaked. The colors I'd seen before were now just different shades of gray.

Coming up on the right was the road home. It was somewhat comforting to know what lay at the end this road. For once I paid so much attention to every little detail I knew just over this hill was home. The rain was like an intimate blessing from the great mother. I could feel the love through each drop that touched my skin. Was it a coincidence that my first recollection was my own mother washing me in the kitchen sink? I didn't know nor did I care because the love was exactly the same.

Whende stopped the carriage by the edge of the steps and looked in the direction of the stable. At once a door swung open held by a shadowy figure. She tapped my leg motioning for me to get down. When both stable doors opened the person began walking to the carriage. I stepped into the shallow mud a few feet from the first step and waited. Whende gave the reins to the young man I saw earlier then dismounted the carriage on my side. When we reached the first stone step the carriage moved in the direction of the stable. She hurried past me up the steps and waited on the porch. I stopped a few steps from the top and turned around to enjoy the rain. Not much could be seen of the landscape through the rain and the ever darkening sky. Only the light from the stable was visible until the doors closed.

Finally I went up the last few steps to the porch then followed her inside. Briskly we walked past the large open space lit by all those candles and down the corridor to her room. Only two candles burned in the darkness with dim light coming from the direction of the bathroom. I stood in the center of the room not knowing what to do next. Whende returned from the bathroom immediately and took me inside. She lit another candle with a long skinny stick then pointed to the tub of fresh water. It was just what I needed and I did not hesitate to remove my clothes. She returned from her room to see me lowering myself into the warm water and placed clean garments on the dresser in front of me.

There I relaxed rubbing the soft water over my face reflecting on all I'd seen today and how much more I would see. It would take some time but I was sure in a few months I'd be able to speak the language. After that I could sail to North America and stand at the top of Sugar Hill. I wasn't sure but I think most of New York City was covered by a glacier at this time.

My mind raced with thoughts of my future and what I could contribute to this society and how could I earn my own money? Sure Whende was wealthy but I was not the type of man to sponge off of her forever.

Shortly before I was ready to get out of the tub, Whende returned. It seemed she had washed in another part of the house. Now she wore a soft peach colored skirt with a short-sleeved matching top. I sat in the tub and looked at her and my breathing grew heavy. She opened a piece of cloth draped over her forearm and held it in front of her like a matador waiting for the bull. Slowly I stood up and stepped out of the tub until she wrapped me in this soft dark cloth. Before I could put my arms around her she smiled and left. Reluctantly I put the garment on she left for me and waited in her room.

Whende came back shortly and pointed to her mouth to see if I was hungry and I shook my head to say no. She seemed to have a worried look on her face. I put my hand on her waist and pulled her closer to me wanting very much to kiss her. We looked at each other and I kissed her lightly on one corner of her lips, and then the other side. She had wide and soulful eyes that could melt the coldest heart. I kissed her again and this time she kissed me back passionately. We were standing a few feet from the hallway and my hands slid down her back. Just before they reached the small of her back she stopped kissing me. With an alluring smile she took my hand and led me to the bed then went in the direction of the bathroom. At this moment I let go of everything I'd left behind. I was happy now, happier than I'd ever been. The princess and I were about to make love and I would leave the future behind me.

The wind had been blowing a little harder with each passing hour since we'd returned. The parrot didn't like the storm either. He was fidgety and pasted back and forth on the perch. I walked to the perch and put my hand up slowly. When I wondered if he might bite me and pulled my hand back but it was too late. He'd already taken his left foot and stepped of the perch onto my extended finger. We looked at each other close-up and I wondered, where do you pet a bird to relax him? I'll try his stomach so he can see what I'm doing. I took one finger and rubbed his little chest. He slowly bent his head down near my finger and nudged it. I rubbed the top of this head ever so gently and he liked it. He opened his mouth like he was yawning and then I saw his black tongue.

Whende returned with an apprehensive look but quickly removed it. I didn't even know how to ask her if something was wrong or was I moving too fast? Maybe there was some form of courtship involved I knew nothing about. She walked up to us extended her hand and the bird jumped on. Then she placed him back on his perch. He nodded his head up and down and said,

"Neia abei, neia abei."

Whende walked away from me with her head down looking at the floor. She always held her head up proud but something was wrong. I walked over to her and touched her arm and she stopped. I turned her around to me and said,

"What's wrong?"

She started to open her mouth and nothing came out. I tried to get her to smile but it wasn't working. Not knowing what to do I moved closer to her and wrapped my arms around her and hugged her. Her head was in my chest while I rubbed the side of her temple. Then the princess looked at me and I kissed her between the bridge of her nose and her forehead and told her everything would be all right. Her lips were so full and beautiful I had to kiss them again, and I did. I held her head in my hands and lightly kissed her face picking a different each time and my passion rose. I could feel her hands closing around my waist. Kissing her again with my mouth parted just touching the middle of her lips with my tongue, her mouth opened and I couldn't stop. The candles flickered around the room as her hands rubbed my back and our bodies pressed closer. I turned my head to kiss and neck. If I had been a vampire like in the movies would I feast on this charming neck? Yes.... yes I would. I opened my mouth and put my lips against her skin and softly bit her. The only sound from Whende was the sound of deep breathing. I kissed a path from her neck to the bottom of her ears. She turned her head and kissed my mouth and all of a sudden she grabbed my bottom lip between her teeth and softly sucked it. To me it was like throwing gasoline on fire and before I knew it my hands were exploring her body. They went past the small of her back and flowed over the curves of her cheeks and there they stayed. The firm softness of her was extensive but there was nothing soft about me anymore and she knew it. Then the wind flared up and the canvas came loose from the ties.

That gust blew most of the candles out so Whende ran over to the doorway and closed the shutters tight. Then she went to the dresser and got some long sticks to re light the candles and left the room.

This scenario topped what I visualized as the perfect place to make love. I always thought a trek to the North Pole inside an igloo wrapped in bear skin rugs with a small fire and a little cognac would be the ultimate.

I sat in the chair and soon Whende returned holding two cups. She handed one to me and I took a sip. It was wine, not very strong and not very sweet. She drank some too then sat on the edge of the bed. Her eyes focused on me with a hypnotic gaze so strong and enticing it pierced my will. I put down the cup and went to her. Taking her cup I drank from it then sat next to her and took her hand. I raised it to my lips and kissed the tip of her pointer finger and then each joint down to her wrist. I put the cup down and moved closer to her. Our lips met again as she laid back. I was almost on top of her and could see her nipples through her garment and touched them. I wanted her now, I wanted to pull my clothes off and hers and make love to her this very minute and I would, but I meant to enjoy her. I would take my time with her like that first meal she gave me only, Whende was the meal and I meant to have her one grain at a time.

The wind roared outside as I removed her top and then mine. I kissed between her breasts while she touched the back of my head. And when her nipples touched my lips I remembered saying to my-self, one grain at a time. She was breathing faster now and I let my hands drift down her body.

We lay naked next to each other. I could feel her guiding me to lie on top of her. Her head was on my arm while my hand was rubbing her thigh. I looked in Whende's eyes and slowly slid my hand along the inside of her and then I touched it. It was all I could do to keep from plunging into her. One grain at a time Bennie remember that, I thought to myself. I was on my knees and she was under me. My lips were in her stomach and the side of her ribs. I didn't know how far I should go? I decided to let her stop me. My mouth was on her belly button and each time I kissed I would go a half-inch lower. I stopped when I reached the hair just kissing her pelvic bone then her hands held my head and pushed it down further. Her fingers were in my hair and each time my mouth touched her I went a little slower. I was almost there as her hips squirmed in front of me. I heard her whisper something and finally my mouth met the lips of Whende's affection.

I pretended not to hear the wind blow something against the side of the house. With her permission nothing could stop me now. I explored her with circular motions, questioned her with incursion, and teased with flickering pauses. Unwillingly she would show me all her desires. Heaven help her when I find what she likes most. And I meant to find out one grain at a time.

The wine tasted much better the second time around. I offered the princess some and watched her drink gradually between breaths. As we lay side by side I felt her take a hold of me like a witch's stare. Her eyes looked into my veins, maybe each and every cell. I felt slightly intimidated. I was in her world, she was the spider and I was the fly. Now it was time to take my painful rigidness away.

Our bodies had become one and the wetness of her was like a morning sunrise. I never wanted to leave this place, this time or this position. We discovered a rhythm, a beat I would never forget. And the feeling was so good I had to control myself if I planned to go deeper. I was as gentle as I could remember to be but my fever was rising. Our bodies were bound by sweat and Whende was changing the rhythm and I was holding on for dear life. She was playing a new game. Who was going to hang up first?

My ego wouldn't let me go first and before I knew it she switched on me again and I could feel my control slipping. I tried to stop, too slow her down but she wouldn't have it. I was like a kid begging not to have that extra cookie. Whende had such a confident smile on her face, and when our eyes met I was sinking fast.

I said,

"Wait, wait a minute."

She sucked my bottom lip and it was over. The sand in my hour-glass was running out but I was determined not to go alone. With her knees around my shoulders I kissed her one last time and selecting a special angle and rhythm of my own. I could feel small shivers that grew stronger and faster throughout her body. Our sand was running out together and when I looked down at her she looked as if she were crying.

A short time after Whende left the bed and went to the bathroom. When she returned she wiped me with a moist cloth and soon returned to bed. We lay with our heads together with our bodies resting like spoons. The darkness of sleep approached while a soft hand caressed mine softly repeating the words,

"Neia abeir Bennie, neia abeir."

Chapter 9

Terri couldn't figure out why the subway sat in the tunnel so long after 116th Street. Two A trains and one D train passed by on the express track. She'd skimmed through two magazines and some office paperwork without knowing what she'd read. Each day that went by without hearing from Bennie was pushing her to the critical level. At one moment her fury was like an explosive volcano spewing fists and kicks, the next moment was followed by a reason to forgive him. On the other hand she sometimes felt like the witch who was doused with water and left to melt into an embarrassing puddle of rejection. Unsure what road her life would take was a lot to handle.

The train lurched forward and Terri lifted her head. Across from her a single light bulb moved slowly in the darkness past the window. She watched until another bulb passed and then another. Finally the train picked up a little speed and for the first time she looked around the train at faces and noticed a man smiling assertively at her. She lowered her head pretending to read and wondered if he was still looking.

Passengers stood up and headed for the doors as the train pulled into the station. The people standing in front of Terri moved to exit exposing the man still smiling at her. He looked to be in his early twenties wearing a white turtleneck sweater, a blue dungaree jacket with matching pants and white sneakers. His eyes wandered from her ankles until they reached her crossed legs. She thought she might be revealing herself so she serenely pulled the hem of her skirt tucking it under her thigh. This action made him smile even more as the train continued to the next stop.

Terri gathered her papers together and walked to the door. She would not look back at him again. Once outside the train station a few feet from the entrance the magazines fell from under her arm. Before she could bend down to reach a hand was picking them up.

"Here you go, Miss," he said politely.

It was the man from the train and now she would have to say something.

Looking at him with poise she said,

"Thank you."

There was not much wind today but the air was chilly. Soon her papers and magazines were neatly put away in her bag and she began to walk away.

"Miss, could I ask you a question?"

Terri wasn't in the mood for any pickup lines today, but she felt his act of chivalry deserved ten seconds of her time.

"What?" She said cautiously.

"Would a decent, intelligent hard working man like me ever stand a chance with you?"

The question caught her by surprise and she was flattered. Just when she thought she'd heard every line that could be said, here was a new one she had no answer for. While she thought of something to say her tension was alleviated. She took that brief moment to look him over and before she knew it, she was smiling again after all these days.

"That's very nice of you," she said.

"No, you don't understand. I'm also trying to apologize for the way I stared at you on the train. You see it's not just your appearance that interests me. I was hoping your qualities were more than just what is on the outside. Does that sound stupid?"

"No it doesn't," she said frankly.

"So would I stand a chance with you?"

Before Terri could answer he said,

"By the way, my name is Trent."

Her mind had been so preoccupied and confused she was reluctant to let go of this momentary diversion.

"My name is Terri."

"It's nice to meet you Terri."

Now they were shaking hands near the corner in front of the elementary school. She had to admit he was nice looking and then asked, "How old are you?"

"I just turned twenty two."

Terri started shaking her head saying no to herself, but he was very determined.

"You still haven't answered my question."

"Listen I don't..."

"Would I stand a chance with you?"

"If I weren't seeing somebody yes, you would."

"I understand," he said in a disappointing tone, "You're married."

"Yes I am."

"He's a lucky man."

Trent's last statement brought her back to reality but she remained unruffled.

"Thank you for asking and I hope you find what you're looking for."

She turned to walk uptown and after a few steps he said,

"Can I give you my phone number if he messes up?"

This made her chuckle silently searching for an excuse to say no and Terri slowed down to a turtle's pace. If Bennie didn't want her why not take his number? Trent fumbled through his pockets for a pen and paper when he approached her he wrote the number down and Terri took it.

"I would like to see you again, Terri."

"We'll see," she said and continued to walk uptown.

There was a new stride in her step. The chill in the air was gone and she'd felt better about herself then she had in days. She walked past the little park and then the church. If she had to start over why not let it be with someone young she could mold. She could teach him how she needed to be treated. Terri never dated a man younger than she was but contemplated it more than once. The more she turned it over in her mind the better it felt. She made a stop at the corner grocery store for some pantyhose and ice cream then walked past the basket-ball court and had a stunning revelation. I met Bennie at the train station and now I meet this mother fucker at the train station. Hell no, she thought to herself, hell no. I'm not going to let this happen again. She reached in her pocket and opened up the piece of paper to make sure it was his phone number then tore it into as many little pieces and she could and tossed it in the corner garbage can.

With her key in hand Terri hustled up the steps to the front door of Bennie's house and quickly went inside. Her actions made her feel like a fugitive on the run. After breathing a sigh of relief from avoiding conversation with anyone she stopped at the mirror in the hallway. Who was this woman she thought she'd known so well? She deliberated on Trent wondering if she'd been too hasty discarding his telephone number. She went into living room kicking her shoes off by the couch as she walked to the mantle wondering if she'd ever feel like this was her home?

Terri looked at the pictures in front of her. Bennie's Aunt Dot was there next to a picture of his sister. Lorraine and Ronald's wedding picture was under a portrait of Bennie's mother and father. A black and white photo of Bennie when he was a year old always made her smile. He was such a cute kid smiling from ear to ear in his shorts, and little round shoes. That was the smile she fell in love with and then she found some relief. Next to his baby picture was one of her and next to that a picture of the two of them taken by some stranger while they were bicycling in Central Park. In the picture, Terri found something that would anchor her and she would not doubt him again. Her picture was here amongst his family and friends and she had to trust him. He told her things would be different when he returned and she would wait.

Terri went to the kitchen and put the ice cream in the freezer. When she got upstairs she checked on the fish and gave them a little food. Then she went to his answering machine to listen to the messages. Upon listening she realized she was not the only one who was worried about him. Aunt Dot's first few messages blasted him for making her worry. His sister left a few of the same with some curse words added. Then there was a call from a vending machine salesman, but no calls from anyone else she could not recognize. She would have followed her first instinct days ago by placing a call overseas to the local police to check on him, but decided against it because she didn't want to appear obsessive. Every message she left at his hotel came with an assurance from the staff that he'd arrived safely and had been seen.

Before Terri settled down she had to check in with Lorraine. They hadn't spoken since the day Lorraine was last here and if it were up to her, she'd never let Lorraine in this house again. The idea of her going through Bennie's personal belongings was unthinkable. Once he returned Terri would address this situation in front of Bennie with Lorraine present.

After Terri took a shower and got comfortable, she picked up the cordless phone and sat on the edge of the bed. The phone rang four times before Lorraine answered and then she laid back. "Hello," Lorraine said.

"Hi girl, how are you doing?"

Terri was calling specifically for information regarding their trip but did not want to appear desperate.

"I got your messages at work but I was on a research assignment."

The truth was Terri was in her office but didn't want to talk to her.

"I got yours too. I've been so busy around here packing and everything."

"How's Ronald?"

"Working hard as usual." Lorraine replied.

Terri thought Lorraine was trying to infer that Ronald did all the work.

"That's Ronald," Terri said.

There was an awkward moment of silence between them then Lorraine said, "Has he called?"

"No, but its fine, I know he's all right."

"You do."

"Yes," she said assertively.

"Well, we're leaving in a few days."

That was all Terri wanted to do was make sure they were still going. If they weren't, she would catch the next flight herself. There were times she got the impression Lorraine didn't care one way or the other about Bennie, but it wasn't a good time to ask Lorraine why she acted that way. Instead she made sure the conversation ended on good grounds.

"Is there anything I can help you with?" Terri asked.

"No everything is okay."

"Do you guys need any money?"

"I don't think so. We're picking up some traveler's checks tomorrow."

"If you think of anything let me know."

"I hear they have nice fabrics and linen. I'll pick out something for you."

That really pissed Terri off. To Lorraine it was just another vacation instead of a possible rescue mission.

"No honey that's all right. I don't want anything."

"Are you sure?"

She fought back to urge to tell Lorraine how she was feeling now and took a deep breath.

"Yes I'm sure and I'll talk to you before you leave."

"Are you all right?"

"Sure girl I'm fine I'll talk to you later. Bye."

Terri pressed the button to disconnect and sat up feeling like throwing the phone against the wall. It was clear Lorraine wasn't worried about Bennie at all, and she found it amazing they were still friends for so long. She also was beginning to realize with each encounter she had with Lorraine her self esteem was chipped away. Each time she made you feel good or did something nice, Lorraine followed it with three or four times of making you feel like dirt. This situation could not continue and when Bennie gets back things will be different.

Back in Egypt the morning was very unusual. I felt like a child waking up the day after Christmas remembering all the new toys I had to play with. I fell asleep last night with Whende in my arms feeling her warm tears rolling down my arm. She never made eye contact with me after we made love. Because of my somewhat weakened condition combined with all the excitement of yesterday I lacked the strength to hunt for an explanation. My only recourse was to hold her close and rock her to sleep.

The storm was over and the sun was up. The room was very quiet and my new friend was missing from his perch. I yawned deeply and stretched in bed. Today I would start learning her language. I remembered thinking of a plan as I drifted off to sleep. With my knowledge of the future I would try to make sure African people stayed the rulers of their continent. I would also make sure somehow that no African would ever be kidnapped from this soil. I didn't know how to do it or where to begin but that was my goal. Maybe it could be a ritual of how to treat strangers placed in their culture. I could develop a method of dealing with strangers who would later be found as invaders, or invent new strategies of war. My limited knowledge of technology might reproduce the first firearm to defend the shores. It sounded so simple now. Improve the present by changing the past.

Someone was coming; the footsteps were fast and more than one person. From the hallway three men came into the room. The first two stood close to the perch not far from the right side of the bed. The third was homeboy who walked around the foot of the bed and stopped near my side. The only thought I had at this moment was how glad I felt not to be totally naked under this blanket. I'd gotten up last night to take a leak and before I got back in the bed I put on the cloth supporter Whende had given me earlier.

The two men stood holding wooden spears with metal tips at their sides. Homeboy wore a wide leather belt at his waist with a holster that held a machete-sized knife. He reminded me of the policeman who pulled me over because he said my car fit the description of one used in a robbery. When he came to the car, he made sure I could see his hand resting on the gun.

Homeboy stood close to the bed trying to intimidate me by opening and closing his fingers around the ivory handle of the knife. I got out of the bed nearly stepping on his feet to look for my sandals. My mistake was taking my eyes off of him and he moved swiftly punching me in the ribs with his left hand. The pain was intense and before I could get my hand out to protect myself I felt a second blow on the side of my face that sent me crashing to my knees. I could see one of his ankles pivoting in preparation to deliver a third strike. I looked up only enough to focus on where I was about to hit him. Taking a quick breath and with a right-handed uppercut I punched him as hard as I could. He didn't even flinch. I thought I'd missed or possibly he was a eunuch and felt no pain. I looked up and when I saw his face I knew I hadn't. He fell to the floor as the two men lowered their spears and came towards me. I pulled the knife from his belt and held it to his throat. Whatever happens now I'm taking homeboy with me. I stared at the space between both tips of the spears. If they moved one inch toward me I would kill this man. The blade at his throat didn't bother him. He just lay in a fetal position holding his groin. Then I asked God for some help. Praying silently I said, you know I'll kill him Lord if I have to. So please show me what to do.

Just then Whende came into the room and my prayers were answered. She shouted at them and the two men withdrew their spears and stood at attention. She looked at me and I knew everything was all right. I stood up and threw the knife on the bed. She spoke to the guards again and they put down the spears and moved closer to see about Homeboy. While they were next to him about to lift him to his feet I tried to walk around them and that's when I got hit. The punches were coming from all directions. I heard Whende yell again and they stopped only after they had both my arms twisted behind my back. I was bewildered by the look of hatred in Whende's face. She walked slowly to me and slapped me as hard as she could. I could taste the blood filling the inside of my mouth. Her eyes fell on the knife I had thrown on the bed and she picked it up, and held it to my chest. Her teeth grinded as she spoke and when she finished the guards dragged me from the bedroom and down the hall pass to two more doors and threw me in a small room the size of a large elevator. Before I could get to my feet they closed a heavy wooden door. From the other side I could hear the sliding of the metal bolt lock me in. I ran at the door with my shoulder and then I tried kicking it until my ankles were sore. Whende and the men were talking just outside the door and I broke my code of silence and started yelling and kicking the door again.

"What happened Whende, what did I do?"

They stopped talking but I knew they were still there.

"Why are you doing this?"

The sound of the footsteps faded away until only a distant murmur could be heard. This was the last place I thought I'd end up. She must be out of her fucking mind. What did I do to make her turn against me and how was I going to get out?

The walls were made of small stone bricks that were cool to the touch. At the opposite side of the door was a small window just large enough for my head. For some strange reason, the floor was covered with a bed of straw and nothing else. When I looked at the door from this side of the room I saw a small panel like a large mail slot at eye level. I looked around the room for something to use as a tool. If I could find something hard enough maybe I could scrape between the bricks enough to loosen one or two. I kicked at the straw and felt around the floor for anything that could help me. I kept trying to think what I had done to make her turn against me. Then I wondered if she had this planned from the beginning.

After several hours of listening at the door I sat with my back against the wall under the window. This was the first time I'd ever been this scared. If homeboy had his way I would be dead now or maybe they were planning my execution. I didn't have to worry about a firing squad but they did have the means to cut off my head. And for a while it was hard not thinking of different ways they could torture me. Maybe they had no intentions of killing me, just removing my eyes leaving me blind. They could cut off my hands or my feet, or use my flesh to feed some hungry animal, or Whende could just leave me here to starve to death.

I stood up in the center of the room facing the door thinking about what I would do if I had an opportunity to escape? Only one person could fit through the door at a time so I began to calculate each scenario. I envisioned my attacker coming through the door so I counted the steps from the door to the center of the room. I decided to stand as close to the entrance to as I could giving one enough room to enter at a time. If he was empty-handed a swift kick to the kneecap or the groin should stop him. While holding a handful of straw concealed behind my back I would throw it in the face of the second man hoping to grab his weapon. If the first man entering had the weapon I would throw the straw in his face and disarm him. They had no idea who they were messing with. I was a warrior too. Hell most of my nightmares were about fighting for my life and if it were Whende's wish for me to die, this would be the place I could offer my best defense.

I could also play possum pretending to be sick or too weak to resist until I was removed from this room to a better place to launch my attack. The only problem was I had nowhere to go and I couldn't communicate with anyone unless I pretended I couldn't speak. Now that might work I thought. If I got away and someone kept me hidden I would pretend I was a mute until I learned the language, then come back for my revenge.

I rehearsed and planned until the sun started falling from the sky.

Then I sat up all night fighting sleep in case someone came in. From the small window I was able to see the night sky without any clouds. I stood by the opening and looked for the Big Dipper or the Little Dipper, the only group of stars I could recognize. The moon had to be here but where was it? I pushed my head in the small square space looking out in all directions and couldn't see it. My view of the night sky was like someone seeing it for the first time. Without the reflection of the millions of lights on the ground, the sky seemed like a clear 3-D image. So many stars could be seen in the night sky they seemed close enough to touch and their combined light shining illuminated the distant trees and mountains. It could have been breathtaking to sit with her under the stars outside listening to the sounds of crickets chirping while having hours of enlightening dialogue.

At this moment I didn't care. I started blaming myself cursing my decision to come here. Why hadn't I'd been satisfied with where I was and what I had become? All I had seen in my brief stay was not worth dying for. I could have stayed in my time and made effective changes there.

Before I left my hotel room I remembered Whende asking me about the Creator. Had we learned more about the Creator? Had we gotten closer to God? She never seemed impressed with the future. Was that the way she tricked me? The more I thought about her, the angrier I became. She wanted to know if we had grown spiritually as a people and if we had found peace? If I ever got my hands on her again I'd show her some peace!

The light of the sun trickled over the distant mountains and so far they hadn't decided what to do with me. I'd stayed awake all night thinking of a way to escape. The house remained quiet all night except for the time I thought I heard someone tiptoeing outside the door. In the darkness of the night I decided not to fight them when they came in. I would pretend I was sick and hurt until I found a chance to escape. My hunger was increasing with my thirst for vengeance. I'd seen the morning come without so much as a knock on the door or any food and I was forced to relieve myself in the corner, and clean up with the dry straw. Whende would pay for that too.

My feet were sore from kicking the door yesterday. Only after a few hours of this useless behavior did I decide to save my strength. The truth was I was glad to see the sun come up again not knowing if it would be my last. I thought about our carriage ride and how nice it felt to hold her. How good her voice sounded in my hotel room and all the things she had told me. And worst of all I actually thought I was falling in love with her.

There were footsteps outside the door. I had nothing but my fists to protect me. My eyes searched the room again for a makeshift weapon. Even a thin sliver of wood the thickness of a pencil was better than nothing. The small slot in the door opened. It was the old woman I saw cleaning Whende's room. She pushed a round clay tray into the slot until it stopped. I tried to pull the tray through the slot and found its oval shape prevented it. The old woman pulled the tray out and when she put it back there was a small piece of bread on it. She gestured for me to eat quickly before anyone saw. I put the piece of bread in my mouth and chewed it quickly. It left a strange aftertaste like lead or metal in my mouth. When I stopped chewing, she closed the little door and walked away. I went to the window and looked outside spending most of the day plotting revenge and escape. Maybe I shouldn't have eaten that bread. If I could go a couple more days without eating or drinking I could escape back to my time. I could leave this awful place and never return.

Shortly I began to feel as if I'd been drinking. My head started spinning and my limbs felt heavy. This feeling was coming on too fast. It was the taste of metal in the bread that was causing it. I went to step forward and fell on the ground. My arms were heavy and the room was tilting to one side. What more could you do to me Whende?

I don't know how long I was unconscious when I heard people talking. They were in the room with me but all I could do was make out shadows. It was like waking up after an operation. Now I was being lifted and I couldn't tell where I was. I kept thinking I was in a hospital being wheeled on a stretcher. We were going outside in the bright sun. I tried to move my head but couldn't. I heard her voice still harsh, and angry like before. The shadows were clear enough to see the guards had their backs to me, and Whende was standing over me. I still couldn't see her clearly but I felt her hand on my face touching where she had slapped me. My mouth was so dry now. Whatever I was lying on slowly tilted higher and higher until I began to slide off headfirst into the water and back into my mother's arms.

Chapter 10

Flight 237 landed in Cairo five hours late with Ronald and Lorraine aboard. They left New York just after midnight on March 23rd. There had been engine trouble found while the passengers were boarding. They spent three hours at the gate watching a movie. When the flight was about to be canceled the problem was corrected and their plane took off.

By the time they landed in Cairo and claimed their luggage it was 3:30 PM. They looked for Bennie in the terminal then Ronald called the hotel. He left a message for him days ago with all their flight information. They sat on a leather loveseat in the lounge until most of the luggage was claimed and the people disappeared. Then Ronald wandered around the terminal until he found the bus that would take them to the hotel. Some moments later the bus pulled into the loop and stopped in front of the hotel. Immediately Ronald went to the desk while the bellboy put their luggage on a cart. Lorraine lagged behind looking and studying every person she saw. Once they were checked in, the hotel clerk gave the bellboy a key for Suite 919 adjacent to Bennie's.

The bellboy pulled the chrome-plated cart full of luggage in the direction of the elevator. Lorraine never acknowledged the elegance of the hotel lobby but before leaving the front desk she asked if there were any messages left for them. The clerk looked in the box marked 919 and told her no.

When they reached the ninth floor Ronald asked Lorraine if she remembered what room I was staying in. When the bellboy stopped at their door Lorraine walked past him to the next door and said,

"It's this one, 917! The one with the do not disturb sign!"

Ronald joined Lorraine at the door and touched the sign pretending to read it standing there to see if they could hear sounds.

"Do you think we should knock and let him know we're here?" She said.

"Let's put our luggage in the room and come back."

The bellboy looked puzzled then asked,

"Is there something wrong, Mr. Jefferson?"

"No our friend is staying in that room," Ronald said.

Then he followed behind the cart when it was pushed inside. After explaining and showing them all the features the suite had to offer Ronald tipped the bellboy and he began to leave. Lorraine stood in the doorway keeping an eye on the hallway then she said,

"How is Mr. Reeves?"

"Mr. Reeves?"

"Yes our friend from America."

"I think I saw him a few days ago."

"So he's in his room now?"

Now the bellboy seemed a bit embarrassed by the questions. It was hotel policy to be discreet and not give too much information about their guests. He shouldn't have said anything but since they all knew each other he offered a bit more.

"I think he's been enjoying his vacation."

"Why would you say that?" Lorraine said with a smile.

"You know how lovers are?" He said with a slight grin.

"Yes I do," she said staring at Ronald.

"He just comes out for clean towels now and then."

"Is that so?" she said watching Ronald.

Lorraine had heard enough. She stepped aside to let the bellboy leave and once she closed the door she said,

"You see," she said, pointing her finger in the direction of his room,

"I knew it! I knew he was down here with somebody!"

"Well he didn't tell me," Ronald said quickly.

Lorraine looked at Ronald in disbelief.

"He didn't say anything... I'm serious," he said again.

"Your boy has been keeping secrets from you."

Ronald walked to the curtains and pulled the string to look at the balcony.

"I'm going to call Terri right now!" She said.

Lorraine put her purse on the bed and reached for the phone.

"Don't call yet," he said.

"This is bullshit. He makes us come down here to check on him!"

"Let's talk to him first."

"For what!? You heard the man. Bennie is doing what he's always done."

"I still want to see him first," Ronald said firmly.

Lorraine put the phone down taking quick strides toward the bathroom. When she got close to Ronald she stopped and pointed towards the direction of Bennie's room again and said,

"You wait till I see him, just wait."

Inside my room I could see the inside of my door and the legs of my bed. I was lying on my stomach and I couldn't feel my hands. My clothes were wet and the room was cold. I tried to move but my feet were tied and my hands were pinned under me. I could see the clock on the dresser but I couldn't focus to tell what time it was. I could hear the maids vacuuming the rooms and closing the doors. I didn't know how but I knew I had been saved and sent back to my room. I tried to yell but could not. A cloth had been stuffed in my mouth. One of the maids should open my door and see me sooner or later.

The noise of the vacuum grew louder while more doors opened and closed. I heard people talking in the hallway and after a time the sound of doors closing and the humming of the vacuum cleaners went away. I grew anxious because I couldn't feel my hands. I needed to turn over to get some of the weight off my arms but every move I made took all of my power. I wanted so much for someone to come in and rescue me. The cloth stuffed in my mouth made it hard to breathe but my vision wasn't so blurred now and I could read the little red numbers on the clock and the time was 1:36pm.

I turned over finally, by steadily rocking back and forth I was able to roll on to my left side facing the door then asked myself, what was the point of tying me up if she knew she was sending me back? I opened my hands and closed them repeatedly until I felt the circulation returning.

Ronald was done showering and changing into his clothes when Lorraine asked when was the last time he had spoken to me?

"Sometime before he left," he said indifferently.

"You haven't spoken to him in all this time? I'm going to knock on his door when we go out," She paused for a moment and said,

"That's just like Bennie to go somewhere and forget all about us. You know he really pisses me off sometimes! He could've met us at the airport."

Ronald put his sandals on and said,

"Our plane was late, he might have been at the airport and left."

While he sat on the bed buckling his sandals he noticed a door on the wall and said,

"I think that is a connecting door to his suite. Why don't you knock and see if he answers."

Lorraine went to the door and opened it to reveal another door. She turned the knob but the door did not open. Then she knocked a few times and waited. She knocked again and yelled,

"Bennie, I know you're in there, it's Lorraine."

She knocked again much harder this time, "Bennie, Bennie! He's not answering."

Finally she closed her door locked it and walked away.

I'd fallen asleep or maybe just passed out. I thought I'd heard knocking from the other bedroom. It was 5:20 PM and when I woke this time I didn't feel right at all. It felt like I had the flu and was coming down with a fever. My clothes were cold and damp like being wrapped in a soggy blanket.

"Bennie, Bennie!"

I heard my name from the other side of the door and could see it shake with each knock.

"Hey man wakeup, you gonna sleep all day?"

It made me feel so much better to hear Ronald's voice. I tried to yell and forgot the cloth was stuffed in my mouth, and all that did was make it slip further down my throat. I was choking on it now and the more I gagged the more it went down. I heard them walk away and I was close to panic. I tried to calm down and breathe through my nose. I knew the sun was setting because the shadows in my room were much longer than before. I relaxed some and prayed for this nightmare to end. I knew Ronald and Lorraine were here and they would discover me, I just didn't know when. I wanted to try and cough the gag from my throat but I was scared it would slip down further and choke me for good.

When they reached the elevator Lorraine looked puzzled.

"Something doesn't feel right," she said.

"Like what?" Ronald replied as he watched the numbers on the elevator panel light up.

The door opened and two people got off and went in different directions but Lorraine and Ronald did not get on.

"Maybe he's not in there and he forgot to take the do not disturb sign off," Ronald said.

The elevator door started to close and Ronald pushed the button to stop it.

"You're right," she said, "I can hear him telling us some story already."

They got on the elevator deciding to have a drink at the bar and an hour and a half and several margaritas later Lorraine went to the front desk to leave a message in Bennie's box. She got a piece of paper from the woman behind the desk and when she finished writing she folded it and said,

"Excuse me, when Mr. Reeves comes in can you give him this message?"

The clerk took the paper and put it into slot marked 917.

"Miss, are all those messages in that box for Mr. Reeves?" Lorraine said.

"Yes ma'am."

"Why are there are so many?"

"Mr. Reeves left instructions for all his messages to be held."

"Held until when?"

"He didn't say."

"This doesn't sound right. Can you look in his box and see if he left anything for me and my husband?"

The clerk looked through all the messages until she found an envelope with Lorraine and Ronald's name and gave it to her.

"When we checked in, I asked if there were any messages for us," Lorraine said furiously.

"I don't know why it was in his box, it should have been in yours, I'm very sorry."

Lorraine faked a smile and said nothing. She went back to the table in the lounge and gave Ronald the envelope. When he opened it they were stunned. It was a letter written like a last request stating if he were not seen again what should be done with his property. After finishing the letter Ronald and Lorraine gloomily looked at each other and headed back to the front desk. Lorraine wanted to get into the room and see what was going on because of the do not disturb sign and came up with a plan.

"Miss, we have a problem. My husband and I are worried about Mr. Reeves. When was the last time he spoke to anyone or was seen?"

"I wouldn't know. Today I started work at 5:00pm and I think I saw him about five days ago."

"Five days ago!" They both interrupted.

"Yes, he came down and sat around the lounge for a while then left."

"Was he with anyone?" Ronald asked.

"No, he was alone."

Lorraine reached in her purse for the envelope. She didn't open it; she just showed it to the clerk.

"This is the envelope you just gave me. It has very disturbing news in it and we want to go up to his room and see if he's all right!"

"I'm sorry Mrs. Jefferson but I can't give you keys to his room."

"Well come with us, we don't care!" Ronald said.

"I can't leave the front desk unattended. Only the manager or hotel security can enter a room without the guest's permission."

"Then get them over here!" Lorraine yelled.

Heads turned in the lobby towards the direction of the front desk.

"Mrs. Jefferson the manager and chief of hotel security are in a meeting. They should be finished within the hour."

"It's almost 8:00pm and we can't wait. Mr. Reeves is a wealthy man, he may have been kidnapped or,"

Lorraine couldn't bring herself to say the rest. Now the young lady seemed flustered and perplexed. Ronald spoke a bit softer this time.

"What is your name?"

"My name is Nancy, sir."

"Nancy, Mr. Reeves and I have been friends since we were kids, we're like family. Now I'm going up to his room with or without your permission, so call the police if you have to."

And with those last words he told Lorraine to come with him. He turned away and began walking to the elevator. Lorraine tried talking to Nancy again in desperation,

"Nancy can you understand we are worried? None of his family or friends has spoken to him in more than a week."
Lorraine put her hand on Nancy's and said,

"I don't want my husband to get in any trouble."

Nancy reached for the phone and finally agreed. Lorraine ran to the elevator to stop Ronald. When they came back to the desk Nancy had just hung up the phone.

"One of the maids assigned to that floor will meet you at his door and let you in."

"Thank you, thank you so much," Lorraine said.

I had been lying on my side thinking of more pleasant times and searching for courage. I could see the sun fading from the Obeni reducing the light in the room even more. I lacked the strength to turn around enough to see it completely. If Whende was there I didn't want to see her and if she had been watching me she never said a word. Just the thought of her made the anger in me rise and swell inside my head and always I had the same question, why.... why Whende?

I closed my eyes and thought I heard voices outside my door. I could hear the lock turning and when I saw the door crack I thanked God for not leaving me. Three sets of legs walked in and then I heard Lorraine scream. Ronald ran over to me and kneeled by my side while Lorraine stood a few feet away with her hands covering her mouth.

"Is he alive?" Lorraine asked.

I looked up at her and then back and Ronald.

"Yes, he's alive," he said.

He pulled the gag from my mouth and bent down closer to my face. I tried to speak but could not. My mouth was moving but no sound was coming out. I tried again until finally I whispered the word, "water."

Lorraine ran into the bathroom. The maid was still in the doorway terrified to come in. Ronald untied the ropes from my wrists and feet. Then Lorraine came back with a glass of water and a hand towel. She gave the glass to Ronald with trembling hands spilling some of the water. Without moving me, he held the glass to my lips and I took a sip and then another.

Lorraine said,

"I'm calling the police!"

Before I took another sip and I was able to speak more clearly and I quickly said in a defiant whisper,

"No police."

Lorraine looked at me strangely and stepped away from the phone. I sat up with a little assistance resting my back against the bed. I took a few more sips then told them to send the maid away and call a doctor.

Within an hour the police came and went along with the manager of the hotel, and the chief of security. It was my guess the maid tipped them off. I didn't answer anyone's questions when they came. I pretended to be to sick and too confused to remember. While the doctor was there he suggested I check into the hospital. His diagnosis was a case of severe dehydration and hypothermia. One or two more days would have killed me. I refused to go to the hospital so he prescribed some of vitamins and a very bland diet for a day or two to give my system a chance to readjust.

Everyone was gone except Ronald and Lorraine. They sat on the couch holding hands across the room watching me lying on the bed. I knew they were waiting for everyone to leave so they could hear the real story and I knew it would be a hard pill to swallow. They continued holding hands never taking their eyes off me. I looked at the Obeni, then back at them and said,

"Thanks for saving my life. I don't know how long I could've held on."

I remembered thinking about all those Africans kidnapped from their land and chained in the bottom of slave ships for months, coming up once a week for exercise and to be washed off. I had called on their spirits to give me strength and they comforted me.

Ronald and Lorraine hadn't said anything yet so I broke the silence.

"You wouldn't believe me if I told you."

"Well let's see," Ronald said, "if it's strange, it's got to come from you."

I Laughed at Ronald's statement hoping it would ease the tension while looking at the Obeni and shaking my head.

"Yes that's an interesting piece. The manager was looking at it for a long time. What is it?" Lorraine asked.

"It's called an Obeni."

"That's nice," she said pleasantly, "now what the fuck happened to you! When we read this note we got worried."
She snatched the envelope from her purse and shook it at me. I was touched by her concern and felt I had misjudged her.

"I'm telling you, you wouldn't believe me."

"Honey, if he says that one more time I'll," Lorraine said while removing her hand from his.

"Okay, okay," I said then took a deep breath, and started to explain.

"For the past three of four days I've been in Egypt. I went back in time to the year 12.820 B.C. give or take a hundred years."
Their heads turned in unison until they were looking at each other. It took one smirk from Ronald and they were laughing uncontrollably doubling over from the pain. I found myself laughing too and it felt good after all I'd been through.

"No I'm serious," I said between my own laughter. "I went through the Obeni and met a princess."

They were hysterical now holding each other trying not to fall off the couch.

"You met a princess," he said jokingly as they both continued laughing.

"How did you do that? Did you fly there on a rocket ship?"

"I told you, you wouldn't believe me."

"Oh no, we believe you,"
He strained to keep a straight face and I tried to be serious again.

"It's not a ship, it's a door."

"Ohhh it's a door, I understand."
By now they were falling on each other holding their sides.

Despite all I had seen in the past few days I was delighted to hear their laughter and glad to be in my time where I belonged. I said nothing more until the laughter subsided. When we started to talk again I asked Ronald to stand on the chair and remove the metal disks from the slots. Whende had lied about something and I wasn't taking any more chances. For all I knew I could wake up and have to confront those bastards again here in my room. Once he'd removed the disks I assured both of them I was safe and promised to explain everything in the morning. I turned over, wrapping myself in the blanket facing away from the Obeni. Ronald and Lorraine left the room through the adjoining door after looking back at me several times. I knew they didn't believe me, but tomorrow morning they would have no choice.

The next morning I woke up filled with regret and got angry again that Whende had sent me away. She threw me back into the water like an unwanted fish. Yes I had opened my eyes this morning from a dream I could not entirely recall but I knew I had been dreaming of her.

I had no idea what time it was when the knock came from the other side of the adjoining door. Slowly I got out of bed went to the door and opened it. Ronald asked how I had slept while he pushed a cart with food into my room. I shook my head not really answering pretending to still be groggy while I stumbled into the bathroom. He explained how their flight was delayed and how they were so late getting there. I looked in the bathroom mirror and saw new lines in my face and bags under my eyes.

When I walked back into the room Ronald was standing next to the cart. When I got close enough to see he took the cover off. It was corn flakes in a bowl with a tall glass of milk on the side. He told me he ordered this because the doctor said I'd need light foods for the first day or so. Then he looked at me and said,

"How long have we known each other?"

"Ahh shit," I said.

I knew it was about to get serious up in here, but I gave my patented answer,

"We were about seven or eight when we met so I figure we've known each other about twenty years or more."

"I told Lorraine I would come over and talk to you first," he said.

I poured the milk in the bowl of cereal and added some sugar. Then I took the spoon and scooped some up but before I ate I said,

"It might be simpler if you get those metal disks and put them back in the slots."

I was still eating when he returned and put the disks in place. Then he stepped down pulling the chair close to me to have a seat.

"What's this all about Bennie?"

"Just give it a few minutes," I said slyly, while I continued chewing.

"The doctor said you've been tied in this room at least three days. Who did this to you?"

"The only way for you to believe me is to show you."

We sat alone while I ate my cereal. Each time Ronald tried to muster up a sentence I stopped him insisting on his patience. I'd finished the cereal and the juice when a single beam of light came from the Obeni. As the light grew it took the shape of the sun and grains of sand grew brighter. Everything was as it was before. Her house was there but the chair next to the pool was gone. I could still see the entrance to her bedroom. Ronald was flabbergasted as he rose from the chair to take a closer look.

"Be careful not to touch the glass. It gives you a freezing burning sensation," I warned.

But he never got close enough to touch it, nor did he want to.

"That's where I've been for the past three days; I found a way to crossover!"

Neither one of us noticed how long Lorraine had been standing in the room. And I was like a spoiled child repeating to her,

"You see! You see it right?"

They both said nothing.

I looked on the cart for something else to eat. There were still two pieces of buttered toast left. I took a bite and began reluctantly to tell them everything. I also knew how long it took to convince myself what I was seeing was real so before anyone could say it was a movie projection I started to ramble.

I told them how I thought the room had been bugged when I first got here. How I thought I was on a game show and this was all a fake, and how I went over every inch of the room for any projection devices. Then I explained my cab trips across town and my argument with Candice from the antique shop. I explained everything as fast as I talked without even giving myself a chance to breathe. My explanation took less than a few minutes to bring them up to date. It would have taken a bit longer but I purposely left out the way I crossed over and I never told them the true nature of my relationship with Whende. It hurt too much to think of the time we'd spent together and the agonizing way she rejected me.

Ronald did the same thing I did when I first saw the Obeni work. He looked all over the room and when he couldn't find anything he sat down. He was about to speak but Lorraine interrupted and said,

"Bennie you're so full of shit!"

She stood with her hands on her hips and said,

"I'll tell you what happened. You were here for a couple of days and you met some woman. You brought her up here and she robbed your ass! And I hope she robbed you before she fucked you!"

"Calm down baby," Ronald said.

"Na, Na fuck that! That's why I always call your ass a dog."

My eyes flared up at Lorraine because she knows I hate being referred to as a dog. My mouth was opening when she started again.

"You got Terri in New York crying her eyes out because you had some woman in your room and couldn't make time to talk to her. Then you refused her messages when she called back!"

I was about to have another one of those heated arguments with her.

"Yeah, you didn't think I knew about that did you Bennie?"

"No one was here!" I replied loudly.

"Who's Dari?" Lorraine asked.

"Dari?"

"Yes mother fucker, Dari?" She yelled holding a small piece of paper.

It felt like I'd been here so long I'd forgotten about the stewardess I'd met on the plane.

"She's someone I met, but I never called her."

"Oh you didn't, cause everyone at the hotel says you have been knocking boots and getting fresh towels every day," she said. Lorraine's head looked like it was about to explode.

"Bennie you must think Ronald and I are stupid. You have to because if no one was here then.... how the fuck did you get tied up? I'll tell you, this woman Dari turned the tables on your ass!" she said still holding the telephone number.

It didn't bother me that she was almost right. What was starting to bother me was Ronald allowing her to yell at me so much. And I accepted it because I knew I wasn't being totally honest with them.

"You scared us half to death, almost sent my husband to jail for breaking your door down, and all you can do is come up with this bullshit story. Well you're not going to ruin our vacation with a magic show!"

She stormed out of the room and through the connecting door and slammed it shut.

"She doesn't believe me," I said.

"Can you blame her? Look what you're asking us to consider. You went back in time like H. G. Wells?"

"Ron look at the Obeni! Can't you see it?"

"I see it," he said, "but what I don't see is how you got tied up."

"I don't want to talk about it!"

"Bennie, is anyone after you?"

"Not anymore," I said sadly.

Slowly I took a seat and stared into the Obeni. I was tired of talking. So much had transpired this week and I just wanted to rest and go home.

He turned and walked towards the adjoining door and before he went through he said,

"Get some rest buddy I'll see you later."

So I sat in the chair looking at the canvas rippling in the doorway from the light breeze. I asked myself again if maybe I had imagined it all. I had only to feel the pain in my ribs and see the rope burns on my wrists to know it had not been a dream.

I stood up to take the disks out when I thought I saw a hand pulling the canvas back so I sat down and waited. If it was Whende I didn't want to see her but I still wasn't able to move from the chair. She came from behind the canvas in a long white sleeveless dress. She looked like the first day I saw her, strong and invincible. She walked to the far side of the pool with her head high in a slow gracious rhythm. I was about to knock on Ronald's door when she looked right at me. She squinted her eyes and moved closer. My heart raced with anticipation and regret bordering on anger. When she got close enough to see me tears rolled down both sides of her cheeks with a sigh of liberation.

"Are you well? I thought I would not see thee more."

I was mystified and I could not understand her reaction. Ignoring her question I gave her a vile stare.

"You must speak Bennie."

"Why Whende?"

"I could not tell you the danger."

"Whende I don't care anymore."

I stood up dragging the chair and walked over to remove the disks. When I got closer I refused to look at her. I stood on the chair to remove the disks and she said,

"Please forgive me, my love?"

I froze and when I looked down our eyes met. Her face was filled with exhaustion and her eyes were bloodshot.

"I could not let you be slain."

"Who would slay me Whende?"

She took a deep breath to steady herself and started to explain. She wiped the tears from her face again then told me that the man who came into her room and hit me was Kfaru and he's in charge of all the guards who protect her. She said he was a jealous man who watched her constantly. Before I came through the Obeni he watched Whende talk to me one day from a distance. He even sent a spy who saw me in the water sleeping in my hotel room. The spy told him there was a spirit in her pool and she had control over it. Whende told me how she regretted keeping the secret from me. Once I was with her she thought she could tell her people I was from the distant island of Mears. She said the people spoke a different language there. Then after I arrived she found out one of Kfaru's spies had seen me sleeping under the water and that excuse couldn't be used. Then she told me after we returned from the carriage ride Kfaru's gave orders I was not to see another sunrise. There was no way for her to warn me, and the only choice she had was to send me back.

I knew homeboy didn't like me and I had no idea jealousy and murder existed back then. Whende continued to tell me how she thought of a plan to send me back. She told the guards I had violated her, which gave her the right to choose my execution.

"Was that why you were crying that night?" I said.

"Yes my love. No man wanted me the way I was. No man has ever listened to me without feeling threatened by my knowledge."

I watched a tear roll down past her nose to the corner of her mouth and down her chin. That tear melted the last piece of ice I had left in my heart.

"That first night you laid with me... no man has touched me the way you did."

"I thought you didn't want me and sent me back."

She put her hand in a leather pouch tied to a waste and pulled out a small gold plate.

"I had the sakeon make it from my memory," she said.

It was the gold piece I saw in the Aswan shop that carried my likeness.

Instantly she started running away and stopped beckoning me to wait. Whende entered the house and returned with the parrot perched on her hand.

"Someone misses you," she said while she rubbed the bird's head and it said,

"I love you, I love you."

For the second time I doubted her and was proved wrong and it showed on my face.

"What troubles you?"

"I forgot to thank you for rescuing me. My life has been saved twice in less than a week, once by you and again by my friends here."

"Two by me," she smiled.

"I don't understand."

Then she explained there was no way I could remember. When I was coming through the Obeni to her side she saw just my hand above the water and my face was in great pain. Once my entire body came through, I sank to the bottom. She said she didn't know what to do so she waited but when I didn't move she jumped in and pulled me out of the pool. She said I wasn't breathing and that she had learned a way to save someone who'd drowned. She said she rolled me on my stomach and pushed on my back until the water came out but I still wasn't breathing. Then she blew air into my mouth until I coughed and started breathing once again. I looked at her having no recollection of what she done but was twice as grateful.

"I wish it could have been different Whende."

She stood there happy now that I was safe but I was still longing to be with her.

"So what will you do now," I said.

"The festival of Simbel is soon. There will be much celebration and I will miss you."

She touched the pouch on her side and asked, "What will you do with the Obeni?"

"I will never live long enough to use it again so I will stay here and talk with you until Yemot's comet is gone."

"No Bennie there is still danger. I cannot see you anymore. They want to see your slain body. I told them I burned you and they think I'm untrue."

There was a knock on the door and when it opened it was Ronald and Lorraine. They walked in and I didn't say anything. I just waited for them to see her. Whende stared at them with the same commanding look she'd given me that first day. Lorraine saw her first and her expression made Ronald look. They were both like statues and I took great satisfaction from their fear and began walking towards the Obeni and Whende said,

"Goodbye my love. I will pray to the creators we meet again someday."

She turned and walked towards the house and never looked back. We watched as she disappeared behind the canvas in the doorway. Ronald and Lorraine rubbed their eyes and foreheads grimacing with incomprehension. They looked comical but it wasn't funny because in them I saw myself, and how I must have looked that first day. At once Lorraine bolted through the adjoining door gasping for air as if she seen a ghost and Ronald took off after her. I thought about following them but decided to let all they had seen sink in. Through the open door I could hear Ronald trying to calm Lorraine down. Whende gave such a chilling look before she walked away giving acknowledgment, but never bothering to speak to them.

After some moments of silence I heard Ronald call me to come in to their room. When I went inside he was standing talking on the phone. When I got a little closer I heard him say,

"Yes Terri he's all right, he's right here."

I stood still not knowing what to do. I knew I had to speak to her but I was not ready. Before he gave me the phone he cupped his hand over the receiver and said,

"We didn't say anything about what happened."

Like that was supposed to make me feel better. When I took the phone Ronald walked to the curtains and unlocked the glass door and stepped out onto the balcony.

"Hi Terri, I'm sorry you haven't heard from me. I tried to call you a couple of times and I left the messages."

"Are you all right?" she said sounding very reserved.

"Yes I'm fine and I know I have a lot of explaining to do."

There was silence on her end. Lorraine exited the bathroom and stood next to me with a spiteful look and said,

"When you finish talking, I want to speak to her."

"Sure," I said.

Then I told her Ronald was out on the balcony.

"Are you still there?"

"Yes," Terri said.

I could think of nothing to say without explaining the whole situation so I asked,

"Where are you?"

"I'm here at your house."

"That's great," I said as the awkward silence continued. I was the one who messed up and it was up to me to make it right.

"Terri, I'm taking the first plane home."

Still she said nothing but I could hear her occasionally breathing.

"I miss you," I said.

"Bennie, do you love me? Cause I want to know right now."

"Yes I do."

I thought I heard a sigh of relief.

"I have a lot to tell you when you get home," she said.

"I kind of got sick while I was here. Maybe it was the food or the water."

"But you're okay now?" Terri asked.

"The doctor said I was a little dehydrated."

"Is there anything I can do?"

"No baby, I just need to eat light and I'll be on the first plane out of here."

"I want you to be healthy when you get here because you know I'm gonna kick your ass."

"Come on baby."

"Do you know how much I worried about you?"

"Yes."

"So when you get here take your ass whipping like a man."

"Okay baby I'll talk to you tomorrow."

I tried to get her off the phone while things were still going good.

"Before I forget Lorraine wants to talk to you," I said reluctantly.

"Tell her I have to run out and I'll talk to her later."

"I'll tell her."

"I love you Bennie."

With some hesitation I said,

"I love you too."

I told Lorraine Terri said she had to go and would talk to her later but she didn't believe me.

Back in my room I was about to call the front desk for a 4:00 AM wake up call and changed my mind. I wanted to sleep until I felt like getting up. I closed the adjoining door and lie across the bed. A half an hour ago I told Terri I loved her and it was too late to take it back.

I looked into the Obeni at Whende's house for the last time and decided to remove the disks. I knew she wouldn't come back to the pool until the comet was gone. Still questions I tried to repress haunted me. If Whende made the mask of me after seeing me, how could the old woman from the Aswan shop have it before I went back in time? If it wasn't me why did it look like me? Most likely it would be a riddle I would never solve. So my mind turned to more pleasant things. What did Dr. Morrison say Whende's life would be like?

When I visited Dr. Morrison at the University a week ago he told me the Princess was the first educated woman of her time and Afermose's favorite daughter. She later married Kfaru and would have children. I also remembered him saying Whende would die an old woman outliving Kfaru. Damn, Homeboy is going to have her after all, but there was some fulfillment knowing Whende would always think of me.

Chapter 11

It was about noon the next day when I answered the phone. It was Ronald calling to tell me they were going out to see the city. I told him I would see them later and tried to go back to sleep but it was useless. My dreams were so peaceful last night. Everything was right and I felt like I'd been given a second chance to enjoy my life as it was. Never would I stand on the banks of the Hudson River like I planned but I was satisfied with the time I had with Whende and all I had seen.

When I was ready to get up, I felt hungry but much better than yesterday. My vigor was returning and the vitamins the doctor gave me were working. From the phone I ordered breakfast from room service. I had no trouble holding down my food yesterday so I decided to order anything I wanted. I asked for pancakes with scrambled eggs and ham, with a side of home fries, toast and coffee. Plus an English muffin with well-done corned beef hash, orange juice, and some assorted fresh fruit. There was no way I could eat all of this food but I didn't care. I just wanted a little of everything. While I was on the phone I asked for all my messages to be brought up with my breakfast and for a reservation on the next flight home. The clerk at the front desk said he would get back to me when he had the information.

While I waited for the breakfast to arrive I took a shower and got dressed. When I looked in the mirror the weight I lost was perceptible. My face was looked gaunt as if I'd been sick. Nothing some food and more rest wouldn't fix I thought.

When I was done showering I went back to the bedroom and turned on the TV. I was still a little weak and wanted to go back to bed instead I sat in the loveseat and put my feet up. This was the first time I turned on the television set since I'd been here. Most every channel was in

Arabic but still I watched a movie and tried interpreting the meanings.

Room service came and the cart was full. I signed the bill and gave the bellboy a tip. After my previous efforts to make everyone think I was just a normal guy, he seemed nervous being here. I can only imagine the rumors that were going around the hotel and I knew they would be more than happy to see me go. I was also glad I moved the Obeni against the far wall and covered it. Then it occurred to me the Obeni would never survive the trip if it were not carefully wrapped. It would have to be packed in a crate and that might take some time and different travel arrangements.

As soon as room service closed the door I headed for the cart and pulled it in front of the loveseat. When I lifted the first metal top from the plate it was scrambled eggs with corned beef hash. There was nobody to impress and I snatched the fork and started eating and this time I ate like a hungry man. I was still chewing when I lifted the next top. All four pancakes were golden brown with a wad of butter melting into center. Reaching for the syrup I poured generously until it ran down the side of the plate. I was so glad no one was here to see me. While tasting the pancakes I wondered if it was too late to order some Belgian waffles. Instead I lifted the next top to unveil a generous portion of sliced ham with bits of onions and green peppers cut up in the home fries. Under a cloth napkin in a basket I found eight slices of buttered toast with assorted freshly baked muffins and a small saucer with packets of jelly. The last basket had fresh oranges, apples, grapes, cherries and strawberries. It reminded me of a still life ready for painting but not for long. So I sat like a king eating some of this and a little of that.

When I finished I reached for the messages. I took off the rubber band that kept them together. The first one was from Terri and the next one was too. Then there was one from Ronald saying he would call back with his flight information. Normally I would have thrown them all away but I had nothing else to do. There was one from my sister and another one from Terri and Ronald. This message gave the day and time Ronald and Lorraine would arrive. There was one more message and it was the most chilling of all. It was from Dr. Morrison. It said please call for more information about the murder of Princess Sakatet.

I read this note over and over again. It had to be a mistake so I quickly reached for the phone to clear it up. I held the note in my hand while the phone was ringing. Why would he say murder?

"Hello, Cairo University," the voice said.

"Hello, may I speak with Dr. Morrison at extension thirty six please." I was put on hold and my head started to pound. It had to be a mistake. We discussed Whende's family that day and he never said anything about anyone being murdered. My finger was in my mouth looking for a nail to bite. He probably looked up someone else and got confused.

"Hello, Dr. Morrison speaking."

"Dr. Morrison it's Benjamin Reeves."

"Yes Mr. Reeves, what can I do for you?"

"Dr., I'm calling about the message you left. I'm just receiving it now."

"Really, I called you a few days ago."

"I'm sorry Dr. I've been away."

"That's quite all right young man. You said it was your first visit to Cairo. Have you seen anything interesting?"

My head was hurting too much and only the right words from him could make it go away.

"Doc, I'm concerned with the note you left me about the murder of Princess Sakatet. She wasn't murdered. You told me she died of old age!"

"I never told you that."

"I'm sorry doctor but you did! You told me she married Kfaru and they had some children."

"Son you're mistaken, I told you Kfaru killed her."

"No you didn't!" I insisted, "You told me she was Afermose's favorite daughter."

"Yes Mr. Reeves I told you that. It's true she was his favorite daughter."

"Doc, I don't understand."

"Mr. Reeves I have been studying Egyptology more than thirty years. There were a lot of kings, queens, princesses and royal families that stretched for thousands of years. I don't make mistakes like that," he said firmly.

191

I didn't want to get him angry and this was getting me nowhere so I politely asked him to refresh me on the Princess.

"Please tell me about her again sir."

"Well let's see, she lived in the year 3200 B.C. and was one of Afermose's favorite daughters."

For someone who studied Egyptology for thirty years he didn't know he had the date wrong, and now was not the time for debate. To try and explain to him it was three times longer than he said I would need to tell him how I knew and I wasn't about to do that, so I let him continue.

"Her mother Kymeka was Afermose's most trusted wife. She convinced Afermose to allow Princess Sakatet to pursue an education. Later Kfaru a high ranking soldier courted her. Sometime before the festival of Simbell, Kfaru accused Sakatet of conversing with a demon from the water. It is written Sakatet brought this demon into the world of the living and copulated with it. The water demon under her command almost killed Kfaru so all the priests who were jealous of her passion for knowledge used this opportunity to accuse her of Devil worship and sorcery. I believe Kfaru's jealousy had the princess killed after the festival of Simbell. Now that's what I told you when I met you right Mr. Reeves. Mr. Reeves are you there?"

What was going on here? I distinctly remember what he told me that first day. If he said Whende was going to be murdered I would have warned her.

"Yes I'm here."

There was such a lump in my throat I couldn't speak at first.

"The reason I left you a message Mr. Reeves was because when we spoke I couldn't recall when they killed her."

Dr. Morrison changing his story about Whende wasn't as bad as him telling me about a conversation I had no recollection of.

"I also searched for the meaning of Obeni. There is one in the museum here in Cairo," he said.

I remember asking him about the Obeni and the books he recommended I read.

"The Obeni is an instrument for measuring time like an hourglass filled with a metal ore of some kind."

I began to wonder if a crazy person knew when they had lost control.

192

The Obeni in my room had always been a secret so I asked, "Doc do you know where the other Obeni is?"

"What other Obeni? Do you think there is more than one?"

"I don't know I just thought..."

"Mr. Reeves how long will you be in Cairo?"

"At least a few more days," I said.

"We may talk again if I find more information on the princess or the Obeni. And please feel free to call me if you have any questions."

"Doc, are you sure she was killed?"

"According to the texts... yes," he answered.

"I can't believe it, I just can't."

"You're taking this quite hard. It was more than five thousand years ago and yes I'm sure. Now if you'll excuse me I must be going."

"Doctor Morrison one more thing, do you know anyone named Ept, or Yemot the son of Jonen."

"In what dynasty?" He asked.

"I'm not sure maybe between 15 or 20 thousand mala ago."

"Did you say mala?"

"I mean years."

"I know," he said astonished, "mala means years in a very old Egyptian dialect. You've been reading some books during your visit I see."

I needed an answer so I said,

"Yes but I'm not sure of what book it was."

"Are you sure about the time? That's pretty far back."

"Yes."

"I'll look it up but right now, no I've never heard those names before."

"Thank you Doc, you've been a big help."

When I put the phone down I was extremely shaken by the news of Whende's impending death. I knew what the doctor was talking about but the reality was hard to face. I alone had changed her destiny and taken away her future. It was my intention to change events but I'd never predicted this. I was the water demon Dr. Morrison spoke of and the guilt was hard to swallow. I would be the cause of Whende's death and I had to warn her or go back and save her.

During the next hour I was in meditation and prayer. My plan was a simple one; make myself believe I could save Whende. The phone rang six times before I answered. This time it was Ronald telling me he was on his way over and now things were falling into place. I would need him to move the Obeni back to its original spot near my bed. I stood up looking for any trace or compression in the carpet where the legs of Obeni had been. The maid vacuumed once and with all the foot traffic there were no imprints left.

When I opened the door for Ronald he could tell I was preoccupied. I know he was telling me about his day but I wasn't listening. I thought of the three days of starvation ahead and cursed myself for thinking about just letting Whende die. Finally I heard Ronald say,

"Are you listening to me?"

"Sure," I said casually removing the sheet from the Obeni.

"Bennie what are you doing?"

"I just want to see something."

I stayed to one side of the Obeni and held the edge and waited for him to take the other side. He grabbed the other side and we moved it back to where I thought it had been.

"Why are you moving this? I thought you were gonna pack it later."

Once we stopped pushing I could tell it wasn't right but finally saw a light impression in the carpet.

"Push it just a little more to the right," I said.

"All right Bennie, what's going on?"

I gave him my full attention and said,

"I have to go back."

He knew what I meant but he asked anyway, "Back where?"

"They're going to kill her and it's my fault. I've got to go back!"

"Kill who?"

"Kill Whende," I said solemnly.

"The one we saw yesterday?"

"Yes."

"You told me she died of old age."

" That's what Dr. Morrison told me before I left. If I didn't cross over she would have lived to be an old woman. I changed her destiny and he's going to kill her because of me."

"Who is?"

"A guy named Kfaru."

194

"How is that possible?"

"They think she can summon evil spirits."

I was pacing the room with nowhere to go just walking continually.

"I'm not going back empty-handed. I need a knife or something."

"Hey Buddy wait a minute. Have you thought about how ridiculous you sound?"

"Yes."

"If you think about it she's all ready dead. She's just a pile of dust now!"

I stopped walking and said calmly with a smile,

"If you think about it she's alive right now."

"Man I can't let you do this. You're in no condition to starve your self again."

"Your right, that's why I'm trying to find a drug I can take to speed up the dehydration,"

When he stood there and I knew he was thinking of something he could say to change my mind.

"Bennie let's say for a minute I believe some of what you're saying. The doctor said you could have died in this room. What hold does this woman have on you?"

"It's not like that."

"Was it because of her we found you tied up?"

"Yes," I said halfheartedly.

The image was starting to appear in the Obeni but it was somehow different. We stood and watched until everything was finally clear and it was not the same place. Whende's house was not in the background. Even Ronald noticed and was somewhat relieved.

"That's not the same place," he said quickly.

"I know," I said looking at the scenery and wondering what I did wrong. In the distant corner I saw the skinny bridge we traveled across.

"That's about four or five miles from her house."

"Are you sure?"

"Oh yeah, I'll never forget that bridge."

Ronald was still talking while I continued to think. This body of water was probably a reservoir for the city. If I came through there it might be too dangerous. It was very secluded and I had no idea how deep the water was or whether I would come through in the middle and have to swim to the edge.

"I don't think this is going to work."

"Thank you! Finally you're listening to me."

I went to the Obeni and looked down at the carpet. One side could be pushed back just a little more.

"Tell me if it changes," I said and began nudging the left side back. "How's that?"

He looked silently then walked to the loveseat. I went to the front of the Obeni and looked for myself. Whende's house was there but it was a little different. Before I only saw only the corner of her bedroom with the two windows and the door in between. Now much more of her house could be seen and the tree that was in the background was gone.

"There it is Homey," I said trying to sound sure of myself.

"Bennie do you love Whende?" He said, "Do you?"

I heard his question but ignored the content.

"No I don't, I mean I could but right now I don't."

"So why risk your life for a woman you don't love?"

I felt like he had not been listening to me all this time.

"Because it's my fault!" I yelled.

"You said that before and it's all bullshit!"

"Haven't you ever..." I searched for the words to explain myself,

"Haven't you ever wanted to be the cavalry? Or be like John Wayne, or better yet Shaft? You know, busting through the window to save the girl."

"You're corny as shit Bennie!"

"No wait a minute, do you remember when we were kids, and we always wanted to be the good guys, especially you Ron?"

I had his interest now and couldn't stop.

"Remember that night we wanted to run those junkies out of our neighborhood? So we all dressed up in dark clothes that night."

I had him smiling now so I continued,

"Nothing was gonna stop us that night remember? We got tired of seeing them come into our block. We knew one day it might be your mother on my mother or Mark's mother who might get robbed by those fools."

"Yes I remember."

"We bought smoke bombs from the store and planned an assault. Then we met after midnight outside in the park when our folks were asleep. I even took my father's .32 from under his pillow. Remember? We were kids then but we were serious."

"I know," Ron said.

"And you remember what we did?"

"Yes."

Our plan was successful and what happened that night was always kept between the group of us. That night six of us from the neighborhood armed ourselves and surprised the junkies sleeping in the basement of a near by apartment building. We were only teens but we threw firecrackers and fired shots into the basement while yelling for them to leave our block.

"Well that's what I'm doing now. I can't let Whende die because of me."

"You know Ben, when I was leaving New York I saw one of the newspapers and the article was about Halley's Comet and..."

I interrupted him furiously, "Yemot's Comet!"

"Yemot?"

"Yes, Yemot. He saw the comet way before Halley was born."

"Anyway the comet is leaving earth's orbit. You told us the Obeni works with the comet. You don't have that many days left. And what are you going to do when you find her? Are you going to bring her back with you?"

"She can't come forward. It would mean death to all she knows."

"So what are you telling me, you're not coming back?"

"I don't know, I haven't thought that far yet."

"I can tell, because if you had you wouldn't be going!"

He put his hand on my shoulder and said,

"You've been like our brother to me and, my best friend so I can't let you go buddy."

"You can't let me go!" I snapped.

"I'm going and there's nothing you can do about it!"

He wanted to say something but changed his mind. Instead he said very strangely,

"You're right, I'll see you later."

Shortly after Ronald left, I removed the discs from the Obeni and hid them in my suitcase with the dirty clothes. The incentive to save Whende's life had brought new meaning to my own. I was not about to wait for Ronald to come back with Lorraine so I could continue arguing. I locked the adjoining door and went to the lobby for a taxi. When I walked past the front desk the clerk told me my plane reservations were ready and I canceled them.

I was about to ask the doorman where I could find a pharmacy but we had caused so much commotion in the hotel lately, I kept my mouth shut. Instead I got the name of the Umall pharmacy from my cab driver. I had just eaten a huge breakfast but maybe instead of starving myself for three days, I could leave in two with the pharmacist's help. Since I didn't have a complete plan or a plausible excuse to use at the drugstore, I decided to go to the Cairo Museum first. Dr. Morrison told me there was an Obeni at the museum and I was curious to see it again. It was possible the museum held clues to a successful rescue attempt.

The museum was a gray four story building with many steps leading up to the main entrance similar to the Museum of Natural History. Once inside I went straight to the information desk and asked the woman what floor would I see Egyptian artifacts? She found my question amusing then told me the whole museum was filled with them. I was more specific this time and asked where they displayed the jewelry Egyptians wore and the furniture they used. Then she told me I could start on the second floor and work my way down.

When the elevator door opened on the second floor I saw the entrance to a tomb the size of a two car garage. A burgundy velvet rope kept spectators from going in or touching the stones. They must have excavated this and brought it back to the museum stone by stone. The smooth columns and rectangular stones where just like the ones in the front of Whende's house. When the people standing in front of the exhibit moved I went over to read the small sign. It gave a brief summary of when it was found and how it was retrieved from the Valley of the Kings. The date it was built was estimated at 2726 B.C. I stood looking at the date admitting to myself how hard it was going to be to rescue Whende. What happened if I got back and couldn't find her? There was no way I could communicate with her once I returned. Then if I were able to rescue her, what would I do then? How could I keep an army of guards from killing us? If I could think of a way to beat all those guards I might have a chance. If I could bring something from the future to help me defend myself it might work.

Whenever I tried to find something it was always in the last place I searched. This time I found what I was looking for in the first room I went to. In the far corner in a display case was the second Obeni. Most of it was broken except for the symbols around the borders. The wooden arch on top that held the discs was intact but empty. To the left of the Obeni frame was a display table five feet long covered in glass. It contained earrings, necklaces, rings, and bracelets made of ivory and semi precious stones. There was a comb with a gold handle that resembled a fancy Afro pick and in the case next to the comb where two discs like mine. Whende said there were three Obeni`s made and I knew I had the only one that worked. With my curiosity solved I left the museum and walked into the hot dusty air. This time my thirst for water exhilarated me. I took it as a sign of the beginning of the rescue and nothing would deter me, not even my best friend.

During the cab ride back to the hotel I thought about the conversation I had with Ronald. I knew he was very upset but he seemed very composed when he left my room. He might as well accept it because there was no way he was going to stop me.

The doorman greeted me at the cab and once inside I felt refreshed by the cool air in the lobby. Casually I headed for the elevator and was called to the front desk by the clerk. She handed me a note from Ronald and before I could open it she said,

"I hope everything is all right when your friends get home."

"What happened, did they leave?"

"Yes they left for the airport an hour ago."

"Did they say why?"

"They said it was an emergency."

I ripped the envelope open and started reading.

Dear Bennie,

Forgive me. I couldn't think of any other way to stop you from going. I took the disks from your luggage and we're catching flight 1233 to New York leaving at 5:00 pm. We left our luggage in the hotel and we will get it on the next flight. Don't call us at home because we plan to travel until the comet is gone. I couldn't think of any other way, sorry,

Your friend,
Ronald.

It was 5:20pm when I looked at my watch then I said,
  "Son of a bitch!"
  "Is something wrong, Sir?"
  I shook my head and ran towards the elevators. He wouldn't have taken them. That was the first lie I told myself. When I got my hands on him he's going to pay, and that was the second lie.
  Fumbling with the key I opened the door and ran to my bag and the discs were gone. Then I opened the hotel safe and found my cash and traveler's checks still there. I never thought he would do this to me. No wonder he was so calm when he left. We had been friends for so long and I trusted him but this really hurt. What gave him the right to make this decision for me?
  I sat on the bed trying not to think of Whende. She was perfect for me and without those disks she was truly dead now. But in the quietness of the moment from deep inside me the question was asked again. Bennie do you love this woman? Yes, the thought came to me. And finally I said it out aloud,
  "Yes I love her."
  There was a moment of deep silence and the pain in my heart was now becoming a reflection that turned into a vision. Heavy gray clouds began drifting apart and when the sky opened I saw the discs where the sun should have been. There were two discs in the museum. A smile came to my face and energy coursed through my veins. I popped up from the bed with only my heart guiding me. There was nothing I wouldn't do short of murder to get those disks. Adrenaline was in my ears, my eyes, and my body. My best friend had betrayed me, but it was all right. No one would stop me from becoming Shaft. I closed my eyes and tried to send a spiritual message. Right now I believed I could do anything and if I tried hard she would hear me. My eyes were shut tightly and in the darkness of my mind I said, I'm coming to get you Whende.

Chapter 12

Today the sun was bright and the air crisp in New York City. The birds chirped a special tune beckoning the listener to enjoy. On a tranquil wave of happiness Terri floated to work. This morning she ignored the rudeness of her fellow passengers all the way downtown. And once she arrived at the office her co workers could see the change in her manner. They also noticed her hair was different. Terri had been to the beauty parlor yesterday in anticipation of Bennie's return.

Even her clothes were cheerful today. She wore a red miniskirt suit with a white silk blouse and red tennis shoes. In her office she kept several pair of high heels in the bottom desk drawer. All the years she worked here she'd never given anyone a reason to complain about her attire, but today she would keep her red sneakers on because they made her feel good.

For the first time in almost two weeks, Terri was glad to be at work. She put her briefcase and her purse down on the couch. When she started to take a seat at her desk, she noticed the lonely and neglected plant in the corner. After Lorraine's visit to her office, she placed the plant as far away from her as she could. Now she began to feel sorry for taking her frustrations out on it. Terri removed the plant from its desolate corner and placed it on the windowsill behind her chair. From her purse she took a bottle of spring water and carefully watered her new friend. She stroked the leaves gently and silently asked for absolution.

Monday mornings were generally busy and after checking her messages and returning a few phone calls she found it hard to concentrate. Terri spun around in the swivel chair looking past the plant and out the window at the cars moving up the Brooklyn Bridge. She crossed her legs and tapped the eraser of a pencil on her knee and began to plan something special for Bennie's homecoming.

Yesterday after leaving the beauty parlor Terri walked half a mile to the supermarket. She thought preparing a dinner at home would give them a chance to be alone. She took a shopping cart from the line and went to the meat aisle first. Unhappy with the look of the pork chops and the steak she decided the chicken looked best. The label said sell by March 27th and that date made her realize her period would come soon. If Bennie didn't arrive shortly all he would get would be a chicken dinner.

Terri put a box of stuffing into the cart and thought about how she would tease him during the night. Her actions and subtle behavior would turn him into a volcano, and if he hadn't been with anyone else, the eruption should be prompt.

She took a container of orange juice and a quart of milk. Maybe he should be punished first for all the worrying she'd done. With a smile of revenge she thought of welcoming Bennie home with passionate kisses, then remain pleasant, sweet and understanding while posing provocatively for him. Finally she would make an excuse to go, leaving him hard as nails with his damn chicken dinner.

From the baking aisle she took a box of cornbread mix and a bottle of syrup for French toast in the morning. Why didn't she stop taking her birth control pills last summer when the idea crossed her mind? If she'd become pregnant, it might have changed everything. That day she was about to start a new prescription and considered flushing her daily pill down the toilet. Terri held that first pill in her hand and time seemed to be suspended. The thought of having a baby with a man who didn't love her was a line she would never cross. Maybe that's what another woman would do to keep a man but it wasn't her style. And she would never bring up the pictures Lorraine showed her, at least not right away.

The fresh collard greens were withered and brown along the edges and the cabbages were too large. The broccoli was fresh and on sale so she took it. In a plastic bag were three hearts of Romaine lettuce and with a few grape tomatoes and some croutons she could make a nice salad. Every day while Bennie was gone she thought about why he said things would be so different when he returned. Was it possible he went away to see how much he would miss her, or was it something less complicated? Did he go halfway around the world to have one last fling to purge it from his system?

A cute little Spanish boy bagged Terri's groceries while she dropped two quarters in a cigar box next to him. Then she took a bag in each hand and left the store. She would never pressure Bennie into marrying her right away because he'd finally said the words she wanted to hear. If he had to go thousands of miles away to have his last fling to understand how much she loved him she could accept it. When he came home if things were better between them like he promised she would be satisfied because, he said he loved her. Her patience and persistence would at last be rewarded by his commitment to her, and she would finally have the man of her dreams.

A news helicopter flew high above the center of the Brooklyn Bridge and the plant Lorraine gave her was coming back to life. Today belonged to Terri and she felt whole city could see her red sneakers from the window. She hadn't been this happy in a long time. Her man was coming home and she couldn't wait to see him and say, I love you.

It was late in the afternoon when I rolled out of bed still over seas. My lips were chapped and my mouth was dry like sandpaper. When I looked in the bathroom mirror my skin looked a bit gray. Truthfully I did not feel as strong as yesterday but I disregarded my symptoms. I brushed my teeth and washed my face ignoring any temptation to drink water.

To my surprise I wasn't angry with Ronald anymore. I'd had most of the day to think and understand why he tried to stop me from going. If the situation were reversed I couldn't honestly say I wouldn't have done something similar. I likely would have offered more assistance to him but it was all contingent upon me believing his story. Even with everything he'd seen as proof, I knew my story was hard to accept. And the fact that I had left out one important detail lessened my anger toward Ronald. I never told him that I was in love with Whende. It made me realize I didn't give him any choice. He was still my buddy but he wasn't going to stop me.

The list of lies I'd told Terri in the past month had grown very long. My heavy burden of deceit was new to me and difficult to carry. I had never in my life acted this way and felt ashamed of the way I was treating her. A force was driving me and I couldn't explain it. I felt I had no choice but to go to Whende the same way those horses followed her commands.

Yesterday I found out the museum closed at 7:30pm and it was 3:00pm now. I had to get ready to leave before Terri called again or Ronald found another way to stop me. It was my plan to get into the museum a few hours before closing and find somewhere to hide then escape from the window.

Hastily I left my suite with the rest of the money I had in the safe and took a taxi to the nearest hardware store. There I bought a small flashlight and a screwdriver, some tape and a small tool for cutting glass. In the corner of the hardware store I saw one hundred and fifty feet of the thin rope mountain climbers used. If there were a way I thought I could sneak it into the museum using the rope I would have bought it. While I stood at the counter to pay, I noticed a white man with dark hair watching me. When I tried to look at his face he turned his back, and walked out the door. He seemed a bit strange but he was gone. From now on I would pay attention to see if I was being followed.

Slowly I walked up the steps to the museum with my sunglasses on. The small items I purchased fit nicely in the huge side pockets of my shorts. Casually I walked around looking for a place to hide. I'd dismissed the idea of smashing the display case glass and running out with the disks, but I kept that in the back of my mind as a last resort.

When I was upstairs, I went into the room of my desire. It was now 5:00pm, and people were still here admiring a statue of Osris. I stood in front of the display case to examine it more carefully. There was a thin line of tape the color of aluminum foil along the edges of the glass. If the glass were broken I'm sure an alarm would go off. Next I walked to the window and looked outside. Even though we were on the second floor it was a long way to jump down to the street level. The window was wired to the alarm system by a switch near the latch. When no one was watching I opened the latch but did not push the window up because this would later be my escape route.

After leaving the room I went into the hallway for more reconnaissance. Groups of people were still walking around when the janitor opened a door in the hallway to replace the mop and bucket he used to clean the floor. I walked past him while the closet door was open and looked inside. It seemed large enough to hide me and the door had a simple slam lock.

Then I went to the third floor even though it held no interest for me. It had to appear I was really fascinated with everything they had and hanging around on the second floor too long was asking for trouble. I walked into each room slowly killing time but while I was up there I took notice of the exits and stairways.

At 5:50 pm, my heart began to race and my palms were sweaty. Very soon they would ask people to leave and I refused to be herded from the museum under their watchful eyes. I went back to the second floor and took a final assessment. Eight people stood around the table looking through the glass at a brown and white beaded necklace. When I went back into the corridor two people turned and walked down the steps and now was my opportunity. I walked to the closet and placed some pamphlets near my feet. If anyone came out I would pretend to be tying my shoe. I took the small screwdriver from my pants pocket and forced it between the lock and the doorway wall. It was quiet now but the voices from the nearby room were growing louder. Straight ahead the number panel lit up above the elevator and began to blink. It was coming from the basement and it did not stop in the lobby. Finally I was able to open the door before the elevator stopped and went inside closing the door behind me. I stood in the dark afraid I'd knock something over if I moved and then I heard people talking. If I were discovered, this mission would be over before it started.

There I stood, frozen like a mannequin with my back to the door. I waited until the only sound I could hear was my heartbeat and the air coming from my nose. Then I took the flashlight from my pocket and switched it on. The closet was huge, filled with rolling buckets and a waxing machine. The mops and brooms hung in a row suspended from hooks and inches from my feet was another metal bucket with a dry mop inside. In the corner stacked against a wall were cartons of wax, and cleaning solution including boxes of toilet paper, paper towels, and liquid hand soap for the bathrooms. I went to the corner to make a place to hide if someone came in. Gingerly I moved each stack of boxes away from the wall and shimmied into the small space. I lay down on the cool dusty floor on my side with my back against the wall and waited. So far, so good I thought to myself and then I remembered I hadn't picked up the brochures from in front of the closet door.

The loudspeaker requested all visitors leave the museum again. Someone came to the door and stopped. Then I heard a set of keys jingling until the door opened and the light came on. I never thought about what I would do if I were caught. Only now did the question enter my mind. The light came on abruptly and the footsteps stopped in the center of the closet. Above me near my waist a box was opened and then another until the light went out and the door closed again. Shortly after that I heard a click and the light from the hallway that once trickled under the door into my little corner was gone. For a long time I waited in the darkness until no voices echoed in the hallways and the faint vibrations of doors closing ceased. How long would it take for all the staff to leave or did someone stay in the museum all night? Still I did not move. I lay on my left side refusing to shift while the circulation slipped away. Finally I turned on the flashlight and looked at my watch to see it was ten minutes after nine.

At 10:00pm I decided it was time, and rose in silent segments like a monster in a horror movie. First I pushed one row of boxes and then another. Inch by inch I moved them until there was enough room to sit up. There I stayed for a few minutes until I moved again. Each time I stirred, I clicked on the flashlight and when I sat still I turned it off. Twenty minutes later I was standing in the center of the closet listening for the slightest sound. I turned the flashlight on and put my hand on the knob and twisted it slowly without making a sound. Before opening the door, I turned the light off again and listened then slowly pushed my head out. The only light shining was from the next hallway but it was just enough to guide me. I left the closet and walked in the room where the disks were. Then taking the glasscutter from my pocket I made a light circle over the disks. Each time I traced the circle it made a deeper cut until finally with a small tap it fell inside the case. It seemed so easy I began to enjoy it. I reached inside and picked up the two disks and put them in my pocket and went to the window. My mistake was moving a smaller cabinet closer to the window so I could step up to climb out.

The alarm made no sound when it went off. Then suddenly I heard footsteps coming in my direction. I reached for the window latch only to discover it wasn't a latch. It was a lock! I looked around the room for something small enough to pick up to break the window but by that time through the darkness a flashlight shined brightly in my face. A voice shouted in Arabic and I didn't move. He shouted again but I couldn't understand what he was saying.

"I don't know what you want me to do!" I said.

"Keep your hands where I can see them!" He commanded.

And that's just what I did.

In contrast to the past few hours that went by slowly as I sat on the floor in the museum closet, events were now taking place at lightning speed. In less than twenty minutes, I had been apprehended and hand-cuffed, hustled from the museum into a police car and locked in a room handcuffed to a desk.

An Arab man wearing a suit introduced himself as Mr. Rabindra. He entered the room with a policeman moments after I was brought in and fumbled with papers from his briefcase. I refused to speak to them or offer any explanation for my actions until I'd seen a lawyer. I'd watched enough police shows to know not to say anything until I knew my rights. But in this country what rights did I have?

Mr. Rabindra leaned back in his chair after receiving no coopera-tion and gathered all his papers and put them back in his briefcase.

"Mr. Rabindra we've been sitting here for a while and I've decided it doesn't matter what I say. I just want to get out of here. I've been sick for a few days and I think I need to go to the hospital! I am willing to pay for all the damages and the trouble I caused if you let me go!" Mr. Rabindra seemed unconcerned with my plea of restitution,

"I'll see what can be done Mr. Reeves."

Then he stood up left and never gave me a second look before closing the door. Ronald was right I hadn't been thinking clearly. I'd made no preparation in case I was caught or arrested. Now if I tried to tell them the truth they'll never let me out of here.

An officer remained in the corner of the room with his arms folded never taking his eyes off me. He wore a white collared shirt with the first button open at the neck. His sleeves were rolled up to the fore-arms and his shirt was wet under the armpits from sweat. He wore a 9 mm pistol in a shoulder holster on his right side. His head was bald in the center with a few strands combed across the top to hide the spot like they do in America. Unwilling to be intimidated I looked in his direction every few minutes. My mind drifted to vague accounts of documentaries, news articles and personal statements of people being beaten in police custody. With my wrist cuffed to the desk not being able to defend myself I wondered if I was about to share their experience?

If they forced me to tell the truth what could I do? If I told them the real story they would have me committed and the lie would put me in prison. I considered this as I sat with my wrists cuffed in the Cairo police station.

It was almost 2:00 am on Tuesday and I still declined to answer any questions. Two hours ago, Mr. Rabindra brought a butted roll and a cup of coffee into the room and I refused it. He placed them on the desk anyway and left again. The site of the buttered roll with small black poppy seeds made my stomach churn with hunger. After reaching for the cup of coffee I thought of Whende and why I was here. Still my plan to save her did not seem hopeless because there were other alternatives to consider. If I had to offer one of the laundries or give up my half of the business to buy my way out of this mess I would. As long as the Obeni was working I had a chance to save her. When the temptation to drink the coffee became too much I hurled the Styrofoam cup against the wall with my left hand and pushed the bread in the same direction.

The policeman in the corner looked upset as the veins between his eyebrows swelled when he looked at the mess, and then suddenly gave me a sinister smile. Was it possible the only reason I hadn't had my skull cracked for not cooperating was because I am an American?

Folding my arms, I rested my head on the desk. In that tiny moment the image of the officer coming towards me made my head raise abruptly. Now was not the time to fall asleep or let my guard down so to keep myself occupied I studied my surroundings.

The walls were made of large bricks painted in two tones. The ceiling and the upper half of the wall was a faded eggshell white and the bottom half, which started at eye level was dark green. The door to the room was made of heavy wood with thin wire mesh running through the smoked glass. Most of the night I watched the shadows walk in the hallway past that glass. Now two figures stood on the other side of the door. Muffled voices could be heard at first and then the sounds grew louder and clearer until I heard someone say,

"Make him understand the penalty for stealing priceless historical treasures is twenty five years in prison!"

A dark haired white middle aged man wearing a charcoal gray double breasted suit and wire rimmed glasses opened the door and from my chair I saw the side of Mr. Rabindra standing in the hallway. The stranger came in with a brown leather briefcase in his right hand and a yellow folder in his left. He closed the door behind him and stood next to the chair across from me. He looked at the officer in the corner of the room then at the shadow of Mr. Rabindra listening from the hallway. He set the briefcase down on the floor next to his chair then put the folder on top of the desk. Without saying a word he took his jacket off and draped it across the back of the chair and sat down. He turned his head to the right and looked at the shadow on the other side of the door but did not speak. He looked at me suspiciously and cleared his throat loudly then turned his attention to the door until the shadow disappeared. At once he opened the folder in front of him and began to speak,

"My name is Robert West and I am here to help you. I'm glad you haven't made my job harder by giving any statements without benefit of counsel."

"Are you a lawyer?"

He shook his head to say no and when I was about to speak he put his hand up in a polite gesture for me to be silent. He turned and looked at the door again before he went on.

"Mr. Reeves you were arrested last night for theft, vandalism and trespassing."

Harshly he looked into my eyes and said,

"You had two metallic objects in your pocket. Furthermore the museum guards testified these pieces were in a display case you broke!" He glanced at the door once more and started again.

"I've checked your background and you've never been arrested or been in any trouble with the law. You are partners in a successful business in the U.S.; surely you must know this is a serious offense. Why would you do this? And before I forget, there was a problem at your hotel two days ago. You were found tied up in your room?"

I took a deep breath and shook my head closing my eyes searching for a place to start,

"I want to tell you but, I... you'll just think I'm crazy. You'll get up from that chair and help them commit me!"

He sat back in his chair and said,

"Start from the beginning.... please." He said.

I tried to relax my shoulders but the handcuff was pinching my wrist.

"Mr. West will you ask them to remove the handcuff? It's been on for hours."

He looked at the policeman in the corner and said,

"Sergeant take the cuffs off Mr. Reeves and leave us alone."

The sergeant reluctantly took a key ring from his belt and removed the handcuff from my wrist but left the other one still locked to the rail on the desk.

"I'm sorry. I hadn't noticed they were still on," said Mr. West.

My trust needed to be placed with someone and Mr. West was quickly becoming my first candidate.

Once we were alone I started to breathe easier touching my hand gently. The handcuff aggravated the bruise on my wrist left from the rope burns. Mr. West smiled at me pleasantly and asked,

"Do I look familiar to you?"

"No."

"I watched you in the hardware store yesterday," he whispered. I never saw the man's face clearly but I always had the feeling of being watched.

"Was that you?"

"Yes and believe it or not, you have a friend here and if you tell me what's going on I'm sure I can help you."

It seemed implausible I could have a friend here when I knew no one. I watched him with suspicion and he looked at me with one eyebrow slightly raised. If I were going to take a chance this seemed like the best opportunity. We were alone and whatever I told him I could deny later if I had to.

"Let me ask you a question?" I said.

I was losing my courage so I forced myself to speak,

"What would you do if you saw a...dinosaur or a...ghost or some-thing?"

"Did you see a dinosaur Mr. Reeves?"

"No, I'm just asking you a question? What would you do if you really saw something that was unbelievable?"

He had to give me an honest answer before I said any more.

"I don't know," he said simply.

"Well that's my problem. I saw something that can't be explained!"

I swallowed some air and touched my crusty lips with my dry tongue.

"Would you like something to drink?"

"No," placing my hands over my face until a compassionate voice said,

"I don't know what I'd do Mr. Reeves, I really don't. But I can prom-ise you this, if you tell me the truth I will fight to help you no matter how weird your story sounds."

The time and my choices were slipping away hour by hour and there was nothing I could do, it was now or never.

"Why don't you start by telling me why you were found in your hotel room tied up?"

"No, I'll start from the beginning."

I looked right in his eyes and said,

"I swear on my family, on the Bible, and on the graves of a hundred dead people I don't even know that what I'm about to tell you now is the truth, so help me God!"

Unlike the version I gave to Ronald and Lorraine, Mr. West was about to hear the whole story in chronological order. Taking my time I spoke cautiously but in a clear low voice. It had taken me several days to accept my circumstances so I was leery anyone would believe this tale immediately especially with no hard evidence. It was impor-tant I appear rational and believable if nothing else and answer all of his questions.

When I told him how the Obeni was first discovered by Remi he seemed pleased. It was at this time Mr. West revealed himself to be a member of the secret society established more than one hundred years ago to document and safeguard Egyptian history. When asked he would not tell me the name of their group or its headquarters. However he did tell me the Aswan shop was always kept under surveillance. From the time I purchased the Obeni until now I had been watched.

Because Mr. West was willing to exchange small bits of information I decided to confide in him. I told him about my trip into the past and everything I'd seen. Never once mentioning the intimacy Whende and I shared, I told him she saved my life by returning me against my will. Because of that they found me in my room tied up and alone. And when I returned I found out I had altered history by causing her death. My plan was to return and save her but my friends stole the disks and left Egypt. Time was running out and I felt I had no other options. My only chance was to commit this robbery and that's why I was here.

Once I finished I felt half the burden taken from my shoulders. There was nothing left to say. Mr. West would believe me, or he wouldn't.

"Is that why you threw the coffee on the floor?"

"Yes," I said in confirmation, "because I can't eat anything now."

He sat in his chair looking at me with suspicion. I felt he didn't believe me and the suspense was unbearable.

"Would you be able to come up with $50,000 dollars?" He asked.

"$50,000 dollars for what?" I asked.

"I think if you paid for the damages, and offered a donation to the museum the charges could be dropped."

"Yes I could get it but I need to hold the disks."

"They won't do that Mr. Reeves."

"Haven't you been listening, I can't go back without them!" yelling furiously.

"Keep your voice down. I'm going to help you," he said.

"How?"

"Trust me but first, we need to get you released with all the charges dropped."

He was right and if I weren't so confused, I'd know it. I felt like one of the horses galloping across the bridge with blinders on seeing only the safety of Whende ahead of me. $50,000 dollars was nothing compared to my love for her. The money was meaningless if I returned and saved her life. If Mr. West couldn't help me keep the disks I would break in to the museum again tomorrow with an army this time to retrieve them.

For the next hour I paced alone in the room silently considering if I had misplaced my trust. Mr. West being a white man had nothing to do with it because I can remember being bullshitted by every people of every race. It was because he made sure when he left the room, the Sergeant locked the door. So if we really trusted each other, he should know I would not try to escape.

The soft pounding in my head that started a short time ago was increasing. In between the thumping, the short spells of dizziness were becoming harder to control. Reaching the first chair I sat down with my back to the door and my head on the desk. Shortly after my prayer to the Creator to give me more strength I heard the door unlock. Turning my head slowly I saw Mr. West standing in the doorway holding it open for me then he motioned for me to follow. Taking a deep breath I stood up and pretended I was not about to fall flat on my face. I followed him down the corridor and through the swinging doors into the lobby of the police station and finally out the front door to a waiting automobile.

The sun was on a downward angle but the ripples of heat rose from every object including the roof of the car. The hot air found its way without delay to the back of my throat swelling my vocal cords. Mr. West opened the back door for me exposing the cool air inside. Declining to speak I offered a sincere smile of gratitude and then he said,

"By the way you owe me $50,000 dollars."

Extending my hand to shake his, I mustered up a scratchy thank you and told him he'd have his money tonight.

The air conditioned ride helped clear my throat so that by the time we reached the hotel I felt much better but decided to limit my words. Before I got out of the car I noticed the glass in the partition was very dark making it impossible for me to see what the driver looked like, and when I got out of the car the driver's window was also very dark.

When I reached the front desk of the lobby I was met with the same strange stares I received during my first week's stay, but this time they came with respect. Mr. West gave me the necessary paperwork to authorize a wire transfer of money from my account to him under the pretense of property I was to purchase. Reading the documents quickly and as carefully as I could I signed them in triplicate with the hotel manager as a witness. The young lady who helped Lorraine and Ronald gain entrance to my room the last time was reluctant to speak which was fine with me.

When the elevator stopped on my floor, we got off and went to my room. Just down the hall a maid I'd never seen before seemed caught by surprise and started fumbling with the towels on her pushcart. Holding them in front of her face, she pretended to fold them. When I stopped to look at her she faced away from me pulling her car behind her.

Once we entered my suite a sigh of relief came over me. The Obeni was still in the corner near my bed full of sand and nothing had been changed even the covers on my bed still thrown back in disarray as I left them.

"Does that woman work for you?"

"That is not important."

"Then tell me this, do you believe me?"

"Yes I do."

"And why are you helping me?"

"That's not important either," Mr. West said unexpectedly.

Now I just wanted him to leave so I could plan another raid on the museum.

"Okay fine, does the museum have their property back?"

"Yes they do, but don't worry your disks are on the way."

"What! How, how did you do that? When will they arrive from the States?"

Mr. West walked away and sat down on the loveseat and looked at his watch.

"Your friends never went home, they simply checked into another hotel across town."

"How did you find them?"

"I told you we have been watching you since you made the purchase of the Obeni. And that includes everyone you come in contact with."

"How did you get Ronald to give them to you?"

"I can't tell you that either"

"You didn't hurt him did you," I said vehemently.

"No, no one was hurt I assure you."

"Can you tell me why you people let me buy the Obeni in the first place?"

"I can only say we exist to ensure a fair and accurate account of history. I really can't say more about us so please stop asking."

"Can you at least tell me why you're helping me save her?"

"I'm not at liberty to discuss it."

Next he told me a messenger was coming here with the disks and some items to help me, and then he asked me to sit down next to him.

"There are some things I need to tell you that you may have already found out when you altered history the first time. When you return to the past you become a virus that contaminates the timeline changing the future. You cannot make any changes or bring modern ideas before their time. Under no circumstances are you to kill anyone. The people you encounter there are direct descendants of us all. If you killed one of the guards he could possibly be your own ancestor or mine."

So far I'd been so caught up in saving Whende and correcting the wrong I caused I never thought about that.

"By killing one guard or two you could change history and wipe out one million people or maybe more, possibly even your own existence. Do you understand?"

"Yes I do."

"Are you sure?"

"Yes."

There was a knock on my door and Mr. West told me to remain seated. Then he went to the door and came back immediately with a small briefcase. Placing the briefcase between us he sat down and opened it. Reaching in carefully he handed me the pouch containing the disks. Then he reached inside again and pulled out a small canister with a white plastic mouthpiece attached to the top.

"This is because you said you could not breathe as you fell and had to be revived after. When you arrive you must destroy all evidence of this canister. It can never be found, understand?"

"Sure."

Next he took out a straight wooden rod the color of bamboo and the length of a flute and handed it to me. It was circular like a garden hose with two holes side-by-side like a double- barreled shotgun.

Then he reached in the bag again and took out a cigar box. The entire box was laminated he said to make it waterproof and inside were thin wooden darts the size of pencils wrapped in heavy plastic.

"This is a blow gun that shoots two darts at a time. In this jar is a harmless tranquilizer, very potent and fast acting. All you need to do is pierce the skin and within four to six seconds the victim will feel drunk and pass out. Do not rub this on your own skin or you will fall asleep."

Mr. West, if that was his real name, showed me how to prepare one of the darts by dipping most of the tip in the small jar of liquid and letting it dry. He suggested I not dip them all until I had practiced shooting a few of them at some targets around the room. He said it had a range of Ten feet but an experienced person could shoot much farther. Then he showed me how to carry them in the little holster he provided which was to be worn around my arm. It was a good feeling to receive his aid but I still couldn't help but wonder why?

"Why are you doing this?" I asked.

"So that you can repair what you have broken and because," He wanted to tell me something else but stopped.

"I think I've already said too much," he said, "and before I forget, on this piece of paper are a few phrases that might help you but I can't be sure of the pronunciation."

"Thank you."

I looked at the paper while he was still in the room. It contained four simple sentences. Where is the Princess? I will not hurt you. Take me to the Princess. When I found her I could say, you are in danger, come with me.

"I'm leaving now Mr. Reeves. We will be guarding your room so that you are not disturbed for the next few days. And remember you are a virus, try not to be seen or say too much. Don't make any changes in the way they live, and most of all don't kill anyone!"

With those last words Mr. West left my suite. It felt good to know there were still people in the world like him. I would do everything he said as long as I could save Whende.

Chapter 13

The sun was shining through my eyelids and without opening them I turned my head searching for a small slice of darkness. Unknowingly I'd slept most of the morning and well into the afternoon. For me sleep was the barricade that kept the hunger and thirst away. As long as I kept my eyes closed and dreamed, everything was perfect in my world. I was twisting against my pillow trying to wake up. The rocking escalated until finally my mind was saying no. If I could sleep for another hour I'd feel better, but my head was still shaking and my mind was still saying no. My eyes opened with a slow flutter making the image of my room look like an old silent picture movie. I'd never felt so bad in my life and wondered if I was dying. The clock on the nightstand read 3:15 pm. I'd slept for more than twelve hours!

Yesterday after Mr. West left, I practiced blowing darts at the pillows from five feet away in a standing position. Every half an hour I moved back one foot refining my accuracy until I could hit the pillow each time from ten feet away without missing. Then I strapped the holster around my forearm and slid a few darts into their individual sheaths. Next I practiced pulling them out quickly loading them into the blowgun. Finally I tried walking around the room and shooting the target until I felt satisfied with my progress. Target practice came to a halt when each puff of air I took scorched the back of my throat and it became difficult to breathe. After that I unscrewed the top of the tranquilizer bottle and dipped all twenty darts placing them on the dresser with the tips hanging off the edge to dry. Then I considered how I was going to keep them dry.

Tomorrow I would wear my sandals and the khaki shorts with the huge pockets on the thighs to hold the cigar box, and the T-shirt with

Harlem embroidered across the chest so I could feel like a superhero.

I sat on the loveseat and rehearsed those phrases Mr. West had given to me but I was having a hard time memorizing them so I disregarded two and worked on those I felt were the most important: "Take me to the Princess" and "You are in danger, come with me".

After an hour of repeating the lines to myself, I walked over to the darts and touched them lightly to see if they had dried. I carefully placed them in the pouch and then in the cigar box with the two arm holsters. Now there was nothing left to do but wait until tomorrow. I had no plan of action to follow and no scenarios to guide me, only the Creator's hand on my shoulder. Before I fell asleep, I cleared my mind by attempting to think of what I was doing last year at this time and couldn't remember. Tonight was March 26 and I couldn't think of anyone famous born today or even tomorrow but this date should be important. It was a significant event the world would never witness or ever believe. Random thoughts crossed my mind during the night like who was the inventor of the match, and what day was the first flight at Kitty Hawk? All of these thoughts had no meaning but my mind rambled until the hunger and thirst went away.

It was 3:26 pm and I sat up like a man about to face the firing squad. With all honesty, I knew I was scared but when my foot touched the carpet I refused to let fear and confusion slow me down. It was as if someone lit a fire to my behind and from that moment on I refused to entertain any thoughts of failure.

The first thing I saw were the sandals and I quickly put them on and then the shorts. The cigar box was too big to fit into the thigh pocket but there was plenty of room to shove it inside my shorts. Now I needed the canister of air before I could leave. Looking at the Obeni full of sand reminded me of the disks. It was my intention to put them in at the last moment and that moment was here. A chill ran through my body when I inserted the disks like the feeling of someone stepping on your grave. If I stopped now I might lose my courage and never forgive myself. Within a few moments, the distorted image of Whende's house appeared with no one in sight. And then I thought about the fall into darkness and my feet felt like concrete blocks, I forced them to obey my will as I stepped closer to the Obeni". This was an essential time to check the canister to see if the air worked.

The black canister had no instructions or labels, just a small round knob on the left side. Stretching the elastic strap over my head I inserted the hollow plastic end in my mouth and bit down to hold it steady and turned the knob. A cool steady stream of air filled my lungs and then I turned the knob to the off position. Taking a step forward my legs felt weighted again. I touched the cigar box to make sure it was closed and before I gave myself a chance to be scared, taking a deep breath, I ran as fast as I could into the Obeni instantly falling into the darkness.

My heart was about to burst from my chest and the hum of a wind whistled past my ears as I searched for that pinhole of light I'd seen before. There was some comfort in knowing I would not crash below and when I expanded my lungs to take the first breath there was no air. During my fall I held the canister tightly against my chest with my left hand and the cigar box against my abdomen. Refusing to let go of the box to turn the knob I tried to relax by counting slowly until I got to 90. I could always hold my breath for at least 90 seconds and by the time I had reached 35 I saw the light at the bottom. When I got to 57 it was still very far away but I told myself I would make it. 78, 79, 80, 81, and the light grew much closer, but when I reached 90 I still wasn't there. I began telling myself I'd make it if I just held on. At 103, the brightness was all around me. Closing my eyes I felt the sensation of warmth that was immediately followed by a chill it reminded me of having an accident in bed as a small child. It felt warm at first, but then suddenly cold is hell. My eyes opened to the blurry burning sensation of water. Instinctively I thrust my head out and took a breath of air.

"Thank you," I whispered softly to the Creator, "thank you."

Wading to the edge of the reflection pool I was about to get out when I saw one of the guards less than fifty yards away walking in my direction. Moving to the corner of the pool I bit down on the mouthpiece and submerged my head underwater. Then I turned the knob and a stream of bubbles floated to the surface. Expecting the noise to attract him I turned the knob off and blew the bubbles slowly out of my nose. I repeated this procedure for several minutes until he was out of sight. Exiting the water, I ran to the shade tree and kneeled behind the chair.

All of the fatigue I felt before was gone. My heart raced, my ears were tuned to the slightest sound, and my eyes were like those of a predatory bird. Quickly I opened the cigar box simultaneously studying my surroundings. Everything inside was dry and with each dart I placed in the sheath, I thanked Mr. West. When I was finished I strapped the holsters around my arms and then the worst thing that could possibly happen did. I had no idea where the blowgun was? I sat behind the tree cursing myself for being so stupid because with all my meticulous planning I forgot to bring it. Now what was I supposed to do, throw the darts with my hands?

After a brief moment of intelligent reasoning I quickly realized there was nothing to do. Returning to my room for the blowgun was out of the question. I was here now and I meant to stay. Turning around facing the house in a kneeling position I looked carefully one more time and bolted across the lawn towards Whende's house. Reaching the outside of the door I removed one dart and listened for movement inside. Opening the door cautiously I went inside closing it behind me. My ears were so sensitive I believed I could hear a pin drop if one fell. It was unsettling to stand in a room that was once filled with so much love. Leaning over I touched the bed with an open hand feeling for the slightest warmth from where I imagined Whende would lay. I would take this as a clue to whether or not she was still alive. However, it did not take a detective to see there had been a struggle here. Aside from the covers on the bed being tossed around, two chairs were on their sides and her clothes were thrown everywhere. I took a step towards the bathroom and saw the parrots perch lying across the floor. Promptly I entered the bathroom to find the same manner of disarray. If I was too late and they had killed her what would I do then?

When I came out of the bathroom I walked right into the face of the old woman I'd seen twice before. The element of surprise was gone and I clutched the dart in my hand and held it behind my back waiting for her to sound the alarm. Both of us stood by the foot of the bed not far from each other. Now was the time to recite one of the phrases I'd memorized but I'd forgotten them too.

All I could say was,

"Whende?"

She smiled and took my hand and led me down the hallway. Before we went further inside she looked carefully around and when she saw no one, she clutched my hand even tighter. We walked briskly to the same room where the guards had placed me before. Then as quietly as possible she lifted the latch and slid the iron bolt back. I pushed the door open with one hand and saw Whende lying on the floor covered with straw under the window. I went inside and knelt down beside her calling her name softly. Her eyes opened and she smiled as if glad to see me, but there was no time to waste.

Taking Whende's hand I pulled her to her feet and we went to the door. Her voice sounded hoarse and scratchy as if she were struggling to speak. While she was talking, I motioned with my hands to tell her we should go for the horses and get away. Not knowing whether she understood me, I started pulling her while she was still talking.

We made it to the front door when I heard someone talking from the other side. Leaning with our backs against a wall we hid behind the door waiting for it to open. My heart was thumping as I pulled another dart from my arm. Looking at Whende I gave her a signal to be quiet and as the first guard opened the door I waited for the second one to come in and once he did I stuck them both in the arm and moved away. The first guard ran to me grabbing my neck powerfully with both hands. I dropped the darts and tried punching his arms to remove his hands. The other guard grabbed Whende by the arm and pushed her against the wall. Everything I tried wasn't working. At last his grip around my neck loosened and he fell to the floor. I turned to help Whende but the tranquilizer began to work and the second guard let her go and fell to the floor. Whende seemed very upset cupping her hands over her mouth muffling her scream. I assume it is because she thought they were dead. I put my hands together placing my head on my hands, closing my eyes in an effort to explain to her that they were only a sleep.

Now we walked to the front door carefully, not knowing who might have heard the commotion. Everything was still quiet in the house and we were almost home free. I took out another dart and peeked around the door to look outside. Taking Whende's hand we walked outside to the patio and looked down the steps to the stable. When we reached the edge of the patio, the young boy I'd seen before who held the reins for Whende walked out from the stable and looked up at us.

We stopped not knowing what he would do but found out quickly. He called loudly to someone inside the stable and from the shadows a man came out. It was Kfaru accompanied by an even bigger man. When he saw us standing at the end of the patio he threw a canvas sack he was holding to the ground so hard it created a small patch of dust. Then he ran back inside and came out with a machete-sized knife. We ran back into the house past the tall columns and the chandeliers filled with candles. When we reached the hallway that led to Whende's room we heard the front door open with a crash. Holding hands and never stopping we ran through Whende's room and out the door. I wanted to go left but she wanted to go right and our hands pulled apart. Stopping for a tiny moment we looked at each other. I extended my hand, which she gladly took again and we ran around the edge of the pool. Kfaru stopped running when he got outside Whende's door and saw us while the other man ran up from behind the house to cut us off. Whende started yelling something at him as he walked closer and closer waiving the knife in his hand never taking his eyes off of me. Whatever she was saying to him didn't matter because I was going to get the first chop. Most likely Homeboy was thinking about when I hit him in the balls the last time.

We backed up near the edge of the pool as both came closer, stalking us. Whende yelled at him persistently with a commanding voice but still he came. I threw the dart as hard as I could and it bounced off his garment and fell to the ground. I held her hand tighter while we stood just feet away from the pool. Then I heard Whende say a phrase I could recall,

"neia abeir Bennie."

Unexpectedly she pushed me with her body into the pool but I was clutching her hand so tight she came in with me. Instinctively I was still trying to save her and I strengthened my grip until the darkness surrounded us and we fell through the Obeni to the plush carpet of my suite.

Lying on my back I tried to inhale and was forced to roll over and expel the water I swallowed. Still clutching Whende's hand, I saw the three of them staring at us in the Obeni. Struggling to my feet I stood up to remove the disks but felt compelled to say something now that they could understand me.

Showing no weakness I walked closer to the Obeni and with a commanding voice I said,

"Never speak of me, and I will not return! Live your life with a light heart, and I will bless you and your children forever."

Then I reached into the arch and removed the disks staring at the red sand inside. Only then did I notice Whende's lifeless body on the floor. Kneeling beside her I fought back the tears. Once again she'd given her life to save mine and I'd given nothing in return.

Chapter 14

Across town as dusk was approaching, Ronald watched the sun begin to disappear through his open hotel window. While he stood quietly, Lorraine walked busily around the room congratulating herself on her latest shopping acquisitions. She'd bought souvenirs for her friends and some clothes for their son Jimmy.

Everything was sprawled across the bed and atop the dresser, from soft Egyptian cotton sheets to jewelry to T-shirts and silk dress shirts for Ronald. When she could no longer ignore the one-sided conversation she was having and her questions about who should receive which souvenir were met with I don't knows she refused the accept his partial silence.

Ronald had barely said two full sentences in a row since he'd taken the disks from Bennie's safe three days ago. Of course they'd gone shopping and had dinner together but his thoughts were elsewhere. They planned to take a tour of the pyramids tomorrow and she wanted his melancholy attitude to end now so she embraced him. Standing behind him she wrapped her arms around his waist and kissed the back of his neck.

"Why are you so quiet, Sweetheart?"

Ronald watched the sun's colors shift from orange to red he responded to her question with only a deep sigh. She knew what was wrong, so why was she even asking, he thought.

"Do you still want to see the pyramids tomorrow?" She asked.

"Sure."

Comforting him wasn't working fast enough so she tried the usual approach...nagging.

"Why are you letting him spoil our vacation?"

"I'm not," he said as he turned to look at her.

"Then what's the matter?"

"I don't feel good about what happened," looking for some support.

"What we did was right! And by keeping the disks with us you saved his life!"

"I should have stayed with him and helped."

"For what?" Lorraine said loudly.

"If we didn't come to make sure Bennie was all right, why are we here?"

"Honey you are too nice to your friends and all they ever do is use you."

"That's not true." He said firmly.

"It is true!" Lorraine rebutted.

"But you saw her!"

"See, that's what I mean."

"What are you talking about?" he asked as if annoyed.

"That wasn't real!"

"Lorraine, you didn't think that lady was there?"

"Hell no! He's fucking with us somehow. I mean come on baby, be serious. You believe Bennie went back in time? Do you really believe that?"

"If I didn't think it was real, I wouldn't have taken the damn disks!" He said loudly.

Then Ronald stared at Lorraine and with a slow distinct he said,

"And I know you believe him too."

The tranquility of the sunset no longer offered comfort and Ronald moved from the window looking for a split second at the meaningless trinkets they had purchased today shaking his head.

"What about Terri?" He asked, "We haven't called her or anyone else to let them know where we're staying."

Raising his hands as a gesture of agreement he said,

"It doesn't feel like a vacation. I feel more like fugitives hiding from our friends," Ronald said.

"We agreed not to tell anyone where we were because Bennie might find out and come here."

"Of course he would. You saw how desperate he was to save her!" Ronald said.

"And do you remember how sick he looked?" She asked.

"Yes."

"Well that's why we did it, to save his life!"

"I know," he said grudgingly.

"So you made a decision for him because he was not rational and you need to accept it. It's done and that's all there is to it."

"Yes that...."

"No, no, no, you saved his life, and that's what you need to consider!"

Unenthusiastically he agreed but it still didn't dissolve the lump of betrayal stuck in his throat. They'd always stuck together often disagreeing but never interfering to this extent. Except today for the first time, Ronald knew he'd crossed the line.

Back in my hotel room I sat on the edge of the bed with Whende's head near my feet pondering all the questions I never asked her and how much more she could have taught me. Less than a minute had gone by since my return when I noticed an insignificant tremble in her body. How could I have been so stupid not to have seen it earlier? She'd revived me on my first trip and maybe that was what she needed.

I fell to my knees shaking her and patting her cheek while calling her name with no response. Rolling her on her stomach I pushed on her back a few times until a clear liquid ran from her lips. Then I turned her over pinching her nose and blowing air into her mouth. Calling her name louder I told her she was strong and she could make it. In my panic, I slapped her face. The sound of the slap was followed by a muffled cry that twisted her face until her mouth opened so wide I could see her tonsils. When she was able to inhale, the next cry was louder and much longer. I was so happy she was alive and I cradled her like she'd done for me but she continued her unusual cry.

It wasn't long before I noticed there was something very wrong. She had little strength in her arms and while her eyes were open they never focused on me or anything in the room as she continued wailing. Had she gone through some trauma during the trip? Maybe she hit her head on something in the room when she fell? While she cried I examined her head for bruises and signs of blood and found nothing but I realized she could not support her head. Peeling back the covers from the bed I took off her wet garments then picked her up and put her in bed under the covers. Whende settled down and fell asleep next to me. I was so happy that I had not lost her.

Against the odds I'd saved her and when she woke we would start a new life here. She pretended to be uninterested in the accomplishments of my time but once she saw for herself there would have to be some amazement. Her people had specific knowledge of celestial bodies but they never seen a picture of Saturn or Mars. They'd never floated above the ground in a hot air balloon or watched the landscape wiz by on a high-speed train. Whende wasn't astounded because she had yet to see first hand what we'd become. In time I would introduce her to everything new and brilliant.

The hours crept by while she slept and I refused to let her go or move from her side. I wanted to be the first face she saw when she opened her eyes just as she had been the first face I saw when I'd entered her world. Yet, I was still haunted by unanswered questions.

In that moment when Whende opened her eyes it shouldn't have taken so long for her to recognize me and know she was safe. She had no strength in her muscles and when she was lifted her body slumped like a rag doll. Had she now become a paraplegic and lost her mind? If she was, how was I going to take care of her? By saving her life and bringing her to the 20th century had I forced her to live the life of a human vegetable?

I thought about Yemot's first sighting of the comet. Then Ept, creator of the Obeni and his warning to those who would try to use it incorrectly,

"Death to all that is known."

Tears rolled down my face and I covered my mouth with my hand so my sobs would not wake her. I swore to myself that if this were true I would take care of Whende whatever the consequences and she would be my responsibility now.

Composing myself I slipped off the bed and went to the bathroom for a few sips of water. Whende would be hungry when she woke because Kfaru had locked her away to starve to death. After using the phone to order room service I went to the bathroom to wash and change into fresh clothes.

I removed the holsters containing the wooden darts from my arms and left them near the sink. When I was finished in the bathroom I went to the bed where Whende was still sleeping peacefully. I forced myself to think positively. I was still alive with no permanent injuries and with some physical therapy Whende might regain the use of her body. No expense would be spared. She would have the best doctors and therapist's money could buy.

I saw the blowgun on the love seat and cursed myself. If I'd thought to take it with me, circumstances might have been different. Then I remembered the cigar box wrapped in plastic. I'd been so upset about leaving the blowgun I forgot to bury the cigar box and the plastic bag. They were still behind the tree and would eventually be found and there was nothing I could do. My only hope was that a small cardboard box and a plastic bag would not alter the future much.

The series of light taps at the door caused Whende to stir a bit. I greeted the gentleman and took the cart, not allowing him to enter the room. I apologized for not having a tip ready and promised I would find him later. Then I pushed the cart close to the edge of the bed. The order I placed was very simple, four bottles of apple juice and a fruit basket to start. Opening one bottle I drank half and went to the bed to wake Whende. I talked to her telling her she had to drink something. Her eyes opened never focusing on anything except the sound of my voice.

"Whende how do you feel?" I said not expecting to understand her.

With no recognition of me, her head turned slightly but not much and she began to cry again. I sat on the bed carefully pulling her up to me allowing her head to rest in the cradle of my arm. Placing the bottle to her crusty lips I poured some juice inside her mouth. All of the liquid ran out and down the sides of her neck and as I watched there was something very familiar. Her mouth was making a sucking motion exactly like that of a newborn baby. She only stopped crying when I put the bottle to her lips. Patiently I worked with small amounts until the bottle was finished. She seemed content and through the covers I could see her arms and legs moving sporadically. At least I knew she had some feeling in her limbs. When I touched her hand her fingers closed around my pinky. I thought about Yemot's warning again. Death to all that is known and decided something had been lost in the translation. It meant the death of all her knowledge but did it mean she could not learn again. It was too early to tell but it looked as if she had the mind of a baby trapped inside a woman's beautiful body.

Looking through the glass doors of the balcony I watched the lights come on in distant windows as night fell over the city. Making several trips to the cart that was left in my room I drank silently and chewed a piece of apple as I formulated a new plan. This time there would be no room for error. I did not feel safe here anymore and there would be no time to relax until I was on familiar ground but I felt I needed Mr. West's help one more time.

I peered into the hallway and saw a dark skinned man with straight black hair wearing a black suit and white shirt standing near the elevator. The maid I'd seen earlier that tried to conceal her face was nowhere in sight. When I looked back at the man near the elevator he seemed surprised and turned his face away, so I closed the door and looked for my hotel key. I had no intention of going very far from my room but I couldn't take a chance of leaving without the key and being locked out. I had a feeling that man was doing more than just waiting for the elevator. With key in hand I opened the door to see the same man standing by the elevator but this time he wore dark glasses. I checked to make sure the door was locked before walking down the hall and pushed the button for the elevator. As I waited, I began to think. If he had been waiting for the elevator why wasn't the button pressed? When the doors opened I wanted him to get on first so I said,

"After you."

"No you go ahead," he said nicely.

"You sure?" I said sarcastically.

"Yes, go ahead."

During our polite conversation the elevator doors closed leaving us still in the hallway and my suspicion was confirmed.

"I need to speak to Mr. West," I said under my breath.

"Who?"

"Mr. West, I need to speak with him," I stated slightly louder.

"I'm sorry I don't know anyone by..."

"Listen, I really don't have time to play around. I need to speak with him please."

Without giving him a chance to respond I walked back to my room and went inside. It was almost 9:00 pm and it had been the longest day of my life. I'd starved myself to the brink of death, traveled through centuries of time and back to save the one person I loved with no reward. In some small measure there was success, Whende was spared a horrible death and slept in front of me. Her eyes rolled back and forth under her eyelids signaling she was dreaming. I wondered what a person with no memory could dream of.

I called room service to place another order. This time, I was more prepared for Whende's needs. I sent for milk and cereal, more juice and fruit, some aspirin for my headache and half a case of bottled water. I wanted to ask if they had baby bottles and nipples in the hotel but it would cause too many questions.

Shortly after the food arrived, Whende woke up making a whining sound. Able to free one of her arms from the covers she sucked on her clenched fist. When that did not offer satisfaction she began to cry, so I was ready with a warm glass of milk. Feeding her was easy, propping her up and holding her steady to burp her was the chore. Afterwards she settled down as I rocked her slowly. She seemed content in listening to the sound of my voice. When she was almost asleep she made a small grunt followed by a nasty smell. I hoped it wasn't what I thought it was but the odor was unmistakable. Though I wasn't prepared this would now be part of her care.

Instead of bringing towels wet with soap it was easier to wash her in the tub with a small amount of water. When that was done I carried her from the bathroom crying and wrapped her in a blanket and left her in the center of the room while I took the sheets off the bed and flipped the mattress over. Then I placed clean towels over the mattress and put Whende on top of them. I was about to cover her but I could not help looking at her nakedness. Less than a week ago we were lovers joined in passion. Her breasts were the same full ones I had so eagerly sucked. She still had that special curve in her hips that excited me the first day I saw her and without question I wanted her again. Looking at her face I wanted to kiss her and lie down next to her and put my lips on hers and after that one kiss I swore to her and the Creator I would never look at her helpless soul with such lust. She was dependent upon me and I wouldn't disgrace the memory of what we had.

In the solitude of my room I rested next to Whende with my eyes closed preparing a list of items we would need: a wheelchair and women's clothes, and some form of diaper to put on her. Suddenly I opened my eyes and went across the room to push the love seat in front of the door in case Mr. West and his group tried to come in without my permission. If they could sneak into Ronald and Lorraine's hotel room and steal the disks, they didn't need a key to get in here.

On my way back to bed there was a knock on the door.

"Who is it?" I asked softly trying not to wake her.

"Mr. West," the voice said.

I pulled the love seat away from the door and let him in.

"Why are you still here?" He asked, "Did you change your mind?"

"No."

"Then what happened?" he said loudly.

"Keep your voice down," I said in a whisper.

It was too late Whende moved a little but did not wake up.

"Who is that?" He asked walking a little closer to the bed.

"That's the Princess."

"What! Are you kidding me?"

Mr. West walked towards me shaking his head. I could see the skin between his eyes bunch up into two thick lines.

"Why did you bring her back?"

Before I answered an idea crossed my mind that he might want to take her from me so I became very defensive and made my explanation brief.

"We were being chased and couldn't get away. She tried to send me back but fell in after me."

"You cannot change the past like this, Mr. Reeves," he said angrily.

"There was nothing I could do!" I said.

Now was not the time to tell him I didn't bury the cigar box and the plastic like I promised.

"What changes you've made now to the future I can only guess," he said in a disappointing tone.

I tried to sound positive before he thought of more to say on that subject.

"Nothing has changed."

"What about the children she would have?"

"I told you she was supposed to have children but I changed that before. Your records indicate at her death she had no children, right?"

"Yes."

"And she doesn't, nothing is changed. Now will you help me get out of here?"

"Sure," he said strangely and went to the phone.

"Who are you calling?"

"A friend of mine," he said calmly.

Beginning to feel like the chase was not over I held his arm preventing him from dialing.

"You are not taking her from me, you hear!"

Now I was raising my voice.

"Let go of my arm," he said calmly.

"Do you understand?" I said staring into his eyes.

"It's you who doesn't understand. She is exposed to all kinds of 20th century germs and must be vaccinated immediately!"

"I know."

Relinquishing my grip I stood close by his side while he spoke on the phone in a language I could not comprehend. For the moment I cursed Ronald for not being with me as someone I could trust. If he were here the odds would be more in my favor in case I was being set up.

When Mr. West finished he went to the loveseat and sat down. I could not shake the feeling of being stalked and I believed it would not go away until I was safely home with Whende. Sitting next to Mr. West on the loveseat I revealed that Whende was a permanent vegetable. Her mind was filled with oatmeal and it was my punishment and responsibility to take care of her.

For the next few minutes Mr. West and I discussed arrangements for my departure. We settled on chartering a private jet with diplomatic status to fly nonstop to Kennedy airport and a limousine to meet us near the hanger. At some point he said I would need a birth certificate and a passport for Whende, which he would provide. With Mr. West's contacts it would be easier to supply these documents if we agreed she was born here.

After 11:00 pm the doctor arrived alone carrying a small black medical bag. Now I had two men to contend with if something went wrong. Before I let him examine Whende I made them both wait in the other room until I dressed her in a T shirt and some of my under-wear. It wasn't because of jealousy; it was her dignity I was looking to protect. She stirred a little in a sleepy state while I dressed her and when I was finished I went to get the doctor.

From what I could see the Doctor performed a legitimate medical examination. He checked her ears and shined a small flashlight in her eyes to check her pupils for reactions. He listened to her heart with the stethoscope under my watchful eyes while I held one of the darts be-hind my back, cupped in my hand waiting for the slightest provoca-tion. When he put the cuff on to check her blood pressure she began to fidget. Then he gave her a vaccination for smallpox and measles that started her crying but by then he was finished. I wanted to comfort her but I had to keep tabs on my visitors.

In the next room I received the doctor's medical report. Whende was in good health but he could offer no explanation for her mental and physical state without further examination. Then he wrote on a piece of paper the type of shots he administered and what should be given next and when. Still on edge I watched both of them intently. The doctor peeled off the latex gloves he wore and dropped them in his medical bag along with the stethoscope and the small flashlight he took from his pocket. In the same shy nondescript manner as everyone who was in Mr. West's circle of influence he said goodbye never mak-ing eye contact with me when he left.

Now it was time to care for Whende so I asked Mr. West to come with me into the next room. While he remained seated near the door I gave her the warm milk I had waiting. An adult body can't survive on warm milk and juice so I would need help at some point formulating a nutritious diet for her. She sucked the rim of the glass like before and when it was finished I patted her back until she burped. Mr. West watched me clean her face and rock her until she fell asleep. It was my opportunity to show him what I would be dealing with for the rest of my life.

He looked on from across the room with wonder, sorrow and ex-pectation. When I was sure Whende was sound asleep I joined him on the loveseat to further discuss our plans. Sitting next to him exhaus-tion was overtaking me but I did not let on. We watched her sleep until the silence was broken with his empathic comment,

"I'm really sorry Mr. Reeves."

"Me too."

"She is a beautiful woman. I could see why you went back for her."

"Yes, but she's not a woman anymore," I said with regret.

"But if you could have talked to her you would really understand what drew me to her," I added.

"Have you spoken to your friends?" He asked.

"No."

"What will you tell them?"

"Nothing."

"We would like to know your progress."

Once I was gone I saw no reason to update him on anything but I said, "Sure."

"Well let's see, we have a jet ready for you at 6:30 a.m. tomorrow. Is there anything else you think you might need?"

"Yes, I'll need a wheelchair and some of those diapers senior citizens use."

He took out a pen and paper and began to write.

"Okay, what else?"

"I don't know, some baby powder, and milk and juice I guess."

"Now what about that?" He asked pointing to the Obeni.

It was the last thing on my mind right now. I had no intention of using it again and I doubted very much I live another seventy six years to see it work.

"I know it belongs to you Mr. Reeves but I have a suggestion."

"What?"

"Let us store it for you and we will keep it safe."

"Fine."

"And you can keep the disks," he said.

By now I just wanted to sleep before Whende woke up and started crying again. Then he said,

"All you have to do is create of a name for her to use on the passport and birth certificate."

My mother's name came to mind but that was no good. As a matter of fact I didn't want to name her after anyone in my family or any women I'd slept with. Finally I came up with the name Linda after a girl who went to my high school. Mr. West stood up to leave when he finished writing and shook my hand. Before he left his next construc-tions sounded like something right out to spy movie. He told me never to speak of him or anyone I saw, or the assistance I received. There would be no telephone numbers and address's given to me. If I wanted to get in contact with him I had to come here personally and once I checked through customs they would find me. I agreed and said thank you closing the door behind him.

It was almost midnight when I laid down next to Whende to sleep. She would wake up two more times during the night and both times she needed to be washed. I fell asleep as soon as Mr. West left and when I woke up to feed her I saw I had not pushed the loveseat in front of the door. I hated to be paranoid but until I saw some friendly faces or stood on familiar soil I could not relax. I was grateful for the few hours of sleep and at 5:00am the phone rang. Mr. West called to say everything was ready and he was coming up.

He arrived pushing a wheelchair inside the room and a large bag slung over his shoulder. He told me my hotel bill was paid and all I needed to do was get ready to leave. He'd set up a wire transfer like before and we had to stop at the front desk and sign it in front of a witness. The charge for my room and the arrangements he made came to $22,624.38. Since I had the money I didn't argue it seemed like a bargain for peace of mind.

I dressed Whende quickly while she slept placing one of the adult diapers on under her dress. I never bothered to change my own clothes or pack any of the shit I brought with me. I just wrapped her in a clean blanket and put her in the wheelchair and by 5:20 a.m. we were ready to leave.

Time moves so fast when you're anxious. Ten minutes later I signed the wire transfer in front of the hotel clerk and we were in the car headed for the airport. The streets were still dark and few people were out. By the time we reached the airport the sun was rising. The car did not go to the terminal instead we went through a guard booth and rode on the inside of the airport restricted for personnel only. The entire time we were in the car Whende cried. She cried while we boarded the plane and during takeoff. We were at thirty five thou-sand feet and she was still crying. It was almost as if she knew I was taking her away but that was impossible. She would not eat and she wasn't wet and I was at a loss of what to do. Luckily the plane had a bed to put her in. Whende cried until she was exhausted and finally after 6:00 am she fell asleep.

Still I was nervous, how could I be sure they were taking me home? I'd made some grave errors in judgment. Never once did I call my sister or any of my family to tell them I was on my way home and how I was getting there. Alone, I thought about what had transpired these last few weeks and how I would never be the same. I was forced to believe in the unbelievable. I had fallen in love for the first time and had it taken away. Now I was forced to live with the reality that the one I wanted most would never know me. If I had to do over again how could I have made it different?

My best friend had frustrated me so deeply. Even though in my heart I knew he did it for love. Would I ever be able to trust him again? Then there was Terri, how was I going to explain this to her, and what would she do? Would she ever forgive me? Every unanswered question hurt my soul and at thirty five thousand feet the only relief from my uncertainty was sleep.

Chapter 15

Nineteen days had passed since I'd left my home in New York and by Thursday March 28th, 12:48 pm, I was back in my living room. It was almost 7:00 am when the jet departed on its sixteen hour non-stop trip back to New York. My anxiety faded some the moment I was back in the old neighborhood and saw my front door. It was pure luck no one was on the block to witness my return.

A half hour after we were inside, Whende had been washed and fed and was sleeping soundly upstairs in my bedroom. Today she seemed slightly stronger and able to lift her head a few inches to follow my movements. Her eyes had begun to focus in my direction when she heard the sound of my voice but otherwise there was no change.

I sat on the couch experiencing the true meaning of the word exhaustion. If I let myself go right now I could sleep through the night and into the next morning. It was still hard for me to believe Mr. West let us go and I wondered if his influence could follow me here. I pulled myself away from the couch; took the cordless phone and went into the kitchen to sit at the table. I called my friend Butch who lives on 121st Street and told him I lost my keys. I needed the locks changed and he said he would be here within the hour. It wasn't that I was paranoid I just felt I had to do everything I could to keep her safe. I had thoughts of armed guards and attack dogs but first I would start with the locks.

To keep myself from falling asleep I started making phone calls to let everyone know I was back. The first call was to my Aunt Dot in Detroit who couldn't tell me enough times how much she worried and how upset she was with me. Yes, she received my postcard two days ago but she reminded me of all the calls she had received concerning my whereabouts. Apologizing after every sentence, I promised I'd never make her worry again.

I called Chris and Raymond at the stores to see how things were and let them know I wouldn't be back for a few more days. I got pretty much the same response from them about my disappearing act and I made even more apologies. After that I called my sister, Demetrice, at work and started with an apology. I think if she weren't surrounded by people, she would have cursed me out; still she seemed glad to hear from me.

Then I made the hardest phone call of all. Terri would be in her office now and I had no idea what I would say to her but I had to call. After being on hold for several minutes she picked up. I told her I was home and when she asked when I got back I was glad I could say it was today. She sounded very reserved but said we needed to talk and I agreed. Then she was interrupted by someone in the office and told me she would call back. The tone of her voice was disturbing. It sounded free from any emotion. She was not mad or happy to hear from me. She'd been hesitant to discuss events in her life concerning disappointments from other men especially those from her father. At times I felt she placed too much emphasis on trust. I knew she had been traumatized and looked for me to help her recover, but from what I never knew.

Butch did not come to change the locks until he walked in the kitchen where I was sitting to let me know he was here. He had his own set of keys for many years in case of an emergency that caught me out of town. Not only did he do plumbing and carpentry around the house he'd been a good friend of the family. Even though he was raising two boys and working a full-time job, he found the time to help anyone who asked. Grateful for a couple of hours sleep, I explained which locks I wanted changed then went upstairs to check on Whende. When I went to the bed she was awake sucking on her finger. I took this opportunity to warm a bottle of milk and this time I added one teaspoon of cereal. Each time she ate more and slept less. It was evident I would need a home attendant to watch and feed her while I was working.

When I finished burping her, she made a slight grunt followed by that familiar smell. While I was in the bathroom running the water I wondered if there was an easier way to keep her clean. So far I'd washed her in the tub five or six times but I wasn't sure she needed a bath every time. Until I figured out a better way, this is what I had to do but the pain in my back from lifting her each time would make me think of something soon.

Placing Whende in the bath I thought about the times I sat on the floor next to the tub while Terri soaked. She would come to my house and be exclusively pampered. I'd add oil and bath beads to turn the water ocean blue then place one Minuet rose in a small crystal vase by the edge of the tub. Then I'd read poems by Nicky Giovanni while we sipped on glasses of wine. After the wine and bath, Terri received a total massage with warm strawberry scented oil. She loved to be pampered with foreplay and I enjoyed making her wait, but those days were over now.

While Butch worked on the front door, Terri approached him with her keys in hand. She wondered why I hadn't mentioned getting the locks changed and felt awkward coming inside. The one item that anchored her faith in my love was those keys.

I thought I heard a voice downstairs and as it came closer I knew who it was. It was my intention to be finished and put Whende to sleep so Terri and I could talk downstairs.

"Bennie what's that nasty smell in here?"

"Terri, wait there a minute!"

"Butch is downstairs changing the locks," she said.

She was in the bedroom now and there was nothing I could do.

"I lost my keys and…"

When I turned around she was standing in the bathroom doorway.

"Who is that bitch?!"

"Terri, wait a minute."

"Sure."

Then she raced inside the bathroom lunging at Whende. I couldn't let Terri hit her so I swung my right arm before she got to close and pushed her back.

"Did you just hit me?"

"No, I just…"

"Motherfucker, did you just hit me?"

She turned and went out of the room and downstairs but her purse was lying near the wall, and then I heard her footsteps returning. She was calm when she took off her coat only then did I see the butcher knife in her hand.

"Terri, wait a minute! Please, you don't understand."

She looked like someone I'd never seen before. Her expressions changed like flashcards from pain to anger to joy and eagerness. I had no idea who this woman was with each slow step she took.

"You fucked up now! I tried to keep her away from you but it's too late!"

Terri held the knife just like I taught her only now she wasn't looking at Whende anymore, I was her target. She waited for me to move closing the distance between us inches at a time. Watch your opponent's first motion, and then strike, I often told her.

"Terri it's not what you think."

"I know, baby," she said smiling moving ever closer.

"She's an invalid... and she's retarded. If I let her go she'll drown!"

Terri stopped just four feet away never taking her eyes off me, but once she did, I kept talking.

"She's my sister and she's retarded... and bedridden. I have to wash her until I get a nurse. Terri please look at her, she doesn't know what's going on, and we are not doing anything!"

It was hard to tell whether I should watch Terri's eyes or the knife for a clue to what would come next.

"Look at her cry. She can't understand," I whispered.

I pushed Whende forward so Terri could see her face.

Terri watched Whende struggle to hold her head still and for a second Whende's eyes stopped to watch Terri as she waved the knife from side to side. Whende stopped crying only because her eyes followed the glint of the knife but had no change in expression.

"See I'm telling you the truth, and I knew you were coming. Why would I be with someone?"

"It still doesn't explain a lot," she said calmly holding the knife.

"I know."

"You think I'm a fool?"

"No, I don't!"

"You don't think I know how to check plane reservations and when you made them! You were never going to take me on that trip with you... were you?"

I opened my mouth and said nothing.

"You brought one ticket two days before you left! Didn't you?"

I played stupid like I had no idea what she was talking about.

"But I tell you what;" as she lowered the knife, "always remember this day. You were the only one that got away. If you see me, don't say shit to me or ever call me again and you'll be safe."

I had no idea what she meant by that but I was clear on one thing. Terri had lost her goddamned mind. Terri smiled at me with the eyes of a comic book villain and said,

"Do you understand?" then waited like a statue for an answer.

"Yes," I said.

Then she dropped the knife on the bathroom floor and walked out. Instantly she returned peeping only her head in and said,

"And by the way, I killed your fucking fish!"

I stayed in the same position unwilling to move, listening to make sure Terri was leaving. When the front door opened I heard Butch speaking briefly to Terri downstairs then I pulled the pin to let the water out of the tub. Strange to think with both doors closed Butch never could hear us fighting upstairs. When only two inches of water remained, I left Whende in the bathroom to check for myself. In the living room I saw the milky green water in the fish tank and an empty bottle of pine-scented ammonia on the floor. I never went up close to look at the fish but I knew they were dead.

Once I was satisfied Terri was no longer in the house I cleaned the bed and dressed Whende and laid down beside her. I never believed Terri would act that way or that she was capable of such violence. But her eyes told me she would never have been satisfied with stabbing me just once or even a few times. I think I would have been able to stop her but I would never be totally sure.

She was the type of person to expand on anything she was taught and most likely she would have stuck me at least once. I couldn't help but think what was in her past to make her act that way, and why I didn't see it coming?

She was always reluctant to discuss her childhood and where she grew up. There were no family photos displayed in her apartment and no picture albums. She kept one picture of her father taken from the casket before he was buried and that was it. It was hard to believe I was the reason for her manic behavior but I was glad to find out now.

Butch finished shortly after Terri left. He'd kept one set of keys for himself and given two sets to me. Before he left he asked about the yelling he'd heard upstairs. I told him simply Terri and I were no longer seeing each other and to never let her in the house again. From his brief observation of her leaving he gave me a bit of advice. He said watch that woman and be careful cause he didn't think she was right in the head. I totally agreed with him and reminded him never to let her in again.

I sat downstairs in the living room holding the picture we'd taken together and reminisced about the good times with Terri. There was only one thing she'd ever done that was a little strange but it was so long ago I'd forgotten.

Before we were intimate I showed up at her apartment unannounced on a Saturday with a bouquet of her favorite roses. I knew she was home because I'd called her and she said she was staying inside that day. When I knocked on the door she opened it after a time and only a few inches. She was reluctant to let me in until I showed her the roses but still there was something very strange. When she finally opened the door, I remembered she had that same villainous smile. Something told me I should leave but I just thought she was playing with me. She wore black jeans and a gray hooded pullover sweatshirt. Her hair was a mess and if I didn't know she was a lawyer I would have thought she escaped from the Creedmoor Mental Hospital. She wore yellow Playtex gloves smeared red around the wrists but the fingers and palms of the gloves were clean like she'd tried to wash them before she opened the door. And the gray sweatshirt was speckled with blood. I asked what she was doing and she said she was cutting up some liver so I paid it no mind.

She wouldn't let me stay long and when I wanted to use the bathroom she said her toilet was stopped up. A few days later she came to my house and asked me if I would tell anyone that asked that we spent all day Saturday together. No one ever asked and I forgot about it, but that should have been my clue to leave her ass alone. Was I so preoccupied with getting into her pants I missed it?

I never missed the other clues women gave, like when Angela offered to cook dinner and fell asleep preparing it. She almost burnt my house down that night. I made sure I never saw her again after that. Then there was Bernice who cursed out the waiter ghetto style in that nice restaurant downtown. I never took her anywhere else except to bed and home. When she was hungry we ate takeout and she stayed in the car when I ordered it.

But Terri's fury, however justified, could not be disregarded. This event was a huge billboard, which read, "Leave her ass alone!" If I saw Terri again I would say nothing but always keep my eye on her.

The next week went better as far as Whende was concerned. I hired a home attendant to look after her twelve hours a day, six days a week. Her name was Yvonne Camps, She was a native of Trinidad and she started on Monday April Fools day.

Yvonne was the best choice out of all the other candidates I interviewed. As her new employer, my instructions were very simple. If the doorbell rang, don't answer it. If the phone rang, don't answer it; let the machine take a message. And most of all don't let anyone see Linda without my permission. As a trained health care professional she was diligent and attentive to Linda's special needs.

Yvonne was in her late forties with brown skin and hair just long enough to curl the edges. She was five feet nine inches tall with a slender build for a woman who had four children. She spoke with a soft, lilting but authoritative Trinidadian accent and as the days went by I learned to trust and depend on her suggestions. There were times when she became overbearing and meddlesome but every time I came home Whende was happy, clean and well fed.

On Tuesday the next day, we moved Linda down the hall and made that room her bedroom. There was some comfort in seeing Whende grow stronger with each day. When I brought her home last week she could barely turned her head or lift her arms but by Tuesday she was lifting her head slightly and holding my hand. I talked to her constantly and prayed she might be in some kind of coma and was fighting to return. So each day I talked to her about where I went and what I did. I told her what I ate, who I saw and what they said to me. I knew she couldn't understand but every night just before she drifted off to sleep I told her to keep fighting.

On Saturday I went to the office and that was the week Ronald and Lorraine returned home. I'd been so busy lately that I never prepared a story to tell. Surely, he was looking out for my wellbeing and I still loved him because we were like brothers. However, his disloyalty would be forgiven but never forgotten.

I spent the afternoon reviewing almost three weeks of receipts. Chris and Raymond performed well during our absence and with Ronald's confirmation I planned to give them both a bonus and some extra vacation time. From the monitor I saw Ronald enter and walk towards the office. When he came in, I stood up from behind the desk and extended my hand.

"What's up man?" He said as we shook hands.

"Everything is good," I said with little emotion.

"How long have you been back?"

"I've been back of more than a week, from last Thursday I think."

He looked around the office before he sat down on the couch.

Thinking about how Lorraine knew Paula's name and what else he'd mentioned about my life bothered me. It was my belief when we spoke about my exploits it was just guy talk that stayed between us. Lorraine knew details she could only have gotten from him, and she probably told her girlfriends too. Because he was married I never told his business to Terri or anyone else. Even if he wasn't, I'd never have talked about what I knew about his life unless he mentioned it first. So from this day forward, I decided not to say anything I didn't want Lorraine to know.

We sat with an awkward silence brewing between us until I decided to break it for the purpose of controlling his suspicions.

"You were right not to help me."

He looked at me in disbelief and gave a sigh of relief.

"I was trippin' but I'm okay now," I said with a smile.

"I wasn't sure I did the right thing."

"No you did, and it's cool."

"Really?"

Determined not to mention anything about bringing Whende home I said, "I stayed for a couple of days and came home."

"You did?"

I knew Mr. West and his colleagues robbed the disks from their room and he might ask me about it.

"Yes I did."

Now it was time for me to see where he was coming from.

"So where did you guys go?"

After a short silence he said, "We didn't go far, just across town to another hotel."

"Another hotel? I thought you left!" I said trying to sound surprised.

If I acted like I didn't know where they went he couldn't ask me about the missing disks. I promptly grew fed up with this bullshit cat and mouse game. The more I thought about what he did the angrier I became, but I held it inside. If I stayed any longer I was bound to say something I would regret.

"Well listen, I've been going over the receipts and the deposits and everything looks good. If it's all right with you I'd like to give Chris and Raymond a thousand dollar bonus, and one week's paid vacation."

"One thousand to split or a thousand for each of them?"

"It's up to you."

"They could have been robbing us blind, but they didn't," I added.

"You're right, give them each a grand."

"Is there anything else?"

"No I don't think so."

"Well then I'm outta here."

When I reached the door I turned around and said,

"I almost forgot. Terri and I aren't seeing each other anymore."

"What happened?"

"I'll tell you later but listen, the girl has a problem and I think you and Lorraine should stay away from her. She poisoned my fish and some other dumb stuff."

"She didn't mess up the house did she?"

"No, the house is fine."

"What happened?" Ronald insisted.

"I'll talk to you later. But seriously if you see her be careful and watch you back."

"Watch my back?"

"Yeah! And be sure to tell Lorraine too."

Yvonne was in the kitchen when I returned home. Linda was resting upstairs and Yvonne took this time to ask me about her condition. I told her I was not sure what happened but she had not always been like this. She did however confirm what I'd seen for myself. Linda was getting a little stronger each day. She was holding her head up more steadily and her eyes focused on your face and other objects when you showed them to her. She would reach out and grasp anything in front of her, and as long as it wasn't heavy she held it. At times, she even put it in her mouth. She also enjoyed shaking the pink plastic rattle I bought from the toy store and other baby toys.

Yes I had noticed she was a little stronger and I wondered if the warning had been misinterpreted with the translation.

"Death to all that is known," could have referred to the mind and not the body, and if that was true could I expect her to make a full recovery? I dared to hope and surely time would tell.

Later on that evening when Ronald arrived home he called to say that everything went well. He told Chris and Raymond the good news, and then asked again about the breakup with Terri. I left out the part about Linda and the butcher knife. Instead I told him Terri threatened me and told me to stay away from her. I also said she was mad with him and Lorraine because she felt they were covering for me. I told him I changed the locks because she poured ammonia in the fish tank. Then I said I was cooking which I wasn't, so I could end the conversation but he pressed for more details.

Speculating what might happen if I told him the truth, I imagined a day Lorraine would confront me and insist Terri's behavior was the result of my neglect. I had a suspicion that as he talked to me on the telephone, Lorraine sat close by listening. At times, during previous conversations Ronald would repeat my sentence while we spoke. It never seemed to bother me until now but with Linda living here my faith in his word was not absolute. I envisioned the government sending a small army of men, some dressed in white lab coats, and others armed with assault rifles storming into my house to take Linda. Sooner or later he would find out I was taking care of her and when he did I would insist to him and everyone who asked she was my long lost sister, a child my father never knew existed. So the dialogue ended with me insisting I smelled my food burning.

Linda went through so many changes in the next two weeks; it was a joy to come home. She cried less and smiled more and soon she could recognize my face from Yvonne's. I could get her to smile each time by lightly touched her cheek with my finger. She was listening to the sound of her own voice and turning over on her own. When Yvonne discovered Linda could roll off the bed I purchased a new one with pull up guardrails.

Her diet changed from the warm milk and cereal mixture to soft food prepared in a food processor. It was wonderful to see the progress she made each day. By her third week in her new home, Linda was able to sit upright, which meant washing her in the tub wasn't so back-breaking.

Towards the end of the month, she began to crawl and although it was good to see, it opened up a world of trouble because she wanted to touch everything. It was necessary to childproof the house by install-ing bars on every window and an iron gate to prevent her from falling down the stairs. I moved anything that was dangerous or poisonous, from pens and pencils to the cleaning products. I moved the silverware and all the stuff she might find small enough to choke on and covered the electrical outlets.

When May came, Linda was walking and the next week she was running through the house and calling me Be Be. There was a day or two when she tried to say Da Da but I couldn't stand it. I had no idea what to expect or if she would ever remember her past. The thought she might always consider me as a brother was bad enough that I did not want her to call me daddy. So I kept saying Be Be to her so when she saw me that's what she said.

Once Linda began to chew her food her diet remained simple. She ate only the foods she would have been accustomed to and everything was organic. I wanted to limit as many chemical preservatives from her food as I could. The poultry was bought live at the chicken house killed and cleaned in front of me. I knew the ancient Egyptians ate poultry, fruits and vegetables along with bread and fish. I also saw cows, goats and lambs while we were in the carriage but until I found evidence she ate beef, and goat meat she couldn't have it.

Linda's food was never warmed in a microwave and if the refrig-erator weren't such a necessity I would have gotten rid of it too. Every-thing she ate was natural and free from preservatives. I didn't give her candy or granulated sugar. She was not allowed to drink soda, milk or processed beverages. Instead I bought a juice machine and blended the juice myself.

Because of her diet, I changed mine too. Eating dinner and drink-ing homemade juice with Linda, I began to have more energy and after a while I knew at least sixty ways to prepare chicken and turkey meat. Only when I was alone, did I sneak into Sherman's restaurant for barbeque ribs and spaghetti.

Shortly after I returned home from Egypt I called pet shops for puppies that evening when I arrived home from work there was a message on the machine from Puppy Palace. They had some ten week old puppies left from a litter of nine pure breed Rottweilers. The next day I went to the shop on Tremont Avenue in the afternoon to look at the pups. From outside I saw them in a large cage next to the window. I stood for a moment study them and feeling good about the decision I was making to have a guard dog. Finally I walked inside and went to the cage. Three of the pups were huddled in the corner sleeping, and one stood by the window uninterested. The other two were excited to see me and battled to lick my finger. A man asked if I need some help and I told him why I was there.

It was hard to decide which one I wanted to hold so he opened the cage and grabbed the first one. It was a male he said when he handed it to me. I held the pup and rubbed his neck and he never took his eyes off me. He was 90 percent black except for the lower part of his legs and his paws were like bear claws. I had an idea he would be big when he grew up. The gentleman asked if I wanted to hold one of the others and I said no, this was the one.

At the store I brought some dog food and vitamins, a collar and a leash. I also needed some bowls for the dog food and the water. The salesman also recommended I buy some pads to place on the floor until the puppy was trained to go outside. He also suggested I take the puppy to a veterinarian as soon as possible for some shots.

Once everything was paid for he placed the puppy in a cardboard box and accompanied me to the car. I put the bags in the back seat then took the box from him and put it in the seat next to me. The puppy was so quiet on the way home that at the first red light, I peeked inside the box to be sure the dog was still breathing. He was fine but when I closed the lid he started to cry. I pulled over near the Cross Bronx Expressway and took him out and drove home with him on my lap.

He showed his gratitude by licking my hand all the way home. So content and grateful, since I picked him I thought we'd have a special bond like Lassie to the little boy on TV. I thought about naming him Mr. Charles and then Mr. Mann because they sounded incisive, finally I said I'll call you Mr. Tibbs because I always liked the way Sidney Portier said that line in the movies. He let you know right away he was not to be messed with. I called him Mr. Tibbs until it started to sound a bit corny so after a day I just called him Mister.

In the distance I could see the building where Ronald and Lorraine lived and my thoughts turned to him. I did not like the strain on our friendship and his birthday was coming in a few weeks and we had a ritual of treating each other to a night on the town. It was never anything fancy. Most times we ended up at a strip bar throwing dollar bills away, or going downtown to a couple of clubs. The last time we went it was my birthday and I got so wasted I came home and threw up in the tub.

He looked out for me that night so I could relax and celebrate my day. It was time I thought more about the good things he did for me and the times we had with each other. I thought about calling him when I got home to arrange a meeting so we could talk. Once we met we'd talk a bit and then I would say how long have we known each other? He would say since we were seven or eight. Then we'd talk until the sun came up. The only problem was I couldn't stop seeing the men taking Linda away from me. If I confided in him, I did not believe he could keep the secret.

It was a beautiful warm day near the end of May. I watched Linda and Mister play in the backyard from the second floor window while Yvonne read the newspaper on the balcony. Except for the backyard, which was fenced in on both sides, she'd never been outside or seen anyone except from the window.

By now Linda could say my name and Yvonne's and her vocabulary began to grow quite quickly as she learned new words each day. She could also tell us when she needed to go to the bathroom and Sunday was the last day I had to wash her. She still needed supervision and that could be done by keeping the door open, glancing in now and then reminding her to keep the water inside the tub.

When she was able to understand I would tell her no one was allowed to see her naked or touch her private place including me. Once her mind caught up with her body she would realize why, but right now even she looked almost thirty years old, she only had the intelligence of a two-year old child.

I tapped on the window to let Yvonne know I was standing inside. She closed the newspaper and came in with a strange look on her face and stood by the window next to me.

"Good afternoon," she said.

"Hi Yvonne, how are you?"

"Fine."

"How is Linda?"

"She's good."

I went to the door and waved at Linda.

"Hi Bennie," she said with a bubbling voice.

"She learns so fast," I remarked.

"Yes, I never saw a case like this before."

"Well I'm just glad she's getting better."

"I spoke to a doctor from my country and he would be more that glad to help with her recovery?"

"She has a doctor" I said trying not to appear defensive.

"I know, but my friend thinks she suffered some kind of trauma?"

"No, she didn't."

"It's just that she..."

Yvonne stammered for the words.

"Have you noticed something?" I asked eagerly hoping Linda's memory was returning.

Without any warning Yvonne said," I have been wondering when her last period was?"

"Her period?"

"Yes man, her period. You know her cycle, her menstruation."

"I know what you mean."

"Well, when was it?"

"I don't know."

"I'm asking because she hasn't had one. I've been here almost two months you know."

I looked at Mister licking Linda's face and wanted to smile. I wanted to jump up and down with happiness at the thought of being a father but the lie I created wouldn't allow it. If I let Yvonne suspect for one second Linda was pregnant by me I'd be in trouble.

"Are you sure?"

"Yes."

"I have to find out," I said calmly.

"Yes we must," Yvonne said.

Something about the we in her sentence bothered me. If Linda was pregnant I needed to get rid of Yvonne without making her suspicious.

"You never said what kind of accident she had?"

"I not sure."

"Did someone do something to her?"

"No."

"Then what happened?"

I told her the only thing I could think of, "Before she came here to live she fell and hit her head. The doctors said it would take time for her to recover and as you see she gets better every day."

"Yes I know but what if she's pregnant?"

"I don't think so, it's probably just because of her injury she's late." I couldn't blame Yvonne for being concerned and if Linda was pregnant there was no way to hide it. To throw off her suspicions I said,

"I'll call the doctor tomorrow and set up an appointment."

"Okay."

Without giving her a chance to ask any more questions I wasn't prepared to answer I made it sound like I would include her.

"I'm so glad to have you here Yvonne, and we'll find out what's going on."

Then I went upstairs to my bedroom to think.

It was after 3:00pm and Yvonne had a few hours before she left for the day, so I left the house and took a cab across the river to the Bronx to purchase a home pregnancy kit. I concealed the box in a brown paper bag and a white plastic shopping bag and returned home. Linda and Yvonne were sitting in the living room watching television. I lied to Yvonne when I told her Linda had an appointment to see the doctor on Monday. Kindly she offered to come with us but I gave her the day off. I reminded her I did not want Linda to watch television. In the past two months I hadn't listened to the radio or watched television in her presence. I kept as much modern technology away from her as possible. Right now while she was still learning, it was my opinion she should only have the stimulus she'd grown up with: music and books, live entertainment, and human interaction. But one day when I felt her mind was strong enough I would do whatever it took to jog her memory. If I had to recreate her room in detail, or hire a seamstress to make the same clothing we'd worn when I'd traveled into the past, I'd do it. I'd even travel with her to Africa and find the place where her house once stood. Most of all I needed patience. One step at a time, I thought, just one step at a time.

That night after Linda went to sleep; I lay awake in bed for hours. If Linda was pregnant, I could not keep Yvonne around. I knew I could not fire her too quickly without arousing her suspicion. However it was beneficial to have a woman around to show Linda the things I could not. While I was able to instruct her how to tie her shoes and explain certain precautions she needed to know as a woman, it was Yvonne who showed her how to put on a bra. Taking one off was easy, I'd done that many times before but I assumed there are secrets of a woman's psyche I could not teach her.

Yvonne also knew I was not dating and tried several times to introduce me to some of her girlfriends. She understood I'd just gone through a breakup with Terri and that was the excuse I used not to meet them.

Then there was the test. How was I going to get Linda to take a pregnancy test? It was necessary to dip a plastic wand treated with a chemical into her urine. If the plus sign appeared the test was positive for pregnancy. How was I going to ask her to pee in a cup after I placed so much importance in using the bathroom, and could she tell Yvonne? Tonight was Thursday and tomorrow was the end of the month. I had all weekend to figure out what I should do. I relaxed and waited for sleep thinking of the last time I kissed her sweet mouth wondering if I would ever be able to do it again.

When Friday morning came, I was ready to leave as soon as Yvonne arrived. It was my intention to be out of the house early and come back just when it was time for her to leave. That way I could avoid long conversations with her until I knew what to do.

The weather forecast had predicted that this Saturday would bring the first heavy rainstorm of the season. Outside, it was a mild 79 degrees with gray skies and gusting winds. I came home early so that Yvonne could leave before the storm hit. I still hadn't figured a way to get Linda to take the test but I had more than two days to come up with something. So after Yvonne left I joined Linda in her room sitting at the table using her crayons.

"Did you come to play with me?" asked Linda.

"Yes I did."

"Oh goody," she said happily, "you can color in this book."

I took a seat across from her and she pushed a coloring book in front of me.

"It's a new one, but let me color Donald okay?"

Just to test her I asked, "Which one is Donald?"

"Here I'll show you."

Then she turned a few pages in the book and stopped.

"That's Donald, isn't he funny?"

"Yeah he sure is, and who's this?"

She stopped coloring and flipped through the pages.

"That's Mickey Mouse and that's Goofy. Goofy's a dog and that's Minnie she's a mouse too."

"You're so smart," I said.

"Yup."

I took a crayon and started to color. After a few minutes Linda said with envy,

"You're good."

"You'll be able to do it to, just keep trying."

I had to find out if she was pregnant and if she was how could I explain it to her? Everything in her room belonged to little girl and as hard as I tried I could not see myself asking her to urinate in a cup. The whole idea made me sick.

"What's wrong Bennie, are you sad?"

"No."

"You look sad. Is it because you don't have any friends?"

"No."

"I don't have any friends either."

"You have me, and Mister."

"Mister is a dog. He can't talk to me."

Linda's voice sounded heartbreaking then she said, "Mickey Mouse has a lot of friends and I don't have any."

She stopped coloring and was about to cry.

"We'll find some friends for you," I said hastily.

"You will," she said with a huge smile.

"Sure."

"Where?"

"Outside at the park."

"When?"

"Monday, I'll take you to the park."

"Oh goody goody."

She leaped from her chair and started kangaroo hopping around the room shaking everything.

"But you have to be good."

She stopped at once, "I will, I will," she said in earnest.

"And there's one thing you have to do for me."

"What?" She said happily.

Now as my opportunity to tell her all she had to do was pee in a cup, but I couldn't find the words.

"What do I have to do Bennie?"

I felt sick inside and I couldn't do it.

"After you finish coloring clean up your room and take a bath."

"That's all."

"Yup."

"I will, I will."

We continued coloring together until 7:30pm then I left her alone to clean up her room.

From my bedroom I heard Linda talking to Mister and I yelled to her and she came running from a room. I asked her to let Mister into the backyard and I would be down in a minute. When I went to the bathroom I got an idea. I turned the water off at the toilet and flushed it until all the water was gone. Now when she went to the bathroom I could do the test.

It was darker than usual and the floodlight in the backyard was on. The trees were swaying in the wind and the first drops of rain began to fall. I asked Linda if she needed to go to the bathroom, and when she said yes I told her the toilet wasn't working and I would fix it later. Then I stood on pins and needles until she finished. When she came out I went inside the bathroom to perform the test. I followed the directions and after awhile I found out she was indeed pregnant.

I turned the water back on and started to fill the tub for Linda. Standing in front of the mirror with the door closed wondered what to do. It felt like I was punished because I was not allowed to be happy about the news. How was I going to explain a seemingly retarded woman having a baby?

Linda knocked on the bathroom door to tell me she was ready for the bath and when I opened the door I found it hard to look at her. Rushing past I went to my room and sat silently until she finished and went to sleep.

During the night the storm intensified. The winds howled and blew metal trashcans around the street. The rain poured and the lightning lit up the room like a photographer's flash. The thunder felt like a bass drum vibrating the house. When the lightning flashed again Linda was standing at the foot of my bed in a white nightgown. For a second I thought back to when I saw her standing in the Obeni and the sun shined through her silky white dress. Her curves were still sensual and I gazed at her beauty. She wiped her eyes and said, "Bennie I'm scared."

"It's just a storm Whende...I mean Linda."

"I know but I'm scared."

"I won't let anything hurt you," I assured her, "go back to bed."

"Can I sleep in here with you, please?"

I should have said no but I couldn't help myself.

"All right but just for tonight."

I lifted the covers on one side and she climbed in next to me. In the dimness I told her some facts about lightning so she wouldn't be afraid. And when the next bolt lit up the room and a thunder followed she moved closer laying her head on my chest and her feet touching mine.

"It's inside the house," she said holding me tighter.

Her breasts pressed against me and we were close like lovers. I fought to control the rise swelling within me but it was too late. Her hair smelled sweet under my nose and when I caressed her head my breathing grew heavy. I called her name and when she looked at me I kissed her forehead and transcended back in time to when we were in her bedroom so many months ago.

"Do you want to go to the park Monday?"

"Yes."

I remembered the sweet taste of her mouth, and the scent of her affection.

"If you're not a good little girl I won't take you!"

"I know... I'll be good."

Terri use to toy with me in that same tone.

"Do you know what I want you to do now?"

"No."

"Turn over and go to sleep."

I turned away until our backs were together and listened to the rainfall.

Chapter 16

This year Ronald's birthday fell on a Sunday so we made plans to celebrate on the Friday before his birthday. That way he could spend the weekend with Lorraine. Even though it was eighty three degrees, the breeze hitting the sweat on my arms immediately gave me a chill. I waited outside the car on 127th street and 7th Avenue with a half case of cold beer on ice and a pint of vodka in the cooler.

At 5:30pm the people from the neighborhood were getting off the buses and trains and returning home from work when I saw Ronald walking towards me. Today was his day and I was determined to show him a good time. As he approached I extended my arm to shake hands. Then I said,

"So how old are you gonna be thirty five, thirty six?"

"Twenty eight," he said with a smile.

"Damn, you're an old bastard," I laughed.

"Shit, you're older than me!" he grinned.

"Are you sure?" I said keeping a straight face.

I opened the trunk and went in the cooler and took out two beers. We walked to a bench outside the park across from the car, opened the cans and touched them together.

"Here's to you. May you have a healthy, happy, and prosperous life, happy birthday."

"Thanks man."

We looked around to make sure no cops were watching, and then we took a long sip.

"That's good," Ronald said.

"Goes down nice right?" I replied.

"Yeah it's ice cold," then he took another sip.

I looked at him and thought how many times we'd done this over the years, and realized he was still the only person I trusted, but I heard that song in my head and it confirmed my uneasiness. "When a man loves a woman, she can do no wrong. Turn his back on his best friend if he puts her down."

As much as I loved Ronald, I knew one day I would be forced to make a difficult shift in our relationship. Each time we got together, his woman, Lorraine, backed me further into a corner over bullshit that had nothing to do with her. As hard as I tried not to let it bother me one day she would add enough straw to break my back.

Like the day I casually mentioned I was going to drive upstate to the cemetery and spend a few minutes at my mother's grave. She felt that since she never went to see her departed ones, I shouldn't go either. I explained how just a few moments cleaning the overgrown grass from the bronze marker gave me some small comfort. Mom had been laid to rest in a peaceful quiet setting over looking mountains covered with green grass and trees in one of the most serene locations I'd ever been. Her grave was set in the middle of a beautiful picture postcard or artist's canvas. I would go there and wait until the wind stopped rustling the leaves and for a brief period there was blissful silence. In those moments, I felt in touch with her and when I left it seemed there was no hurdle I couldn't climb and no project I couldn't accomplish. With Ronald standing quietly beside Lorraine in their living room she insisted I was wasting my time and preceded to tell me there was only a shell buried under the bronze marker. I told her if it made me feel good what difference did it make. Still that didn't matter, she just went on criticizing me until I left their house. That day I knew whatever I did to appease her would never be enough so I stopped trying.

"What's been going on with you?" I asked.

"Nothing much. We're looking for a car."

"Yeah, what kind?"

"I don't know," he changed the subject, "How's your sister?"

"Oh Demetrice is fine," I said.

We were both making uneasy small talk when it wasn't necessary.

"So what do you want to do, Homey? Today is your day." I asked him.

"Let's start at the Wren's Nest and then we'll go check out Al's," he said.

"Cool and don't worry about nothing, I got your back," I told him.

We sat and chilled on the bench talking about music and sports. The conversation shifted to old friends and people in the neighborhood: who was doing what and who still wasn't doing shit. A fly sister in a tight orange dress smiled at us when she walked by, and we kept watching until she was out of sight. When we finished the last two beers and the evening approached we left and headed downtown to the east side.

It had been a while since we'd spent time together. We used to hang out almost every day and we biked twice a month but since my return I'd seen him only once or twice. We had a lot of catching up to do and I was looking forward to the meeting. Ronald was my best friend first, and then my business partner and I could never forget that. Even when we were teenagers he knew the right thing to say. He was the one that told me life was like a roller coaster, a series of ups and downs.

One day, some idiot ran a red light and hit the first car I ever owned, a two door sky blue Dodge Colt with black vinyl interior. It wasn't much but like a first kiss or a serious love it held particular meaning. That day a man named Jesse assumed responsibility for the damage to my car and offered to pay for the repairs. After a few weeks of him giving me the run around, I went to small claims court to sue him for the damages. It was the first time I had ever gone to court and I needed a person to serve Jesse with an order to appear. Ronald was the only one of my friends that volunteered to hand Jesse a piece of paper, and it was instances like those that made us friends. We had too much history to let anything come between us. I just wished sometimes he would tell Lorraine to mind her own damn business.

After circling around for fifteen minutes, I found a parking space on 93rd Street and 2nd Avenue. From there we walked the rest of the way to the Wren's Nest. One Friday about a year ago, we started at 125th Street and walked stopping at different stores to buy beer to drink as we ran out. Each time we reached a corner, whichever direction peaked our interest was the way we headed. Out of all the guys I grew up with Ronald and I were still tight and we could walk and talk and laugh and just be buddies. That day we found ourselves in the 90's on the East side and heard music from a corner bar and looked through the window. The place was jumping with excitement from a mixed crowd of young working folks so we went inside.

The bar was on one side of the room while rows of tables and chairs were on the other. The walls were wood paneled decorated with pictures of sports figures and other celebrities. In the corner, close to the ceiling hung a six foot plastic alligator mounted on the wall. At the end of the bar was a small kitchen large enough for three people to prepare burgers and fries, hot wings and mozzarella sticks. It was called Wren's Nest and we've come back ever since. After going a few times we became familiar with the bartenders Jenny, Gloria and Max. Ronald labeled Jenny Ms. Vogue because she was always flipping her long curly hair around and she had hips like a sister even though she was Jewish.

Ronald and I enjoyed celebrity status when we entered the Nest because we were regulars. Besides feeling pretty good, a night away from home was just what I needed. Ronald and I stood until seats became available then we sat at the corner of the bar. We ordered two Coronas with a twist of lime and two shots of tequila from Jenny. I placed $100 bill on top of the bar knowing it would stay there all night and mentioned it was Ronald's birthday. Jenny opened her arms and hugged him, kissing his cheek and saying happy birthday. When we finished the third round of Coronas, I ordered a large platter of extra spicy Buffalo wings and two large frozen margaritas. Then Ronald looked at me with apprehension and said,

"How long have we known each other?"

He must have figured out what I did in Egypt, or one of the neighbors told him a nurse has been coming to the house for the past two months.

"I don't know, since we were seven or eight," I said.

"I gotta say something," then he paused," I know Lorraine gets on your nerves at times and...well I just wanted to say thank you for putting up with it, I know you only do it cause of me."

I was surprised to hear him say it out loud but glad that he did, I wanted to say it was all right and that her meddling behavior didn't bother me but it was time for truth.

"Yeah dude but don't worry about it, everything's cool. As long as she is making you happy, that's all that matters."

I felt like asking him how Lorraine knew about Paula but I already knew that answer and tonight was his night.

"She's always been a handful," said Ronald.

"Really?"

"Yes and it's not just you. So don't think you're the only one she argues with, she treats all my friends like that."

"Like what?" hoping he would say more.

"You know...the way she just jumps in your case. Like last summer when we went to Great Adventure and she argued with the man in charge of the water gun game for ten minutes because her gun started a second or two after the rest. When he offered her a free game that wasn't enough, she insisted on the stuffed duck."

"I didn't know, so what happened?"

"After ten minutes of arguing he let her play the game over and she lost. Then I heard about it for the next half an hour."

We stopped talking because Jenny came with two more Coronas and tequila shots. This time she stayed and had a drink with us. I had been meaning to take her out one night but I just kept letting her simmer until she was ready to boil; besides she liked Ronald more. Jenny told us she would be on a break soon and would come sit with us. When it was her time she came from behind the bar and wedged herself between us. She and her girlfriends took a liking to us and my suspicion was because we were black, but as long as the free drinks and the Jell-O shots were coming I didn't care.

One night last year, just after Thanksgiving, Ronald and I went to the Nest for drinks and Jenny was working at the second smaller bar in the back next to the pool tables. The place was crowded, as usual, and we went to the bar to order. That night Jenny catered to us exclusively and seemed bothered when others came to order drinks. Whatever we wanted to hear, she played on the CD player and whatever we wanted to drink she brought. When a customer asked to hear a particular CD she said no, claiming he didn't have the juice we did. That night there was a girl walking through the crowd with long silky black hair selling Jell-O shots for two dollars. We bought two shots and Jenny asked Ronald to feed the Jell-O to her. She guided his hand to her mouth and sensually ate the Jell-O from the paper cup. When she finished she used great technique to suck the whipped cream from each of his fingers. Then she made a date with us and said she'd bring the Jell-O shot girl with her. After the display with the whipped cream we could hardly say no.

Jenny stayed until her break was over and went back to work behind the bar and we continued our conversation. I must admit I felt guilty because Ronald confided with me and I was reluctant to reciprocate.

"Hey man, don't worry about it, just talk to her." I said slapping his shoulder.

"I've been thinking about leaving her, Bennie."

"What?"

"Yeah, I get tired of the arguing and the bullshit, but I'm scared she'd make my life miserable."

"Hold on a minute now, she loves you man," I said quickly.

He looked at me to see if I really believed what I was saying.

"She really does and if I didn't think she loved you I'd say so, but she does. So just talk to her!"

In my heart I did believe she loved him so I never pushed him to cheat on her or set him up on dates with women. Anything he did was because he wanted to and he never needed any coaxing from me. But he was my buddy and if I thought for one minute Lorraine didn't love him I would have said so. When I think about it, it's a funny thing. There were so many times Lorraine accused me of trying to break them up she would never believe I was sitting here trying to talk him out of it.

I changed the conversation by needling him about the Knicks and asked him when he thought they'd win their next championship. Ronald reminded me he was a diehard Knicks fan and they were going all the way this year. Then I saw the back of her head and became uncomfortable. It was Terri with two other women standing fifteen feet away from us in the crowd. I tapped Ronald on the hand and pointed in her direction. We watched her make a way to the end of the bar. I recognized one of the women with her as Trina, a co-worker who frequently joined her for lunch.

"Do you think she saw you?" Ronald said.

"Not yet," I replied.

"How'd she know about this place? Did you bring her here?"

"Nope, and I never mentioned it."

We kept a few fun spots to ourselves in case Lorraine or Terri felt like tracking us down.

"Are you going to say something?"

"Hell no! And don't you say anything either."

We watched her take a drink from the glass and turn around to face her friends. She seemed happier and much calmer than the person I'd seen in my kitchen threatening my life. And I began to wonder if I should buy her a drink just to say I'm sorry.

"Hey Ron, you think I should send some drinks over there?"

"If you want to," he said like it was a dare.

When Jenny got close I called her and it was then Ronald said, "She's looking over here."

Jenny heard him and turned around to see who we were looking at but she couldn't tell right away. Terri's eyes were cold and menacing when she looked at me.

"Do you know her?" Jenny asked.

"Yes," I said.

"Why are they staring at you?" Jenny meddled.

"That's my ex girlfriend," I said looking into my drink.

"So what's up?" she said looking at our bottles to see if they were empty.

Terri's expression assured me sending her a drink would not make things any better between us.

"When you get a chance come back and have a drink with us," I said to Jenny.

"Sure," then she looked at Ronald and asked, "Are you staying till I get off?"

"I don't know," Ronald said.

Then Jenny looked at the end of the bar where Terri was.

"They seem a bit strange," Jenny said while she pouted with a smile flipping her hair as she left.

Terri's expression had changed. It was no longer happy and calm; it was the same wicked twisted face I'd seen in the bathroom. Her friends were tapping her shoulder and pulling her arm but she didn't hear them. Then she smiled at me like a shark ready to bite. Even Ronald noticed the strange behavior.

"What the fuck is wrong with her? She looks like she wants to kill you!"

"She does look that way. Just remember Ron... don't say anything to her," I said under my breath trying not to seem uneasy.

"Don't worry I won't. I think you should stay away from her cause she's way out there now!"

He would get no argument from me. I was uncomfortable playing this staring game with her. Trina pulled Terri's arm until she had her attention and all three started for the back room where the pool tables were. Our focus was on them until they disappeared into the crowd but I felt like there was a volcano in the distance ready to erupt. Ronald had no idea what Terri was capable of but from a brief glimpse of her changed personality he felt as concerned as Butch had the day Terri and I had our blow up at the house.

I tried to relax and get back into the spirit of the celebration but Terri's appearance was like a flash flood at a picnic. The fear I had was not of her but the problems she might cause and the unnecessary drama she could put me through. If she wanted to stay here it was okay by me but it was time for us to leave. So when we finished our drinks I suggested to Ron we go to Al's and hang out there. Jenny gave us a sad face when we stood up to leave and asked were we coming back. we always said yes even if we didn't and tonight was no exception. She held Ronald tight and kissed his mouth briefly but with much fondness and I heard her tell him if we came back she had a very nice birthday present for him.

Al's was only five blocks away on Second Avenue in the eighties so we started walking. Without realizing I was doing it, I looked behind me every hundred feet or so. Ronald laughed and asked me if I thought Terri was coming after me. It was funny the way he said it and we both laughed out aloud but I did feel I needed to be very mindful of her from this day on.

Ray the bouncer at Al's was standing outside smoking a cigarette when we walked up. Ronald and I stood outside and talked with him for a few minutes. In this ten to twelve block area everyone working knew each other. The same bouncer or bartender who worked at one bar wound up months later down the street working at the next one. They were interchangeable like sports figures playing on different teams. Once the bouncers and bartenders knew you by name most times you never paid to get in or to drink.

Al's was similar to Wren's Nest, a kitchen and two pool tables in the back except they had better music and a small dance floor. They had twenty different beers on tap and the lights were dimmer in the back lounge. We would meet women and after a few drinks take them in the back where it was cozier.

It was not unusual for us to have six or seven different types of drinks in one night as long as we paced ourselves. Ronald ordered Long Island ice teas in 20 oz. glasses but I knew it was my last drink for the night. We had been drinking for almost six hours and my inebriated condition made me paranoid witnessing Terri's anger again. Ronald went to dance with two women while I stood guard near the door looking for Terri. I wondered if her fury could be directed at my family or friends. If anything happened I would never forgive myself for not telling Ronald what she was capable of. So when he returned from dancing we stepped outside to talk. Leaning on a car parked a few feet away from Al's I told him Terri tried to kill me with a knife several months ago, and that's why I kept looking over my shoulder. Without saying anything about Linda, I went into details and ended my story with a warning to stay away from her. It seemed after my conversation we were both a bit more sober and decided to leave Al's. My car remained where it was and we took a taxi to his house, and then I went home.

Linda was doing well and no longer needed a nurse and that was my reason for letting Yvonne go. Subsequent to telling Yvonne that Linda was not pregnant I let her stay one more week while I interviewed prospective babysitters. The way Linda behaved it was my opinion she was about six years old and did not need the professional care Yvonne used to provide. The first babysitter's name was Karen. She was twenty one years old attending college at Columbia with a major in business administration. After a few days I realized Karen and I had too much sexual attraction, so I decided on a woman in her sixties.

Janice Bertrand was a retired grandmother married forty one years.

She and her husband put three children through college and she only worked part time to keep busy until her husband retired in ten months. With Janice I made up a new story about Linda's condition. Linda was still my sister and her husband died in a car accident. The trauma caused her memory loss but it was returning slowly. If questioned Janice was to deny any knowledge about Linda's past life, she was simply to tell Linda to ask me. My instructions were always the same. Never let anyone in the house while I'm gone. Don't discussed Linda's condition with anyone, and don't let her watch television.

My request seemed bizarre to Janice in the beginning and I anticipated Linda was months away from asking any complex questions. My foremost concern was what I would tell her when the baby started to kick? So far everything had gone smoothly and with each problem I established a way around it. Luckily the schedule Ronald and I made allowing us to manage the stores on alternate weeks which helped immensely.

It seemed like only yesterday Linda was making goo goo sounds and now she was talking. I'd done a good job adjusting to her growing intellect, teaching her at home on nights and weekends but I never knew when her mind would unexpectedly leap forward a few months or even a year. When that occurred she became bored with everything from the coloring books and the floating toys at bath time, to the posters on the wall in her room and the way she wore her hair.

I knew it was time for me to become her primary teacher so we started first by singing the alphabet. Then I brought construction paper and we drew each letter from A to Z. She caught on so quickly by the time I let Yvonne go, Linda was writing her name and most four and five letter words from memory. I kept her fascinated about learning through encouragement and love. I made it a big deal when she mastered something new and her rewards came quickly. If she wanted to go outside or asked for a new toy she got it. I'd start by saying,

"When you can read this Cat in the Hat book to me, I'm going to bring something really nice home for you."
Linda would be so excited her eyes would light up and she'd say,

"What is it?"

"It's called... math!" I'd say making its sound like it was something new she had to have.

"Math! What's that?"

"Ohh! It's what everyone needs, you'll see."

Still smiling and looking a bit mystified she asked, "What does it look like? Can I play with it?"

"Yes you can play with it and when you know how to use it well you can go to the store."

"Really?"

"Sure you can, and when you finish with math I'll show you science!"

This was how I kept Linda happy and intrigued about learning, but it wasn't easy keeping up with the changes in her development. And as time went on I thought more about the relationship we once had.

If her memory never returned, she would forever see me as her older brother and her affection towards another was inevitable. But worse than that, in my efforts to raise her as a strong independent woman, my love for her was slowly changing. I had reached inside myself and torn every fiber of sexual attraction I had for her out and placed it on a raft that night she got in bed with me during the thunderstorm. With her body next to mine I stood on the shore and watched the raft drift out to sea. And each night before I went to sleep I stood on the shore to make sure I could see it but each passing week it drifted farther away.

On the first of July, Mister was four and half months old and weighed 37 lbs. He rarely barked and did all of his business in the backyard, which was cleaned three times a week. Except for my neighbors adjacent to me no one had seen him.

Mister and Linda were best friends and I never regretted the choice I made at the pet store. He had the soul of an older dog and the willingness to be training. Mister watched us all the time and a few weeks ago he started doing something totally unexpected I guess from watching me. Each night when we were ready to go to sleep Mister would check the house. He would go downstairs and walk past each window and every door and when he was satisfied we were safe he came upstairs and slept in the hallway between our rooms.

In the three months Linda had been with me she was quite easy to deal with but July was a nightmare. Her body along with her emotions changed slightly. Her weight gain was noticeable and she became a bit more irritable. Last month she asked questions concerning her body and why her breasts felt heavy so the time was approaching when she had to be told about the birds and the bees.

Late in the afternoon two days ago Linda spent a long time in the bathroom. I thought nothing of it until she did it again last night. It had been months since I'd seen her naked and had no desire to. Once I knew she wouldn't drown in the tub I allowed her to close the door respecting her privacy. When I asked why she was in there so long Linda told me she was just taking a bath, but I didn't believe her. The next time she went in the bathroom I heard the water running and when it stopped I stood near the door. Ten minutes went by and I still didn't hear splashing in the tub so I turned the knob went in. Linda sat undressed on the toilet with both lids down and her head arched back inserting the head of a small yellow plastic duck in her vagina.

"Linda, what are you doing?" I said in a somewhat raised voice.

"Nothing," she answered fumbling for her robe. I knew what she was doing and I felt embarrassed when I caught her.

"Why are you in here so long? What are you doing?"

"I don't know," she said putting each arm in the sleeve.

She said she didn't know and I believed her, I had to. Her illness was a medical mystery and I was quite sure no one knew what to expect from this mature woman with a child's mind. I tried not to appear mad or disappointed with her but I had to do something.

"Did you take your bath yet?"

"No."

"Then get in the water and stop playing around!"

"Yes Bennie," she said pulling off the robe and stepping into the tub. Immediately turning away to leave I said, "Wash up and go to sleep. We'll talk about this later."

Pulling the knob leaving the door half closed, I had to talk about it later because I had no idea what else to say.

I went in my room and turned on the television set which hadn't been on in months and turned the volume down low. When Linda finished she came out of the bathroom and went to sleep. Nothing could have prepared me for this but I guess it was the sort of crisis parents occasionally faced. I'm just glad my parents never caught me.

Subsequently the issue of what she was doing had to be approached carefully. If I said nothing I'd be giving her a license to masturbate. If I was too hard and inconsiderate of her mind-set she might refuse to talk to me when she really had a problem.

The next morning we planned to go shopping for new clothes. Previously I'd purchased all her clothes a size larger and loose fitting to avoid temptation but a size eight was becoming too tight on her.

I was down stairs early in the kitchen about to make waffle batter. Linda came down dressed in blue jeans and sneakers wearing a pink T-shirt. She walked slowly to the table and stood behind it. Mister knew something was wrong and started to jump at Linda licking her hands for attention.

"Linda don't play with the dog while I'm fixing food in the kitchen. Mister," I said firmly looking at him,

"Go sit down... go on."

He looked at me then left Linda standing alone.

"Did I ever show you how I make waffles?"

"No," she said in a whisper.

"Well wash your hands and you can help me."

I had no idea what I was going to say so I decided to be pleasant. She washed her hands in the sink next to me and waited.

"You see that box."

"Yes."

"Give it to me."

I put the mix into a measuring cup and told her to put the box back in the cabinet. When I added all the ingredients into the bowl I plugged in the mixer and turned it on.

"See that little bottle over there, give me that too."

I opened the bottle and put it to her nose.

"That smells nice," she said with a minor smile.

"It's vanilla extract."

I added a few drops into the mix then checked the turkey sausages.

"How do you feel?" I inquired.

"Fine,"

"Did you sleep well?"

"Yes."

"Good," I said smiling at her.

When the waffle iron was hot I opened it pouring some batter in the center then looked at my watch. Then I turned around smiled at Linda and said,

"What were you doing in the bathroom last night?"

"Nothing," she said looking at the floor.

"You were doing something, why?"

"I don't know."

What did I expect her to say? I knew she was doing it because it felt good.

"Linda, look at me."

Her eyes began to water and one teardrop rolled by the side of her nose. She was a physically mature woman with a child's mind feeling sensations she didn't understand.

"I'm not mad at you, but you can not stick things in your vagina," I said firmly, "you could really hurt yourself. Do you understand?"

"Yes." I opened my arms and hugged her then said,

"Okay, now let's check this waffle and after we eat, we're going outside."

She could never comprehend how hard it was for me to talk about what she'd done, and I can only trust I handled it right. And that morning we ate our breakfast and our bond was back to normal.

Because I never kept her isolated she saw things outside that were beyond my control. The next few months I called the question months. Linda asked me how did birds fly, and were airplanes big birds that carried people? What made the wind blow, and why she couldn't answer the telephone? Why is the sky blue, and how does it rain? And there was the time we saw two dogs humping in the street and she asked about that. I told her one dog hurt his leg and the other one was carrying him home. She wanted to know about Christmas, and if Mister would eat Santa Claus? Linda questioned why she had to wear a dress sometimes, and I didn't have to? Why was my underwear different from hers, and where did this stuff go when she flushed the toilet? Why she wasn't allowed to go to the store by herself, and how come boys stand when they make pee pee.

Linda never got the impression she asked too many questions because I always encouraged her. I wanted her intellect to catch up with her body and then I would start the process of jogging her memory. How I would do that hadn't come to me yet but I had a few ideas. Until then she kept doing problem solving puzzles and workbooks.

She finished the third grade math and English books by the beginning of August and was working on the fourth grade ones when she stunned me. I came home from work Monday and Janice and Linda were waiting in the living room. Janice said Linda talked back to her and was very rude. When I asked what happened Janice said she asked Linda to come down for lunch and Linda told her she wasn't her mother and didn't have to listen to her. Janice was about to leave when I grabbed Linda by the hand and made her apologize. Never had I yelled at her the way I did but I was glad she felt intimidated. I knew a day would come when she would refuse to pay attention to me but I was determined it wouldn't be today.

Linda said she was sorry and when Janice left we sat in the living room and talked. I told her our mother and father were dead and that they loved us very much. We never discussed death before because I preferred to deal with issues when she asked about them. I did not tell her that I believed one day when I passed away I would be with my parents again and all my loved ones. I simply said death happened when a person got old or very sick. It was like going to sleep forever. But I was careful to tell her it could happen to anyone at any time if they were not careful. I gave her an example of me crossing the street without looking for cars and being run over. Then I said a person could fall from a high place and die too. I never mentioned that people could cause one another's deaths because I had no intentions of letting anyone close enough to her to cause harm. She would find out eventually and come to understand but for now I used death as a way to make her be careful and not do anything foolish.

There were questions churning in her head and I waited until one came out. Linda wanted to know if people could come back from death. I told her no because I didn't want to scare her like I'd been all those years thinking my jacket was a headless man in my room. I ended our conversation early by explaining how she'd hurt Janice's feelings by being rude and she would need to think of a way to make it up.

Linda's symptoms of pregnancy were almost nonexistent as far as I was concerned. She threw up a few times and that was it and near September she started to show.

She was reading on or near the seventh grade level and demanding to be more active. Her competitive daredevil nature was blooming with her stomach. It started with her wanting to race to see who was the fastest. She craved speed and when she ran I saw the same smirk in her face she had when she drove the horses across the bridge. Linda also asked for a pair of roller blades and a bicycle. Fortunately she didn't understand finances so I told her I didn't have the money but I would save up for one. At home she rearranged her bed and two heavy dressers without my knowledge and her running and heavy lifting made me a nervous wreck. It couldn't persist so I was compelled to explain her condition.

The day after Labor Day, Linda and I walked up the street into the park. We followed the iron fence until I saw a long rock in the shape of a couch. Ten years had gone by since I'd sat here with my friends and nothing had changed. We sat down on the rock enjoying the sunshine and began to talk.

"My friends and I used to come here a long time ago," I said.

"What is this place?"

"Just a spot we had to hang out," I said leaving out how much fun Ronald, Jasper, Cheese, Archie and the rest of us had rolling joints and smoking here.

"I hear you speak to Ronald on the telephone, is he still your friend?"

"Yes he is."

"When can I meet him?" She asked and right away she was calculating new questions.

I t was then I realized she hadn't grasped the concept of time. Linda's questions had been about whom, what and how but never how long or where. No doubt she was becoming more analytical and the perception of time was the missing element. My palms were sweaty and I was nervous about the outcome but we would not leave here until she understood a life was growing inside her.

"Linda, how old are you?"

She smiled searching for an answer then said confidently,

"I'm studying seventh grade work and kids start school at six so I should be...thirteen, right?"

"Well not quite but we'll get back to that. Do you know where babies come from?"

"Yes they come from mothers."

I'd opened the door and couldn't go back so my only recourse for the time being was to control her source of information.

"Today I'm about to tell you some things that are very important. If it doesn't make much sense now it will later on so try to listen. You are not thirteen years old, you're about twenty six. In March you had an accident which made you forget most of your life."

I stopped and gave her a moment for it to sink in and to gauge her reaction. Her eyes grew small and she held the side of her head from the pain of uncertainty but said nothing.

"You don't have to worry," I said patting her hand, "you're going to be fine," and still she said nothing.

"You've been getting stronger and smarter every day. Trust me you'll be all right."

Unsure of what Linda was feeling I waited for her response. She stood up on the narrow dirt walkway in front of us and paced a few feet then walked back.

"Linda please sit down I don't want you to fall."

It wasn't dangerous up here but you could trip and fall if you weren't careful.

"What happened to me, Bennie?"

"I don't know exactly, but it's nothing to worry about. Like I said you're getting better every day. Just take your time and everything will come back to you."

"Is that why I don't remember our parents?"

"Yes."

"But it will come back to me?"

"Of course it will, but don't rush it! Don't make yourself upset trying to remember, just take it slow," I suggested.

She retained current events quite well, so from this day forward truth was mandatory. I didn't want Linda to presume one day she couldn't trust me by exposing a previous lie.

"Okay," she said.

"Now I know I've just told you a lot but you also need to know why you can't have the bicycle and the skates yet."

"I know because we don't have the money right now."

"That's part of it but there's more."

She sat prepared to hear the reason, "Do you know where babies come from?"

"Yes, they come from mothers."

"That's right from mothers, and you are going to be a mother."

"Yup, someday I'll be a mother and..."

"No, that's what I'm trying to tell you. When you got hurt you forgot," I reached and touched her stomach rubbing it gently, "you're going to have a baby."

Linda looked down at her stomach then put her hand next to mine and pressed.

"There's a baby in here in my stomach?"

"Yes."

Her thoughts raced, and the skin above the bridge of her nose wrinkled with questions.

"I don't feel anything, what does it...I mean how?"

"Relax Linda upsetting yourself is not good for the baby, you must try and take it easy. Everything will be fine. I won't let anything happened to you."

"I know you won't Bennie, I just don't feel so good."

"Sure I understand, we'll sit here for a few more minutes and go home."

"Will you help me get it out?" She asked.

"Get what out?"

"The baby," Linda said innocently and she never looked at me with such dependence until now.

"Of course, but it's not time yet, the baby is still growing."

"How will I know when it's time?"

"Your stomach will get bigger and you'll feel some pain but that won't be for a few more months."

"Is it going to hurt a lot?"

"Yes, but it won't be so bad."

I wanted to give her encouragement instead of dread so I said,

"You should start to feel the baby moving soon, like little tickles inside your stomach, but don't worry. I'll prepare you and you'll do just fine," I said with a comforting smile.

Linda took a relaxing breath then told me she loved me. We sat on the rock silently listening to the children playing in the park below and then left to go home.

When we returned Mister was waiting in the hallway to greet us. I went to the living room and returned with a detailed book on reproduction and gave it to Linda. I told her it would answer any questions she might have about where babies come from. As usual she was eager to open it and went straight to her room. No doubt after she read it she'd have more questions for me tomorrow.

After being home only a couple of hours I found Linda's questions couldn't wait until tomorrow. That evening I was in the shower when Linda knocked on the door. I pulled the shower curtain back sticking out my head to answer her. She told me she needed to speak to me and her voice was very persistent on the other side of the door. I asked if there was a problem and she said no only she needed to speak with me. I told her to give me a few minutes and I'd meet her in the living room. When I finished I put on my pajamas and went downstairs. Linda was sitting on the couch still dressed from this afternoon. I forced a smile and sat down next to her.

"Have you read this book?" she asked.

"No not that one."

"But you know what it's about?"

"What is it Linda?"

"This chapter is confusing. It says this squiggly thing called a sperm fertilizes an egg then after nine months a woman gives birth out of her vagina."

"Yes," I answered showing no emotion.

"So what if I use the bathroom and forget to look, I could flush it down the toilet and not know, then how would we get it?"

"That won't happen," I said intrigued by her growing thought processes,

"You have more than three months before the baby is due."

She appeared relieved then turned the pages backward until she stopped saying,

"I don't understand this either."

With her finger following the words she read aloud, "It says a man uses his pen is to...."

"It's pronounced penis," I interrupted.

"His penis to, what's this word?"

I looked in the book and read the sentence for her, "Impregnate the woman through intercourse. Yes, that is correct."

Linda sat looking at the page and in a crackling voice she said,

"You must be disappointed with me."

"No I'm not, why would you say that?"

"Because you told me not to stick things in there," she said with her head held down.

"That's different because you were a grown woman then and you knew what you were doing. There's nothing wrong with two people who love each other to be together like that. Since you had the accident it's up to me to show you what's right until your memory returns. So I'm not mad with you at all, I love you very much."

"So what I did was all right?"

"Yes Linda."

"And who was this person...did I love him?"

"Yes you did," I said reluctant to answer any more of her questions.

"Where is he?"

I gave the only answer I could think of that was close to the truth,

"I'm not sure who he is but I know he will return when your memory returns."

"I hate not being able to remember my parents or how I got pregnant."

"I know."

I closed the book and took her by the hand to go upstairs. She would do no more reading tonight if I could help it. We said goodnight to Mister and went upstairs. Mister did his usual checks of the house and by the time I was in my bedroom he was coming up the stairs. Linda absorbed a lot of information today and I was confident I'd done the right thing. Once the baby was born I would begin the process to jog her memory. Since there was no way of telling how she would react or what she might do I refused to start while she was pregnant. But with a little more than three months to go it was hard to control my anxiety.

That night I tossed in bed staring at the clock every half an hour wondering why I wasn't asleep. It was my intention when Linda regained her memory and I could at last call her by her given name and honestly say she'd been the last woman I'd touched. She would then understand how deep my love went and how hard I fought temptation. That's what I told myself but each week I found it harder to stick to the plan. It was the summer and the sisters in Harlem were looking damned good and even a few of the old ladies. Masturbating was a ritual I hated each time it was performed and I doubted I could hold on much longer, and starting a relationship was the last thing I wanted. Besides there was herpes and a new disease people were starting to talk about called AIDS and once you contracted them there was no cure.

Two weeks into the school year I felt Linda no longer needed a babysitter so I thanked Janice for all her help and support and paid for a two-week cruise to the Bahamas for her and her husband. That evening I told Linda I was going out for a few hours and not to wait up for me. It was my intention to have a drink downtown but I never made it. I stopped the car and went in a store near 125th Street for a beer. In line in front of me was a dark skin woman with a ponytail wearing black spandex pants and maroon T-shirt that just covered her hips. She was a slim five feet four inches tall and extremely shapely. When she placed her beer on the counter she turned and smiled to reveal a missing canine tooth on her left side. I smiled back and when I finished at the counter she was standing outside. My mouth opened before I could stop myself,

"How you doin'?"

"I'm doin good," she said looking me up and down and flirting as she slowly licked the beer from her lips.

"So what are you doin?" I asked.

"Nothing."

"You wanna hang out with me?"

"Sure, why not," she said after a concise pause.

"Then let's go my cars over here."

We walked across the street and got in the car. I hadn't been driving more than a few blocks when I said politely, "Yo baby, I want some head."

"You want some head?" She said sounding very pissed off.

"Yeah baby I..."

"Hey motherfucker I ain't on no stroll!"

I was embarrassed as hell. I'd never spoken to a woman like that unless I already knew she was willing. Right away I started to apologize while pulling to the curb.

"Listen I'm sorry," I said with both my hands up in a nonthreatening gesture.

"All right then," she said.

I waited for her to open the door instead she took another sip from the can and said,

"I'm not on anybody's stroll. But if I like you, I'll suck your dick." Wow, I thought to myself pulling away from the curb this is going to be an interesting night.

Her name was Thomasina and as I drove we found ourselves on the west side of 125 street under the parkway. Other cars were parked near the water facing the Jersey shore so I felt content to stay there. A chill was in the air as darkness fell turning our make shift living room into a picturesque and serine location. To the left individual lights blushed across the George Washington Bridge like a strand of pearls. Ahead across the water at the New Jersey shore car head lights moved like horizontal pin drops in three parallel levels.

Thomasina started talking about her life, husband and their two daughters. How he could never keep a job for longer than a few weeks and why he was just plain trifling. I said nothing about being an entrepreneur, instead I told her I was an over the road truck driver who grew up here and kept an apartment in Harlem. Then I told her I just went through a nasty break up and I wasn't in the mood for any games and she agreed.

Thomasina did most of the talking and I knew tonight she just wanted someone to listen. It was easy sitting with her and as the night progressed I found it mistakable the way I first approached her. An hour went by and I found I was honestly enjoying Thomasina's conversation when she told me she was hungry. There was a little all night fried chicken place under the train station a couple of blocks away so we went there for a bite to eat and returned to the waterfront where we continued talking. It was going on 11o'clock and I was ready to go home so I said,

"Thomasina I had a nice time with you."

"Me too."

"But I'm gonna go home now. Where can I drop you?"

"Already? It's not even eleven."

"I know but I have to get up in the morning."

"You can't leave yet because I've figured it out."

"Figured out what?"

"I like you, and your gonna get what you want," she said with a grin.

Without hesitation she began to please me and I should have let that be enough but the more I squeezed that round butt of hers the more I wanted it.

"Thomasina... I want some of this," I said after some time.

She stopped long enough to say,

"So do I," then kept going.

"Wait, we have to go to the store for some rubbers."

"Well let's go," she said sitting up in her seat.

We left and drove to the nearest bodega where I stood on line waiting to purchase the condoms through a small revolving plexiglass door. On the outside I appeared restrained and deliberate but underneath my hormones were a level five twister. By the time I reached the window to order I'd calculated seven different positions to put Thomasina in which demanded more room than I had in the car. When I went back to her I asked if she'd come to my house suggesting she might want to use the shower. With a suspicious look she told me she had just taken a bath but agreed to come. I decided to take her to the apartment I kept when I spent time with Paula on 122nd street.

When we arrived I told her this was my apartment instead of saying I owned the building. Thomasina made her self at home and after some short meaningless talk we had sex three times but never kissed. As soon as it was time to take her home she asked if it had been good and would I want to see her again. If I had no intention of seeing her again I would never have said, but if a couple of nights a month could keep me focused and relieve some tension it might work.

We left the house and drove to 127th street between Madison and Lexington and double parked in front of her stoop. At no time during the night did Thomasina ask for money so I didn't see the harm in giving her some now. I took sixty dollars from my wallet and handed it to her and she said,

"What did I tell you?"

"I know but that's not what I'm trying to say. Just give it to the kids."

She took the money graciously and responded,

"Now here's my phone number," she said placing a small piece of paper in my hand.

I thought this odd so I questioned her,

"You said you have a husband. Don't you?"

"Listen don't worry, I'll say you're my sister's oldest boy."

"What?"

"My sister is older than me. You could be her first child, you know my nephew."

"Thomasina this is crazy, you and I are the same age!"

"So, dat nigger don't know all my family."

"I don't know...it's too,"

"There he is in the window," she said pointing to the second floor near the fire escape.

I couldn't see much just a guy looking up and down the block. Then the most extraordinary sensation took over me. I'd never acted this way with a woman and I knew it was wrong, but I didn't care. It was kind of thrilling looking at this dude after just boning his wife and I took on a new personality.

"Let's get out and you can meet him," she said and I sensed she was experiencing the same feelings I was.

"No, not yet. You didn't tell me your sister's name?"

"It's Angie," then she began feeling for the handle.

"What if he asks me questions?"

"I told you don't worry."

What I was becoming took over and I said daringly,

"I'm not worried about a damn thing. It's you and that motherfucker who'll have a problem if he starts fucking with me!"

Thomasina sat immobile gauging my expression.

"What do you mean by that?" she said adding a little defiance in her tone.

I said it slow this time,

"You heard me. If any shit happens you... and that motherfucker will be sorry!"

I didn't care that she was nervous or if I ever saw her again but her agitation turned into a sexy submission.

"Okay you can meet him later but I promise its fine. You can call me at home and if he answers tell him you want to speak to your aunt."

"I don't know," I said thinking about the fun we'd just had.

"I want to see you again," she smiled and I saw the space where she was missing a tooth.

"Fine, I'll call ya."

"Good, and don't forget to wave at him when you leave."
She opened the door and walked to the stoop loudly saying to her husband,

"That's my nephew he gave me a ride home."
Then she looked back waving bye to me. I started the car then let the window down to wave to her husband. Despite my misgivings about the situation I felt good, and was sure I'd call her again.

The next morning Linda was excited by the sensation of the baby moving inside her. She told me that she had let me sleep late and quoted my entrance time as 3:50 am Now that I was awake; she bubbled with joy and more questions. I understood she now had a concept of time. She wanted to know how long this house was here, when was it built, who built it and how was it done? I answered to the best of my knowledge then she moved on to the city. How many cities were there, and how many people were in them and where did they all come from? It was good to hear her questions and I began to think that soon she would be my intellectual equal and if her hunger for knowledge endured she would undoubtedly surpass me. I put Linda's questions on hold and had her follow me to the living room where I presented her with a book on American history. I also warned her that the material in that book was subject to interpretation and scrutiny and gave her an example.

We sat on the couch and turned to the chapter on Christopher Columbus. I told her the dates and locations were correct but the discovery of America did not belong to Columbus because he was not the first person to inhabit this land. She would need to read this book to understand and later find the discrepancies by cross referencing this information with other books to find the truth. Linda appeared perplexed but I made it sound more interesting by telling her it was like solving math problems.

I also found it increasingly hard to keep her from twentieth century technology. She wanted to listen to music and watch television and eventually I complied, but her interest in entertainment was short. Linda still favored reading and to keep her creativity flowing we went to the art supply store and set her up with a beginner's paint set and canvas.

So far her rebellions were minor but I had to start letting her go out by herself and be more on her own. My dread was that I couldn't limit what she saw and how she interacted with people. There were so many dangers and scams she could fall for it seemed as if I had turned her loose in a swamp and neglected to say beware of the alligators. That's why I followed Linda without her knowing whenever she asked to go out. There would come a day when she would leave without asking. Often I wondered if Mr. West and his group had been watching us and how far their influence stretched. Did they know she was pregnant or were they waiting like I was to see the outcome and then snatch her?

One Sunday morning, I came downstairs and Linda was watching T.V. in the living room. She always said good morning and when the silence persisted I went in. Unaware of how long she'd been up or what she'd heard I sat next to her and listened. When the preacher finished and the program went off she said,

"Didn't you tell me no one could come back from the dead?"

"Yes I did and it's true," I said looking at her because of her tone. She appeared angry because she thought she had been deceived.

"Then why does this man say Jesus came back?"

"Because it's called religion and it depends on what you want to believe."

"So tell me about religion."

"Well let's see, there are a lot of religions... how many I'm not sure, but there is Judaism they might also call it the Hebrew I'm not sure. Then there's Hinduism and Christianity, along with Islam and Seventh Day Adventists and some I can't remember."

"So which..."

"Wait, I'll tell you everything I know. Now where was I...oh yes the different religions. I am not sure about the specifics of all of them but I think most believe in a supreme being or beings. One thing I can tell you is they all believe their worship is the right one."

It was almost as if I could tell what she was thinking so I said,

"And you must respect the beliefs of other people."

"Who did the man on television mean when he said Father Almighty?"

"He is called God and he created everything, the earth and sky, the stars and all the planets. All of our emotions, strengths and weakness' come from him. He knows all that will happen in the future as well as the past. Everything you do he sees and he's with us all the time."

Linda looked around the room and up to the ceiling.

"Is he here now?" She said timidly.

"Yes but don't be afraid because he loves you and would never hurt you."

Suddenly I recollected the part of the Bible where God caused some destruction and I wanted to end this conversation before Linda asked my source of information. The way she thirsted for knowledge she was bound read the Bible for herself and ask me about this contradiction.

"So, "he" looks like us?"

"Yes, we were made in his image but like I said each religion believes something different. Like when and how we should worship and what we should eat."

If I knew for sure what her people believed at the time and their God's names I would've explained that to her.

"What do you believe?" Linda said humbly.

"I know there is a Creator and he guides me. I draw my courage and strength from him and you must too."

I knew just how to mull her questions and now was the time.

"Next week I'll take you to a building where every book you would want to read is kept. It's called the library and they have hundreds and hundreds of books."

The library was another thing I couldn't keep from her for long. And as I predicted she grew so eager about other subjects she stopped her inquiries about religion.

Over the next few months Linda spent most days reading at the library on 135th street and I spent more time with my so called aunt. I had a meeting with Thomasina's husband the second time I picked her up. It was 7:00 pm on a Saturday when I went to her house and they were both standing outside. I got out the car expecting a confrontation but nothing happened.

Derrick seemed like a nice enough fellow, a bit quiet and a few inches shorter than me with lighter skin. She introduced me as her nephew and he shook my hand without asking any questions. Thomasina told Derrick I was dropping her in the Bronx and would pick her up when she finished visiting with her cousins. I played along with the charade by asking Thomasina about one of her cute neighbors crossing the street. She quickly dismissed the idea saying the woman was too fast and loose so Derrick agreed. I always watched him closely to see if he was catching on but nothing ever happened. After we got in the car and drove away Thomasina mocked him saying she was going for a ride, but not the ride he thought.

I didn't like the way she used Derrick and in a strange twist of fate I treated her the same way, with on respect. When we got to the house if she started to complain about him I'd tell her to save it. Then walk in front of her and unzip my pants to remind her why she was here. Though I was never verbally cruel I remained insensitive to her emotional needs. Thomasina was just a loan from Derrick until Linda could find her way back to me.

Tonight after four encounters with Thomasina, I was satisfied and ready to take her home. She tried several times during the night to kiss me but I turned my head and kept my lips closed. There was only one person I longed to kiss again and it wasn't Thomasina. While I drove her home I found myself making absurd requests to see how far I could push her. I told her she couldn't give her husband head any more, only straight sex. When she complied I told her she was going to do all the acts for me she wouldn't do for him. This caught her attention and she said inquisitively,

"Like what?"

"Don't worry about it. The next time you come to my house, you'll find out!"

Thomasina sat mutely smiling at me until we reached her block and as always Derrick was in the window looking for her. I pulled over and doubled parked across the street from their house.

"So when will I see you?" she asked.

"I'm going out on town for a few weeks, I'll call ya."

I looked across and up the window and gave Derrick a wave and he returned it.

"He's up there?"

"Yup," I said getting somewhat irate."

"I wish he'd get a job."

The whole idea sounded impractical since she wasn't working either.

"Bennie, do you have a couple of dollars? I want to get my hair done."

"How much do I need?"

"Forty or fifty dollars?"

After I gave her some money I started to wonder if he was pimping her and playing me for a trick.

"Thomasina that nigger knows I'm fucking you, don't he?"

No, he don't."

"You so full of shit!"

"Bennie, he don't know."

"I'm gonna get out and tell that motherfucker right now cause both you motherfuckers are trying to play me!"

There was desperation in her voice and she begged me not to say anything.

"Baby please, he does think you're my nephew!"

I sat quietly with my hand on my chin staring at her.

' I swear on my dead son's grave. He don't know!"

Now I was having satisfaction through her anxiety otherwise she might think I was as stupid as he was. At the same time I was seeking vengeance for him because of her infidelity.

"Something just isn't right," I said.

"Look I gotta go upstairs before he comes down."

"Let that motherfucker come down here and see what happens! I told you before; I'll bust a cap in both your asses. Let him start some shit!"

Never would I have harmed them but she had to believe I was capable.

"I wouldn't lie to you. I promise he doesn't know."

And when I felt I'd taken her off her high horse I said,

"Yeah, alright."

Thomasina opened the door and stuck one leg out and said with a smile,

"When you come back in a few weeks I'll be ready for you. And don't forget to say goodbye to Derrick when you leave."

I watched her walk up the steps and to the door, then I waved to Derrick and left. Thomasina and I would have one more night some weeks later shortly after Thanksgiving. Afterwards I broke it off because Linda's due date was coming close.

The story I told my sister Demetrice and my Aunt Dot about Linda was that Linda was a woman I fell in love on vacation. Because of an accidental fall she lost her memory. I expressed my regrets for not telling them sooner but I thought it necessary because in her confusion Linda believed I was her brother. I told them meeting other family members too soon would add to her problems and it was her doctor's recommendation to limit all personal contact. Unlike my Aunt Dot, Demetrice had many questions about the way I choose to handle Linda's trauma but I persuaded her to trust me and assured them they would meet her as soon as the doctor said it was best.

On December 12th, Linda went into labor at home and on the 13th she gave birth to a healthy baby girl at Harlem Hospital. I wanted to be in the room but my legs would not move when the nurses called.

The baby was 7 lbs 11ozs and 21 inches long with beautiful curly black hair and when she stirred she looked like my mother. I wanted to cry from joy. I wanted to tell everyone I was a father and pass out cigars but that was unfeasible. There was no one I could articulate my new feelings of fatherhood to, and no one who could congratulate me. In the waiting area I got down on my knees and thanked God for my happiness and asked for guidance to bring Whende back to me.

When I saw Linda that day I told her she had done well and the baby was fine. She was exhausted and saw the worried look on my face and tried to make me laugh. She told me I had lied to her when I said it wouldn't be much pain but she would forgive me in a few years. We laughed and soon after she went to sleep.

The next morning when I got to her room she was breast-feeding the baby and didn't see me so I waited outside. She looked much better and I couldn't wait until she finished so I could come inside. Finally with the baby in my arms I asked,

"How are you feeling?

'A little tired but I'm okay. How's Mister?"

"He's fine. He wonders where you are."

"Really?"

"Sure, he walks by your room and looks for you," I said.

"No kidding. He's a smart dog," Linda said.

"So, what will you name her?"

"There are so many nice names, but what do you think of Tiffany?"

I held the baby close enough to smell her newborn scent and said, "Tiffany's a good name, I like it. What made you call her Tiffany?"

"I heard it a couple of times and I liked the way it sounded," Linda said.

"Then Tiffany it is," I said with Linda smiling at me.

I held her and did not want to give her back but she was hungry and wanted some milk. Linda said,

"You don't have to leave. You're my brother, I'm not ashamed."

So I stayed and while the baby was breast fed, Linda asked the strangest question,

"Would you ever hurt this baby?"

"Linda what are you talking about?"

"You would never hurt this baby right?"

"Of course not, I love her!"

"What if God asked you to?"

Now I knew what Linda was talking about, she'd been reading the Bible. Her mother's instinct was in full effect and she watched me for the slightest hesitation.

"Not even if God asked me. As a matter of fact why would a God who loved me ask such a thing?"

"So why would God ask a man to kill his son to prove his love?" she asked.

"I don't know Linda. I can only say no one could make me hurt this child."

"Well that's one religion I will not follow," she said defiantly, "And another thing, why did Adam listen to Eve and eat the apple. Didn't he have his own mind? The book makes it sound like a woman was the blame for Adam's fall from grace."

"I know, but let's talk about it later. I want to hold the baby again."

I looked at this little girl and understood how Linda felt. I felt an overwhelming need to protect her. She was my first child and I wouldn't let anyone or anything harm her as long as I lived. And Linda was at last showing signs she was a critical thinker. It made me more conscious of the fact I would need to read more in order to keep up with her. My only worry was when she finally remembered all that had happened would she still love me?

Chapter 17

Linda and the baby were discharged from the hospital several days later in perfect health. While Linda was in the hospital I used that time to switch our rooms and clean the house. I gave Linda and the baby the master bedroom and I took hers. Linda was happily surprised with the changes I'd made. Inside she found a white wicker bassinet near the bed and a changing station for Tiffany. I substituted my clothes with a gross of white cloth diapers and lots of baby blankets and towels. Together we would pick up a crib in a few days and whatever else Linda wanted.

Then there was the task of getting Mister acquainted with the new baby. I made clear to Linda we couldn't neglect Mister right now. He was a close member of our family and had to be showered with attention so he would not become jealous of Tiffany. The first few days Mister was very curious but not allowed inside Linda's room. After that he was permitted to smell the baby occasionally, and look at her from a distance. At no time did he ever show aggression but we never took any chances. It would take time for him to understand there was another person to protect.

At times when I held Tiffany the clandestine joy of fatherhood was a burden I acknowledged as temporary. The contemplation of never being able to claim her as my daughter was heart wrenching but I had not endured all of these problems in the past months to fail now. And I dreamed of the day when she could call me daddy.

The first time I saw Tiffany sleeping through the glass window of the nursery at the hospital my mentality shifted to plans of her well being. Suddenly the world had to be a place fit for her to live, free from the growing evil and perversion that only seemed to grow daily.

When I was a kid I could walk to the store at five years old and not have my parents worry whether I was coming back. It's possible I was too young to notice the dangers, but now it seemed there were more disgusting people who would deny children their blissful lives. The news reports come from all over the country about missing children and it sickened me. My child would not be walking to the store by herself until I was satisfied it was safe.

At the hospital as a father, I swore death to anyone who might even try to harm her and let only God judge me for my actions. A side from that I planed to teach her about life from my mistakes. Tiffany could attend any college she chose to and have everything I could not. As a child I remember accepting my father's challenge many years ago. He said I had to surpass him by being a better father than he was. His words filled my head and I was in that strange place between sadness from missing him to the joy of showing him how I would succeed. That was all he ever wanted and I knew one day we would meet again and I could say,

"Look daddy, see what I've done. I listened to you and you were right. You told me the easy road wasn't always the right one, and to stand up for myself. I know I could have done more but, I have planted a seed on earth and together we will watch her grow into a woman. She will not disappoint us because I've taught her everything you taught me."

That day at the nursery I put my hand on the glass in and effort to send her some of my love and in my mind I heard my father say,

"I'm proud of you son."

In the passing weeks Linda and I doted over Tiffany, taking turns looking after her, which resulted in a small decrease in Linda's consumption of knowledge, but it didn't last long. Two weeks after we came home each time I went out at her request and brought back specific books on childrearing, economics and world religion. With the onset of motherhood Linda had now become my intellectual equal but still needed me to fill in the blanks.

One day after Tiffany had gone to sleep Linda asked me to show her some of her old pictures. She said she'd seen albums with photographs of our parents and me but none of her or us together. I told her all those pictures were destroyed in a fire. It was questions like those that made it increasingly hard to stay ahead of her thoughts. My greatest fear was she would catch me in one of those lies before I could restore her memory.

Linda also started using the telephone more. She called the Pediatrician and found out when it was safe to stop breast-feeding the baby and made her own doctor's appointments. There was no way to stop her from using the telephone, but I could control who called.

I told Demetrice and Aunt Dot to only call me at work. They were not going to see or speak to Linda yet because they could unwittingly discuss matters that would unweave the tales I'd spun. Lorraine and Ronald hadn't spoken to Linda either because I told them I was staying at my other apartment to avoid Terri who I'd seen in the block once or twice. Ronald could leave his nightly message on the answering machine at 122nd street and I would return it minutes after.

On the other side of town Thomasina kept leaving messages. I heard from my tenant Mr. Smith and he told me she'd come by and left a note under the front door. Then she came back a few days later and asked if she could go upstairs and knock on my door but he said no. I had no interest in seeing her again but I returned her calls once in a while from a pay phone to say I was in Texas or Florida with the truck. Thomasina would make me talk to Derrick for a hot minute to make it look good.

Between Linda's reading and painting her period started its regular cycle and she questioned me more about religions. I'd always told her to follow her heart and believe what she thought was right. She wondered why her gift of menstruation was referred to as a curse. She felt that any society or religious group that made women feel unclean and inferior was not for her then she went on to quote a few.

One day in February I came home and Linda revealed her painting of a pyramid like none I'd ever seen. It was surrounded in the distance by tall sloping trees in a green landscape. All the sides were smooth and covered with a marble slate, which gave the structure a shiny glow. When I questioned her about it she said, she just closed her eyes and that was what she saw. Now I knew what the glow in the distance was that day when we were in the chariot and she was pointing at the sky. Her memories were gradually coming back and I could only hope for the best.

I was so happy seeing the painting I couldn't sleep that night. The first idea I had to bring my love back was to have a tailor design the outfits Linda wore when I first saw her. Then I would take her to the museum where the Egyptian artifacts were kept and expose her to whatever else I might think of from jewelry, to her original hairstyle. Tomorrow I'd wake up in the morning and sing Earth Wind and Fire to her at breakfast. Maybe with any luck she'd sing along.

During the night Linda woke me up with what would be the foundation of her returning memory. She never experienced dreams before and her first one was a nightmare. She ran in my room with the baby in her arms and said in a terrified voice,

"There's a man in my room!"

Still groggy and went to investigate. If someone came in why didn't Mister bark? I called to him and he came from down the hall where he slept and I said,

"Mister, check the house."

He turned and went downstairs and came back in a few minutes and sat down.

"Linda there is no one here."

"But I saw him."

"What did he look like?"

"I couldn't see him well but I saw a dark figure."

"Why don't you start from the beginning, what happened?"

"I went to sleep and then I was sitting in a chair looking at this gloomy man who kept moving like a worm. Then I was running in the backyard but the yard was different."

"The yard was different?"

"Yes and ..."

"You had a dream Linda that's all."

"A dream, is that what is was?"

"Yes, you never had one before?"

"No, I know what they are but it seemed so real."

"Well relax you just had you first one."

"But it was so scary and I couldn't see who he was!"

"Always remember Linda, dreams can't hurt you."

"But it seemed so real. He was right there!"

"I think your memory is coming back," I said encouragingly.

292

Linda sat on my bed with a frown on her face holding Tiffany who was still asleep.

"So finish telling me what happened?"

"I was running in the back yard and there was a pool and the man had my hand and he pulled me under the water and tried to drown me!"

"Why do you think he tried to drown you?"

"Because I couldn't breath and he wouldn't let go. He must be the same man who caused my accident."

"Now wait a minute Linda. Dreams don't always make sense. Nobody hurt you; you fell and hit your head."

"But how? Maybe I was running from someone who was trying to get me."

"I don't think so," I said in a persuading voice.

I wondered if she believed me so I said,

"Not all your dreams will be unpleasant, you'll see. Some of them can be like wishes taking you off to distant places or make you feel as if you have control of the impossible."

"Like what?"

"Lets see when I was a kid I'd dream I could change from my size to the size of a giant, or become as small as an ant. I could also become invisible and walk around the city."

I didn't tell her the dreams of invisibility were during my adolescent wet dream phase, when each night I went around rubbing women's behinds and feeling up attractive movie stars.

"But trust me dreams are not all bad. As a matter of fact I read that dreams serve as a way to clear your mind of useless clutter and anxiety."

This was one of those times she would listen to me and still do the opposite.

"Do you mind if we sleep in here tonight?"

"Linda you're older now. You don't have to be scared."

"I know but just the same I want to stay," she said and she wasn't taking no for an answer.

"Sure why not."

We got in bed and pulled the blankets over us with Tiffany in between and turned out the light. It took a few seconds to settle down and out of the fading darkness Linda said,

"I remember coming in here when I was scared of the lighting."

"You do?" I said with astonishment.

"Yes, and you always knew how to make me feel better. Thank you for being my brother. I don't know what I would do without you"

"Thank you, that's nice to hear."

It was quiet for a while and then she said, "I love you Bennie."

"I love you to Whende," I said.

"Who?" she said sitting up in the bed.

"What?"

"You called me Whende."

"No I didn't."

"Yes you did. You called me Whende, Who's Whende?" she said in a playful voice,

"Is she some woman you know?"

"Nope."

She rolled closer hitting me lightly with her elbow,

"Come on who is she?"

"Know one; I think it means sister in Japanese."

"Yeah, that's the next thing I want to do is learn another language."

I could never slip like that again and say her real name, there was too much to lose.

The next morning Linda was up before me and was making breakfast when I came downstairs. When she saw me she talked about finding out how big the earth was and how many people were living on it? Why were some people poor and starving if the world was big enough to feed everyone? I told her it was because of greed. Some people have hundreds or even thousands of times more than they could ever use and they still want more. Then she wondered why men have wars and how many had been fought? By now she was only thinking out aloud. She relied on me less for answers because she had learned how to find out for herself.

When I sat down at the table and started humming that's the way of the world just like I'd done before. Linda never stopped cracking the eggs to turn around she only listened. When I was done she said that was a nice song and that she liked the words but there was no change in her manner. There was some disappointment but I figured it would take time.

It was March of 1987 and Tiffany was three months old. It was like raising Linda all over again without the speed and quick recognition. It had been almost one year approached since I left for Egypt and so far all my efforts to return Linda to her rightful mind were unsuccessful. The trips to the museum and the recreation of her clothes had no effect. The books on Egypt and the pictures of the temples and statues didn't assist in her acknowledgment of the past. But I refused to give up and assumed it was one of those slumps Linda hit every so often when her brain needed time to assimilate new knowledge. And as it turned out that's precisely what it was.

I came home in the after noon because I'd left my wallet and found Linda standing in the hallway in front of the large mirror. She never moved aside or turned her head when I opened the door. I took a moment to gaze at her sensuous profile. Her body returned to its normal size and was shapelier than before. For months Linda had been picking her own wardrobe and she stopped wearing loose fitting dresses and pants. Today she wore a red cotton dress, which clung to her exquisitely. I spoke to her commenting how nice she looked and walked around her to go in the kitchen when I turned back. Linda never answered or acknowledged my words so I stepped back to see why. She watched her reflection with pain and her eyes stayed fixed on herself as if she couldn't believe what she saw.

"Linda what's wrong, why are you standing here?"

She said nothing but kept looking at herself like I wasn't there.

"What are you doing?" and still she said nothing.

I moved closer and put my arm around her shoulder until we were standing together and shook her softly and she came out of her trance and smiled at me.

"Are you okay?" I said very concerned.

"Sure, why, and when did you come in?"

"I've been here a little while."

Seeing the tension on my face she asked,

"What happened?"

"You were standing here and I thought there was a problem."

"No, there's no problem. Do you like this dress?" she asked moving from side to side.

"Yeah it's looks nice on you."

"Thank you, now why are you here?"

"I left my wallet."

"Bennie what's the matter with you? You'd forget your head if it wasn't attached."

Then she said, "Do you have plans tonight when you come home?"

"No."

"Good, will you watch Tiffany when you come home? I want to go out."

"Out!"

"Yes."

"Where?"

"I met a nice woman at the library the other day who attends City College. She was reading a book on economics for school and we got to talking. You know I think I'm going to college too. But anyway her name is Sonya and she told me there was a nice area downtown called the Village. She asked what I was doing for the weekend and since I wasn't going anywhere I said I would go."

"I see," I said trying not to sweat.

"Have you ever been there?" she asked me.

"Yes many times," I said grudgingly.

"How was it?"

"It was okay," I said not wanting to give any details.

"And did you know women call Friday and Saturday Date Night?"

Hell no, she wasn't going I thought. Not in that dress!

"No, I didn't know that."

"Yes she said I should put on a sexy outfit and a little makeup and go out. And who knows I might meet a nice man."

"Does Sonya have a boyfriend?"

"No, why do you want to meet her?"

"I will one day."

"You should come with us tonight. We haven't done anything fun in a while."

"Then who will watch Tiffany?"

"We can call Mrs. Bertrand"

"That might be too late for her but I will call her and see."

I had nine hours to think of a way to stop her from going so I didn't worry. I just retrieved my wallet and ran out of the house.

Later that night I called Linda at 9:30pm from a pay phone and told her I had a flat tire. I said I tried to call Mrs. Bertrand to come over to baby sit but she was not feeling well. I said as soon as the tow truck came I would be home. Before Linda could ask why I didn't change the tire myself I told her I lent the jack out and forgot to get it back. So by the time I got home at 3:00am it was too late to go anywhere, but I knew she'd plan to go out again.

Over the next several weeks the dreams became more vivid and the trances more frequent. Until even Linda knew there was a problem. Two times I witnessed her break from reality after the first time in the hallway, though she has claimed to have many more.

The second time I saw was just like the first. Linda was in the hallway in front of the mirror trapped in her reflection. This time I didn't disturb her, determined to see how long it would last. She stood there for more than two hours as if she was trying to speak. Only the voice of Tiffany crying upstairs brought Linda back. At least there was no fear of her ignoring the baby. She could hold Tiffany and look in the mirror without losing herself because she was aware of the baby's presence.

It also appeared small mirrors had no affect, only large ones near to the size of the Obeni. The next time it happened was near April. Linda and I were outside at the corner on the sidewalk waiting to cross the street. I had the stroller when a truck that delivers plate glass windows over shot the red light and stopped in the crosswalk. I went to walk around the truck and Linda didn't move nor did she hear me call to her. When I stood behind her I could see her entire reflection in the glass. The light turned green and when the truck moved she was back to normal never remembering it happening.

The realization of these trances happening outside when Linda had to focus on obstacles around her was petrifying to me. I was in over my head and admitted to myself, I needed help. I made an appointment with Dr. Donnell Jase a prominent black psychologist to make sure I wasn't doing harm to her psyche by ignoring the trances.

After his second session with Linda he came to a startling diagnosis. Dr. Jase said Linda was delusional and at times lost touch with herself. He had no explanation why the mirrors triggered the reaction but I had a good idea. He said he'd never come across a case like this and pressed me for more details about her accident. He got the same story I gave Linda because he would have had me committed if I told the truth. However he did feel that her memory was fighting to return. His instructions were to be patient and notify him of any significant changes in her behavior between her secessions. He said Linda trusted me more as a father than a brother and to be tolerant of her shifting personality. Then Dr. Jase wrote a prescription for her I never intended to fill and we left.

Why I thought I knew more that the Doctor was a mistake and in little more that a month I totally screwed it up. Two weeks after the Doctor's visit her nightmares became worse. Linda would run into my room hysterical every other night complaining of the same squiggly man chasing her. We'd talk about her dreams until one day she said she didn't belong here and the nightmares stopped. When the night-mares stopped she began to view me with suspicion. I suggested she take up a second language but that compounded the problem.

Linda picked Swahili and as she learned more, her hatred for English grew. She became frustrated because I didn't learn it with her. It was a bad time for both of us. Linda was irritable and I was horney as hell. The one constant joy we held close was Tiffany.

Then on April 27th the worst action I could have possibly taken occurred. It had been weeks since I'd seen her lose herself inside the mirror and when I came home Linda was standing in the hallway star-ing at her reflection. I went to her side and looked in the mirror with her and when she saw me she smiled and turned to face me. Her arms came up and held me around the shoulders and she buried her head under my neck. I never uttered a word, and it was so good to hold her after so much arguing I rocked her in my arms holding her tighter. Linda's looked into my eyes and said,

"Neia abeir Bennie."

The rest of the words I couldn't understand and it didn't matter, my Whende was back. A single tear rolled down her cheek and to the corner of her mouth and I kissed her. We held each other in the grip of obsession until we reached the couch in the living room. I lie down on top of her looking at the warmness in her eyes and unbuttoned her blouse kissing her neck and her chest until I had to have her.

She whispered,

"No, no."

All at once there was repulsion in her eyes. Linda looked down to see her breasts reveled and was horrified.

"No!" she said what are you doing? Get off of me!"

I moved and she covered herself.

"Have you lost your mind?" she said pulling her dress down and running to the other side of the coffee table.

"Wait a minute it's not what you think!"

"You were trying to have sex with me!"

I began to shudder and I couldn't make sense of what happened then she walked away crying.

"Linda hold on a minute," I ran to take her arm.

"How could you!" she yelled at the top of her voice,

"Don't you ever touch me again!"

She ran upstairs weeping and slammed her door. Mister came from the kitchen looking at me for instruction. He was excited and on guard from Linda's tone. How could I have been so stupid? I wanted to run up stairs and tell her the whole story but I had to let her calm down. After a half an hour I went to her door and knocked.

She yelled from the other side,

"Go away."

Standing outside I said,

"I'm going now and I'll be back tomorrow. It's not what you think Linda, I could never hurt you."

I left and went to the other apartment and sat in the living room by the window. The phone rang once but I didn't pick it up and all the messages were erased from the answering machine without listening to them. I should have tested her to see how long she would remember. Now Linda would never trust me again. That night I went over all the mistakes and how I could have done it differently. What was she thinking and if she would forgive me? If I'd slept with Thomasina a few more times maybe I wouldn't have been in such a rush. What happened to the guy who impressed her by eating so slowly that day? He was here alone, and clueless.

The next morning I went back home and Linda was gone. Her letter was short heartbreaking and to the point. The note she left said she accepted some of the responsibility for what happened between us. She knew what she was doing and felt powerless to stop me. She wrote how she no longer trusted me with Tiffany and to leave her alone. Then she thanked me for the money I'd given her and all that I'd taught her but teaching her to be a whore wasn't her idea of love.

Chapter 18

After almost a year of searching by myself and coming up with nothing I hired Mr. Queen. He spent four months on my case and came up empty. Misery could not describe my condition or my appearance. I'd found it hard to eat or concentrate and had lost several pounds. There were so many things I never got a chance to warn her about like street cons and how to spot dangerous people. I never told her when she goes out never to leave her glass unwatched because someone could spike it. I never told her always keep her eyes on Tiffany at all times so she wouldn't be taken. But most of all I was sorry for the events I would miss.

I would never get to walk Tiffany to school or witness her first steps. She would never get to call me daddy or Uncle Bennie. There would be no PTA meetings with her teachers and I'd never get to see the little performances kids put on every year. Worst of all no one could understand what I was going through.

That first day I met with Mr. Queen and walked home with Mister I tried to think of a plan B incase Mr. Queen could find them. It wasn't until years of agony and two more unsuccessful attempts with detectives did I come up with and idea. Linda's appetite for books might be the only way to get in touch her. I was sure she was still a voracious reader and to keep from loosing my mind, I wrote this book as an effort to find you and convince you to come back home.

Linda I promise that as hard as it might be for you to believe this story it's true. I can take you the Egypt and show you the Obeni as proof but you could never see it work again in your lifetime. I could take you to the Aswan shop where I brought it and you could speak to Farisha. She will show you the gold mask of my face. Her Grandmother has since died, but she is still a witness to what Candice told us that day.

We can speak to Dr. Morrison here in New York and he can confirm my meeting with him and our telephone conversations when I went to Egypt. I could show you the discs I keep in a safe deposit box at the bank and we could have them carbon dated. This is why you have had those feelings of not belonging. I'm the squiggly man in your dreams. I admit I've lied to you but never about keeping you and Tiffany safe.

On the other hand my story would be hard for any sane person to trust so I won't ask you to believe if it is too difficult. Take it as a sign of my desperation to have you back home. I am so sorry for what I've done and if you come home I swear on my mother's grave to never touch you again, that is my word. I will be your brother and never mention our incident again. If this book finds you please call the publisher and leave a message to say that you are all right or just come back home. Love always,

Bennie.

www.ingramcontent.com/pod-product-compliance
Lightning Source LLC
Chambersburg PA
CBHW070305260626
47160CB00003B/729